The Wedgwoods

SALZWASSER
VERLAG

Llewellynn Jewitt

The Wedgwoods

Reprint of the original, first published in 1865.

1st Edition 2022 | ISBN: 978-3-75259-060-9

Verlag (Publisher): Salzwasser Verlag GmbH, Zeilweg 44, 60439 Frankfurt, Deutschland
Vertretungsberechtigt (Authorized to represent): E. Roepke, Zeilweg 44, 60439 Frankfurt, Deutschland
Druck (Print): Books on Demand GmbH, In de Tarpen 42, 22848 Norderstedt, Deutschland

THE WEDGWOODS.

THE WEDGWOODS:

BEING A

LIFE OF JOSIAH WEDGWOOD;

WITH

Notices of his Works and their Productions,

MEMOIRS OF THE WEDGWOOD AND OTHER FAMILIES,

AND A HISTORY OF THE

EARLY POTTERIES OF STAFFORDSHIRE.

BY

LLEWELLYNN JEWITT, F.S.A.

WITH A PORTRAIT,
AND NUMEROUS ILLUSTRATIONS.

LONDON:

1865.

TO

THE RIGHT HONOURABLE

WILLIAM EWART GLADSTONE, M.P.,

HER MAJESTY'S

CHANCELLOR OF THE EXCHEQUER,

AS A SLIGHT TESTIMONY TO HIS
MATCHLESS TALENTS AS AN ORATOR AND A STATESMAN;
TO HIS HIGH AND NOBLE PRINCIPLES,
PRINCIPLES WHICH HAVE MADE HIM ONE OF THE
BRIGHTEST ORNAMENTS OF THE AGE;
TO HIS INNATE AND BOUNDLESS LOVE FOR THE BEAUTIFUL IN
NATURE AND IN ART;
TO WHOM AND TO WHOM ONLY,
(FROM THE PROMINENT AND PRAISEWORTHY PART HE
TOOK IN FURTHERANCE OF
THE WEDGWOOD MEMORIAL INSTITUTE),
A MEMOIR OF THAT GREAT AND GOOD MAN CAN WITH
PROPRIETY BE INSCRIBED;
AND IN
GRATEFUL ACKNOWLEDGMENT OF MANY ACTS OF KINDLY
COURTESY RECEIVED AT HIS HANDS,
THIS VOLUME IS, BY EXPRESS PERMISSION,
DEDICATED.

LLEWELLYNN JEWITT.

INTRODUCTION.

Yielding to no one in love for the beautiful in Art and in Nature, or in veneration for whatever is great and good and noble in the human family, the preparation of the life of the man whose works are pre-eminently entitled to be classed with the former, and whose whole life and character so imperatively demand for him a proud place amongst the latter, has to me been a "labour of love," and one in which I have taken more than usual delight.

The task has been one of serious labour, but fully commensurate with that labour has been the pleasure I have felt in prosecuting and completing my task. To me, in literary matters, it has ever appeared that the heavier the toil, the pleasanter will be the result. There is, in my opinion, but little credit and less satisfaction in accomplishing a work which takes no trouble. It is the hard literary digging —the throwing up of heavy spadesful of soil, in the hope of finding even one little bulb which may germinate and add its beauties to those that are already garnered or are yet to come—which brings with it enjoyment and satisfaction. It is but small merit to compile a work from data and materials ready "cut and dried" to one's hand. It is the getting together of those materials that constitutes the credit, and brings with it a gratifying reward.

It is in holding these views that I am enabled to say the preparation of my present work has to me been "a labour of love." Had its subject been less worthy than it is, and had the actual toil been short of what it has been, the pleasure I have felt in its preparation and continuance would undoubtedly have been far less than that I have experienced. How I have succeeded, it is for others to judge. That my work may contain errors, I am prepared to believe, and that it may not be so full and complete as some may have desired, I can readily understand; but in future editions, should they be called for, I hope to correct whatever there may be of the former, and successfully to accomplish the latter.

Mr. Gladstone, speaking of the subject of this memoir in his admirable address on occasion of his laying the foundation-stone of the "Wedgwood Memorial Institute," at Burslem, said, "Surely it is strange that the life of such a man should, in this 'nation of shopkeepers,' yet at this date remain unwritten; and I have heard with much pleasure a rumour, which I trust is true, that such a gap in our literature is about to be filled up." That "gap" I have endeavoured in this work to "fill up"—I hope with satisfaction to my readers; and I trust also that what I have now for the first time brought together, may be found useful, and at the same time instructive, to collectors, while it may be read with pleasure and profit by all. A large mass of original letters of, and documents relating to, Josiah Wedgwood, are fortunately—despite the wreck of the papers which were with reprehensible thoughtlessness sold, destroyed, or lost some years after his death—preserved in the hands of my friend, Mr. Joseph Mayer, F.S.A. These having been unreservedly placed, years ago, by Mr. Mayer, in other hands, for the purpose of their forming the groundwork of a different publication on Wedgwood, have been a "sealed book" to me. I have never sought to see them, or even inquired of what they consist, but, on the contrary, have scrupulously avoided any allusion or reference to them. It is my sincere hope that they may be carefully and properly edited, and may form a work which may worthily supplement my own, which has been prepared independently of any such aid.

It is right to say that the groundwork of this—my Life of Wedgwood—is to be found in the chapters on "Wedgwood and Etruria," which form a part of the series of Histories of the Porcelain and Earthenware Manufactories of this Kingdom, which I am regularly giving in the pages of that admirably conducted and exquisitely beautiful publication, the *Art-Journal*, to whose learned and able editor, my kind friend, Mr. S. C. Hall, F.S.A., I have to express my deep and lasting obligation for favours most kindly conferred upon me. The chapters, however, which appeared in the *Art-Journal* do but form the groundwork of the present volume. The whole has been re-modelled and re-written, and the additional matter has swelled it to more than double its original size. It is hoped that the narrative I now present to the public will be found to be a history of the "great Josiah," his family, and his works, which shall form as pleasing and lasting a "Wedgwood Memorial" as any of the others that have been projected.

DERBY, MARCH, 1865.

CONTENTS.

THE EARLY POTTERIES OF STAFFORDSHIRE.

THE WEDGWOODS.

CHAPTER I.

CHAPTER II.

CHAPTER III.

CHAPTER IV.

CHAPTER V.

CHAPTER VI.

CHAPTER VII.

CHAPTER VIII.

CHAPTER IX.

CHAPTER X.

CHAPTER XI.

CHAPTER XII.

CHAPTER XIII.

CHAPTER XIV.

CHAPTER XV.

CHAPTER XVI.

CHAPTER XXI.

CHAPTER XXII.

CHAPTER XXIII.

CHAPTER XXIV.

LIST OF ILLUSTRATIONS.

PORTRAIT, AUTOGRAPH, ETC., OF JOSIAH WEDGWOOD.

THE WEDGWOODS.

THE EARLY POTTERIES OF STAFFORDSHIRE.

CHAPTER I.

INTRODUCTORY.—GRADUAL PROGRESS OF THE ART IN THE DISTRICT.—THE CELTIC PERIOD.—CINERARY URNS.—DRINKING-CUPS.—FOOD-VESSELS.—INCENSE-CUPS.

The history of the important and truly beautiful art of "pot making," so far as regards our own country, which has not yet been written, must and will one day—it is hoped ere long—form one of the most pleasing and instructive works which can be produced. The deep and undivided research of the patient antiquary, the graphic powers of the skilled biographer, the thoughtful comparative experiences of the collector, and the matured observations of the practised manipulator, will need all to be united in the production of such a work; which, if properly carried out, cannot fail to present a more vivid and more pleasingly instructive picture of English industry and English art—both allied and independent of each other—than it has fallen to the lot of any one as yet to attempt to depict.

Extending uninterruptedly through several centuries from a period long antecedent to historic times, down through every change of race and of peoples to our own day—followed in one way or other in almost every district throughout the length and breadth of the land—gradually extending itself from the first rude and coarse clay vessels for receiving the ashes of the dead, to every conceivable appliance of the table, the toilet, or the drawing room of the living—from the thick and clumsy half-baked urn, to the finest, most costly, and exquisitely beautiful porcelain services and ornaments—the art of the potter has been associated with every race, with every age, and with every occupation of the occupiers of the soil, and has thus been connected with their everyday life, their homes, and their callings. A history of this art, then, must, more than any other, illustrate the history of man, and the progress of his intellectual development, and must form, when properly considered, a key to his civilisation and to his social advancement.

This history, as I have said, has yet to be written, and will, sooner or later, form a work of surpassing interest and value. Introductory to the memoir of one of the greatest potters the world ever saw—JOSIAH WEDGWOOD—I have thought that a slight sketch of the progress of the art in the earliest times in the district which gave him birth, and in which he "lived and moved and had his being," could not fail to be interesting to his countrymen, who enjoy to so great an extent the results of his talents, his skill, and his industry; and I have therefore thrown together the following notes, to give an insight into the state of that art, and to show with what success it has been followed in that one district of our kingdom which has earned for itself the proud title of "*the* Potteries."

The early fictile history of the important district to which I have referred, and which is universally known as the "Staffordshire Potteries," is naturally, like that of every place or seat of manufacture, involved in mystery. That mystery, however, happily is not altogether impenetrable. By the constant labours of the antiquary, and the discoveries which from time to time he is enabled to make, a light is every now and then thrown on the productions of the early inhabitants of the place; and thus new links in the chain which connects the present with the past are continually being formed. It is, indeed, an occupation of intense interest to examine these links as they appear, and, by following their ramifications back to the most remote time, take up the thread of history, and connect the early efforts of primeval man, with his rude and clumsy vessels of coarse clay, with those of his successors at the present day; with their wondrous and marvellously fine productions in earthenware and porcelain. It is always interesting to trace out the gradual progress of an art, whatever that art may be; but in the case of pottery that interest is increased an hundred-fold. The art of pot making is essentially a homely one; its vessels are for the "people," and for every occupation of the people, and therefore tell more of their manners and customs, their occupations and their inner or home life, than anything else does or can. But few things indeed so well and effectively illustrate the progress of a nation or a race as its pottery; and certainly there is nothing that better shows the gradual development of its civilisation, and of its "mind," than does a chronologically arranged series of its fictile productions; and the following slight sketch of the history of early fictile art in Staffordshire at different periods will be useful in assisting the collector to understand the progress and development of that particular manufacture for which it is so "world-famous."

That pottery has been made in the district from a very early period there can be no doubt, and that in course of time a continuous chain of examples, from the most remote ages down to the present time, might with care and attention be still got together, is equally certain. This collection would be of great advantage to the district, and not only to it but to the country at large: and it is much to be hoped that in the new Wedgwood Institute and Museum, at Burslem, this suggestion may be fully carried out.

The four great divisions into which the history of the Ceramic Art of this country is to be divided (leaving out the modern manufactures) are, of course, those of the *Celtic* or ancient British, the *Romano-British*, the *Anglo-Saxon*, and the *Mediæval* periods. To each of these periods a separate volume, to do the subject even a shadow of justice, ought to be devoted. My present purpose, however, is only, as I have stated, to glance at their principal characteristics, and to illustrate them, as far as may be, by Staffordshire examples.

In the CELTIC, or ancient British, period, the pottery consists mainly of cinerary or sepulchral urns, drinking-cups, food-vessels, and incense-cups. These were undoubtedly made on the spot, or near the spot, where found. They were, no doubt, the handiwork of the females of the tribe, and occasionally exhibit no little elegance of form and no small degree of ornamentation. They are formed of the coarse common clay of the place where made, occasionally mixed with small pebbles and gravel. They are entirely wrought by hand, without the assistance of the wheel, and are, the larger vessels especially, extremely thick. From their imperfect firing, the vessels of this period are usually called "sun-baked," or "sun-dried." This, however, is a grave error, as any one who will take the trouble to examine an example will easily perceive. If the vessels were "sun-baked" only, their burial in the earth—in the barrows wherein they were deposited, and where they have remained for a couple of thousands of years—would soon soften them, and they would, ages ago, have returned to their old consistency. As it is, they bear evidence of the action of fire, and are indeed sometimes sufficiently burned for the clay to have attained a red colour. They are mostly of an earthy-brown colour outside, and almost black in fracture; and many of the cinerary urns bear internal evidence of having been filled by the burnt bones and ashes of the deceased, while those ashes were of a glowing and intense heat.

The *Cinerary Urns—i.e.* such urns as have contained, either inverted or otherwise, the burnt bones and ashes of the deceased—of Staffordshire, like those of Derbyshire, vary considerably in form from those of many other districts. Their principal characteristic is a broad or deep overlapping border or rim. They vary in size from nine or ten up to sixteen or eighteen inches in height; and their ornamentation, always produced by indenting twisted thongs into the pliant clay, or by simple incision, is frequently very elaborate. This ornamentation usually consists of diagonal lines, or of "herring-bone" or zigzag lines, arranged in different ways, and producing a remarkably good effect. Of these interesting vessels some excellent examples have been found in Staffordshire, and these were, without doubt, made on the spot. They are, therefore, the very earliest examples which

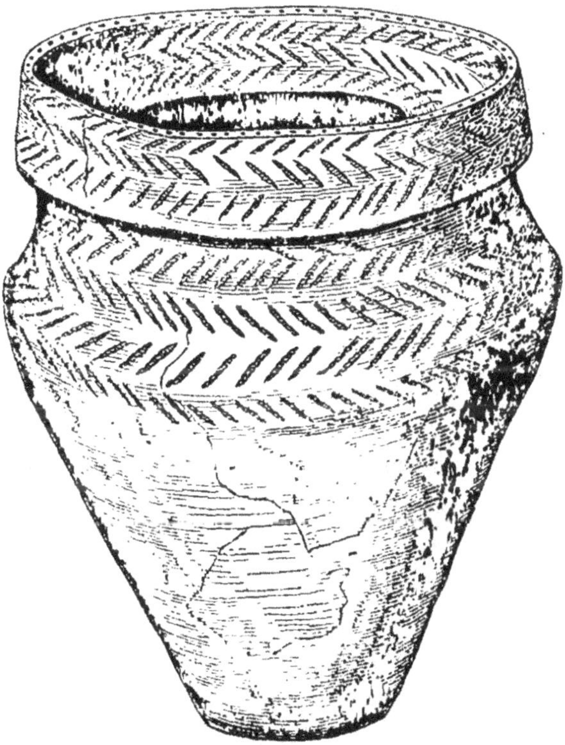

can be produced of Staffordshire pottery, and date back to the time when that district was inhabited by the Cornavii. Of the form of Staffordshire pottery of this early period the best idea will be gleaned from the accompanying engravings.

The first is a remarkably fine cinerary urn, discovered in

a barrow, along with other pottery to be hereafter noticed, at Trentham. It is richly ornamented in the usual manner, with lines formed by indented twisted thongs, and is of remarkably good form. It is in the possession of my friend, Dr. J. Barnard Davis, F.S.A. The next example is from

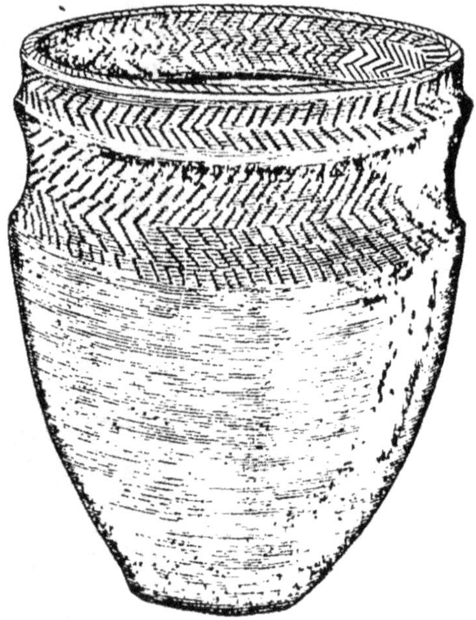

Stone, where it was discovered some years ago. It is, as will be seen, a fine urn, and is elaborately ornamented with incised lines. Like the Trentham urn, this one was filled with burnt bones when found. The third one was discovered, in fragments, by Mr. Redfern, the historian of Uttoxeter, at Toot Hill, near that town. It is ornamented with indented twisted thongs in the usual manner.

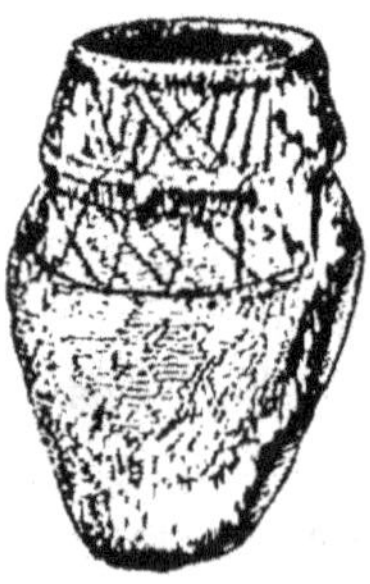

At Yoxall, some years ago, it is recorded about forty cinerary urns were discovered, but were, unfortunately, nearly all wantonly destroyed. They appear to have been of the usual form, with somewhat elaborate zigzag ornaments. An urn, with the upper rim punctured

in three rows, was also, many years ago, found at Over Tean.

It is interesting to note that besides the urns here engraved and described, several discoveries of similar kinds of pottery have been made in other parts of Staffordshire, principally by Mr. Bateman and Mr. Carrington; and that even in the very centre of the potteries—at Shelton—while digging the foundations of the Shelton Blast Ironworks, which are now blasting the health and happiness of the inhabitants so efficiently, a barrow containing an urn, unfortunately not preserved, was discovered.

The next engraving shows a remarkably good cinerary urn from the neighbouring county of Derby, which will be seen to be of the same general form as those of Staffordshire.

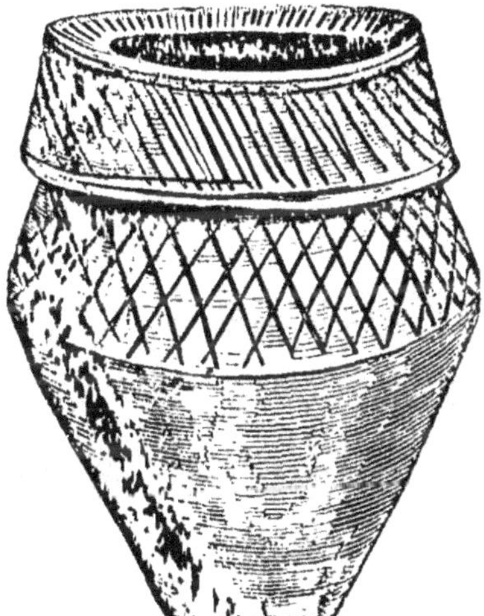

It was discovered, along with many interesting relics, in a barrow at Monsal Dale, where it was inverted over a deposit of calcined bones, placed on surface stones, and a bone pin was found among the remains. Two other urns, a part of a most interesting discovery of five such vessels and other remains in a barrow at Darley Dale, are also shown on the engravings on next page. They will be seen to vary somewhat

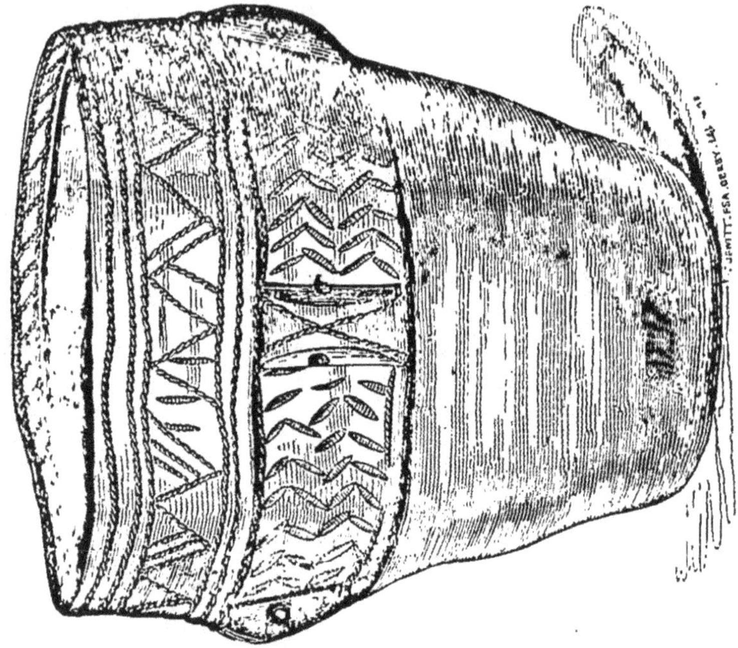

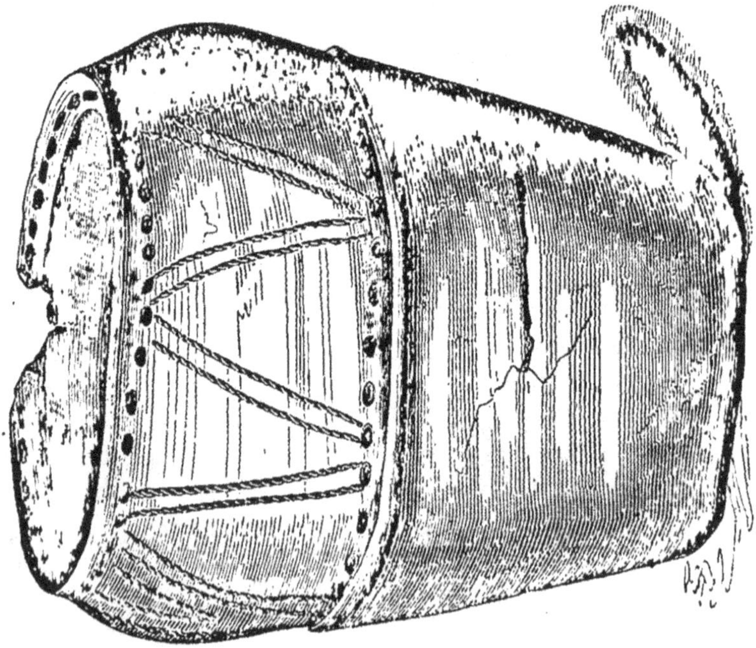

in general form from those with the usual overlapping rims, and one of them has the peculiarity of looped ears at its sides. They may possibly have been the work of the females of a migratory tribe.

The Celtic *drinking-vessels* found in the Staffordshire and Derbyshire barrows are generally from about six to nine inches in height, tall in form, contracted in the middle, globular in their lower half, and expanding at the mouth. They are usually very richly ornamented with indented lines in different patterns; are carefully formed by hand, of fine and well-tempered clay, mixed with fine sand, and are well fired. They are the finest and best productions of Celtic fictile art. Two examples from barrows in the adjoining

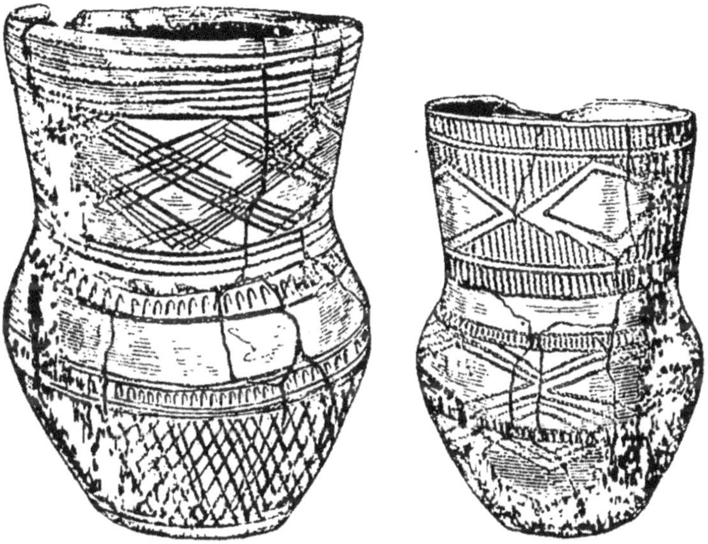

county, Derbyshire, will show the form of the "drinking-cups" of this district. The first one was found in 1851, in a barrow called Bee Low, near Youlgreave. It was six inches and three quarters high, and carefully ornamented with indented twisted-thong patterns. It lay in the cist, as is usual in the barrows of this district, in front of the skeleton, which, as is generally the case, lay in a contracted position, with its knees drawn up, on its left side. The next one shows a different kind of ornamentation, still produced by twisted thongs. This beautiful vessel was found in a barrow at Hay Top, Monsal Dale, along with a skeleton and other interesting remains.

The *food-vessels*—small urns so called because they were apparently intended to contain an offering of food—vary very considerably both in form and in character of decoration, from the rudest to the most elaborate. These vessels are usually wide at the mouth, tapering gradually downwards, until quite small at the bottom. They are formed of clay of much the same quality as the cinerary urns, and are baked to about the same degree of hardness. A very plain and

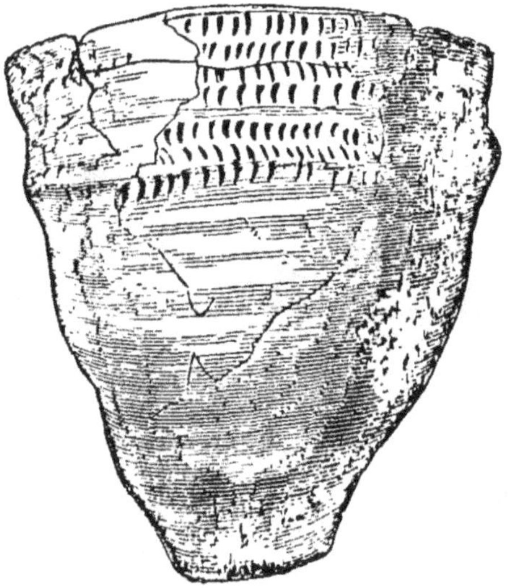

rude example from Trentham, Staffordshire, is here shown; and for the sake of comparison some other elaborately ornamented examples from Derbyshire barrows, and one from Wetton, Staffordshire, with loops at its sides, are also given.

The first of these, on the next page, is a beautiful vessel with ears, somewhat richly ornamented with indentations. It is five and a half inches high, and was found with a skeleton in the usual contracted position, along with a bone pin, and other interesting remains.

The other engravings exhibit two vessels from an interesting discovery made in a barrow on Hitter Hill,* where they

were found in stone cists along with skeletons lying in contracted positions. They are in the possession of my

friend Mr. J. F. Lucas, whose collection contains many interesting examples of fictile art.

* For an account of this discovery see the "Reliquary Quarterly Archæological Journal and Review," vol. iii. p. 159.

The engraving here given shows a remarkably formed

vessel from Wetton, Staffordshire, which is peculiar by having looped ears at its sides.

The *incense-cups* of Staffordshire, like those of Derbyshire, vary in form and in style of decoration. They are very small vessels, not more than from an inch and a half to three inches in height. The ornaments are, as in the other remains of this period, incised or indented lines. Their usual forms are seen in the accompanying engravings.

The first, a remarkably fine example, was found in a

barrow at Throwley, in Staffordshire, by Mr. Carrington, and is preserved in the Bateman Museum, at Lomberdale House. It is ornamented with incised lines, and is three inches and a half in diameter, and two inches and one eighth in height.

The second is from the barrow at Darley Dale, which has before been spoken of; the third is from a barrow on Baslow Moor; and the fourth from a similar tumulus on Stanton Moor.

CHAPTER II.

THE ROMANO-BRITISH PERIOD. — VARIETIES OF VESSELS.— ANGLO-SAXON PERIOD. — CINERARY URNS. — DOMESTIC VESSELS. — NORMAN PERIOD. — PITCHERS AND OTHER VESSELS DISCOVERED IN DERBYSHIRE.—PAVEMENT TILES. —MEDIÆVAL POTTERY.

THE second great division into which the subject of the history of the early fictile productions of the pottery district is to be divided, is that of the ROMANO-BRITISH period—a period in which, although most of the finer vessels used in England were imported by that conquering people, a large variety of wares were made of native clays in different districts which they inhabited. In this period, although it is tolerably certain that wares of some kind or other were made in Staffordshire, there is no positive evidence of such being the case. I am not aware of any authenticated Roman kilns * having been discovered, though it is generally believed that some of the interesting remains exhumed many years ago at Fenton and other localities are to be ascribed to this period. Certain it is that kilns bearing the characteristics of Roman use are recorded as having been exhumed; and equally certain is it that vessels, and fragments of vessels, of undoubted Roman workmanship, have frequently been dug up in the neighbourhood. It must also be borne in mind that in the

* It is stated that a Roman kiln was found many years ago at Burslem, in which were remains of pottery, but as no authentic record of the discovery has, unfortunately, been preserved, too much reliance must not, perhaps, be placed upon the circumstance.

adjoining county of Salop a considerable pottery existed, and that the clays of Staffordshire must have been well known to the Romans. Chesterton, by Newcastle-under-Lyme, was a Roman station, and a Roman road traversed the district of the present potteries. On this line of road fragments of the different wares of that people have frequently been found; and, as I have just stated, there can be but little doubt that many of them were made on the spot. I am inclined to believe that at least some of the finer kind of red ware, commonly known as "English Samian," were made in Staffordshire. At all events, the clay would produce that ware, and many remains of it have from time to time been found in the district.

At Cauldon, at Wetton, and in many other parts of Staffordshire, Romano-British pottery has from time to time been found, some at least of which there is reason to believe was made in the district. The accompanying engraving shows an urn from the neighbourhood of Uttoxeter.

Some of the more usual forms of Romano-British pottery,

though not examples made or found in Staffordshire, are shown on the accompanying engravings, which may, perhaps, be of assistance to the collector in appropriating the specimens in his possession.

The pottery of the ANGLO-SAXON period—the next great division of my subject—was undoubtedly, like that of the ancient Britons, made near the places where the remains

have been discovered. The pottery of this period consists almost entirely of cinerary urns, and their form is somewhat peculiar. Instead of being wide at the mouth, like the Celtic urns, they are contracted, and have a kind of neck instead of overhanging lip or rim. Their general form will be best understood by reference to the accompanying engraving of two urns from Kingston. The pottery of this period is usually of a dark-coloured clay, sometimes nearly black; at others dark brown, and occasionally of a slate or greenish tint. The vessels appear to be hand-made (*i.e.* without the use of the wheel), and are tolerably well baked.

The ornaments usually consist of encircling incised lines in bands or otherwise, and vertical or zig-zag lines, arranged in a variety of ways, and not unfrequently knobs or protuberances are to be seen around the urns. Sometimes also they present evident attempts at imitation of the Roman egg-and-tongue ornament. The marked features of the pottery of this period is the frequency of small punctured ornaments introduced along with the lines and bands, with very good effect. These ornaments were evidently produced by the end of a stick cut and notched across in different directions, so as to produce crosses and other patterns. This novel and early mode of decorating pottery will be best understood by the accompanying engraving, in which I have endeavoured to show one of the notched stick

"punches," such as I have reason to believe were used for pressing into the pliant clay, and also one of the indented patterns so produced. In some districts the vessels are ornamented by small patterns painted on the surface in white; but those of the midland counties, so far as my knowledge goes, do not possess this peculiarity.

Among the Anglo-Saxons the bowls were principally of metal or wood (generally of ash), and the drinking-vessels of horn and glass.* These two essentials, the food-bowls and the drinking-cups, being of wood or metal, and of glass, left but little for which clay could be used, except the funereal urns which I have just described. For culinary purposes the Anglo-Saxons seem to have had a dislike to the use of clay; but nevertheless some other varieties of their pottery occasionally occur, and show that the wheel was sometimes used. One of their forms I here show, and others approaching in shape the basins and unhandled cups of our own day have been found.

Of pottery of the Norman period I am not at present aware that any authenticated examples have been found in Staffordshire, though I have no doubt that in that period the Norman potters worked the clays of the district, and produced vessels for various uses. These consisted principally of bowls or basins, pitchers and dishes; the bowls or basins being used for drinking purposes, as well as for placing the cooked meats in, and the pitchers for holding and carrying the wine, ale, mead, water, and other liquors, to the table. In the neighbouring county, Derbyshire, a most interesting discovery of a Norman pot-work was recently made by myself,† and one or two of the forms of vessels therein found are given in the engravings on the two following pages. The clay is usually of a coarse kind, and the vessels in some, or rather in most instances, bear evidence of the wheel having been used. In colour they are sometimes of a reddish-brown, at others of a tolerably good red, and at other times, again,

* These were the origin of our "tumblers;" the glasses then made being *rounded* at the bottom, so that they must be filled while held, and could not be set down until emptied, without spilling.

† This pot-work is the only one either of the Anglo-Saxon or Anglo-Norman periods which has ever been discovered, and is therefore of great interest and importance. A notice of the discovery will be found in the "Reliquary," vol. ii. p. 216.

nearly black; and one great peculiarity is, that many of the pitchers, or jugs, are covered with a green glaze. They are

usually devoid of ornament, with the exception of having the ends of the handles rudely foliated by the pressure of the fingers of the workman. On one large vessel which I had the good fortune to exhume, however, and which is represented on the preceding page, were the horse shoes, &c., the badges of the Ferrars family, laid on in slip, and a kind of herring-bone ornament scratched into the soft clay. On

other examples heads were rudely formed, as were also, occasionally, figures of horses and men.

Kilns for the manufacture of *tiles* existed in Staffordshire from an early period; and the name of Telwright, or Tilewright, is one connected with the pottery district for many centuries. At Great Saredon, a few years ago, a kiln, where tiles had been made, was exhumed. The manufacture of ornamental paving tiles was one of considerable importance till within the last two centuries, and many religious houses had their own tile-works and kilns within their precincts. The manufacture, however, became gradually lost, and has been entirely discontinued until of late years, when it has, with considerable success, been re-introduced. The principal makers at the present day of these encaustic tiles are, of course, Messrs. Minton, of Stoke-upon-Trent, and Messrs. Maw, of Broseley. The mode in which the old and remarkably interesting tiles which are still to be seen in the pavements of many of our old churches were made was this: the quarry of soft clay was made to its proper size in a wooden frame, and then, the pattern (being first carved on a flat square of wood in relief) was pressed into the red clay to a sufficient depth, and the indented pattern then filled in with a slip of yellow clay. The usual processes of baking and glazing were next, of course, gone through, and the effect produced, of a yellow pattern on a red ground, or *vice versa*, was very pleasing. The devices impressed on tiles were extremely various, and among others consisted of armorial bearings, foliage, grotesque figures, inscriptions, &c., and the patterns not unfrequently extended over four, nine, twelve, or more, tiles.

The MEDIÆVAL vessels made in Staffordshire, like those of other districts, were chiefly confined to pitchers and jugs, of much the same form as the Norman ones just given, and to costrels and other similar productions. Dr. Shaw, in his history of the potteries, says, "there exist documents which imply that during many centuries considerable quantities of common culinary articles were made from a mixture of different clays found in most parts of the district." It is certain that throughout the whole of the middle ages, as in the earlier and later times, the potter's art was practised in this district; and examples of different periods are in existence, showing the progress of that art from one time to another.

In the account of expenses of Sir John Howard, in 1466, is the following entry, which shows somewhat curiously the cost of "potes" in those days:—"Watekin, bocher of Stoke, delyvered of my mony to on of the *poteres* of Horkesley iv^s.^ vi^d.^ to pay hemselfe and his felawes for xi dosen potes," *i.e.* about 4¾*d.* per dozen.

The pottery of the Tudor period—so far as is known of English make—for it must be remembered that the greater part of the wares in use were imported—consisted of costrels (one of which, for the sake of showing the form, is shown on the accompanying engraving), and other vessels for ordinary use. They were coarse in material, but generally thickly coated with glaze, and the surfaces well mottled. Ornaments were not often introduced, but occasionally heads, grotesquely formed, decorated the handles; and other equally rude devices were laid on in different clays. Excellent examples of this period may be seen in various collections, and are well worthy of extended notice.

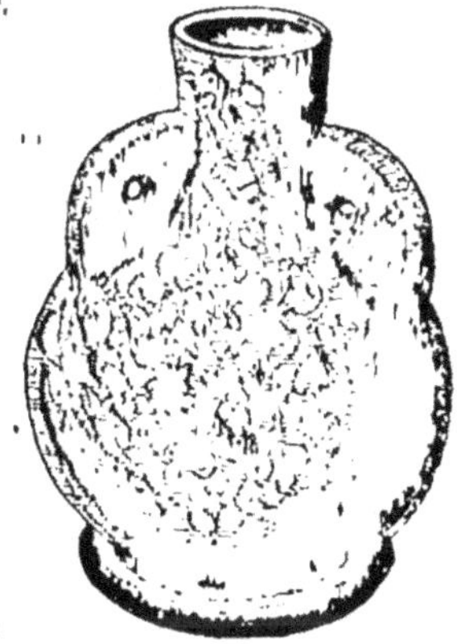

CHAPTER III.

PRODUCTIONS OF THE SIXTEENTH AND SEVENTEENTH CENTURIES. —DISHES OF TOFT, SANS, AND TAYLOR.—TYGS.—THE BUTTER TRADE.—BUTTER-POTS.—CLAYS.—DR. PLOT'S ACCOUNT.—COMBED WARE.—BELLARMINES AND ALE-POTS.—WHITE STONE WARE.—"DRINKING STONE POTTES."—EARLY PATENTS.—SALT GLAZING.—CROUCH WARE.—THE BROTHERS ELER, FROM NUREMBERG; THEIR SECRET DISCOVERED BY ASTBURY AND TWYFORD.

In the sixteenth and seventeenth centuries the fictile productions of Staffordshire were, like those of other districts in which the potter's craft was followed, confined to the manufacture of the common vessels for everyday use—though but few were used, for wooden trenchers and bowls, pewter-plates and dishes, black-jacks of leather, and metal flagons, &c., almost usurped their place. Large coarse dishes, tygs ot various forms, with one, two, three, four, or more handles, pitchers, and other vessels, were however made, and are not unfrequently to be met with in the hands of collectors. In the seventeenth century these large coarse dishes and other vessels were made at Burslem and the surrounding places. The material is a coarse reddish or buff-coloured clay, and the ornaments are laid on in different coloured clays, and the whole is then glazed thickly over. One of these large dishes, now in the Museum of Practical Geology, is shown on the accompanying engraving. The body is of buff-coloured clay, with the ornaments laid on in relief in light and dark brown. The border is trellised, and in the centre is a lion rampant, crowned. On the rim beneath the lion is the name of the maker, THOMAS TOFT. In the same museum is a fragment of another similar dish, with the lion and unicorn. A very fine dish of a similar kind, and by the same maker, is preserved in the museum of my late friend, Mr. Bateman, at Lomberdale House, and is engraved on the next page. It is twenty-two inches in diameter, and bears a half-length crowned portrait of King Charles, with sceptre in each hand, and the initials C.R. Below the figure, on the rim, which,

as usual, is trellised in red and black, is the name THOMAS TOFT. In the same museum is another remarkably fine dish bearing two full-length figures in the costume of the Stuarts, the gentleman holding in his hand his hat and feather, and having "petticoat breeches," tied stockings, and high-heeled boots with ties, and the lady holding a bunch of flowers. Between the figures are the initials W. T., and on the rim at the bottom, in precisely the same manner as the Toft dishes, is the name WILLIAM : TALOR. Another dish of this kind is in the possession of Mr. Mills, of Norwich.

The dish is nineteen inches in diameter. It bears three heads in ovals, with foliage, &c., and the name RALPHOFT, or Ralph Toft, the H and T being apparently conjoined. The ground is buff, and the ornaments are laid on in dark and light brown clay. It is engraved on the next page. Another maker of this period, whose name occurs in the same manner as those just described, was WILLIAM SANS.

Of the makers of these dishes, it is interesting to observe that Toft is an old name connected with the pottery district, and that members of the family are still potters in the neighbourhood. It is also an old Derbyshire name, being connected with Youlgreave and other places in that neighbouring county.

The "Tygs," of which I have before spoken, appear to

have been made in considerable numbers, and, indeed, to have constituted one of the staple manufactures of the potters of that day. They were the ordinary drinking-cups of the period, and were made with one, two, three, four, or more handles. The two-handled ones are said to have been

"parting-cups," and those with three or four handles "loving-cups," being so arranged that three or four persons drinking out of one, and each using a different handle, brought their lips to different parts of the rim. Examples of some of the forms of these tygs are here shown. The two first which are engraved were found in a long disused lead mine at Great Hucklow, where they must have remained for about a couple of centuries. The third has three handles and a spout, and is ornamented with bosses of a lighter colour, bearing a swan, a flower, and a spread eagle. The fourth, a two-handled cup, is of the same

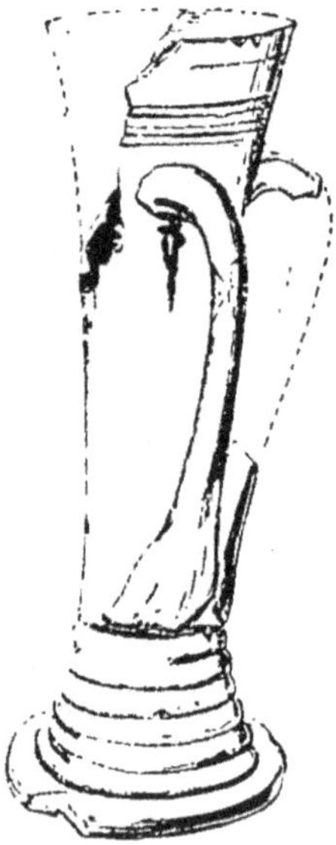

general form as those with one handle, and is, as will be seen, of elegant shape. These two latter specimens are in the Museum of Practical Geology.

A curious candlestick, here represented, said to be of Staffordshire make, is preserved in the Museum of Practical

Geology. It is of much the same kind of ware as the tygs, and has its ornaments in white clay. It bears the date 1649, and the initials E. M.

The manufacture of BUTTER POTS was an important branch of the potter's art at Burslem at an early period, and it may be well to say a word or two upon them, for the purpose of exploding an opinion which I believe has gained very general credence, that, till the time of Josiah Wedgwood, none but these coarse vessels were made in the potteries. Nothing could possibly be further from the truth than this, and I trust that this glance at the history of the Staffordshire potteries will prove that the potters had a far higher aim in their art than the production only of such rude but useful utensils. Butter pots had been made long anterior to the year 1670, in which year the attention of Government was called to the frauds carried on by means of the pots not being of an uniform size and thickness. An Act was accordingly passed,* compelling the Burslem potters to make their pots of a size to hold 14 lbs. of butter, and sufficiently hard not to imbibe moisture; for it appears that, by being porous, the dealers soaked them in water, and thus the buyer did not get nearly his proper weight of butter.

* 13 and 14 Charles II. cap. 26, 1661.

In 1686, Dr. Plot published his "Staffordshire," and thus spoke of the butter trade, and butter pots then made :*—

"From which Limestone Hills, and rich pastures and meddows, the great Dairys are maintained in this part of Staffordshire, that supply Uttoxeter Mercat with such vast quantities of good butter and cheese, that the Cheesemongers of London have thought it worth their while to set up a Factorage here for these commodities, which are brought in from this, and the neighbouring county of Derby, in so great plenty, that the Factors many Mercat days (in the season) lay out no less than five hundred pounds a day in these two commodities only. The Butter they buy by the *Pot* of a long cylindrical form, made at *Burslem,* in this county, of a certain size, so as not to weigh above six pounds at most, and yet to contain at least 14 pounds of Butter, according to an Act of Parliament made about 14 or 16 years agoe, for regulateing the abuses of this trade in the make of Pots, and false packing of the Butter; which before was sometimes layed good for a little depth at the *top,* and bad at the *bottom;* and sometimes set in *rolls* only touching at the *top,* and standing hollow *below* at a great distance from the sides of the pot. To prevent these little Moorlandish cheats (than whom no people whatever are esteemed more subtile) the Factors keep a *Surveyor* all the Summer here, who if he have ground to suspect any of the *Pots,* tryes them with an instrument of Iron, made like a *Cheese-Taster,* only much larger and longer, called an *Auger* or *Butter-boare,* with which he makes proof (thrusting it in *obliquely*) to the bottom of the Pot; so that they *weigh* none (which would be an endless business) or very seldom; nor do they *bore* it neither, where they know their customer to be a constant fair dealer. But their *Cheese,* which comes but little, if anything, short of that of Cheshire, they sell by weight as at other places."

In reference to this, Mr. Redfern, the historian of Uttoxeter, says :—

"Butter pots are mentioned in the parochial records of the town forty years before Dr. Plot wrote; for five pots of butter were sent from Uttoxeter to the garrison of Tutbury Castle, and had been bought at the sum of 12*s*. As this was seventeen years before the Act of Parliament for the regulation of the sale of butter in pots, it is difficult from this to judge of the exact price of butter per pound

* Probably written about ten years before printed.

at Uttoxeter at that remote period. And yet it may be reasonably inferred that the pots of 1644 were of the size of those manufactured after 1661; for it appears the Act was passed more for the prevention of any irregularity in the size of the pots, and the mode of packing butter in them, than for any actual alteration of the size the pots were understood to be. If so, butter then at Uttoxeter was worth but about twopence a pound, supposing the five pots of butter sent to Tutbury, costing 12*s.*, contained fourteen pounds of butter each. About fifty years before butter was retailed throughout the kingdom at sevenpence per pound; but this was regarded as an enormous price, which, Stowe says, 'was a judgment for their sins.' It is highly probable, therefore, that the pots contained fourteen pounds of butter, which consequently was twopence per pound at Uttoxeter, when the five pots were bought, especially as it corresponds with the price of cheese at that time in the town, as to which the old parochial accounts have preserved very distinct information, the sum of £7 15*s.* 10*d.* having been paid for 8 cwt. 2 qrs. 7 lbs., which was also for the besieged at Tutbury."

The following entries, from the churchwardens' accounts of Uttoxeter, illustrate this interesting subject:—

		£	s.	d.
	c. q. lb.			
1644. May 7.	For 8 2 7 of cheese to Tutbury . . .	7	15	10
	For 5 *potts of butter* to ditto	0	12	0
1645. June 25.	Bread, beer, cheese, *a pot of butter*, and a flitch of bacon, for Lieut.-Col. Watson's men quartered at Blunts Hall . . .	2	5	6

The butter pots were tall cylindrical vessels, of coarse clay, and very imperfectly baked. They are now of great rarity, but specimens may be seen in the Hanley Museum, and in the Museum of Practical Geology. Their form will be understood by the engraving on the next page, which exhibits one example from each of these museums. It is worthy of remark that even yet, as it was in Shaw's days, Irish or Dutch butter, which is generally imported in casks, and is in most places known as "tub butter," is, in the potteries, usually called "pot butter."

Of the state of the Staffordshire potteries at this period, the latter half of the seventeenth century, Dr. Plot gives a most interesting and valuable account, in which he shows not only what clays were then used, but also speaks of the glazes, and describes the modes of manufacture of some of

the vessels. The clays, it appears, were mostly procured from the coal measures, and fine sand to temper and mix with them was procured from Baddeley Edge, Mole Cop, and other places. The following is Dr. Plot's account:—

"25. Other potter's clays for the more common wares there are at many other places, particularly at Horsley Heath, in the parish of Tipton; in Monway field, above mentioned, where there are two sorts gotten, one of a yellowish colour, mixt with white, the other blewish; the former stiff and heavy, the other more friable and light, which, mixt together, work better than apart. Of these they make divers sorts of vessels at Wednesbury, which they paint with slip, made of a reddish sort of earth gotten at Tipton. But the greatest pottery they have in this county is carried on at Burslem, near Newcastle-under-Lyme, where for making their different sorts of pots they have as many different sorts of clay, which they dig round about the towne, all within half a mile's distance, the best being found nearest the coale, and are distinguish't by their colours and uses as followeth:—

1. *Bottle clay*, of a bright whitish streaked yellow colour.
2. *Hard fire-clay*, of a duller whitish colour, and fully intersperst

with a dark yellow, which they use for their *black wares*, being mixt with the

3. *Red blending clay*, which is of a dirty red colour.
4. *White clay*, so called it seems, though of a blewish colour, and used for making yellow-colour'd ware, because yellow is the lightest colour they make any ware of.

All which they call *throwing* clays, because they are of a closer texture, and will work on the wheel.

"26. Which none of the three other clays they call *Slips* will any of them doe, being of looser and more friable natures; these, mixt with water, they make into a consistence thinner than a Syrup, so that being put into a bucket it will run out through a Quill. This they call *Slip*, and is the substance wherewith they *paint* their wares, whereof the

1. Sort is called the *Orange Slip*, which, before it is work't, is of a greyish colour, mixt with orange balls, and gives the ware (when annealed) an orange colour.
2. The *White Slip:* this, before it is work't, is of a dark blewish colour, yet makes the ware yellow, which being the *lightest* colour they make any of, they call it, as they did the clay above, the *white slip*.
3. The *Red Slip*, made of a dirty reddish clay, which gives ware a black colour.

Neither of which clays or slips must have any gravel or sand in them. Upon this account, before it be brought to the wheel, they prepare the clay by steeping it in water in a square pit till it be of a due consistence; then they bring it to their beating board, where, with a long *Spatula*, they beat it till it be well mixt; then, being first made into great *squarish* rolls, it is brought to the *wageing board*, where it is slit into thin flat pieces with a *wire*, and the least stones or gravel pick't out of it. This being done, they *wage* it, *i.e.* knead or mould it like *bread*, and make it into round *balls* proportionable to their work; and then 'tis brought to the wheel, and formed as the workman sees good.

"27. When the potter has wrought the clay either into hollow or flat ware, they set it abroad to dry in fair weather, but by the fire in foule, turning them as they see occasion, which they call *whaving*. When they are dry they *stouk* them, *i.e.* put ears and handles to such vessels as require them. These also being dry, they *slip*, or *paint* them, with their severall sorts of slip, according as they designe their work; when the first slip is dry, laying on the others at their leisure, the *orange slip* makeing the ground, and the *white* and *red* the paint; which two colours they break with a *wire brush*, much after the manner they doe when they *marble* paper, and then *cloud* them with a *pencil* when they are pretty dry. After the vessels are painted they *lead* them with that sort of *Lead Ore* they call *Smithum*, which is the smallest *ore* of all, beaten into dust, finely sifted, and strewed upon them; which gives them the *gloss*, but not the colour; all the colours being chiefly given by the variety of slips, except the *motley colour*, which is procured by blending the *Lead* with *Manganese*, by the workmen call'd *Magnus*. But when they have a mind to shew the utmost of their skill in giving their wares a fairer gloss than ordinary, they lead them then with lead calcined into powder, which they also sift fine and strew upon them as before, which not only gives them a higher gloss, but goes much further too in their work than the lead ore would have done.

"28. After this is done they are carried to the oven, which is ordinarily above 8 foot high, and about 6 foot wide, of a round copped forme, where they are placed one upon another from the bottom to the top; if they be ordinary wares, such as *cylindricall butter pots*, &c., that are not leaded, they are exposed to the *naked* fire, and so is all their *flat ware*, though it be leaded, having only *parting shards*, *i.e.* thin bits of old pots, put between them to keep them from sticking together; but if they be *leaded hollow wares*, they doe not expose them to the *naked* fire, but put them in *shragers*, that is, in coarse metall'd pots made of *marle* (not *clay*) of divers formes, according as their wares require, in which they put commonly three pieces of clay, called *Bobbs*, for the ware to stand on, to keep it from sticking to the *shragers;* as they put them in the *shragers*, to keep them from sticking to one another (which they would certainly otherwise doe by reason of the leading), and to preserve them from the vehemence of the fire, which else would melt them downe, or at least warp them. In twenty-four hours an oven of pots will be burnt; then they let the fire goe out by degrees, which in ten hours more will be perfectly done, and then they draw them for sale, which is chiefly to the poor *Crate-men*, who carry them at their backs all over the countrey, to whome they reckon them by the piece, *i.e. Quart*, in *hollow ware*, so that six pottle, or three gallon *bottles*, make a *dozen*, and so more or less to a *dozen* as they are of greater or lesser content. The *flat wares* are also reckoned by pieces and dozens, but not (as the *hollow*) according to their *content*, but their different *bredths*."

The vessels marbled, mottled, or "combed," in the manner here so well described by Plot, were dishes and other things for domestic use, and were, it seems, carried about the country, as pancheons and other coarse ware are now, by hawkers. The collector will find fragments of this kind of ornamented ware in the museums at Stoke and at Hanley, and others are in my own and other private collections. A dish of this "combed ware" is shown on the accompanying engraving. Some of the examples are so delicate and minute in their "combing," that it would be difficult to show the pattern in so small a size. The one engraved is therefore

one on which the pattern is of large proportions, and has been produced by a very wide and coarse comb.

The lead mentioned by Plot as used for glazing was the lead ore procured from the lead mines of Derbyshire, which was powdered, or "punned," according to the native dialect, and dusted on to the clay vessel before submitting it to the action of fire.

In 1685 Thomas Miles, of Shelton, made a white stone ware, and at the same time brown stone ware was made at the same place. The stone ware then made was probably somewhat akin in appearance to the "Bellarmines," &c., at that time imported in considerable numbers from Holland and Germany.

As many of my readers may not know to what kind of vessels I allude under the name of Bellarmine, I here give an engraving of two examples to show their form and usual

style of decoration. The *Bellarmine*, or *Long Beard*, as it was commonly called, was a stone-ware pot of bottle form, mostly with a handle at the back and ornament on the front. The neck is narrow, and the lower part, or " belly," as it is technically called, very wide and protuberant. They were in very general use at the "ale-houses" to serve ale in to customers, and were of different sizes—the *gallonier*, containing a gallon; the *pottle pot*, two quarts; the *pot*, a quart; and the *little pot*, a pint.

These jugs were derisively named after Cardinal Bellarmine, who died in 1621. The cardinal having, by his determined and bigoted opposition to the reformed religion, made himself obnoxious in the Low Countries, became naturally an object of derision and contempt with the Protestants, who, among other modes of showing their detestation of the man, seized on the potter's art to exhibit his short stature, his hard features, and his rotund figure, to become the jest of the ale-house, and the byword of the people. Allusions to the Bellarmines are very common in the productions of the English writers of the period.

Ben Jonson, among other allusions, says:—

> "Whose, at the best, some round grown thing, a *jug*
> *Faced with a beard*, that fills out to the guests."

Again, in his "Gipsies metamorphosed," he gives the following, which is a somewhat different and more amusing version of the origin of these vessels:—

"Gaze upon this brave spark struck out of Flintshire upon Justice Jug's daughter, then sheriff of the county, who, running away with a kinsman of our captain's, and her father pursuing her to the Marches, he great with justice, she great with jugling, they were both for the time turned into stone upon sight of each other here in Chester; till at last (see the wonder!) a jug of the town ale reconciling them, the memorial of both their gravities—his in beard, and hers in belly—hath remained ever since preserved in picture upon the most stone jugs of the kingdom."

In another play is the following:—

> "Thou thing,
> Thy belly looks like to some strutting hill,
> O'ershadowed by thy rough beard like a wood;
> Or like a larger jug that some men call
> A *Bellarmine*, but we a *Conscience;*
> Whereon the lewder hand of pagan workman
> Over the proud ambitious head hath carved
> An idol large, with beard episcopal,
> Making the vessel look like tyrant Eglon."

In the curious play of "Epsom Wells," one of the characters, while busy with ale, says:—"Uds bud, my head begins to turn round; but let's into the house. 'Tis dark, we'll have one *Bellarmine* there, and then *Bonus nocius.*"

Numberless other allusions might be quoted, but these are sufficient to illustrate the name of the Bellarmine, and to show its common use, and that the ale-pots, by being formed somewhat on the model of his corpulent figure, and with his "hard-mouthed" features impressed in front, became a popular and biting burlesque upon the cardinal after whom they were named.*

* The vulgar name of "mug" for the human face is most probably derived from this source—the face on the "ale-*mug*," or "ale-pot."

The ordinary ale-pots, the pint-jugs, were, like the grey-beards, principally at first imported, but were afterwards undoubtedly made in Staffordshire, and other places in this kingdom. They were usually ornamented with incised lines, scratched into the soft clay with a sharp point, in form of scrolls, flowers, &c., and then washed in with blue. Not unfrequently a pattern was impressed from a mould on the front, somewhat in the same manner as those on the grey-beards, but consisting usually of a flower or of initials. One of these ale-pots, from an example in my own collection, is

here engraved. In the reign of Elizabeth these "stone pots" were proposed to be made in England, as is shown by the following curious document preserved in the Lansdowne Manuscripts:—

"The sewte of William Simpson, merchaunte—Whereas one Garnet Tynes, a straunger livinge in Acon, in the parte beyond the seas, being none of her ma^ties^ subjecte, doth buy uppe alle the pottes made at Culloin, called *Drinking stone pottes*, and he onelie transporteth them into this realm of England, and selleth them: It may please your ma^tie^ to graunt unto the said Simpson full power and onelie license to provyde transport and bring into this realm the same or such like drinking pottes; and the said Simpson will putt in good suretie that it shall not be prejudiciall to anie of your ma^ties^

subjects, but that he will serve them as plentifullie, and sell them at as reasonable price as the other hath sold them from tyme to tyme.

"Item. He will be bound to double her ma^ties^ custome by the year, whenever it hath been at the most.

"Item. He will as in him lieth drawe the making of such like pottes into some decayed town within this realm, wherebie manie a hundred poore men may be sett a work.

"Note. That no Englishman doth transport any potts into this realm but onlie the said Garnet Tynes, who also serveth all the Low Countries and other places with pottes."

In 1626 a patent was granted to Thomas Rous, *alias* Rius, and Abraham Cullen, for the manufacture of "Stone Potts, Stone Juggs, and Stone Bottells." As this patent very curiously illustrates this part of my subject, I make the following extract:—

"Whereas we are given to understand by our loving subjecte Thomas Rous, als Rius, and Abraham Cullyn, of London, marchante, that heretofore, and at this present, our Kingdome of England and other our Dominions are and have beene served with stone potte, stone jugge, and stone bottles, out of foreign parte from beyond the seas; and they have likewise shewed vnto vs that by their industry and charge, not onely the materialle, but also the arte and manufacture, may be found out and ·pformed—never formerly vsed in this our Kingdome of England, by any which proffitable intencon they have already attempted, and in some goode measure have proceeded in and hope to pfecte, whereby many poore and vnproffitable people may be sett on worke, and put to labour and good ymployment for their maintenance and reliefe, of which they will make further tryall at their own charge for the good of our realmes; and in consideracon thereof they have humbly desired that we would be graciously pleased to grant vnto them our royall priveledge for 'The sole making of the Stone Potte, Stone Jugge, and Stone Bottle,' within our Dominions, for the tearme of fowerteene yeares, for a reward for their Invencon; and they have also voluntarily offered vnto vs for the same a yearely rental of five pounde towarde the increase of our revenue soe longe as they have benefitte by this our grant; neyther doe they desier by vertue of such priviledge to prohibite or hinder the imporcacon of these comodities by others from foreigne parte, but that they may still bring in the same from beyond the seas as they have formerly done.

"Know ye that we graciously tendring and effecting the generall good and benifitt of our kingdomes and our subjecte of the same, and to the end that as well the said Thomas Rous, als Rius, may receave some convenient recompence and proffitte out of their owne labours and endeavours as reason requireth, as also that other our loving subjecte may be thereby encouraged in the like laudable service and endeavours for the comon good of their country, and for other consideracons vs herevnto moving of our especiall grace, certeyne knowledge and meare mocon we have given and granted; and by these presente, for vs, our heires, and successors, doe give and grant full and free lycence, priviledge, power, and authority, vnto the said Thomas Rous, als Rius, and Abraham Cullin, and eyther of them, their and eyther of their executors and administrators, and their, and every, or any of their deputies and assignes having authority from them or any of them in that behalfe, that they and every or any of them, and non others, shall and may from tyme to tyme, and at all tymes, for and during the tearme of fowerteene yeares nexte ensueing the date hereof, within these our Realmes of England and Ireland, and the Dominions thereof, at their or any of their liberty and pleasure, vse, exercise, practise, and put in vse the arte and feate of frameing, workeing, and makeing of all and all manner of potte, jugge, and bottell, comonly called or knowne by the name or names of stone potte, stone jugge, and stone bottelle, whatsoever, whereof the like hath not heretofore beene vsually made or wrought within our said realmes and dominions, and also to make, erecte, and set vpp in any ground, place, or places whatsoever, within our said realmes and dominions, with the consent, agrement, and good likeing of the persons to whome the same shall belong, any fornace or fornaces whatsoever, concerning the said feate or arte of frameing, workeing, and makeing of stone potte, stone jugge, and stone bottell, and the same soe made to vtter and sell in grose or by retayle, or otherwise to doe away or dispose of the same at their or any of their will and pleasuer, and to their or any of their best comodity and proffitt, during the said tearme of fowerteene yeares; and therefore our will and pleasure is, and we doe by these Presente for vs, our heires, and successers, straightly charge, and prohibite, and forbidd all and every person and persons, as well our naturall borne subiecte, as aliens, denizens, and strangers whatsoever (other than the said Thomas Rous, als Rius, and Abraham Cullin, and eyther of them, their and eyther of their executors, administrators, and assignes, and such as shall by them or any of them be sett on worke, licenced, or authorised), that they or any of them doe nott during the tearme aforesaid presume, attempte, or take in hande to make, frame, practise, vse, or exercise, within our said Realmes of England or Ireland, or the Dominions of the same, the said arte, feate, or way of makeing, frameing, or workeing of any manner of the said potte, jugge, or bottelle, comonly called or knowne by the name or names of stone potte, stone jugge, and stone bottelle, whatsoever, not heretofore vsually made or wrought within our said realmes or dominions, and to be put in use and practise by the said Thomas Rous, als Rius, and Abraham Cullin, or eyther of them, their or eyther of their executors, administrators, or assignes, or to counterfett the said arte or feate by them or any of them soe to be putt in vse and practise, nor to presume, attempt, or take in hande to make, erecte, frame, or sett vpp any furnace or furnaces to that purpose, vpon payne of forfeyture of all and every such potte, jugge, and bottelle, soe to be made, wrought, or counterfetted, contrary to the true intente and meaning of these psente, and also vpon payne of breakeing and defaceing of all and every the said furnace or furnaces to be made or erected contrary to the tenor hereof; and, further, vpon payne of our high indignacon and displeasure, and such further penalties and imprisonment as may by the statute or lawes of the said realmes or dominions, or any of them, can or may be inflicted upon them or any of them for their contempt and disobedience in breakeing and contemning our comandement and prerogative royall."

Glazing by salt appears to have been discovered about 1680, and gradually took the place of the lead glaze before used. The account given of this discovery is that "at Mr. Joseph Yates', Stanley, near Bagnall, five miles east of Burslem, the servant was preparing, in an earthen vessel, a salt-ley for curing pork, and during her temporary absence the liquid boiled over, and the sides of the pot were quickly red hot from intense heat; yet, when cold, were covered with an excellent glaze. The fact was detailed to Mr. Palmer, potter, of Bagnall, who availed himself of the occurrence, and told other potters. At the small manufactories in Holden Lane (Adams's), Green Head, and Brownhills (Wedgwood's), salt-glazed ware was soon afterwards made." "The ovens employed for the purpose being used only once weekly, and the ware being cheap, were large in diameter and very high, to contain a sufficient quantity to be baked each time, to cover all contingent expenses. They were constructed with a scaffold round them, on which the firemen could stand, while casting in the salt through holes made in the upper part of the cylinder, above the bags or inner vertical flues; and the saggers were made of completely refractory materials, with holes in their sides, for the vapourised salt to circulate freely among all the vessels in the oven, to affect their surfaces." The ware thus glazed, and made from the common clay, with a mixture of fine sand from Mole Cop, was called "Crouch ware," and in this all the ordinary articles of domestic use, including jugs, cups, dishes, &c., were made. At this time, it is stated, there were only twenty-two ovens in Burslem and its neighbourhood. "The employment of salt in glazing Crouch ware was a long time practised before the introduction of white clay and flint. The vast volumes of smoke and vapours from the ovens entering the atmosphere, produced that dense white cloud which, from about eight o'clock till twelve on the Saturday morning (the time of 'firing up,' as it is called), so completely enveloped the whole interior of the town, as to cause persons often to run against each other, travellers to mistake the road; and strangers have mentioned it as extremely disagreeable, and not unlike the smoke of Etna or Vesuvius. But a smoky atmosphere is not regarded by the patriotic observer, who can view through it an industrious population, employed for the benefit of themselves and their country, and behold vast piles of national wealth enhanced by individual industry."

In 1688 two brothers named Eler, or Elers, traditionally believed to have been potters, from Holland, are said to have followed the Prince of Orange (William III.) to England, and two years later to have settled at Bradwell and at Dimsdale—two very secluded situations, far from turnpike roads, and scarcely discernible from Burslem or Red Hill—where they erected kilns, and commenced the making of a fine red ware, in imitation of the oriental red porcelain, from a vein of clay which, by some means, they had discovered existed at this spot. Here they produced remarkably fine and good red ware, of compact and hard texture, good colour, and of very characteristic and excellent designs. They were men of much skill and taste, and their productions so closely resemble those of Japan as to be occasionally mistaken for them. An example,

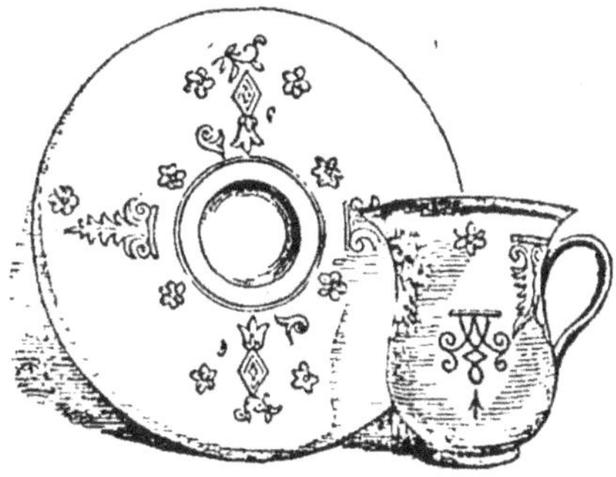

from the Museum of Practical Geology, is here shown. The Elers, besides the red ware, also produced an exceedingly good Egyptian black, by a mixture of manganese with the clay; and this was the precursor and origin of the fine black bodies of Josiah Wedgwood and others. "Their extreme precaution," says Shaw, "to keep secret their processes, and jealousy lest they might be accidentally witnessed by any purchaser of their wares—making them at Bradwell, and conveying them over the fields to Dimsdale, there to be sold, being only two fields distant from the turnpike road, and having some means of communication (believed to be earthenware pipes, like those for water) laid in the ground between the two contiguous farmhouses, to intimate the approach of persons supposed to be intruders—caused them to experience considerable and constant annoyance. In vain did they adopt measures for self-protection in regard to their manipulations, by employing an idiot to turn the thrower's wheel, and the most ignorant and stupid workmen to perform the laborious operations, and by locking up these persons while at work, and strictly examining each prior to quitting the manufactory at night—all their most important processes were however developed, and publicly stated for general benefit. Mortified at the failure of all their precaution, disgusted at the prying inquisitiveness of their Burslem neighbours, and fully aware that they were too far distant from the principal market for their productions—even had not other kinds of porcelain been announced, which probably would diminish their sales—about 1710 they discontinued their Staffordshire manufactory, and removed to Lambeth, or Chelsea (where is at this day a branch of the family), and connected the interests of their new manufactory with those of a glass manufacture, established in 1676 by Venetians, under the auspices of the Duke of Buckingham. Others, however, have stated that their removal was consequent on misunderstanding and persecution because their oven cast forth such tremendous volumes of smoke and flame, during the time of glazing, as were terrific to the inhabitants of Burslem, and caused all its (astonishing number of *eight*) master potters to hurry in dismay to Bradwell."

I shall, later on, show how the secret was surreptitiously obtained by two persons named Astbury and Twyford, and give some interesting particulars relating to them. It is interesting to add that the oven erected and used by the Elers was in existence as late as the beginning of the present century, and that the place, in an old account book in my possession, is called the "Eller field."

The two potters who had wormed out the secret of the Elers are said each to have commenced business on his own account at Shelton, and to have made "RED," "CROUCH," and "WHITE STONE" wares from native clays, using salt glaze for some of the vessels, and lead ore for others.

So little has hitherto been known of the Elers, and of the important part they played in improving the potter's art in Staffordshire, that a few words more concerning them must become interesting to my readers, especially when it is remembered that these brothers produced the finest kind of ware which had at that time been made in this country, and that their biography has until now been entirely neglected. The family of Elers is one of considerable antiquity in the northern part of Lower Saxony, where several places, as for instance Elersdorf, Elersdorpt, and Elerswolf, bear their name. In Hamburg, hereditary posts of honour and distinction were long attached to the family. Of this family was Admiral Elers,* who was commander of the fleet at Hamburg, and who married a princess of the royal house of Baden. By this marriage it appears the Admiral had one son, named Martin Elers, born in 1621. After his father's death, this Martin Elers is said to have asserted his claim to some of the Baden family honours and distinctions, which were made the subject of long and expensive litigation, and in the end judgment was given against him in the Aulic Councils of the Empire. Disappointed at the result, and affected by the great expense attending the litigation, Martin Elers at once removed into Holland. In 1650 this Martin Elers married a daughter of Daniel Van Mildret, a rich burgomaster of Amsterdam, with whom he is said to have received a tun of gold as dower. In the house of this burgomaster, the queen of King Charles I., Henrietta Maria, is reported to have sought an asylum, and to have frequently nursed their daughter on her lap. By this marriage Martin Elers had two sons—John Philip and David; the first one being named after the Elector of Mentz, who was his godfather (Queen Christina of Sweden holding him in her arms at the baptismal font). Martin was a man of considerable ability and learning, and was appointed ambassador to several courts.

John Philip Elers was a good chemist and an excellent mechanician, and was held in much esteem by Boerhave. On the Revolution of 1688, he with his brother accompanied the Prince of Orange, afterwards King William III., to England. The Prince, however, did nothing to further the

* For much of the information contained in this notice of the family of Elers, I am indebted to Major Lacy, whose wife is a lineal descendant of this Admiral Elers.

fortunes of the family, except the granting of a pension of three hundred a year to the sister of the Elers, who became the second wife of Sir William Phipps, the founder of the house of Mulgrave. Elers, or rather, I believe, the two brothers, settled in Staffordshire, John Philip having married a Miss Banks (whose sister had married into the Vernon family), in August, 1699. The story of the success of their manufacture of pottery, and of the not very creditable means used to worm out their secret, I have already told. On leaving Staffordshire, John Philip Elers settled for a time at Battersea, or Vauxhall, and from thence removed to Dublin, where he embarked in commercial speculations. David Elers became a merchant in London, and, dying unmarried, was buried at Battersea.

John Philip Elers left a son, Paul, born in Dublin, who was brought up to the bar, and had his chambers in the Temple. Of this gentleman a somewhat amusing anecdote is told. He had, it seems, an intimate friend, a member of the family of Grosvenor. Mr. Grosvenor being on the point of marriage to an heiress of the Hungerfords, of Black Bourton, Oxfordshire, had arranged with his friend, Mr. Elers, to go down with him to draw up the marriage settlements. While this was going on, Mr. Grosvenor and his bride-elect quarrelled, and the lady transferred her affections and her estates to Mr. Elers. They were shortly afterwards married, and Mr. Elers gave up his profession, and retired to the estate he had thus acquired. He soon, however, became involved, and ultimately, after cutting off the entail, the estates passed into the hands of the Duke of Marlborough. Mr. Elers had a family of nine children—Paul George, lieutenant of the 70th Regiment; John, in the navy; Maria, married to Richard Lovell Edgeworth, and consequently mother to Maria Edgeworth, from whom she inherited her talents as well as her name; Louisa, married to the Rev. Alexander Colston; Charlotte, married to the Rev. John Kirby; Diana, married to the Rev. R. Welchman; Rachel, married to Capt. Hopkins, R.M., who was killed on board the *Bellerophon*, at the Battle of the Nile; Amelia, married to D. Baldey, R.N.; and Jane, who died unmarried. The eldest son, Paul George Elers, married a Miss Debonaire, and by her had three sons, one of whom was a major in the 43rd Regiment; another (George) was captain in the 12th regiment; and the third (Edward) a lieutenant in the navy, who married Eliza Younghusband. By this lady he had four children. Mr. Elers died while the children were yet young, and his widow afterwards married Admiral Sir Charles Napier, who gave the children his own name in addition to that of Elers. The name of Elers has thus, in the direct line, become extinct. These children are—Major-General Edward Hungerford Delaval Elers-Napier; Elizabeth Ann Elers-Napier, married to Colonel Cherry, 1st Madras Light Cavalry; Capt. Charles George Elers-Napier, R.N.; and Georgiana Elers-Napier, now the wife of Major Lacy.

CHAPTER IV.

MANUFACTURE OF TOBACCO-PIPES.—CHRONOLOGICAL SERIES OF EXAMPLES.—TILES FOR GARDEN KNOTS.—THE WEDGWOODS. —JOHN WEDGWOOD.—PUZZLE JUGS.—EARTHENWARE CRADLE.—DELFT WARE.—ENGLISH DELFT WARE.—UNIVERSALITY OF BLUE IN POTTERY.—EMBOSSED STONE WARE.—DISCOVERY OF THE USE OF FLINT, BY ASTBURY.—PATENTS FOR GRINDING FLINT.—PATENT FOR DAMASKING, ETC.—RALPH SHAW.—LITIGATION WITH OTHER POTTERS.—POSSET POTS.—DR. THOMAS WEDGWOOD, JUNIOR.—RALPH WOOD.

AMONG the many descriptions of fictile art made in the pottery district, TOBACCO-PIPES had, from many years before Plot's time, been made at Newcastle-under-Lyme, and Astbury, soon after he commenced at Shelton, appears to have begun to use the Biddeford pipe-clay, for coating over and washing the insides of vessels. By constant improvements on this, the white dipped ware, or white stone ware, was soon produced. The maker of tobacco-pipes at Newcastle-under-Lyme, in 1676 and thereabouts, was Charles Riggs, of whom Plot makes mention.

It may be interesting to my readers, while thus alluding to the manufacture of *tobacco-pipes* in the potteries, to know something of their forms at the time when Plot wrote, as well as in preceding and later times. This will be best done by aid of the following illustrations. In the reign of Elizabeth, the pipes—which are now and then dug up, and are in our day, from their small size and peculiar shapes, known as "fairy pipes," and other similar names—were usually, it appears, of the elongated form. Pipes of this shape are correctly appropriated to the reign of Elizabeth, through examples being known bearing makers' names, who are

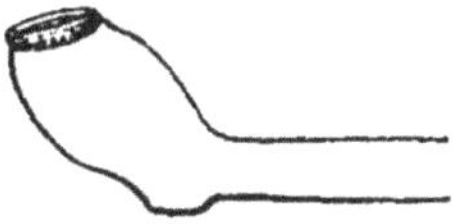

proved to have lived in that reign. The next, here shown, is of the time of James I. or Charles I., in which reigns there appears to have been a considerable diversity of form, as here shown from engravings of the period; the dates being, Fig. 1, 1630; Fig. 2, 1632; Fig. 3, 1640; Fig. 4, 1642. The latter, it will be seen, is of the same shape as those of the preceding reign, and was in general use for a long period.

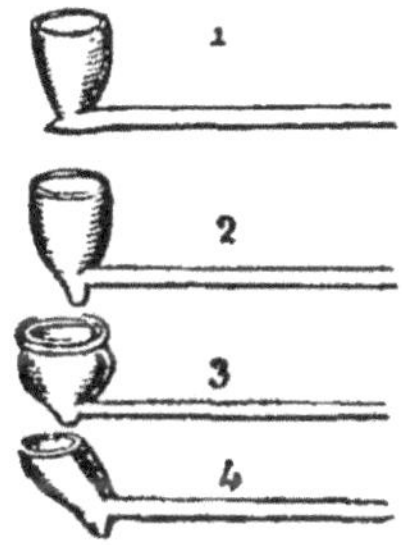

The next examples show the prevailing shapes in the time of the Commonwealth, and the reign of Charles II., the five smaller engravings being selected from traders' tokens of the period, of the following dates:—

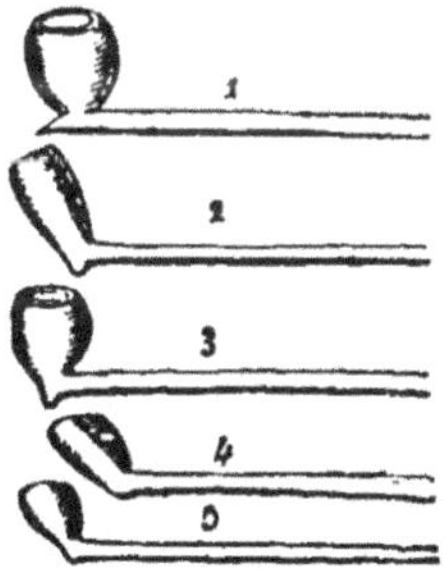

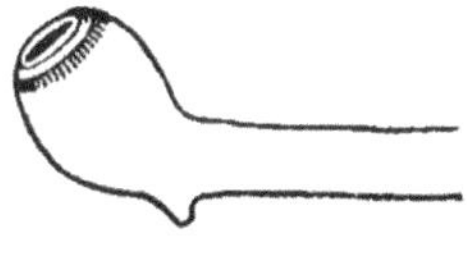

Fig. 1, 1650; Fig. 2, 1666; Fig. 3, 1668; Fig. 4, 1668; and Fig. 5, 1669.

Pipes of an elongated form, such as next shown, are usually ascribed to the time of William III., and, being found more plentifully in those localities where his Dutch troops were stationed, this is probably a correct supposition. Barrel-shaped bowls were, however, then in use, and a very

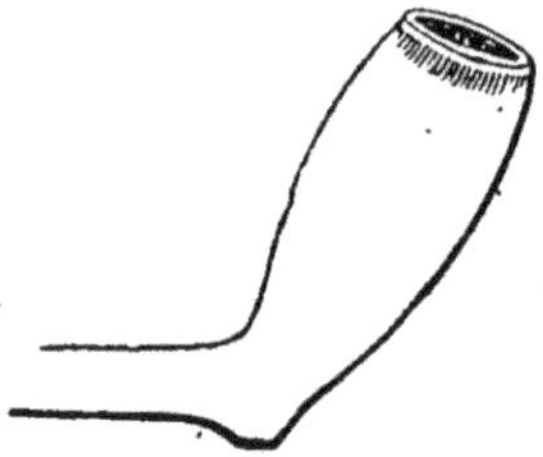

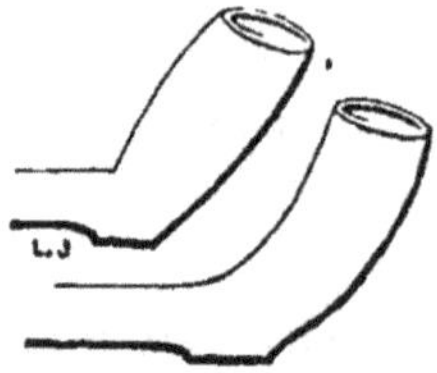

interesting example is here engraved, bearing the date 1689.

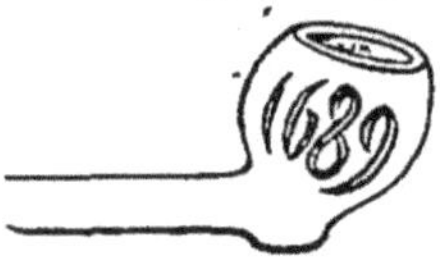

Pipes at this time were, to some extent, imported from Holland, but by far the greater part used were of English make, to which Newcastle-under-Lyme contributed no small quantity. From this time downwards, the shape of the pipe gradually merged from the bulbous into the elongated form just shown, and so on to the wide-mouthed shape of the present time. It may be well to note, that instead of the old pipes being, as is commonly believed, of Dutch manufacture, Holland was originally indebted to England for the introduction of the art into that country.

With reference to this Charles Riggs, the pipe-maker of Newcastle-under-Lyme, I am pleased to be enabled to say, that from recent researches I am justified in believing the pipes engraved on the next page to have been made by him. Nearly a hundred of these pipes, each bearing the *initials* of C. R., found in the neighbourhood of Newcastle, and at other places in the pottery district, have come under my notice, and are, I think, without doubt, of his workmanship. They are peculiarly interesting too, as showing the transition, in the lifetime of one maker, from the flat heel to the pointed spur. The first example on the engraving on the next page has the flat heel,* bearing the stamp of the maker, C. R., with crescent above and below. The second illustration

* The flat heels served as rests for the pipes; the old-fashioned smokers resting them on the table while they enjoyed the "weed."

shows a pipe with the pointed spur, bearing the same stamp on the front of the bowl. It is thus shown, that on the

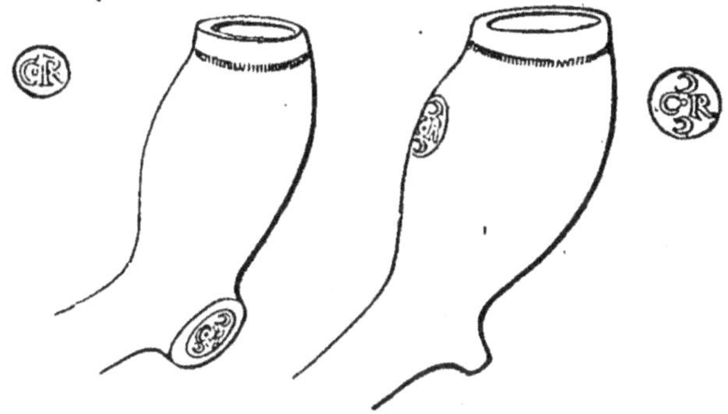

change of fashion, the maker being unable to place his "mark" in its usual position, was compelled either to abandon it altogether, or to impress it on the bowl. Another mark used by Riggs (also shown on the engraving) was simply his initials C. R., and this, too, occurs on pipes of both shapes.

Plot, speaking of the clays of the pottery district, says—

"As for *Tobacco-pipe clays*, they are found all over the county, near Wrottesley House, and Stile Cop, in Cannock Wood, whereof they make pipes at Armitage and Lichfield, both which, though they are *greyish clays*, yet burn very white. There is *Tobacco-pipe* clay also found at Darlaston, near Wednesbury, but of late disused, because of better and cheaper found in Monway field, betwixt Wednesbury and Willingsworth, which is of a *whitish* colour, and makes excellent *pipes;* as doth also another of the same colour, dug near the salt water poole in Pensnet Chase, about a mile and a half south of Dudley. And *Charles Riggs*, of Newcastle, makes very good *pipes* of three sorts of clay, a *white* and *blew*, which he has from between Shelton and Hanley Green, whereof the blew clay burns the *whitest*, but not so *full* as the *white*, *i.e.* it *shrinks* more; but the best sort he has is from Gruffer's Ash, being *whitish*, mixt with *yellow;* it is a short, brittle sort of clay, but burns full and white; yet he sometimes mixes it with the blew before mentioned."

As a further illustration of this interesting subject, the accompanying engraving, which exhibits a number of forms of pipes made in the adjoining county, Shropshire, is given.

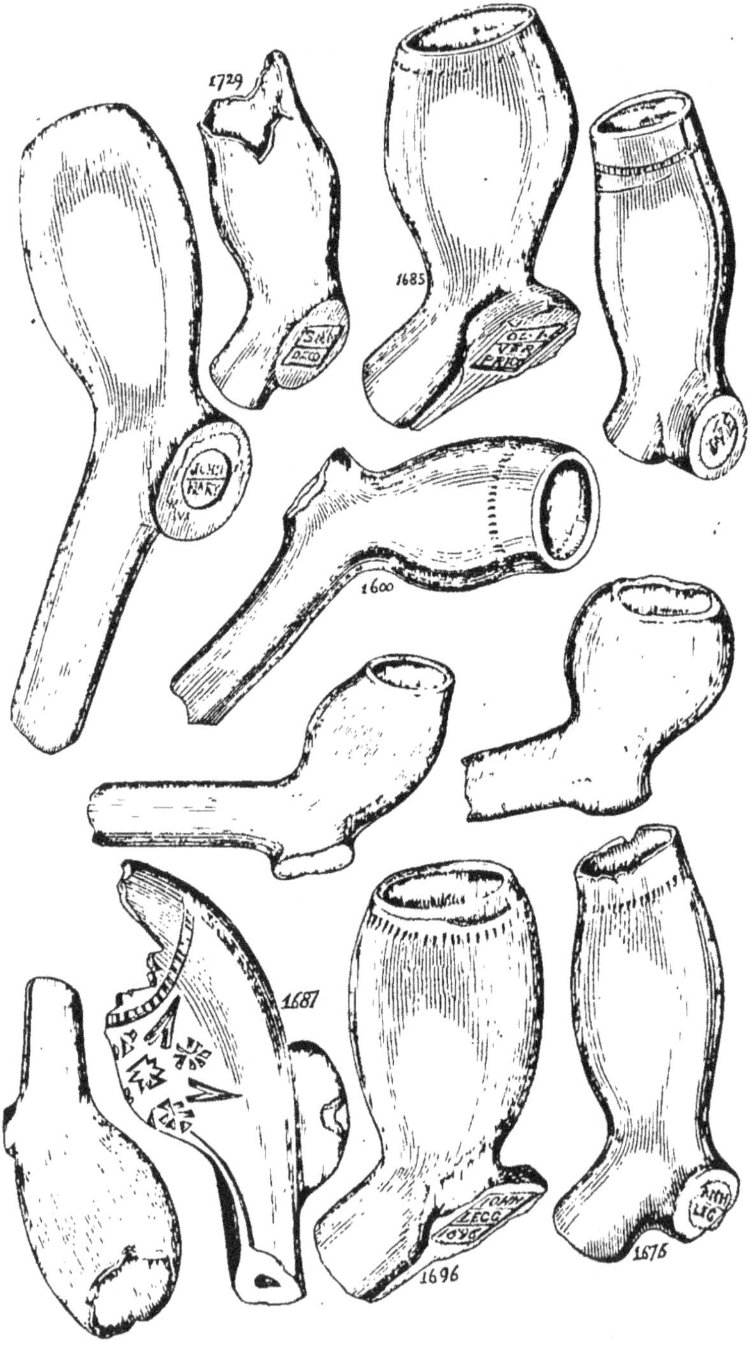
1729
1685
1600
1687
1696
1676

Tiles for garden edgings were at this time made at Newcastle-under-Lyme, and must have had extensive sale, as the gardens of the better kind were, in those days, always laid out in "knots" of more or less elaborate design. Plot, speaking of this branch of manufacture, says:—

"Also at Newcastle-under-Lyme, the *Tiles* burnt in a *Kill* the usual way being found not to last, one *Mr. Thomas Wood* of the same Towne, first contrived to burn them (which we may look upon as an art relating to Fire) in a *Potters' Oven;* wherein he made them so good and lasting, that notwithstanding they have been put to the hardship of dividing the parts of *garden knots,* to endure not only the perpetual moisture of the earth, but frost, snow, and all sorts of weather; yet they few of them decay, scarce five tiles in five hundred having failed in twenty yeares' time; so that now he has been followed by all the countrey thereabout."

Long before the period about which I am now writing, the Wedgwoods, as I shall show in the course of this work, were potters in Burslem, and produced most of the varieties of wares then in use. The family was one of considerable note, and branches of it were settled in different localities. One of these settled in Yorkshire, and for several generations were potters there; and other branches settled in Cumberland, Westmoreland, and other districts, and carried on their family trade. One interesting piece of earthenware, connected with the Wedgwood family, has recently been added to the Museum of Practical Geology, and as it is dated of the period to which in my narrative I have now arrived, I have introduced an engraving on the following page which I am enabled, through the courtesy of Mr. Reeks, who has supplied the drawing, to give. It is a "Puzzle Jug," of brown ware, bearing the name of an early member of the Wedgwood family. It bears the name incised—

JOHN WEDG WOOD 1691.

The jug is more simple in construction than many are, the hollow channel merely passing up the handle and round the upper rim, which has three spouts.

And here it may be interesting, perhaps, to say a word or two on "puzzle jugs," which are curious and very interesting vessels, about which but little is known even by collectors. The puzzle jug was an ale jug, and was so contrived, by perforations in various parts, and by open work in its neck and spout, as to render it impossible to use it like other jugs.

The liquor being drawn into the jug by the tapster, the puzzle was for the customer to drink it all without spilling. It became a prolific source of wagers, and most ale-houses found it to their advantage to keep one or more of different forms for their visitors. The handle usually sprang from near the bottom of the jug, and was carried up its "belly" some distance, when it bowed out in the general form, and was attached to the rim at its top. The handle and rim were made hollow, opening into the inside of the jug near the bottom, and around the rim were attached a number of little spouts, differently placed, according to the whim of the potter. The ale could thus only be drunk by carefully covering up with the fingers all the spouts but one, and through this one the liquor would have to be sucked into the mouth. Beneath the handle a small hole was, however, usually made, through which, if not carefully and closely covered, the ale would spill, and thus cause the discomfiture of the drinker and the loss of his wager.

In my own collection I have the good fortune to possess several interesting examples of puzzle jugs, some of which are of remarkably good form and construction, and of different dates. One of them bears the motto—

> "From mother earth i took my birth,
> Then form[d] a Jug by Man,
> And now stand here, fill[d] with good cheer,
> Taste of me if you can."

The accompanying engraving of a puzzle jug of Delft ware, in Mr. Mayer's magnificent museum, will show by its motto

the kind of wagers which were laid over these curious pots. The verse runs thus—

> "Here, gentlemen, come try y[r] skill,
> I'll hold a wager, if you will,
> That you Dont Drink this liq[r] all
> Without you spill or lett some Fall."

Another one, which bears the name of A. NORRIS, has a somewhat similar verse—

"Gentlemen, now try your Skill,
I'll hold you Sixpence, if you will,
That you dont drink unless you Spil."

Another one which I have seen has simply the characteristic motto,

"The Ale is good, taste,"

around it; implying that it is of good taste if you can but get it!

The accompanying is the representation of another puzzle jug of Staffordshire make, and of different construction,

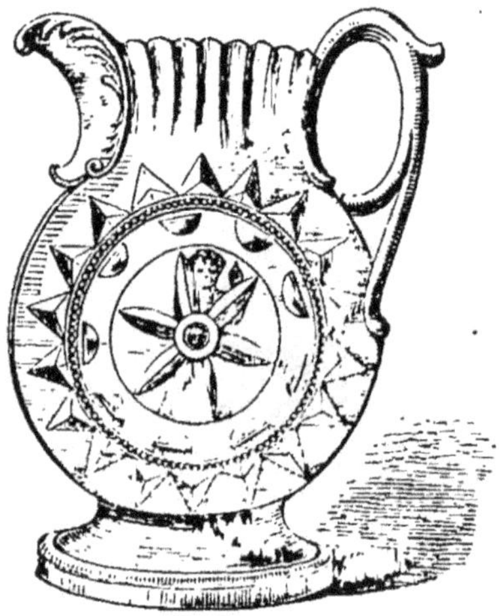

preserved in the Jermyn Street Museum. It is, as will be seen, pierced through the centre.

In some instances a tube is passed from the handle down, inside the jug, to the bottom, and thus adds to the difficulty of drinking,

"Without you spill or let some fall."

In one in my own possession, too, the inside of the jug is made funnel-shaped, with double sides, which is a very unusual mode of construction.

The same kind of ware as the Toft dishes, given on a preceding page, was made in the potteries throughout the latter half of the seventeenth and most part of the eighteenth centuries. Of this kind of ware is the highly interesting

relic which is here engraved. It is, as will be seen, a small earthenware cradle of excellent form, and elaborately ornamented. It is of brown ware, similar, but of finer quality, to the dishes. The ground is a rich reddish brown, the ornaments of buff and black. It is peculiarly interesting, as bearing the date on its top of 1693. This valuable example of English fictile art, which is $7\frac{3}{4}$ inches long, and $4\frac{3}{4}$ inches in height, is in the Bateman museum at Lomberdale House, where there are several other interesting specimens, to some of which I shall yet have occasion to refer.

In all these pieces the ware is first coated over with its ground colour, and the patterns then drawn on in "slip," one colour on the other, and afterwards glazed. The outlines are generally of the darkest coloured slip, with dots, or pellets of buff.

Delft ware was made in Staffordshire about the period of which I have been writing, and continued to be made until its use was superseded by the other bodies. Examples of English Delft ware from different localities are now and then to be met with, and some excellent specimens are in my own possession. Others, for comparison, may be seen in the Museum at Hanley, and the Museum of Practical Geology. In 1710 Mr. Thomas Heath, of Lane Delph, manufactured this kind of ware, and was very successful. His productions were of a good blue-greyish white, and were decorated in the usual Delft fashion, with landscapes and other blue patterns rudely drawn by hand.

Delft ware was originally, as its name imports, made at Delft, in Holland, where it is stated the manufacture of earthenware was carried on as early as 1310. In the middle of the seventeenth century there were, it is stated by Chaffers, "nearly fifty potteries in operation at Delft, employing more than a fourth part of the entire population, viz., about 7,000 persons, and this was the most flourishing period of its existence. In the middle of the eighteenth century they were reduced to twenty-four, yet making a considerable quantity of pottery. At the present day, of all this number of potteries only one remains, and its productions are of a very inferior character, being of a yellowish pipe-clay, devoid of any attempt at ornamentation." Of this great change Von Bleswych says that the Delft pottery "was so famous, not only in these provinces, but also in Brabant, Flanders, France, Spain, and in the West and East Indies, that in a few years twenty-eight potteries were established in Delft alone; the number was afterwards increased to thirty. But these, like all similar establishments, had their turn of prosperity; for in 1702 the number had decreased to twenty. In another twenty-six years more were given up. In 1808 six only were in existence, and in 1849 we are informed that only two remained. The hard paste wares of Wedgwood were found to be as superior to those of Delft as those of Delft had been to the soft wares of the preceding epoch. This naturally caused the decline of this celebrated production, which now gave place to the English wares."

For a long period the bulk of the pots used in England were imported from Holland, but Dutch workmen coming over and settling here, and English workmen prosecuting their researches and experiments in a successful manner, soon altered this state of affairs, and the home market became stocked with home-made goods. Thus, instead of looking to foreign states for a supply of wares, England so successfully competed with them in their production as soon to be able to export at a cheaper rate than they could manufacture. Delft ware, although not generally known to have been made in England, was, as I have on another occasion shown, undoubtedly made in several localities. Liverpool produced its Delft ware of excellent quality, and there its manufacture continued till quite a late period, as many examples in Mr. Mayer's museum, and in my own collection, testify. London, Bristol, Lowestoft, and indeed several places besides the Staffordshire district, produced the same kind of ware during the last century. The peculiarity of the Delft ware is that the body is formed of a soft buffish-coloured clay, and then washed on its surface with a fine slip of a blueish or greenish-white tint, on which the pattern is painted—generally in blue—and then glazed over. The effect produced is extremely soft and pleasing, and the better pieces have a nearer approach in softness and brilliance of appearance to Oriental porcelain than most wares have.

The accompanying engraving of two plates of Delft ware, from my own collection, will serve to show the commoner and more homely kind of goods of that peculiar kind made in this country; and the next illustration will show an example of the Delft ware to which I have alluded as being said to have been made in Liverpool, from the splendid museum of my friend Mr. Mayer, F.S.A. It is one of a pair

of flower-pots of Delft ware richly decorated in blue, and having heads at their sides.

Dated examples of Delft ware are not uncommon, and the engraving on the following page, of the central pattern from a plate belonging to Mr. Mills, exhibits one very favourite style of ornamentation—that of having the names, &c., of the parties for whom the piece was made painted on them. A good specimen of English Delft ware is shown in the inscribed puzzle jug engraved on a preceding page.

Sometimes the colours introduced on Delft ware were other than blue, green, yellow, or red. Blue was, however, the prevailing colour for all decorations, and continued in use till the ware ceased to be made. So accustomed had the Staffordshire potters become to "blue and white" ware, from the time of the manufacture of "Delft ware" downwards, through the different improvements of earthenware to the introduction of "blue printing," that it became, as it were, almost a part and parcel of their manufacturing creed. I have heard it related of one manufacturer (whose name is well known in

the district) of the last century, who was a light-hearted merry fellow, always fiddling, dancing, and humming tunes, that if any of his potters came to ask him what he was to do with any piece then in progress, he would go on fiddling and dancing, while he sang out the reply—

> "Tip it wi' blew,
> An' then it'll dew."

This the children of the neighbourhood soon caught up, and it became a popular rhyme about the place.

Another important variety of ware made in Staffordshire was the white ware—a dirty, creamy looking white—which is usually, though erroneously, called "ELIZABETHAN WARE." Of these a plate, for the purpose of exhibiting the raised border, is shown on the accompanying engraving, from an example in the Museum of Practical Geology. The centre of this example is, of course, printed, and is of later date than the plain examples. Of this ware I possess some excellent specimens, and others will be found in various collections. The ware was impressed from *metal* moulds, some of which, of extreme interest, are preserved in the Hanley Museum.

In 1720 the discovery of the use of flint was made by Astbury, as will be shown in a future chapter, and to this introduction may be dated many of the improvements which afterwards took place. Soon after this period the "sun-pans," or tanks, in which the clay was allowed to lie until it became fit for use, were superseded by "slip-kilns," in which the clays were prepared.

In 1724 a patent was taken out by Redrich and Jones for "a new art or method, as well for staining, veining, spotting, clouding, damasking, or otherwise imitating the various kinds of marble, porphiry, and other rich stones, and tortoiseshell, on wood, stone, and earthenware, and all and every such goods, wares, utensils, and things as are made, cut, or fashioned thereout, as for the making, marbling, veining, spotting, staining, clouding, and damasking any linen, silks, canvas, paper, and leather."

In 1726, and again in 1732, patents were taken out for methods of grinding flints, &c., which were of much importance. The first of these, by Thomas Benson, is described as "an engine or new method for the more expeditious working the said flint stone, whereby all the said hazards and inconveniences attending the same will effectually be prevented." It is stated that in the making of "white pots," flint stone is "the chief ingredient," and that the method hitherto used in preparing it "has been by pounding or breaking it dry, and afterwards sifting it through fine lawns, which has proved very destructive to mankind;" and this invention is to obviate it, and is as follows:—The flint stones are first wetted, then crushed as fine as sand by two large wheels, of the bigness and shape of millstones, of iron, and made to turn upon the edges by the power of a water-wheel. This material is afterwards conveyed into large circular iron pans, "in which there are large iron balls, which, by the power of the water-wheel above named, are swiftly driven round: in a short time the operation is concluded, and by turning a tap the material empties itself into casks."

The next one, by the same Thomas Benson, taken out in 1732, was described as—

"A new engine, or method for grinding of flint stones, being the chief ingredient used in making of white wares, such as pots and other vessels, a manufacture carried on in our county of Stafford, and in some other parts of this our kingdom; that the common method hitherto used in preparing the same hath been by breaking and pounding the stones dry, and afterwards sifting the powder through fine lawns, which hath proved very destructive to mankind, occasioned by the dust suckled into the body, which being of a ponderous nature, fixes so closely upon the lungs that nothing can remove it, insomuch that it is very difficult to find persons to engage in the said manufacture, to the great detriment and decay of that branch of trade, which would otherwise from the usefulness thereof be of great benefit and advantage to our kingdom; that by the petitioner's invention the flint stones are sprinkled with water, so that no dust can arise, then ground as fine as sand, with two large stones made to turn round upon the edges by the power of a wheel, worked either by wind, water, or horses, which is afterwards conveyed into large stone pans, made circular, wherein are placed large stone balls, which, by the power of such wheels are driven round with great velocity; that in a short time the flint stones so broken are reduced to an oily substance, which, by turning of a cock, empties itself into casks provided for that purpose; that by this invention all hazards and inconveniences in making the said manufacture in the common way will be effectually prevented, and in every particular tend to the manifest improvement and advantage thereof, and preserving the lives of our subjects employed therein."

In 1733 (April 24th) Ralph Shaw, potter, of Burslem, who, like many other potters of the district, had long adopted the improvements introduced by Mr. Astbury and others, took out a patent for employing "various sorts of mineral, earth, clay, and other earthy substances, which, being mixt and incorporated together, make up a fine body, of which a curious ware may be made, whose outside will be of a true chocolate colour, striped with white, and the inside white, much resembling the brown China ware, and glazed with salt." The *secret* was merely *washing* the inside, and forming broad lines on the outside of the articles, with a very thick slip of flint and pipe-clay. "To keep his process more secluded and secret, he was accustomed to evaporate his mixed clays on a long trough, in a place locked up under cover, beneath which were flues, for the heat from fire applied on the outside. This also kept the clay free from any kind of dirt; and the idea is supposed to have been gained from the tile-makers' method of drying their tiles in stoves. A pair of flower-pots, excellent specimens of this person's manufacture, which had been received as a present from the maker by his wife's grandfather, were in the author's possession till very recently. Mr. Shaw became so litigious and overbearing, that many of the manufacturers were extremely uncomfortable, and prevented improving their productions. Not content with the success he experienced, and the prospect of speedily acquiring affluence, his excessive vanity and insatiable avarice incited to proceedings that terminated in his ruin. Unwilling to admit the customary practices of the business, and to brook any appearance of competition, he was constantly objecting to every trifling improvement as an infringement of his patent, and threatening his neighbours with suits in equity to protect his *sole* rights; till at length self-defence urged them to bear the expenses of a suit he had commenced against J. Mitchell, to try the validity of the patent, at Stafford, in 1736; and very aged persons, whose parents were present, give the general facts of the trial:—All the manufacturers being interested in the decision, those most respectable were in the court. Witnesses proved Astbury's invention and prior usage of the practice, and a special jury of great intelligence and wealth gave a verdict against Mr. Shaw. The learned judge, after nullifying the patent, thus addressed the audience—'Go home, potters, and make whatever kinds of pots you please.' The hall re-echoed with acclamations, and the strongest ebullitions of satisfaction from the potters, to the indescribable mortification of Mr. Shaw and his family, who afterwards went to France, where he carried forward his manufactory, whence some of his family returned to Burslem about 1750." This event is thus characteristically spoken of in native tongue, in the "Burslem Dialect," by Mr. Ward:—

Terrick. Dust moind, Rafe, owt o' th' treyal at Staffurt o' Johnny Mutchil for makkin Rafy Shay's patten ware?

Leigh. Oi just remember, bu oi wur ony a big lad at th' teyme. It had bin mitch tawkt abaht, an when it wur oer, they aw toud'n wot th' judge sed to th' mesters—"Gooa whoom, potters, an mak wot soourts o' pots yoa loiken." And when they coomn to Boslem, aw th' bells i' Hoositon, an Stooke, an th' tahn, wurn ringin loike hey-go-mad, aw th' dey.

The kind of ware just described was sometimes known as "bit-stone ware," from "bits" of stone being used to separate the pieces in the oven. This was, of course, prior to the use of "stilts," "triangles," or "cockspurs."*

* The marks produced by these ingenious little contrivances for keeping the pieces of ware from sticking to each other while under the action of fire, may frequently be noticed on pottery. It has been absurdly said that three spots on the bottoms of old pieces of china denoted it to be

One description of vessel made in the pot-works of Staffordshire and Derbyshire—for Chesterfield, in the latter county, produced some of the best—may not be generally known to the readers of this volume, and therefore a few words concerning them may appropriately be introduced. I allude to *posset pots*. These have been made and regularly used in these and some neighbouring counties from an early period until the last few years. "Posset," my readers will need to be told, is an excellent mixture of hot ale, milk, sugar, spices, and small slices of bread or oat-cake. In Derbyshire and Staffordshire, and their neighbourhood, this beverage was formerly almost, if not quite, universal for supper on Christmas Eve, and the "posset pot" was thus used but once a year, and became often an heir-loom in the family. A small silver coin, and the wedding ring of the mistress of the family, were generally dropped into the posset when the guests were assembled, and those who partook of it took each a spoonful in turn as the "pot" was handed round. Whichever of the party fished up the

coin was considered certain of good luck in the coming year, while an early and happy marriage was believed to be the certain fate of the lucky individual who fished up the ring. A posset pot, here engraved, of much the same kind of ware

Chelsea, and was indeed the distinguishing mark of that celebrated make. Those three spots were simply the marks of the stilts, not of the manufactory, and may be seen on Delft, and indeed almost all other kinds of ware, and of every period.

as the cradle before illustrated, is in the Bateman Museum, and is dated 1711, and bears the words—

GOD : SAVE : THE : QUEEN : 1711 :

the queen alluded to so loyally being, of course, Queen Anne.

For the purpose of showing that the same general form has obtained to our own time, I here give two other examples, the first one bearing the date of 1750, and the next that of 1819. They are both of the hard brown stoneware

made at Chesterfield and Nottingham, and, as is not uncommon, bear the names of the parties for whom they were made, incised, *i.e.* scratched into the soft clay with a fine point.

One of the principal potters in Burslem in the early part of last century was Dr. Thomas Wedgwood, junior (son of Dr. Thomas Wedgwood, also an eminent potter), who produced imitation agate, marble, and other coffee and tea pots, &c., and made a remarkably fine and good white stone ware, beautifully ornamented with raised patterns, produced from the metal or "tough tom" moulds to which I have before alluded. One of the most skilful cutters of these moulds was Aaron Wood, who was apprenticed to Dr. Thomas Wedgwood in 1731. The following is the indenture of this apprenticeship, and will serve to show the wages then paid, and many other interesting particulars relating to the potter's art:—

"This Indenture, made the three-and-twentieth day of August, in the fifth year of the reign of our Sovereign Lord King George the Second over Great Brittaine, &c., Anno Dni. 1731, between Ralph Wood of Burslem, in the County of Stafford, miller, and Aaron Wood his son, of the one part, and Dr. Thomas Wedgwood, of Burslem aforesaid, potter, of the other part; Witnesseth that the said Aaron Wood, with his own free will and consent, and to and with the direction and appointment of his said father, Hath put himself, and doth hereby bind and put himself apprentice unto the said Dr. Thomas Wedgwood, the art, trade, mystery, and occupation of a potter to learn; that is to say, turning in the lathe, handling and trimming (throwing on the wheel being out of this indenture excepted), and with him the said Dr. Thomas Wedgwood, to worke from the eleventh day of November next, being Martinmas day, for during and until the full end and terme of seven years from thence next ensuing and following, and fully to be compleat and ended, and during all which terme and time of seven years the said Aaron Wood, as an apprentice to his said master, will and faithfully shall serve, his secrets shall keep, his commands lawfull and honest everywhere shall do, the goods of his said master he shall not inordinately waste, nor them to any one lend without the said master's lycence, from the business of his said master he shall not absent himself, but as a true and faithful servant shall, during the said terme of seven years, behave and demean himself towards his said master and all his. And the said Ralph Wood shall, during the said terme of seven years, find and provide for his son all sorts of apparell, whether linen, woollen, or other, as also meat, drink, washing, and lodging, fitting and necessary for an apprentice to such trade as aforesaid. And the said Dr. Thomas Wedgwood, in consideration thereof, and of the said seven years' service, doth hereby covenant, promise, and agree, that hee, the said Dr. Thomas Wedgwood, shall and will during the said terme of seven years, teach and instruct, or cause and procure to be taught and instructed, him the said Aaron Wedgwood, his said apprentice, in the business of the said trade aforesaid, so far as turning in the lathe, handling and trimming, as much as thereunto belongeth, or the best way and method he can.

And the said Dr. Thomas Wedgwood doth also promise and engage to pay unto his said apprentice, the said Aaron Wood, for every weeke's worke done by the said apprentice in the first, second, and third year of his said apprenticeship, the sum of one shilling weekly, of good and lawfull money of Great Brittaine, and for every weeke's work done by the said apprentice in the fourth, fifth, and sixth year of his said apprenticeshipp, the full sum of one shilling and sixpence, and for every weeke's work done by the said apprentice in the seventh and last year of his said apprenticeshipp, the full and just sum of four shillings of lawful money of Great Brittaine; and the said Dr. Thomas Wedgwood doth hereby further covenant, promise, and agree that he, the said Dr. Wedgwood, shall and will over and above the weekly wages aforesaid, give yearly to the said Aaron Wood his said apprentice, one pair of new shoes, during the terme of seven years. In witnesse whereof the said parties aforesaid to these present Indentures, have interchangeably put their hands and seales the day and year first above written.

"RALPH WOOD.
"AARON WOOD.
"DR. THO. WEDGWOOD.

"Sealed and delivered in the presence of

"SARA × WOOD.
her mark.

"JOS. ALLEN."

At the conclusion of this term of apprenticeship he was engaged as a journeyman, at five shillings a week, for five years. At the end of that time, in 1743, he engaged himself with John Mitchell, of Burslem, for seven years, at seven shillings per week, and to work by himself. After a time the introduction of plaster moulds, which I shall have to refer to later on, found him constant employment for different masters, among whom was Thomas Whieldon, who afterwards became the partner of Josiah Wedgwood.

Of the general state of the potter's art at the time when Josiah Wedgwood sprang into existence I shall give a glance in the next chapter, and it will therefore be unnecessary here to allude to it. I shall also, later on, show when the manufacture of China was first introduced into the district, and so give a general insight into the progress of the fictile art in Staffordshire.

My object has been to show, what has never before been shown, a continuous chain of evidence of pottery having been made in the district from the earliest—the pre-historic—times, down through every successive change of periods and of races, to the present, and to bring my narrative down to the time of the great Josiah Wedgwood, and to give a slight—and but a very slight—insight into the state of the art at the time when that famous master of his craft first entered into existence.

I have shown that the art of potting was practised by the ancient British inhabitants of Staffordshire; have given reasons for believing that it was followed in the district by the Roman occupiers of the soil; have shown that the Anglo-Saxons practised it in the neighbourhood; and that through the whole of the mediæval period, and without intermission to the present day, pot making has continued in the locality. I have given illustrative engravings of some of the characteristic examples of the different periods, for the purpose of enabling the collector to appropriate correctly such specimens as may come into his hands; and having done this, I proceed in the next part of my work to speak of the great master of his craft, Josiah Wedgwood, and to trace by the events of his life the progress of the art which he dignified and brought to perfection. Other great potters—the Turners, Booths, Woods, Spodes, Mintons, Mayers, Neales, Yateses, and other art-heroes—and the important parts they have played in bringing the district to its present flourishing position, and the manufacture to the high state of perfection it now enjoys, must be left for a future work.

THE WEDGWOODS.

CHAPTER I.

BURSLEM A HUNDRED AND FIFTY YEARS AGO.—WOLSTANTON.—JAMES BRINDLEY, "THE SCHEMER."—THE WEDGWOODS OF HARRACLES AND THEIR ALLIANCES.—HAZELRIGG, VENABLES, AND FENTON FAMILIES.—HORTON HALL, CHURCH, AND MANOR.—THE DE BURSLEM FAMILY: THEIR ALLIANCE WITH THE WEDGWOODS.—GILBERT WEDGWOOD AND MARGARET BURSLEM.—BURSLEM WEDGWOOD.—DESCENT OF THE "OVERHOUSE," "CHURCHYARD," AND "BIG HOUSE" FAMILIES.—THOMAS WEDGWOOD AND MARGARET SHAW.—WILLS OF THOMAS, RICHARD, AND MARY WEDGWOOD.

BURSLEM, the birthplace of Wedgwood, is called the "mother of the potteries," while Wedgwood himself is usually styled the "father of potters." With these two close relationships to the potters of England my narrative of the career of the "great Josiah" will, of course, begin, and as it proceeds will trace out the progress of the one and the works of the other, and show how the perseverance, the industry, the energy, and the taste of the latter have conduced, not only to the prosperity of the former, but to that of the whole district and of the commerce of the kingdom. During the early part of the century which saw the birth of Josiah Wedgwood, and in the latter portion of the preceding one, the potters of Burslem, which in Plot's time was the principal seat of the trade, had, as I have already shown, made much progress in improving their art. Men had risen up amongst them who produced wonders when compared with what had been done by their forefathers, and they began to feel that their art, as yet in its infancy among us, would grow strong and healthy, and become one day what it soon proved to be, a successful rival to foreign workers in the plastic art.

At the time of which I write—a hundred and fifty to two hundred years ago—Burslem was a small, unassuming, straggling little place, with the houses and pot-works, few in number, scattered about in its gardens and by its lane sides. In its centre was a huge May-pole,* around which the "jolly potters" danced and held their festivals, and in every direction were clay pits† and "shard-rucks,"‡ where, from time immemorial, their ancestors had dug the native clay, and thrown by their "wastrels"§ till they had accumulated to a considerable size. Pitfalls and hillocks, the results of the hard labours of the early potters, were thus the principal features of the place, where now the busy and thriving town, raised by the increase of their trade, so flourishingly stands. The wares then made in the district were the coarse brown ware, the finer cane-coloured ware, also made from native clay, Delft ware, crouch ware, a comparatively fine red ware, and clouded, mottled, or marbled ware; and some of the productions, years before the birth of Josiah Wedgwood—who is by many people popularly believed to have been the *founder* of the art in Staffordshire—are of remarkably good form, of excellent workmanship, and are indeed such as it would almost puzzle even an experienced potter of the present day to reproduce. I name this *en passant*, because I wish to remove the impression which seems in some places to prevail, that until Josiah Wedgwood's time the productions of the neighbourhood were confined to the manufacture of coarse brown butter-pots, porringers, and other clumsy vessels alone,

* The May-pole stood where the Town Hall now stands.

† Pits from which the native clay for the manufacture of earthenware was dug by the potters.

‡ *Shards*, broken pots; *rucks*, heaps. Thus "shard-ruck" was a heap of broken pots—a rubbish heap, in fact, made up of the refuse from the pot-works.

§ Pots spoiled in their manufacture.

and that anything approaching towards art, or even moderate utility, was unknown. Of some of these early potters I have already spoken, and have endeavoured to show that Staffordshire could boast not only of master-minds, but of skilful and expert hands, long before the period to which the first approach to art in the district is generally ascribed.

The family of Wedgwood, for many generations before the birth of Josiah, had been potters at Burslem, and indeed a considerable portion of the place belonged to one branch of them, having passed into their hands by marriage with the heiress of the De Burslems, the original owners of the place, in the beginning of the seventeenth century. They were thus people of note in the district, and it is affirmed that one-third of the inhabitants of Burslem at one time bore the now honoured name of Wedgwood, or were descended from them.

The Wedgwoods originally, I believe, were of Wedgwood, a parish in the township of Wolstanton, in the very centre of the Potteries. The church of St. Margaret, Wolstanton—a fine and particularly interesting building—standing on the summit of a high hill, forms one of the most conspicuous and pleasing objects in the district. It lies on the high road from Burslem to Newcastle-under-Lyme, and commands one of the finest views which can anywhere be obtained of the busy hives of potting industry by which it is surrounded. In this church James Brindley, the engineer—or "the schemer," as he was popularly called—married, when half a century old, his young, loving, and priceless wife of nineteen, Anne Henshall, on the 8th of December, 1765; and in the same parish, at New Chapel,* not far from his residence at Turnhurst, he was buried, in less than seven years afterwards, after passing a most worthy and industrious life, and earning for himself a name and a fame which are

* Brindley was buried in the churchyard at New Chapel, his tombstone bearing the simple inscription—

"In Memory of James Brindley, of Turnhurst, Engineer, who was Interred here, September 30, 1772, Aged 56."

imperishable. The Wedgwoods appear to have been seated at the township bearing their name, from a very early date, and in 1370 (13 Edward III.) Thomas de Weggewood was frankpledge, or headborough, of the hamlet of Weggewood. When they left their original patrimony is not known; but about the year 1470, John Wedgwood, of Blackwood, or Dunwood, "descended from a family that took its name from Wedgwood, in Wolstanton parish, whence they came," married Mary, daughter and heiress of John Shawe, and had with her Harecels (Harracles, in the parish of Horton, near Leek), to which I shall have occasion again to refer later on.

Richard Wedgwood of Harracles married Jane Shirrot, and had by her a son, John Wedgwood, who became High Collector of Subsidy in 1563; and another son, Richard Wedgwood, of the Mole in Biddulph, who married, on the 14th of September, 1567, Margaret Boulton, and had by her three sons—Richard, Randle, and Gilbert, the latter of whom (baptised at Biddulph, November 6th, 1588) married Margaret, daughter and heiress of Thomas Burslem, of Burslem; by his wife, Mary Ford, and had by her Burslem Wedgwood, baptised at Burslem, December 11th, 1614, and Thomas, who became ancestor of Josiah Wedgwood.

John Wedgwood, the High Collector of Subsidy, married Anne, daughter of William Bowyer, of Knypersley (whose sister married William Ford, of the Mosse, about the year 1565), and had by her John Wedgwood, of Harracles, who married Mary, daughter of Thomas Egerton, of Walgrange and Horton, "with whom he had part of the mannour." This John Wedgwood, who died April 6th, 1589, had by his marriage with this lady, who died September 5th, 1582, eight children—viz., John, of whom presently; Egerton, who died without issue; Ralph, married to Alice Leighe; Mary, married to Ambrose Arden; Anne, married to James Gibson; Margaret, married to Thomas Smith, of London, goldsmith, and afterwards to Richard Rand, of London; Eliza, married to Richard Foxe, and afterwards to William St.

Andrew, of Gotham, in Derbyshire; and Felix (*qy.* Phillis), married to Richard Hilders. The eldest son, John Wedgwood, married his cousin, Margaret, daughter and heiress of William Forde, of the Mosse, near Leek. He died April 5, 1658, aged 87, having had by his wife, Margaret Forde, three sons—John, Egerton, and William—and four daughters. Of these, John, the eldest, who died in 1651, married Jane, daughter of Sir Thomas Hazelrigg, of Mowseley, and brother of the celebrated Arthur Hazelrigg, one of the five commoners in whom the generalship was invested by the Rump Parliament, and who was impeached in 1641-2. He died in the Tower of London, January 8th, 1661. He was

> "The activ'st member of the five,
> As well as the most primitive."—*Hudibras.*

This John Wedgwood had issue by his wife, Jane Hazelrigg, four sons—William, of Harracles, who died in 1677, aged 42; John, Arthur, and Egerton; and two daughters. William Wedgwood,* the eldest son, married Elizabeth, eldest daughter of Mills Cotton, of Bellaport, by his wife, Joyce, daughter of Sir Thomas Bromley, of Holt Castle, and had by her William, who died young; and John, second son, who succeeded his father in the estates; and a daughter, Joyce, who married John Hollins, of Mossleigh, and was grandfather to Sir Brooke Boothby, whose family eventually inherited the Wedgwood estates. John Wedgwood, who died January 11th, 1757, aged 88, married Susanna, daughter of Sir Charles Wolsley, Bart., and had by her Charles Wedgwood, of the Inner Temple, who died without issue, aged 35, in 1729; William Wedgwood, who died in 1715, aged 19, also without issue; and five daughters, three of whom, Elizabeth, Susanna, and Dorothea, became his co-heiresses. Of these daughters, Elizabeth, the eldest, married Robert Venables, of the Mere, of the

* This William Wedgwood, who died December 10, 1677, aged 42, was buried at Leek, where his monument, still remaining, bears the arms of Wedgwood and Cotton.

family of Venables, of whom Drayton, in his "Battle of Blore Heath," wrote—

"There Dutton Dutton kills; a Done doth kill a Done;
A Booth a Booth; a Leigh by Leigh is overthrowne:
A *Venables* against a *Venables* doth stand,
And Troutbeck fighteth with a Troutbeck hand to hand;
There Molineux doth make a Molineux to die:
And Egerton the strength of Egerton doth trie.
O Cheshire, wert thou mad? of thine owne native gore
So much untill this day thou never shedst before."

This lady died in 1784, without issue.* The second daughter, Susanna, married John Fenton, of Newcastle, nephew of Elijah Fenton, the poet, of the old Staffordshire family of Fenton and Shelton, and had one daughter, Susannah Fenton, married to John Daniel, of Daresbury, and died without issue in 1770. The third daughter, Dorothy Wedgwood, married Dr. John Addenbroke, Dean of Lichfield and Rector of Sudbury, and died without issue in 1772 The Dean and his lady were both buried in Sudbury Church, where a tablet bearing the following inscription is erected to their memory:—

"Here lie the bodies of the Rev. Dr. Addenbroke, Dean of Lichfield and Rector of this Parish, who died Feb. 25, 1776, aged 64; and Dorothy his wife, 3rd daughter of John Wedgwood, of Harracles, Co. Stafford, Esq., who died March 27, 1772, aged 64.

The estate at Harracles, by the death of these three coheiresses, passed as before indicated, to the Boothbys, from whom, by sale, it passed through the hands of Mills and Cave to Davenport.

In Horton Church is a monumental brass to John Wedgwood, bearing the arms of Wedgwood with Egerton, and other quarterings, and figures of the deceased, his wife, and children. The inscription is:—

"*Hic jacent sepult̄ corpora Johīs Wedgwood, de Haracles, armigeri, et Marie uxoris ejus, filie Thomæ Egerton, de Walgrange, armigeri,*

* For a part of this information I am indebted to my friend Mr. Sleigh, the historian of Leek.

qui obierunt, hic sixto die Aprilis, Ann° Dom̄. 1589; illa quinto Septembris Anno Dom̄ 1582. Sobolem post se relinquentes filios tres, filiasque quinque, quorum animas cum justis remanere speram̄. Johēs duxit Margaret Forde, Egerton celebs mor̄. Radus duxit Aliciam Leighe. Maria nūpt Ambrō Arden. Anna nūpt Jacob Gibson. Marga nūpt Thō Smith. Eliza nūpt Ricō Foxe. Felix nūpt Ricō Hilders,"

Horton Hall, of which I give a view in the accompanying engraving, as having been in somewise connected with the Wedgwoods and their alliances, is a handsome Elizabethan building, belonging to the family of Fowler, of Leek and Horton. The whole of the manor of Horton appears to have belonged, by descent and purchase, to John Wedgwood, who, by will, dated July 29th, 1749, left his real estates to Phœbe Hollins, wife of Brooke Boothby, and the manor of Horton was sold in 1796 by Sir Brooke Boothby to Thomas Harding, from whom it has passed by purchase to the Antrobus family. The house at Harracles, still standing, is a picturesque and interesting building.

The alliance of the Wedgwoods with the De Burslem family, to which I have alluded, took place in the persons of

Gilbert Wedgwood and Margaret, one of the co-heiresses of Thomas Burslem, who were married about the year 1612. The Burslem family was one of considerable note and of long standing in the district, having been settled at Burslem from an early period. In the court rolls the name occurs as early as 5th Henry V. John Burslem, of Dale Hall, who was foreman of the leet jury in 1563 and 1569, was a man of substantial means, holding extensive lands in Burslem and other places in the district. He died in 1596, and was succeeded in his estates by his eldest son, Thomas Burslem, who died in 1619. This Thomas Burslem had two sons, Thomas, who succeeded him, and William, from whom are descended, by female lines, the families of Smith-Child, Biggs, and Earl of Huntingdon. Thomas Burslem, the eldest son, married Mary Forde, of the Mosse, in 1590, and had two daughters, co-heiresses—Margaret, married to Gilbert Wedgwood, and Catherine, married to William Colclough, by whom she had a son John, who died without issue. By this Catherine Colclough some lands were, at her death, devised to her nephew, Thomas Wedgwood, who also purchased lands from his cousin, Burslem Wedgwood.

Gilbert Wedgwood and Margaret (Burslem) his wife had, it appears, a family of six sons and two daughters—Joseph, who died without issue; Burslem, of whom presently; Thomas, ancestor of Josiah Wedgwood; William, who left issue; Moses, who left issue; Aaron, who was ancestor of the "Big House" branch of the family; Mary, married to Broad; and Sarah, married to Daniel. The eldest, Joseph, died without issue, and the issue of the eldest surviving son, Burslem Wedgwood, became extinct in the male line in the third descent. By his wife, Margaret, he had two sons, Burslem and Thomas, and four daughters. This Thomas Wedgwood died without issue, and Burslem Wedgwood having married Elizabeth Cross, had three sons, who all died young, and four daughters. The second surviving son of Gilbert and Margaret Wedgwood, Thomas, having, in 1653, married Margaret Shaw (who survived him, and afterwards married Francis Fynney), had a family of several sons and daughters, and was the ancestor of the families known as the "Overhouse Wedgwoods" and the "Church Wedgwoods," of which latter Josiah was a member. He died in the year 1678. By his will, which is dated February 14th, 1678, it appears that he had then a family of three sons and five daughters living, seven of whom were under age. The sons were John, of whom presently, Thomas, of whom also more presently, and Timothy; and the daughters were Margaret, Margerie, Catherine, Mary, and Sarah.

This Thomas Wedgwood was a man of considerable substance, owning a large part of Burslem, with three or four pot-works. He resided at "the Upper or Over House," which at that time appears to have been a goodly mansion, with a "long table and forms thereunto belonging, standing in the hall place of the house," and with barns, outhouses, stables, cowhouses, yards, folds, orchards, gardens, fishponds, fields and crofts, and kiln yard for the pot works, belonging to it. This estate was his own property, and besides it he owned the "housing and lands lying at the Churchyard side in Burslem," which were formerly in his own possession and that of his father-in-law, Shaw; a horse-mill and buildings attached; large pot works, consisting of workhouses, shops, pot ovens, and all kinds of implements "belonging to the art or trade of potting," which he had erected on land which he had purchased of one William Keen, of Crow Borrow; houses, gardens, &c., and, I believe, pot works called the "Almshouse;" fields of land in various parts, coal mines, and other property. His will, which is a particularly interesting document, I here for the first time make public:—

"In the name of God, Amen. The fourteenth day of February, in the one and twentieth year of the reign of our Sovereign Lord Charles the Second, by the Grace of God, of England, Scotland, France, and Ireland, King, Defender of the Faith, and Ann. Dom. 1678.

"I, Thomas Wedgwood of Burslem, in the County of Stafford,

Potter, being weake in body, but of sound mind, perfect memory (praised be God therefore), do make this to be and continue my last will and Testament, in manner and form following: first, I commend my soul into the hands of Almighty God my Creator, hoping through the only merits of Jesus Christ my dear Redeemer to obtain life everlasting; & as for such worldly and outward estate it hath pleased God out of his superabundant Goodness to bestow upon me, I give and assign the same in manner and form following, that is to say, I give and devise unto Margaret my loving wife, so long as she remain sole unmarried after my decease, for the time of her natural life, all the dwelling house wherein I now inhabit, called the Upper or Over House, with all barns, outhouses, stables, cowhouses, yards, folds, orchards, gardens, thereunto belonging, with the fish-pond and fish ; and also the Oxley Crofts, the great Old Field, the little Old Field, the Oxley Croft Meadow, the Kill yard, with all and every of these appurtenances & privileges which are situate in Burslem aforesaid, for and during her widowhood, in full recompense of her jointure and dower, of all my lands and tenements and under this proviso. Also that my said wife do and shall relay & release all her title and interest in all my housing and lands lying at the Church Yard side in Burslem aforesaid, which were formerly or are in the holding of myself & father-in-law, Shaw, one or both of us, or to my Son John during her said widowhood, and no longer. I give and assign unto my said wife for her natural life my horse mill, with the buildings wherein it now stands, for a further help to her & for the educating and maintaining of my younger Children until they come to the age of one and twenty years, to be disposed of in marriage or receive their portions. Item I give and assign unto my said wife all my workhouses, shops, ovens, which I have erected and built upon a certain piece of ground which I lately purchased of William Keen of Crow Borrow, with all and every their appurtenances lying in Burslem aforesaid, until such time as my Son Thomas Wedgwood shall accomplish the age of Twenty One years, and for no longer time, to keep her, the better to maintain and educate my younger children. I give and assign unto my said Son Thomas Wedgwood, his heirs and assigns for ever, when he shall come to the age of one & twenty years, all the said work-houses, & pot ovens, & folds or yards belonging to the same, all and every their appurtenances & privileges; also the said house, mill, with the buildings thereunto belonging after the determination of my wife's estate. I give unto my Son Thomas when he shall attain the said age of one & twenty years, all the plank boards & shelves which are at the said workhouse, & all other implements whatever at the said workhouse, belonging to the art or trade of potting. I give and assign unto my Son Timothy all my right, title, interest, claim, and demand, which I have in and to all that housing, barns, stable, cowhouse, and backside, & gardens, and all & every their appurtenances, called by the name of Almshouse, situate in Burslem aforesaid & now in the holding of one Paul Shelton & Wm. March. And my will is that my said Son Timothy shall enter upon and enjoy the same when he shall accomplish the age of one & twenty years. I give and devise unto my daughter Margaret Wedgwood, & to my Son Thomas Wedgwood, & to my daughter Margarie Wedgwood, their heirs and assigns for ever, all those several parcels or pieces of land called the Smallthorns, situate & being in Sneyd Hamel, within the parish of the said Burslem, which land my aunt Catharine Colclough deceased gave unto me, and also that parcel of land or meadow grounds called the 'Digged Lakes,' lying in Burslem meadows aforesaid, which I lately purchased of my Cousin Burslem Wedgwood; to the intent that my said daughters Margaret Wedgwood, Margarie Wedgwood, and my Son Thomas Wedgwood, may leece and raise the sum of two hundred pounds out of the said several pieces of lands & meadows, grants by sale of the same, or by any other way that they may find prudent for to raise the said sum of two hundred pounds, to be paid and distributed in manner and form following. For the portions and perferment of my said three children Margaret, Margarie, & Thomas, that is, to my said daughter Margaret the sum of fourscore pounds of lawful money, to my said Son Thomas the sum of Fourty pounds when he shall accomplish the age of one & twenty years; to my said daughter Margerie the sum of fourscore pounds when she comes to the age of one & twenty years. And my mind & will is that my said children shall marry to and with the consent of my said wife, provided nevertheless it is my mind & will that if my Son John Wedgwood shall within some reasonable time after my decease, either pay the said two hundred pounds to my said three children Margaret, Thomas, & Margerie, or give them good security to pay the said sum of £200 or their several parts & proportions thereof at the ages, days, & times above mentioned & limited, that then my will is, that my said Son John shall have to him and heirs for ever, the aforesaid parcels of lands called the Smallthorns & Digged Lake Meadows. I give unto my daughters Katherine Wedgwood, Sarah Wedgwood, Mary Wedgwood, and my said Son Timothy Wedgwood the said sum of £200, to be raised out of all the buildings and lands by me in this my last will given, bequeathed, and devised to my said wife if she keep her widowhood for her life, so soon as it can be raised out of the said lands & buildings, my said Wife's interest & term therein, & applied & paid to my said children, Katherine, Sarah, Mary, & Timothie, when they shall respectively accomplish the age of one and twenty years, or be disposed of in marriage, which shall first happen, if my Wife's estates therein be then determined, and to be paid unto my said children in manner & form following, that is to say, to my daughter Katherine three score pounds of lawful money, to my daughter Sarah three score pounds, to my daughter Mary three score pounds, to my Son Timothy twenty pounds, which last said £200 to my four last mentioned children, I will shall be paid out of all the said lands devised to my said Wife in manner aforesaid, & I charge all my said lands with the payment of the said £200 to my four last mentioned children, so soon as it can be raised & paid in manner aforesaid; & my mind & will is that if any of my younger children in this my will mentioned shall die in their minority or before they be married, or receive their portion or portions, that then such deceased child or children's parts or portions shall go and be equally paid & distributed amongst all my surviving younger children; & after the determination of my said Wife's Estate therein & the said last named £200 paid to my said children, I give the said lands to my said Son John and his heirs for ever; but in case my said Son John shall make default paying the last mentioned £200 to my four last named younger children, at such time and in such manner as is expressed in this my last will, then my will is my said children shall have, hold, and enjoy all the said houseing & lands in this my last will devised to my Wife for her life for so long time, due term of years, as until they my said children have raised the said sum of £200 to be paid as afore expressed. I give and assign to my said wife for the term of her natural life if she keeps her widowhood, all my rights & interest which I have in any coal mine or coal mines within the said parish of Burslem or elsewhere, for the keeping of her as to her comfortable living & the educating of my said younger children, & after determination of my said Wife's estates in the coal mines I give the said coal mines & all my claim & interest in the same to my Son John Wedgwood. I give to my said Son John the long table with the forms thereunto belonging standing in the hall place in the house wherein I now do inhabit. I give unto my Son John all the rikes that are in the mill house below the entre where I now inhabit. I give unto Mr. Geo. Hargreaves, minister of God's Word, ten shillings to preach my funeral sermon. I give unto my Cousin George Hawson of Wolstanton, 12/.; my debts, legacies, & funeral expences, & all such monies as shall be neçessary to be expended about the due execution of this my last will & testament being first paid and discharged. I do for the better education & maintainance of my five younger children until they shall respectively accomplish the said age of twenty-one years, or be married, or receive their portions, & for the due maintainance of my wife's livelihood & subsistence during her widowhood, give unto my executors herein named all the residue & remainder of my personal estate, my goods, monies, plate, cattle, chattels, & personal estate whatsoever; & my will is my said youngest children shall be educated & maintained out of the same residue & remainder of my said personal estate aforesaid. My mind & will further is that what remains of the said residue of my personal estate after my wife's estate or interest therein determined & my said children educated as aforesaid, shall go to be equally divided amongst all my said seven children. Lastly, I do hereby nominate, constitute, & appoint Margaret my loving wife, and my said Son John, & my said Son Thomas Wedgwood, to be the executors of this my last Will & Testament, hoping they will faithfully perform the same; & interest my loving friends the said Mr Geo. Hargreaves & Geo. Hawson to be overseers of this my last will & testament & to aiding & assisting my said executors. In witness thereof I the said Thomas Wedgwood have hereunto set my hand & seal the day and year first mentioned in this my last will.

"THOMAS WEDGWOOD.

"Signed, sealed, published & declared to be & contain the last will and testament of me the said Thos. Wedgwood, in presence of, & all the interlineations done before the sealing thereof, in presence of Geo. Hargreaves & Geo. Hawson."

"Proved 4th April, 1679, on the Oath of Margaret Wedgwood, widow, John Wedgwood, & Thos. Wedgwood, the Executors named therein."

The eldest son of Thomas and Margaret, to whom I have alluded, was John, who appears to have been born in 1654, and to have died in 1705. He married in 1679, and had by his wife, Alice, a daughter, Catherine, who married her cousin Richard, of the "Overhouse" branchd and had by him John, an only child, who died a minor. This lady, who survived her husband, married, secondly, Thomas Bourne, and, thirdly, Rowland Egerton, and died a widow in 1756.

This Richard Wedgwood was, like the rest of the family, a potter, and owned considerable property in Burslem, as is evidenced by his will, here for the first time given.

"In the name of God, Amen. I, Richard Wedgwood, of Burslem, the County of Stafford, Earthen Potter, do make and advise my last will and Testament in manner and form following. Impri^{s}, I give, devise, and bequeath unto my dear and loving wife all y^{t} my Messuage, Cottage, or Dwelling-house, being in Burslem aforesaid, now in the holding of Samuel Malkin, together with all out-buildings, barns, stables, gardens, orchards, ways whatever, and backsides to the same belonging, together with a certain piece of land called the Towncroft, lying in Burslem aforesaid, and also all those pieces or parcels of land called the two Brownhills, in the holding of Stephen Cartlidge; to hold the said Messuage, or Cottage, lands, tenements, Hereditements, and premises, to my said wife Catherine Wedgwood for and during her natural life. And after her decease, I give, devise, and bequeath all the aforesaid Messuage, or Cottage, Lands, Hereditaments, and premises aforesaid to my Son John Wedgwood, his heirs and assigns for ever. Item, I give, devise, and bequeath to my said wife all y^{t} my workhouse, being in Burslem aforesaid, now or late in the holding of Ralph Simpson, for her life; and after her decease, I give, devise, and bequeath the same to my son John Wedgwood, his heirs and assigns for ever. Item, I give to Henry Mountford, of Burslem aforesaid, twenty shillings. Item, I give to Margery Mountford, wife of the said Henry, ten shillings. Item, I give, devise, and bequeath unto my dear wife one parcel of ground called the Service Yard, during her life; and after her decease I give the same to my said son John, his heirs and assigns for ever. Item, all the rest and residue of my Goods, cattle, Chattels, and personal Estate whatsoever, after my debts, Legacies, and funeral expences are paid and satisfied, I give to my said wife Katherine. Lastly, I constitute and appoint my said wife executrix of this my last Will and Testament, hereby revoking all former wills by me at any time heretofore made. In witness whereof, I, the said Richard Wedgwood, the Testator, have hereunto put my hand and seal, the second day of

November, in the fifth year of the reign of our Sovereign Lord King George, Sovereign of Great Britain, &c., Anno Domini 1718.

"Richard Wedgwood, his × mark.

"Signed, sealed, published, and declared to be and contain the last will and Testament of Richard Wedgwood the Testator, and afterwards attested in his sight by Margaret Richards, Margaret Wedgwood, Thomas Bourne."

"Proved 23rd April, 1719, on the Oath of Catherine Wedgwood, Executrix."

The second son of Thomas and Margaret, Thomas Wedgwood, was born in 1660, and married, in 1684, Mary Leigh. He resided, and had his pot-works close to the churchyard at Burslem, where they still exist. By his wife, Mary Leigh, he had a family of four sons and five daughters. The sons, as named in her will, dated 1718, are Thomas (the father of the great Josiah Wedgwood), John (a son Abner appears to have died young), Aaron, and Daniel; and the daughters—Catherine, married to her relative, Dr. Thomas Wedgwood, jun.; Alice, married to Thomas Moore; Elizabeth, married to Samuel Astbury; Margaret, married to Moses Marsh; and Mary, married to Richard Clifton. Mary Wedgwood (Mary Leigh) survived her husband, and by her will, dated January 1st, 1718, devised her personality as will be seen in the following interesting document:—

"In the name of God, Amen, the first day of January, Anno Domini 1718. I, Mary Wedgwood, of the Churchyard, in the parish of Burslem, in the County of Stafford, widow, Being weak of body, But of sound and perfect disposing mind and memory, thanks be therefore given to the Almighty for the same, Doe make and ordaine this to be and containe my last will and testament, In manner and fforme ffollowing (that is to say) ffirst and principally I commend my soul into the hands of Almighty God my Creator, hopeing through the merritts, death, and passion of my Saviour Jesus Christ, to receive free and full pardon of all my sins, and to Inheritt Life eternall, and my body to be decently Interred according to the discretion of my Executors hereinafter named. And for such Temporall Estate it hath pleased God out of his superabounding goodness to bestow upon me, I give and devise the same as follows.

Imp[s]. I will that my debts and funerall charges be paid and discharged. Item, I give and bequeath to my son John Wedgwood Three pounds and tenn shillings, and gave to him in my lifetime Sixteen pounds tenn shillings, w[ch] makes his the sume of Twenty pounds. Item, I give and bequeath to my son Aaron Wedgwood ffifteen pounds, and gave to him in my lifetime ffive pounds, w[ch] makes him the sum of Twenty pounds. Item, I give to my son Daniell ffive pounds, and five pounds I gave him in my lifetime, w[ch] makes his the sume of tenn pounds. Item, I give and bequeath to my daughter Mary Wedgwood the sume of Twenty-three pounds of Lawful English money, to be paid to her within six months next after my decease. Item, I give and bequeath to my Daughter Elizabeth Wedgwood the sume of Twenty pounds. Item, I give and bequeath to my Daughter Alice Wedgwood the sume of Twenty pounds. Item, I give and bequeath to my daughter Margarett Wedgwood the sume of Twenty pounds—w[ch] three last Legacies to my three youngest Daughters, I will they shall be paid as they each of them shall attain the respective age of twenty-one years. And each of them to receive yearly interest for their Legacies towards their maintainance and education. Item, I give and bequeath to Thomas Wedgwood, my son-in-law, one Cow. Item, It is my will and mind that if any of my children dye or depart this life before they attaine the age of one-and-twenty years of age, that then such Child or Children's portions shall be equally divided amongst my surviveing Daughter or Daughters. Alsoe it is my will and mind that what overplus (if any be) after my debts, funeral expenses, and Legacies are paid and discharged, the same to be for the maintainance and education of my three youngest Daughters. Item, Lastly, I nominate, constitute, and appoint, my loving brother Thomas Leigh, and my loveing son Thomas Wedgwood, to be the Executors of this my last will and Testament, hopeing they will faithfully execute and performe the same. In Witness whereof I the said Mary Wedgwood, Testator, have hereunto put my hand and seale, the day and year first above written.

"MARY WEDGWOOD, her marke × and seale.

"Sealed, signed, published, and declared to be and remaine the Last Will and Testam[t] of me, Mary Wedgwood, in the presence of David Gibson, Henry Mountford."

"Proved on the 23rd of April, 1719, by the Oaths of Thomas Leigh and Thomas Wedgwood, the Executors therein named, having been first sworn duly to administer."

It will be seen from this interesting document of the grandmother of the great Josiah, that his father (who inherited the pot-works and other property) was made executor to the will along with his uncle, Thomas Leigh. This Thomas Wedgwood, the eldest son, was born in 1687, and married Mary Stringer, by whom, who survived him, he had a family of thirteen children, seven sons and six daughters. The daughters were, I believe, Maria, born in 1711; Anne, born in 1712; Mary, born in 1714; Margaret, born in 1720; Catherine, born in 1726; and Jane, born in 1728; while the sons were Thomas, of the Churchyard and Overhouse, born in 1716; Samuel, in 1718; John, in 1721; Aaron, in 1722; Abner, in 1723; Richard, in 1725; and Josiah, in 1730.

Most of these Wedgwoods were, of course, potters, and carried on, in the different places in which they were located, the ordinary business of the district. One branch of the family settled at Yearsley, in the Yorkshire wolds, at an early date, and commenced pot-making, which was carried on successfully for some generations. In 1682 John Wedgwood, of Yearsley, was "buried in woollen," as were also in 1692 William Wedgwood, and in 1690 Isabell, who was wife of one of these. John, the son of this John Wedgwood, who died in 1707, was, I have reason to believe, the John Wedgwood whose name appears on the puzzle jug engraved on the following page, with the date 1691.

The ware made by the Yorkshire Wedgwoods was the common hard brown ware, made from the clays of the district, and consisted, of course, mainly of pitchers, pancheons, porringers, and other vessels of homely kind. From researches I have made, I have succeeded in tracing out, with tolerable accuracy, a pedigree of the Yorkshire Wedgwoods for seven or eight generations, ranging from the middle of the seventeenth century down to the present time, when their descendants are still living in the district, not as potters, but in other equally useful walks of life.

So well known were the Wedgwoods of this district, that

one member of the family has been immortalised in song, thus :—

> "At Yearsley there are pancheons made
> By Willie Wedgwood, that young blade."

For this interesting fragment of a Yorkshire ballad I am indebted to my friend, the Rev. Robert Pulleine, Rector of Kirkby Wiske.

Pancheons, it may be well to note, are thick coarse earthenware pans, made of various sizes, and used for setting away milk in, and for washing purposes. They are made in several localities, and, besides being sold by earthenware dealers, are hawked about the country by men who make their living in no other way.

CHAPTER II.

BIRTH OF JOSIAH WEDGWOOD.—HIS FATHER AND GRANDFATHER.—BOYHOOD AND EARLY LIFE.—INDENTURE OF HIS APPRENTICESHIP.—ABNER WEDGWOOD.—THE ASTBURYS.—THE SECRET OF THE ELERS DISCOVERED BY STRATAGEM.—DISCOVERY OF THE USE OF FLINT.—THOMAS WEDGWOOD.—THE "CHURCHYARD" WORKS, BURSLEM, AS THEY WERE, AND AS THEY ARE.—DESCENT OF THE PROPERTY.—MESSRS. BRIDGWOOD AND CLARKE.—PRODUCTIONS OF THE WORKS.—CHARACTER OF JOSIAH WEDGWOOD AS AN APPRENTICE.

JOSIAH WEDGWOOD, it will have been seen, was—like another self-made man, Sir Richard Arkwright, who was born only two years later—the youngest of a family of thirteen children; and therefore, whatever patrimony there might be in the family, it is tolerably certain the usual fate of younger sons—that of having to work out the problem of their fortunes—must have awaited him. How successfully he solved that problem future chapters will amply show.

He was born in July, 1730, and was baptised on the 12th of that month, as will be seen by the following extract from the parish register of his native place, Burslem:—

"1730.—Josiah, son of Thomas and Mary Wedgwood, bap[d] July 12th."

His father was, as has been shown in the preceding chapter, Thomas Wedgwood, eldest son of Thomas Wedgwood, potter, of the Churchyard House and Works, by his wife Mary Leigh. Thomas Wedgwood, the father of Josiah, was baptised at Burslem in 1686-7. The following is the entry in the register of that parish:—

"Thomas Wedgwood, filius Thome et Marie uxoris ejus, baptizatus fuit 11 die," January 1686-7—

His father and mother having, as will be seen from the following entry, married in 1684 :—

"Inter Thomam Wedgwood et Mariam Leigh, 26 die."

The father of Josiah was therefore, it would seem, in his forty-fourth year at the time of his birth, and had had a family of thirteen children, most if not all of whom were then living.

At the time of Josiah's birth, as for many years before, his parents occupied the house and pot-work closely adjoining the churchyard of Burslem, which had belonged to their fathers before them, and in that house the man whose memory all delight to honour was born. The house stood, I have reason to believe, near the site of the slip-house shown in the view of the Churchyard Works given on a succeeding page; but it has been taken down many years, and not a vestige of the building now remains. I believe in those days there was an open pathway through the churchyard, and that there was also an entrance to the works and house from the churchyard. It is well to note, while speaking of the birthplace of Josiah Wedgwood, that the house near the works, now known as the "Mitre Hotel," in Pitt Street, has, but erroneously, had that honour assigned to it. This error has, no doubt, arisen from the fact of the house having been built and inhabited by one of the Wedgwood family, but at a somewhat later date. It has, however, been occupied since then as a residence by a later owner of the Churchyard Works, Mr. Green, and this has, doubtless, strengthened the belief that the father of Josiah Wedgwood had previously lived in it.

Of the boyhood and early life of Josiah Wedgwood, as a schoolboy, we know, unfortunately, literally nothing, beyond the fact that he was an amiable, thoughtful, and particularly intelligent child, ever quiet and studious, and delighting more in thoughtful occupations than in the games and rough exercise of the boys of that, and indeed of every, time. At this period, or rather thirty years later, there was but one school in Burslem, and that so ill adapted to the purpose "that two parts of the children out of three are put to work without any learning, by reason" of that school being "not sufficient to instruct them." Probably to the only school in Burslem, Josiah Wedgwood was sent, but whether there, or under the tuition of his excellent father and mother, he must have made exceeding good progress, for, at the age of fourteen, he wrote, not a boyish, but a fine, firm, manly hand, as will be seen by the fac-simile I give of his signature at that age. We are told that at the early age of eleven Josiah was put to the family business of a potter, as a thrower; and thus he had not much opportunity of gaining extended knowledge in any branch.

About midsummer, 1739, when Josiah was barely nine years old, his father, Thomas Wedgwood, died, and was buried a few days afterwards in the churchyard at Burslem. And here it may be well to correct an error which has crept into all the accounts hitherto published of this remarkable man. Mr. Smiles says, "His father was a poor potter at Burslem, barely able to make a living at his trade. He died when he was only eleven years old." It will be seen that Josiah was only nine years old, not eleven, when he lost his father; and the statement regarding the poverty of his father is equally erroneous. I believe him to have been a well-to-do tradesman, and this is borne out by the fact that the house and pot-works were his own property, and, apparently, were inherited by him from his father. This error, and the statement which follows it, that at the time when Josiah began "to work at the potter's wheel, the manufacture of earthenware could scarcely be said to exist in England," are so glaringly wrong, that it is well to point them out in this place. The latter assertion my preceding chapters will already have fully refuted, and the former ones this memoir will put in their proper light.

The will of this Thomas Wedgwood—a document which

I now for the first time make public—is dated June 26th, 1739, and was proved at Lichfield, the 25th of October in the same year. It shows him to have been possessed of landed property, and to have been a man far above the station of a "poor potter." The following is a copy of this interesting document.

"In the Name of God, Amen. I, Thomas Wedgwood, of Burslem churchyard side, make this my last Will and Testament, in manner & form following: Imp^{s} I give and bequeath to my Son Thomas, All my Real Estate, chargeable & to be enter'd on as hereafter mentioned, viz., my Will is that the produce of that part of my Real Estate which is not settled on my Wife, shall be laid out by my Exec$^{rs.}$ hereafter mentioned, in the bringing up of my younger children, & in raising the sum of Six score pounds, which I hereby charge my real estate with. And my Will is that the said sum be equally divided among my six younger children, viz., Margaret, John, Aaron, Richard, Katherine, & Josiah; and that in paying the said sums, the elder shall be still preferred before the younger. My Will likewise is that my Ex$^{ors.}$ shall have power to mortgage any part of the said Estate not settled, or the whole thereof, in order to raise the Six score pounds or any part thereof. And my will further is that my Son Thomas shall enter on the Estate not settled on my wife, when the said several sums are paid as above, and not sooner. And that if my Wife shall die before the payment of the money to my children as above, then my Son Thomas shall enter on the other part of my Real Estate, and pay of it twenty pounds apiece to all & each of my younger children above mentioned, that shall then be unpaid; & the said Sums he shall pay them as they shall severally arrive at the age of twenty years; my mind, however, in this is, that if my younger children are all twenty years of age when my Wife shall die, my Son Thomas shall enter on the whole Estate paying as above. But if any one then under the age, then he shall only enter on that wch is my Wife's Jointure, & make up to my said younger children twenty pounds apiece as they arrive at the aforesaid age, reckoning first what is raised by my Exe$^{ors.}$ towards it. I likewise give my said Son Thomas that Leas^{d} tenement now in the holding of Jn$^{o.}$ Warburton, lying in the parish of Burslem. Item, my will is that my debts, except on mortgage & fun^{l} expenses be paid out of the rest of my personal Estate, except my household goods, wch I leave to my Wife to use during her life, and at her decease to be divided equally among all my children except my daughter Ann. Item, if anything remains out of my personal Estate besides what will discharge my debts that are not secured on my land, my Will is that it be equally divided betwixt all my younger children except my daughter Ann. Item, if by my marriage settlement I have not power to charge Six score pounds on my Estate, my will is that what I have power to charge be equally divided among my six children above mentioned, and raised as above. And I appoint Samuel Stringer, of Newcastle-under-Lyme, & John Wedgwood, son of Aaron Wedgwood, of Burslem, Excrs. of this my Will. Witness my hand, this 26 day of June, 1739. "T. WEDGWOOD.

"Sealed and delivered, these words being first interlined (due of real the other of my the rest of) (except on mortgage) in the presence of us, who signed this in the presce of the Testator, E. Latham, W. Willets, R. Mansfield."

"At Lichfield, on the 25th day of October, 1739, Administration (with the Will annexed) of the personal Estate and Effects of Thomas Wedgwood, deceased, was granted to Mary Wedgwood, Widow, the relict, a Legatee named in the said Will, she having been first sworn; Samuel Stringer and John Wedgwood, the Executors therein named, having renounced."

By this will it will be seen that the sum of twenty pounds was left to Josiah Wedgwood, to be paid to him on his coming of age—a small fortune for that eminent man to start life with.

The father of Josiah, I have shown, died at midsummer, 1739. His eldest son, Thomas, who succeeded him, carried on the business at the Churchyard, and probably continued to reside there until his marriage, between two and three years afterwards. To him Josiah was bound apprentice on the 11th day of November, 1744—soon after he had attained his fourteenth year. The indenture of apprenticeship is fortunately still in existence, and I am enabled, for the first time, to make it public by presenting the following literal copy to my readers. The indenture is written on the usual foolscap paper of the period, and is duly stamped with three sixpenny stamps impressed at the top. It is carefully framed and preserved, as such an important and interesting historical document ought to be, in the museum of the Hanley Mechanics' Institution, at Hanley, along with other interesting relics relating to the great Josiah. The indenture is endorsed—

Josiah Wedgwood
To
Thomas Wedgwood
Indenture
for 5 years
Novembr. 11th, 1744.

It reads as follows:—

"*This Indenture, made the Eleventh day of November, in the Seventeenth year of the Reign of our Soveraign Lord, George the Second, by the grace of God, King of great Brittain, and so forth, and in the year of our Lord one Thousand Seven Hundred forty and four, Between Josiah Wedgwood, son of Mary Wedgwood, of the Churchyard, in the County of Stafford, of the one part, and Thomas Wedgwood, of the Churchyard, in the County of Stafford, Potter, of the other part, Wittnesseth that the said Josiah Wedgwood, of his own free Will and Consent to, and with the Consent and Direction of his said Mother, Hath put and doth hereby Bind himselfe Apprentice unto the said Thomas Wedgwood, to Learn his Art, Mistery, Occupation, or Imployment of Throwing and Handleing, which he the said Thomas Wedgwood now useth, and with him as an Apprentice to Dwell, Continue, and Serve from the day of the Date hereof, unto the full end and term of five years from thence next Ensuing, and fully to be Compleat and Ended; During which said Term, the said Apprentice his said Master well and faithfully shall serve, his secrits keep, his Lawfull Commands Every were gladly do: Hurt to his said Master he shall not do, nor willfully suffor to be done by others, but the same to his Power shall let, or forthwith give notice thereof to his said Master; the goods of his said Master he shall not imbezil or waste, nor them Lend, without his Consent to any: at Cards, Dice, or any other unlawfull Games he shall not Play; Taverns or Ale Houses he shall not haunt or frequent; Fornication he shall not Commit, Matrimony he shall not Contract; from the Service of his said Master he shall not at any time depart or absent himselfe without his said Master's Leave: but in all things as a good and faithful Apprentice Shall and Will Demean and behave himselfe towards his said Master and all his, During the said Term, and the Said Master his Apprentice the said Art of Throwing and Handleing which he now useth, with all things thereunto, shall and will Teach and Instruct, or Cause to be well and Sufficiently Taught and Instructed after the best way and manner he can; and shall and will also find and allow unto the Said Apprentice Meat, Drink, Washing and Lodging, and Apparell of all kinds, both Linen and Woolen, and all other Necessaries, both in Sickness and in Health, meet and Convenient for such an Apprentise During the Term aforesaid, and for the true performance of all and Every the said Covenants and Agreements either of the Said Parties Bindeth himselfe unto Each other by these presents, in Witness wereof they have Interchangeable Set their hands and Seals the Day and year before mentioned.*

"JOSIAH WEDGWOOD.
"MARY WEDGWOOD.
"THOS. WEDGWOOD.

"*Sealed and Delivered in the presence of*

"SAMUEL ASTBURY.
"ABNER WEDGWOOD."

This indenture, by which it will be seen Josiah Wedgwood was bound apprentice to his eldest brother, Thomas, for a period of five years, "to learn his art, mistery, occupation, or imployment of Throwing and Handleing," is signed by himself, his mother, and brother Thomas, as the three parties to the deed, and attested by Samuel Astbury and Abner Wedgwood. Of these signatures, so historically interesting, I give on the next page a carefully engraved fac-simile.

Abner Wedgwood, whose signature here appears, must have been either uncle or brother to Josiah—for there were two Abners—but I am inclined to believe the latter, who was seven years the senior of Josiah, and had therefore already attained his majority. Samuel Astbury, the other attesting witness, was uncle to Josiah, having married his

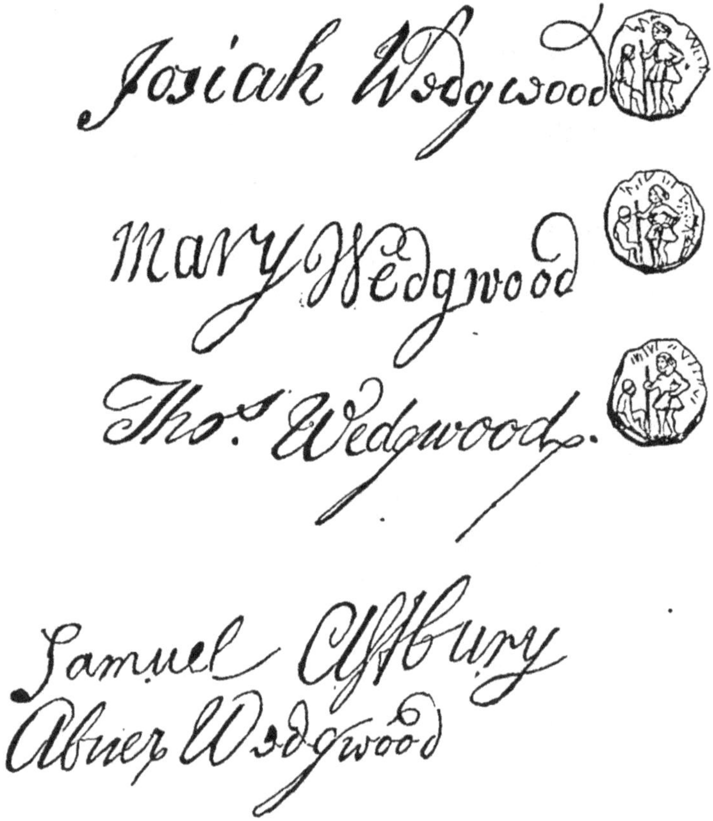

father's sister, Elizabeth Wedgwood. He was one of the family of Astbury to whom the potters were indebted for the discovery of so many improvements in their art, some of which it may not be out of place briefly to notice.

Towards the close of the seventeenth century, when the brothers Elers, to whom I have before referred, had begun their manufacture of fine red ware at Bradwell, and had surprised their neighbours with their productions, and excited their jealousy by their success and the care with which they guarded their secret, a potter of Burslem named Astbury determined to discover their process, and accordingly took means to do so. To accomplish his end he is said to have assumed the garb and manners of an idiot, and then sought the hovel of the Elers, and with every appearance of vacant idiotcy made it understood that he was willing to work. Here he "submitted to the cuffs, kicks, and unkind treatment of masters and workmen, with a ludicrous grimace, as the proof of the extent of his mental ability. When food was offered to him, he used only his fingers to convey it to his mouth; and only when helped by other persons could he understand how to perform any of the labours to which he was directed. He was next employed to move the treadle of an engine lathe, and by perseverance in his assumed character he had opportunity of witnessing every process, and examining every utensil they employed. On returning home each evening he formed models of the several kinds of implements, and made memoranda of the processes, which practice he continued a considerable time (nearly two years is mentioned), until he ascertained that no further information was likely to be obtained, when he availed himself of a fit of sickness to continue at home, and this was represented as most malignant, to prevent any person visiting him. After his recovery he was found so *sane* that Messrs. Elers deemed him unfit longer to remain in their service, and he was discharged, without suspicion that he possessed a knowledge of their manipulations." The information he had thus surreptitiously and dishonestly acquired, he soon turned to such good account that the Elers, "mortified at the fact that their precaution had been unavailing, and disgusted at the inquisitiveness of the Burslem potters" (for another potter named Twyford had also discovered their secret), found that their trade was fast leaving them, and removed at once from the neighbourhood. Astbury commenced business on his own account, and soon became a "man of mark," and took journeys to London to sell his wares and to procure orders. On one of these journeys, it is said, he accidentally discovered the use of flint as an ingredient in the plastic art. This circumstance is thus recorded:—On one of his journeys, on arriving at Dunstable, he found the horse on which he rode so much affected in its eyes, that he feared blindness would result. Having spoken to the ostler at the inn, he recommended burnt flint, and having put a piece of flint in the fire, and kept it there until red-hot, allowed it to cool, and then powdered it. Some of this powder he blew into the eyes of the horse, and relieved it. Mr. Astbury, who had watched the process carefully, was much stuck with the pure whiteness which the flint attained on being burned, and the ease with which it might be reduced to powder; and having also noticed its clayey nature when moistened in the horse's eyes, immediately conceived the idea that if mixed with clay in his trade, it would produce a finer and whiter kind of ware than any which had been yet produced. Having procured some flints on his return home, he profited by his observation, and the result of his experiments was more than satisfactory to him. He soon obtained a preference for his ware over others, and amassed a comfortable fortune; and thus flints became a general ingredient in the potter's materials. Samuel Astbury is said to have been a son of this eminent potter; and thus was united to the Wedgwood family the ability and skill of the Astburys.

It will be noticed that in the indenture of apprenticeship, both Mary Wedgwood, the mother of Josiah, and Thomas, his brother, to whom he was bound, are described as "*of the Churchyard, in the county of Stafford,*" the town, or village as it then was, of Burslem not being named. It is probable, from this fact of *both* being described as "of the Churchyard," that not only was Josiah, as a matter of course, at that time living with his mother, but that Thomas, the eldest son, and successor of his father, also resided under the same roof. Whether this were so or not is, however, a matter of grave doubt; for, although in the indenture of apprenticeship executed in November, 1744, he is described as "of the Churchyard," yet in his marriage settlement with Isabel Beech, dated October 12th, 1742, two years previously, he is described as "of the Over House, Burslem, Potter." By this deed the Churchyard house and works, then his property, are settled, as will soon be shown.

THE "CHURCHYARD WORKS," BURSLEM.

The probability is, that Thomas Wedgwood resided at the Over House at the time when Josiah was apprenticed to him, that he carried on his potter's business both there and at the Churchyard (which was his own property), and that he was in the indenture described as "of the Churchyard," because at those works, where his mother resided, it was intended that Josiah should serve his time, and thus, with nearly the whole of her large family, continue under her roof, and consequently under her careful and watchful eye.

The "CHURCHYARD WORKS," at which the boy Josiah was apprenticed, are, in their present state, shown in the preceding engraving, from a drawing recently made by myself. The sketch is taken from the large graveyard which surrounds the old church of Burslem. The manufactory, it will be observed, forms the boundary of the churchyard on its north-east side. The building with the bell-turret, seen above the works, is the National Schools.

Since the time of Wedgwood, these works have, naturally, been much altered and enlarged; but the site is the same, and some of the buildings now there are what stood and were used in his day. The house in which he was born—which, as I have said before, there is reason to believe stood near where the present slip-house now stands—has been taken down many years, and the site has since been occupied by fresh buildings. New hovels and other conveniences have recently been added to the establishment, which is now a very complete and commodious manufactory.

These historically interesting works, which seem for several generations to have belonged to the Wedgwoods, are described in 1698 as belonging to Thomas Wedgwood, "of the Churchyard House," to whom they appear to have passed on his father's death. His son Thomas, eldest brother of Josiah, inherited this property on his father's death in 1739, and three years later, on his marriage with Isabel Beech, by marriage settlement dated 12th October, 1742 (in which he is described as Thomas Wedgwood, of the Over House, Burslem, Potter), the "messuage, with the appurtenances situate and adjoining the churchyard, Burslem, and all outhouses, *work* houses, &c., then in the occupation of the said Thomas Wedgwood, or his under tenants," were settled upon the children of this marriage. On the death of Thomas Wedgwood, in 1772, this property, and the other he had acquired, descended to his son Thomas, of the Over House, subject to portions to his younger children, under the settlement of 1742. The works were for some time carried on, along with the "Bell Works" and "Ivy House Works," by Josiah Wedgwood. On his removal to Etruria, they were occupied by his second cousin, Joseph Wedgwood (brother of Aaron, and nephew of the Aaron Wedgwood who was partner with William Littler in the first manufacture of porcelain in the district), who lived at the house now the Mitre Hotel, near the works. This Joseph Wedgwood, who made jasper and other fine bodies under the direction of, and for, Josiah, occupied the works until the time of their sale to Mr. Green, when he removed to Basford Bank. About 1780 "the Churchyard premises were sold to Josiah Wedgwood, then of Etruria, who, in 1787, conveyed them to his brother John, also of Etruria, who, in 1795, sold them to Thomas Green, at which time two newly-erected houses near the pot-work were included in the sale." Mr. Green manufactured earthenware at these works, and for some time resided at the house near the works, now known as the "Mitre Hotel," which had been built by one of the Wedgwood family. The property remained in Thomas Green's hands until his bankruptcy in 1811, when it appears to have been purchased by a manufacturer named Joynson, or Johnson, from whom it again passed, some years later, to Mr. Moseley, its present owner. While in his hands, the pot-work has been held by various tenants, and until about seven years ago it was let off in small holdings to different potters. About that period Mr. Bridgwood, of Tunstall, became the tenant of the premises as a general earthenware manufacturer, and was soon afterwards joined in partnership by Mr. Edward Clarke, whose large practical experience has tended much to increase the reputation of the works. This firm, having taken a lease of the premises, remodelled many of the buildings, and erected others, and greatly improved the whole place, by bringing to bear many improvements in body unknown and unthought of by their predecessors. Since Mr. Bridgwood's decease, which took place in 1864, these works, and the large establishment at Tunstall, have remained in the hands of the surviving partner, Mr. Clarke, who is gradually withdrawing the manufacture from them to Tunstall, where his operations will be concentrated. The productions of the Churchyard Works at the present day are like those of the Tunstall works, principally intended for the American market, where they very successfully compete with the French porcelain, and where, being opaque porcelain of the finest and hardest quality, they are known by the name of "white granite." Many of the goods, as services, &c., are embossed in excellently designed patterns, and the greater proportion are sent off white, and are then decorated, on the glaze, in the States.

One of the most notable features in the manufactures at these works, is that of artists' materials, for which they rank deservedly high. Their palettes, tiles, slabs, saucers, &c., possess all the requirements of hardness, evenness, and durability of glaze, and are consequently much esteemed. Another prominent feature of the productions is that of door furniture, which is here manufactured to a large extent both in black and in white, and highly gilt and decorated porcelain, the peculiar hard and fine nature of the body being well adapted for these useful and elegant articles. The firm gives employment to nearly four hundred hands. They have lately turned their attention to the home markets, in addition to the American trade, and are gradually extending their connections, and producing services faultless in style and material. The body, which is remarkably fine and compact, is of good colour, the glazing hard and fine, and the decorations of elegant design and artistic finish. My readers who see the impressed mark of "Bridgwood and Clarke," or the printed mark of a royal arms, with the words "Porcelain Opaque, B & C, Burslem," will be gratified to know that these are made at the works at which Josiah

Wedgwood was born, and at which he served his apprenticeship.

Having traced, briefly, the history of the works in which Josiah Wedgwood was born, at which he was apprenticed, and at which he grew up to man's estate, down to the present day, it will be necessary to again revert to the time when he there learned the "art, mistery, occupation, or imployment of Throwing and Handleing." Of the period of his apprenticeship, of the habits of the boy, of his occupations when away from the wheel, or of his progress *at* the wheel or the mould, but little is known. It is not mere conjecture, however, to say, that his boyhood, and the years which he passed in growing up to man's estate, were spent in the most exemplary manner, and that he grew up a credit to himself, an honour to the place which gave him birth, and a blessing to his friends and relatives. I have heard it from those best able to know—from some of the oldest inhabitants of the place—that in their boyhood, at the end of the last century, they were continually admonished by their parents and grandparents to be good, as Wedgwood had been, and to lead such a life as he, as a youth, had done before them. It is pleasant to put this fact on record, and to hear this kind of testimony given to the character of this great man, even when young, that he was held up to the youth of his native place as a pattern for emulation.

CHAPTER III.

BOYHOOD OF JOSIAH WEDGWOOD.—ATTACK OF SMALL-POX.—MR. GLADSTONE'S NOTICE OF THIS ATTACK.—AMPUTATION OF HIS LEG.—JOSIAH WEDGWOOD AS A "THROWER."—ENOCH WOOD.—WILLIAM LITTLER AND AARON WEDGWOOD.—DEATH OF THE MOTHER OF JOSIAH WEDGWOOD.—TERMINATION OF HIS APPRENTICESHIP.—COMMENCES MAKING AGATE KNIFE HANDLES, ETC.—ENTERS INTO PARTNERSHIP WITH JOHN HARRISON.—PARTNERSHIP WITH THOMAS WHIELDON.

DURING his apprenticeship, probably about his sixteenth year, Josiah Wedgwood was seized with illness—a violent attack of the small-pox, it is stated—and was laid up for a considerable period with that complaint. By this illness, and the weakness which followed it, he was incapacitated from following, to any extent, one branch of the art to which he had been bound—that of a thrower—and thus, fortunately, his ever active mind had more time, and more opportunity, to develop itself in the other and more ornamental branches of his trade. The Right Hon. W. E. Gladstone, in his able and truly eloquent address at Burslem, on occasion of his laying the foundation stone, as Chancellor of the Exchequer, of the Wedgwood Memorial Institute in that town, thus strikingly and pleasingly alludes to this affliction—or, rather, blessing—which visited the boy-genius:—"Then comes the well-known attack of small-pox, the settling of the dregs of his disease in the lower part of the leg, and the amputation of the limb, rendering him lame for life. It is not often that we have such palpable occasion to record our obligations to the small-pox;

but in the wonderful ways of Providence, that disease, which came to him as a twofold scourge, was probably the occasion of his subsequent excellence. It prevented him from growing up to be the active, vigorous English workman, possessed of all his limbs, and knowing right well the use of them; but it put him upon considering whether, as he could not be that, he might not be something else and something greater. It sent his mind inwards, it drove him to meditate upon the laws and secrets of his art; the result was that he arrived at a perception and a grasp of them, which might perhaps have been envied, certainly have been owned, by an Athenian potter. Relentless criticism has long since torn to pieces the old legend of King Numa receiving in a cavern, from the nymph Egeria, the laws that were to govern Rome; but no criticism can shake the record of that illness and that mutilation of the boy, Josiah Wedgwood, which made for him a cavern of his bed-room, and an oracle of his own inquiring, searching, meditative, fruitful mind.

"From those early days of suffering—weary, perhaps, to him as they went by, but bright, surely, in the retrospect, both to him and us—a mark seems at once to have been set upon his career. But those who would dwell upon his history have still to deplore that many of the materials are wanting."

It would be far from my wish to destroy, or to entrench, even in the slightest degree, on the true poetry of this relation; but as its sentiment cannot be altered, or its beauty impaired, by correcting one of the statements, I do not hesitate to say, what I have every reason for believing to be the case, that the amputation of the leg was not altogether the result of the small-pox, which had produced a disorder and weakness in that limb, but of an accident; and that it did not take place during the boyhood of the great man, but at a much later period of his life. The boy had genius and thought, energy and perseverance, in him, which wanted not the bodily affliction to become developed, and to bring them to active perfection. His mind was such as would have surmounted every obstacle which manual employment could offer, and would have risen above every unfavourable circumstance by which he might be surrounded. The small-pox, it is true, at that early period gave him leisure and opportunity to think, to experimentalise, and to form those ideas which in after life he so successfully and beneficially, both to himself and to the world, worked out; but he would have become a great man even without that ailment to help him on.

The small-pox left a humour which settled in the leg, and on every slight accident became so painful, that for one half of the time of his apprenticeship he sat at his work with his leg on a stool before him. The same cruel disorder continued with him till manhood, and was at one time so much aggravated by an unfortunate bruise, that he was confined to his bed many months, and reduced to the last extremity of debility. He recovered his strength after this violent shock, but was not able to pursue his plans for some years without frequent interruptions from the same sad cause. At length the disorder reached the knee, and showing symptoms of still advancing so as to endanger his life, he was advised to undergo amputation, and submitted to it, it is said, about the 34th year of his age. From this period he enjoyed a tolerably good state of bodily health and activity, and has been known to attribute much of his success of life to his confinement under this illness, because it gave him opportunities to read, and to repair the defect of an education which had, as I have shown, been necessarily narrowed by circumstances.

It is recorded that during his apprenticeship he worked in the same room, as a thrower,* with his brother Richard,

* A "thrower" is the man who forms at the "potter's wheel" the vessel by hand from the moist clay. The "ball" of clay being placed on the disc, the boy, or girl, employed for the purpose, turns the wheel quickly or slowly, as occasion requires. By this means the disc is made to rotate horizontally, and the "thrower," who is seated, forms the vessel by hand, and by the aid of guides for shape which he has prepared for the purpose. The throwing, it will thus be seen, is the first and most important operation in the forming of the vessels.

who was five years his senior, and who, it is fair to presume, was also an apprentice, having probably been bound to his father during his lifetime. Richard, however, unlike his thoughtful brother, appears to have left his employment, and enlisted as a soldier. A fragment of an interesting little memorandum in the handwriting of the late eminent potter, Enoch Wood, which I saw, and copied, at Hanley, gives an interesting reminiscence of the boyish days of Josiah Wedgwood. It was written in 1809, and appears to read thus (it refers to a piece of early porcelain made by Littler)—"This was given to E. Wood by Wm. Fletcher in Jany., 1809. He informs me he remembers it being made by Mr. Wm. Littler,* at Longton, near Stoke, about 55 years ago—say in the year 1754. It has never been out of his possession during that time, and is highly valued. This Fletcher says he used to work at the Churchyard works, and made Balls † for two of the Throwers at the same time, namely, Richd. Wedgwood and Josiah Wedgwood, both of whom worked in one room for their father, who was the owner of the works. William Fletcher, within named, was in my employ during part of the last years of his life, and said he was about the same age and size as Josiah Wedgwood, and generally had his old cloaths, because they fitted him well. E. Wood." "Fletcher was a 'Stouker'‡ by trade. I gave him a pint of ale to show my handlers the old way of 'Stouking.' He did so, and the men gave him a few pence, with which he bought more ale and got tipsy, and took a cold, and never recovered, but died soon after,

* Although only stated to be made by Littler, this piece was doubtless the joint production of William Littler and Aaron Wedgwood, his brother-in-law. These two potters having observed how closely in some respects the fine "white stone ware approached to porcelain," united their skill and means to prosecute experiments in the manufacture of "china." Their experiments were eminently successful, both in the body and in the liquid glaze discovered by Wedgwood; but heavy losses were the result, and the work was given up. The information they had gained was afterwards imparted to Josiah Wedgwood by his relative.

† Balls of clay ready for throwing.

‡ A "stouker" was the man who formed the handles of vessels.

and was buried by the parish officers." As an interesting illustration of the rate of wages in the days of Wedgwood's apprenticeship, it may be mentioned that Fletcher,—who "made balls" for the two brothers working at two corners of a small room, he being placed between them and supplying them alternately,—received *fourpence* per week for his first year, sixpence for the second, and ninepence for the third. Of these rates of wages I shall yet have more to say later on.

While yet in his apprenticeship, Josiah lost his mother, who died, it is said, at Burslem, early in the year 1748, when he was between seventeen and eighteen years of age. She was buried near to her late husband, in the graveyard adjoining the works—the graveyard shown in the engraving of the "Churchyard Works," where the burial-place may be seen to the left—but the tomb in which they were both doubtless interred has been despoiled of its inscription. Close beside it are other tombs of members of the family. After the death of his mother, to whom Josiah was, I believe, most deeply attached, he is said to have continued to reside with his brothers and sisters in the same house in the works, and to have applied himself most sedulously to the improvement of his art.

While yet an apprentice he had made great progress in his art, not being content to follow simply that branch practised in his brother's works. He particularly made himself master of the method of colouring wares with metallic calces in imitation of agate, tortoiseshell, &c. During this period, too, he first made advances in his afterwards famous cream-coloured ware. He thus, however, spent so much of his time in experiments, and in trying new applications of his art, that his brother became uneasy, and continually exhorted him to give up these flights of fancy and confine himself to the beaten track of his ancestors—an exhortation which, happily for himself and for the world, was of no avail. At the expiration of his apprenticeship Josiah Wedgwood pointed out to his brother many modes of increasing their trade, and made proposals to be received into partnership. His brother, however, did not think it right to put his wealth at stake in the pursuit of projects which he deemed to be visionary, and declined the proposition.

The term of Josiah Wedgwood's apprenticeship for five years naturally expired on the 11th of November, 1749, when he was a little more than nineteen years of age, and it appears more than probable that, for a short time at least, after he was "out of his time," he remained at his old home as journeyman to, instead of as he had hoped partner with, his brother. It will have been noticed that by the terms of the indenture, no wages were paid him during those five years, his brother merely covenanting to find him in meat, drink, lodging, and clothes. He had at this time, as will have been seen by his father's will—*i.e.*, when he should attain the age of twenty years—the legacy of twenty pounds to begin life with, and we next find him, having left home, lodging with a Mr. Daniel Mayer, a mercer, at Stoke, and engaged in making mottled earthenware knife handles, in somewhat rude imitation of agate, tortoiseshell, and various kinds of marble, which he supplied to the hardwaremen of Sheffield and Birmingham.

Here, at Stoke, in 1752, Josiah Wedgwood entered into partnership with John Harrison, of Newcastle, afterwards of Cliff Bank, Stoke, a man possessed of some means but little taste; and the two commenced business in manufacturing the same kind of goods as I have just named. Harrison was not, it appears, a practical potter, but was taken into partnership by Wedgwood for the advance of capital. Wedgwood, it is said, found the brains, and Harrison the money, and the craft to appropriate to himself the lion's share of the profits. The partners carried on their manufactory at what was Mr. Aldersea's pottery, at the top of Stoke, and opposite to the works belonging to Mr. Hugh Booth. Here, besides agate and other knife hafts, they made the ordinary kinds of wares then in demand, both "scratched and blue," and no doubt, but for "the cupidity of Harrison," the works here would in time have become as celebrated as the later ones of Wedgwood have done.

The works at Stoke are not now in existence, having been destroyed many years ago. They were, I am informed, at the failure of Harrison, bought by Josiah Spode, who pulled them down, and built cottages in their place.

In 1754 Wedgwood and Harrison entered into partnership with Thomas Whieldon, the most eminent potter of his day. The partnership with Harrison, however, continued but for a very short period, and in two years from Wedgwood first joining him (in 1752), he went out of the concern altogether, and the two remaining partners, Wedgwood and Whieldon, continued in partnership for five years. The basis of this union was the secrets of the trade which Wedgwood possessed, and was to practise for their common benefit without any stipulation to reveal them.

"Mr. Wedgwood," says a document I have before me, "spent six months in preparing the models, moulds, and other necessary apparatus for this work, and the first fruit of his genius was a new GREEN earthenware, having the smoothness and brilliant appearance of glass. He made principally of this ware services of dessert; the forms were different kinds of leaves, and the plates were moulded with fruits grouped in a very fanciful way, and they had a considerable sale. He also made toilet vessels, snuff-boxes, and many different toys for mounting in metals, coloured in imitation of precious stones. When he offered these things to the jewellers of London and Bath, they considered them as the productions of some valuable discovery, the nature of which they could not guess at. But there was one of them, among the first at that time in fashion, who, having bestowed many encomiums upon them, excused himself from encouraging their sale when he heard the low price at which their maker estimated them. It was during this connection that he was so much reduced by his complaint, and rendered incapable of attending to business. He was then under the necessity of communicating the knowledge of his mixtures to a workman, and these two first works soon became a general manufacture in the neighbourhood."

In 1754, then, Josiah Wedgwood became the partner of Thomas Whieldon, at whose works at Fenton Low the two carried on their business, bringing to bear on the concern their united skill and united taste. Whieldon at that time was a man of substance, and had been in business as a potter for many years. "In 1740," says Shaw, "Mr. Thomas Whieldon's manufactory at Little Fenton consisted of a small range of low buildings, all thatched. His early productions were knife hafts for the Sheffield cutlers, and snuff-boxes for the Birmingham hardwaremen to finish with hoops, hinges, and springs, which himself usually carried in a basket to the tradesmen, and, being much like agate, they were greatly in request. He also made toys and chimney ornaments, coloured in either the clay state or biscuit, by zaffre, manganese, copper, &c., and glazed with black, red, or white lead. He also made black glazed tea and coffee-pots, tortoiseshell and melon table plates (with ornamented edge and six scollops, as in the specimens kept by Andrew Boon, of the Honeywall, Stoke), and other useful articles. Mr. A. Wood made models and moulds of these articles; also pickle leaves, crab stock handles, and cabbage-leave spouts for tea and coffee-pots, which utensils, with candlesticks, chocolate-cups, and tea-ware, were much improved, and his connections extended subsequently, when Mr. J. Wedgwood became his managing partner. He was a shrewd and careful person. To prevent his productions being imitated in quality or shape, he always buried the broken articles, and a few months ago we witnessed the unexpected exposure of some of these by some miners attempting to get marl in the road at Little Fenton. The fortune he acquired by his industry enabled him to erect a very elegant mansion near Stoke, where he long enjoyed, in the bosom of his family, the fruits of his early economy. He was also sheriff of the county in the twenty-sixth year of the late reign. The benevolence of his disposition, and his integrity, are honourable traits of character, far superior to the boast of ancestry without personal merit. He died in 1798 at a very old age, and in 1828 his relict was interred beside him in Stoke churchyard. Of the four apprentices to Mr. Whieldon, three commenced business, and were eminently successful: Mr. Josiah Spode (the first), Mr. Robert Garner, Mr. J. Barker, and Mr. Robert Greatbach," &c.

Whieldon had already acquired a reputation for his wares far exceeding that of most, or almost any, of the potters of his day, and was thus as desirable a partner for Wedgwood, as Wedgwood, with his exquisite taste and skill, was for him. He had increased his works very considerably, and was employing many hands, some of whom became eminent and wealthy potters. I have now before me the original account-book of hirings, and lettings of land and houses, &c., of Thomas Whieldon, in which all the entries are in his own handwriting, and show him to have been a man of precise and careful business habits, and of good education. From this highly interesting book, in which the entries extend over the period from 1747 to 1754, with some entries of a still later date, I shall in my next chapter make a few extracts, to show the rate of remuneration paid to potters in the days when Josiah Wedgwood first began business, and the curious bargains and customs which were usual at hirings, which, it may be well to remark, were always, among potters, from Martinmas to Martinmas.

CHAPTER IV.

THOMAS WHIELDON.—THE ENLARGEMENT OF HIS WORKS.—"HIRINGS" OF WORKMEN.—EXTRACTS FROM WHIELDON'S ACCOUNT-BOOK.—JOSIAH SPODE: HIS APPRENTICESHIP AND AFTER HIRING.—TORTOISESHELL WARE.—EXPIRATION OF PARTNERSHIP BETWEEN THOMAS WHIELDON AND JOSIAH WEDGWOOD.—WEDGWOOD COMMENCES BUSINESS AT BURSLEM.—TAKES THE "IVY HOUSE" POT WORKS.—DESCENT OF THE IVY HOUSE PROPERTY.—JOHN AND THOMAS WEDGWOOD OF THE "BIG HOUSE."—BURSLEM SHAMBLES, ETC.

HAVING traced the career of Josiah Wedgwood from his birth down through the period of his apprenticeship and his affliction, and so on, through his short partnership with Harrison, at the start of life, to the time when he was fairly embarked in business with his second partner, Thomas Whieldon, at Fenton, it will now be interesting to give some few further particulars relating to Whieldon, and to his works, and to the varieties of wares produced by him; and I am enabled to do this partly by the aid of the original account-book kept by Whieldon, which is now in my possession.

In 1749, Thomas Whieldon built for himself an addition to his works, and as these were the works at which Wedgwood, as a partner, carried on his business, the following account of the "Expenses of the new end & Seller of the Over Work-house," copied from the curious old account-book to which I have alluded, will be found to possess much interest:—

1749.			£	s.	d.
June	10.	John Wood, at sinking Seller,* 8 days	0	8	0
,,	,,	Hancock, 8 days	0	7	4
,,	,,	Stananer, 2 days	0	0	10
,,	17.	Wood, 3 days	0	3	0
,,	,,	Hancock, 3 days	0	2	9
,,	,,	Boys to help	0	2	0
,,	,,	Stanner, 2 days	0	1	8
,,	19.	Ed. Shaw, 4½ days.			
,,	,,	Thos. Shaw, 4½ days.			
,,	,,	Jno. Shaw, 4½ days.			
,,	,,	Saml. Hardy, 4½ days.			
,,	,,	His boy, 4½ days.			
,,	,,	Henny, 4½ days.			
,,	,,	Mearheath, 5½ days.			
,,	,,	Saml. Astley, 4½ days.			
		At serving Masons—			
,,	,,	Jno. Cressall, 6 days.			
June	12.	Jarvis Forister carrd. 4 load. Brick from Brickd.			
,,	,,	Isaac Greatbach card. abot. 5 load. 1 load sand brt. wth. him.			
,,	13.	Jarvis, 2 load Brick. 2 load sand from Bridge.			
,,	,,	Isaac, 4 load brick.			
,,	14.	Isaac wth. one Team most the day.			
,,	15.	Jarvis Forister, all day wth. standing tumbrell, but come late.			
,,	16.	Jarvis Forister, 1 day wth. one Tumbrel.			
,,	17.	do. card. abt. 5 or 6 load.			
,,	,,	Ed. Shaw.			
,,	26.	Pd. for pilinge for thack	0	16	8
,,	,,	Wm. Daniell, 2 days.			
,,	,,	Jno. Wood, a day wrkg.			
,,	,,	Pd. for Springles*	0	1	0
,,	,,	Do. for getting Clay out of Sellor .	0	4	9
,,	,,	Ale at Rearing	0	2	0
,,	,,	Casements, 5½ lbs.			
,,	,,	Barrs for windows, abt. 4½ lbs. from Heaton.			
,,	,,	Pd. for glazing to Hatton, 30 foot @ 6d.	0	15	0
,,	,,	Pd. John Heaton	0	6	0

* Cellar.

			£	s.	d.
June	26.	Pd. John Wood, for drawing ten thrave pileings* for thaching the Over Wk. house	0	3	0
,,	,,	Thos. Payne, 184 foot 1¼ in. thick popr.† Board. 400 foot 1 in. 81 foot Popplary, 1 in. thick			
,,	,,	Moses Stockleys team card. brick & loam 2 hour qtr. One a Clock to Six, but no man wth. it.			
,,	,,	In 4 windows 30 foot glass by Jno. Hatton, 6d.	0	15	0
,,	27.	Moses Stockleys team, 1 load timber from Boothen Green.			
,,	,,	2 or 3 load Shawds,‡ & 2 or 3 load brick to the wall.			
,,	28.	4 load Shawds to wall.			
,,	,,	12 load brick.			
,,	,,	7 load to wall.			
July	1.	3 to Wk. house.			

From this same curious and highly interesting account-book the following extracts will show the small amount of wages paid in those days as compared with the present, and the singular and amusing bargains between master and workman, regarding gifts of "earnest money," "old cloaths," testaments, &c., which were made and agreed upon at "hirings" among the potters, from a hundred to a hundred and fifty years ago:—

1749.			£	s.	d.
Jany.	27.	Hired Jno. Austin for placeing white, &c. pr week	0	5	6
		Pd. his whole earnest	0	3	0
Feby.	14.	Then hired Thos. Dutton	0	6	6
		Pd. 1 pr. Stockins	0	3	6
		Earnest for vineing ‖	0	15	0

* "Thraves of pileing." Piling was straw, and the thrave was twelve sheaves; thus there were ten thraves led in this account, which would be 120 sheaves.

† Poplar.

‡ *Shawds*, pot shards, *i.e.*, broken pots for the foundations.

‖ Veining, same as in the combed and tortoiseshell wares.

		£	s.	d.
Feb. 14.	1 pr. Stockins	0	2	6
	Pd. in part	0	1	0
	Pd. do. in 7 yds. cloth	0	8	9
„ 16.	Hired Wm. Keeling for handleing *	0	6	0
	Pd. his whole earnest	0	1	0
„ 20.	Hired Wm. Cope for handleing & vineing cast ware, for	0	7	0
	Pd. his whole earnest	0	10	6
„ 28.	Then hired Robt. Gardner pr week	0	6	6
	Earnest	0	10	6
	Pd. him toward it	0	1	0
	I am to make his earnest about 5s. more in somthing.			
March 8.	Then hired Jno. Barker fr ye huvels† @	0	5	6
	Pd. earnest in part	0	1	0
	Pd. it to pay more	0	1	0
„ 24.	Hired ...... Low for making Slip	0	5	3
	Pd. him in part of his earnest	0	2	6
	To pay more	0	2	6
„ 26.	Then hired George Bagnall, for fireing for this year, for	0	5	3
	Full earnest, 5s.			
	Pd. in part, 2s, 6d.			
	Hired for 1750	0	5	6
1749.				
April 9.	Hired Siah Spoade, to give him from this time to Martelmas next 2s. 3d., or 2s. 6d. if he Deserves it.			
	2d year	0	2	9
	3d year	0	3	3
	Pd. full earnest	0	1	0

This entry is of considerable historical interest, as being the first hiring of the great Josiah Spode, the founder of the family which rose to such great eminence in the art. The "hiring," which appears to have been the apprenticeship, or, what was tantamount to it, the learning of the trade, would, from this entry, appear to have been for three years. The first at 2*s.* 3*d.* per week, "or 2*s.* 6*d.* if he deserves it," and the succeeding years at a rise of sixpence per week each. There are two other entries in this same book relating

* Making and putting on handles, &c.

† The kiln.

to Josiah Spode, which I here give, as they relate to future hirings after the expiration of the first term:—

		£	s.	d.
1752.				
Feby. 22.	Hired Josiah Spoad for next Martlemas, per week	0	7	0
	I am to give him earn.	0	5	0
	Pd. in Part	0	1	0
	Pd. do.	0	4	0
1754.				
Feby. 25.	Hired Siah Spode, per week . . .	0	7	6
	Earnest	1	11	6
	Pd. in part	0	16	0
1740.				
June 2.	Hired a boy of Ann Blowrs for Treading ye lathe, per week	0	2	0
	Pd. earnest	0	0	6
1751.	Then hired Elijah Simpson for Turning, he is to have pr week .	0	8	0
	Whole earnest	2	2	0
	Pd. in part	1	2	0
Jany. 11.	Then hired Saml. Jackson for Throwing Sagers and fireing, pr week .	0	8	0
	Whole earnest	2	2	0
	Pd. in part	1	2	0
	Pd. more	1	1	0
Feby. 9.	Hired Jno. Edge, for per week .	0	6	0
	He is to have earnest	0	5	0
	& a new pr. stockins	0	2	0
	Pd. in part	0	1	0
	Hired his son Saml. for	0	1	3
April 6.	Hired Wm. Kent, per week .	0	7	6
	To give for earnest	0	12	0
	Pd. in part	0	1	6
	To give a new Shirt at 16d. per yard.			
	Hired Ann Blowrs Girl & Boy—			
	Girl	0	0	9
	Boy, Joseph	0	2	0
	To give earnest, Testament.			
Decr. 26.	Then hired Cupit, pr week . . .	0	2	3
	Pd. earnest	0	0	6
	I am to give him a old pr. stockins, or somthing.			
1752.				
July 22.	Hired George Bagley for 2 years.			
	1st year	0	3	6
	2d year	0	4	0
	To give him a pr. shoes each year.			

		£	s.	d.
1753.				
June 21.	Hired Wm. Marsh for 3 years. He is to have 10s. 6d. earnest each year, and 7s. per week. I am to give a old Coat or somthing abt 5s. value.			
Augt. 29.	Hired Westabys 3 children.			
	per week	0	4	0
	Pd. earnest	0	0	6
	Hired John Everal, pr week	0	4	6
	Pd. earnest, 2 pr. stockins	0	4	0
	1 shillin in Cash	0	1	0
	To have a handkershef.			
1760.				
Decr. 3.	Hired Joseph ——— son to look after my flint mill. He is to have six shillings pr Ton for grinding, & to find his own Candles. To pay £3 a year for the Mill House.			
	Pd. Earnest	0	0	6
	Nothing further, unless I chuse to give him a old coat—he is to work for me at any time when I want. His father is to assist him in any thing he cant do about the mill.			
1752.				
Augt. 24.	Hired little Bet Blowr to learn to flower.*			
	1st year, per week	0	1	0
	2d year	0	1	3
	3d year	0	1	6

From the same document the prices charged for some of those beautiful and peculiar wares for which Whieldon and his partner Josiah Wedgwood were so famed, may be gathered. They are of great interest to the collector, and are as follows :—

To send Mrs. Davison.

6 ½ pt. mugs, white, 2d.
1 flat candlestick, Tor.†

* To paint the simple little sprigs which decorated the pottery.

† Tortoiseshell, the famous ware for which these early potters were celebrated.

Mr. Thos. Fletcher, Dr.

	£	s.	d.
To 1 doz. Plates, Tor.	0	8	0
„ 2 ½ do. plate	0	2	6
„ 2 2 dishes	0	2	0
„ 1 do. painted	0	2	0
„ 1 do. Cream Colr.	0	1	8
„ 5 pails	0	2	6

Mr. Davison.

1 pail	0	0	6

Mr. Broad.

32 desert handles.*

To make for Mr. Green.

4 Tor. Teapots, all Toys.
4 Coffee Pots.
4 Slop Bowls.
4 Ewers.
4 Sugar boxes, China make.
4 Mustard pots, high.
8 Salts, high feet.
12 2 Dishes, Tor.
5 doz. pails.
2 doz. piggins.
6 doz. large plates.
4 doz. round do.
8 doz. a size less
7 of ym round wth. Ribd. edge
1 do. sqr.
3 doz. Bread & butter plates, Ribd.
3 Qt. Coffee Pots.
6 pints.
4 2nd size dishes.
2 larger.

The Mr. Green for whom these goods were ordered, was of Hovingham, near Eylsham, Norfolk.

The goods manufactured by Whieldon, both during his partnership with Wedgwood and afterwards, were of remarkably good quality, of excellent form, and were well "potted" in every respect. They are now very scarce, and are highly and deservedly prized by collectors. I have in my own col-

* Probably the imitation agate knife handles.

lection, among other examples, a fine "tortoiseshell plate" and a small "cauliflower jug," which have passed into my hands from the present aged descendant of Uriah Sutton, who is named in more than one place in the document just referred to as being "hired" by Whieldon. The tortoiseshell ware is beautifully mottled, sometimes by the rich, reddish brown colour, which belongs to the original, and at other times by a fine green, or deep purplish tinge. The glaze is invariably good, and the potting itself of thoroughly good quality. In my own collection is a jardiniere of this kind of ware, of large size, and of excellent design. In the accompanying engraving are shown two of these remarkably

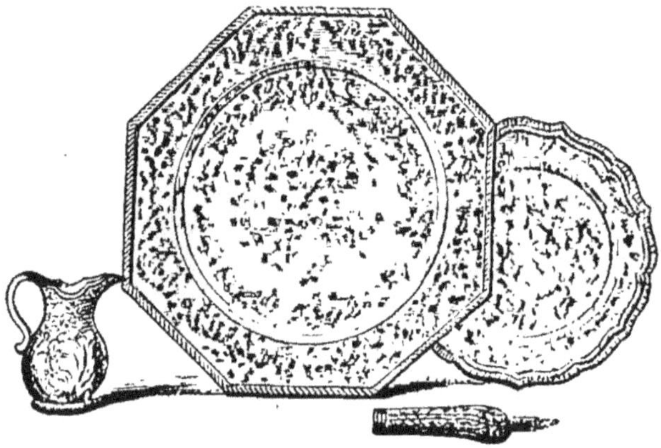

TORTOISESHELL WARE.

fine plates—the centre octagonal one measuring in its largest diameter fifteen and a half inches—a small green "cauliflower jug," and an imitation agate knife-haft, from my own collection. These are all highly characteristic examples of the manufacture of this period.

I have it from excellent authority that as early as 1745—when only in his fifteenth year—Josiah Wedgwood had begun to make a few trial articles of that improved kind of ware which afterwards obtained for *him* the distinction of "Queen's Potter," and for the *ware* itself that of "Queen's Ware;" and these trials and improvements he continued to make and to carry on during the remaining years of his servitude, and afterwards until he brought it to perfection. Whieldon, however, it seems, doing a large business in his own peculiar wares, did not care to embark much on the "new-fangled ways" of his young partner, although he evidently fell into some of those ways in a very profitable manner.

In 1754—the year in which he became the partner of Whieldon—Josiah Wedgwood, after many patient trials, succeeded in producing his admirable green glaze, and this invention did more, it is believed, to augment the already rising fortune of Whieldon than any other ware did. Whieldon in the end acquired a large fortune by his trade, and in 1786 was High Sheriff of the county of Stafford.

In 1759, the term of five years, for which he had by agreement become the partner of Thomas Whieldon, expired, and Josiah Wedgwood immediately returned to his native place, Burslem, with the full determination of prosecuting his own favourite pursuits, and of bringing the schemes and the experiments he had so long tried to a successful issue. Here, at twenty-nine years of age, he commenced business entirely on his own account, and soon showed to the world, not only the extraordinary capacity of his ever active mind, but the extreme skill, intelligence, and taste which he brought to bear on every branch of his native and chosen art.

On his first returning to Burslem, Wedgwood, for a time, I believe, occupied the old pot-work at the Churchyard, where he had been born and apprenticed, and here, untrammelled by partners with views adverse to his own, and by the surroundings of jealous and watchful eyes, he set himself earnestly to the work of improvement his whole heart had longed for, and took leisure to carry on his grand design of raising the potter's art above its then standard of excellence, and of successfully rivalling in earthenware not only the more costly productions of foreign countries of his day, but those of long past ages. Here he was so eminently successful that he soon found himself obliged to extend his operations, and he entered on a pot-work nearer to the centre of the town, and within a stone's throw of the works of his cousins, Thomas and John Wedgwood, to whom the premises belonged.

This, the second pot-work occupied by him, with the house belonging to it, and which was called the "Ivy House," from the fact of its being covered with ivy, was situated where the butchers' shambles now stand, the old buildings having been purchased by the market commissioners, and taken down for the erection of the present market in 1835. The "Ivy House," with the pot-works belonging to it, are shown in the engraving on the next page, from a sketch kindly furnished to me by the oldest member of the Wedgwood family.* These premises belonged to Thomas and John Wedgwood, of the "Big House," to whom Josiah became tenant, covenanting by written agreement to pay for the house and the pot-work attached to it the yearly rent of ten pounds—a rent which, in those days, when Burslem was but a village, and when its pot-works were scattered about the almost waste lands, might be deemed good, but which, at the present day, for similar premises, would have to be multiplied by at least ten, before a tenant could have possession.

The "Ivy House" and works were situated nearly in the centre of the town, or rather village, of Burslem. The premises stood at the corner of what was then, as long afterwards, known as *Shoe Lane*, or *Shore Lane*, now called *Wedgwood Street*, which at that time was a narrow way, only wide enough for a single cart to pass along, and as rough and uneven as well could be. The visitor to Burslem who desires to know exactly the site of this historically interesting house should stroll up to the fine modern-built shambles, or

* Mr. Aaron Wedgwood, of Burslem, an artist of very considerable talent, and a most worthy man, who is lineally descended from Aaron Wedgwood, who, with William Littler, was the first maker of china in the district. Mr. Wedgwood's father, too, was a clever modeller and painter.

THE IVY HOUSE, BURSLEM.

"butchery," as it is sometimes called, and while he stands at the corner facing down Swan Square, he may rest assured that he is standing on what was the little enclosed garden in front of Wedgwood's house; that the outer wall of the building at his back goes diagonally across the house from corner to corner, one half being under the shambles and the other where the street now is; that the site of one of the kilns is just beneath the centre of the shambles, and that another kiln was about the middle of the present street at his back; the surrounding workshops being partly where the street now is, and partly where the building at present stands.

The "Ivy House," so called, as I have said, because it was covered with a profusion of ivy, might originally have been roofed with thatch or mud, like the other buildings of the district, but it was afterwards tiled, as shown in the engraving. In front was a small garden enclosed with a low wall, and a brick pathway led from the gate to the doorway. The front faced the open space called the "Green Bank," where the village children played to their heart's content among the clay and shards which, even in those days, had no doubt usurped the place of the "green" grass from which it took its name. Adjoining the house was a low, half-timbered, thickly-thatched building, afterwards known as the "Turk's Head," and beyond this again was the maypole, on "Maypole Bank," of which I have before spoken, and which stood on the site now occupied by the Town Hall. At the opposite side of the house from the "Turk's Head" was a gateway leading into the yard of the works, which made up one side of Shoe Lane, the pot-works of John and Thomas Wedgwood, with which these were connected, being on the opposite side of the lane, where some of the buildings are now occupied by Messrs. Harley and Dean. These works and house have the reputation of being the first roofed with tiles in the district—the usual roofing being thatch, or, oftener still, mud.

The Ivy House and Works Josiah Wedgwood rented, as I have stated, from his relatives, John and Thomas Wedgwood, of the "Big House," at the annual rental of £10, and here, the Churchyard Works not being sufficient to meet his expanding views and extending trade, he carried on the manufacture of his ornamental goods, his more ordinary ware, I believe, being produced at the Churchyard. At the Ivy House Works he produced many things far in advance of his day, and such as, when he had previously foreshadowed them to his brother, were considered by him and others to be wild and visionary schemes, unlikely to lead to profit, and only to be indulged in at the expense of time, money, and connections.

To the Ivy House itself, too, Josiah brought home his bride, and there lived happily with her for several years. It was after being established here for a little time, and "feeling his way" onwards, that Josiah Wedgwood proposed to purchase the works, and also those of his relatives at the "Big House," with which they were connected, but was unsuccessful. The property, therefore, remained in the hands of the "Big House" Wedgwoods until sold by their descendant, Thomas Wedgwood, in 1831 and 1834. In the former year the portion of the property sold for the purpose of enlarging the market-place—the sum paid for which was £1,400—consisted of four buildings on the side of the property nearest to the Town Hall, which were taken down and their site thrown open to the market. In 1834, it was determined by the market trustees to purchase and take down the remainder of the buildings on this part of the Wedgwood property lying between the market place and Shoe Lane, and to erect the present convenient and spacious market-house on its site. Thus the Ivy House, with its kilns and workshops, the Turk's Head, and other buildings, were swept away. The price paid for this portion of the estate was £2,600, making in all £3,000 paid for taking away one of the most interesting memorials of Josiah Wedgwood which the neighbourhood possessed.

CHAPTER V.

THE "OVERHOUSE."—THOMAS COLCLOUGH.—MADAM EGERTON—THOMAS WEDGWOOD AND THE "OVERHOUSE" BRANCH.—THE "OVERHOUSE WORKS"—OCCUPIERS OF THE WORKS.—ALLMAN, BROUGHTON, AND CO.—JOSIAH WEDGWOOD.—JARDINIERES, MEDALLIONS, ETC.—DIFFICULTIES WITH WORKMEN.—MATTHEW BOULTON OF THE SOHO WORKS.—CALLING WORKMEN BY SOUND OF HORN.—CUPOLA AND BELL.—THE "BELL WORKS:" THEIR OWNERS AND OCCUPIERS.—WEDGWOOD'S "QUEEN'S WARE."—PRESENTS A CAUDLE SERVICE TO QUEEN CHARLOTTE.—APPOINTED "QUEEN'S POTTER."—THE "QUEEN'S PATTERN" SERVICES.—CREAM-COLOURED WARE.—ENGINE LATHE.—"QUEEN STREET" TAKES ITS NAME FROM HIS WORKS.

THOMAS WEDGWOOD, the elder brother of Josiah, and to whom, indeed, the boy was, as I have already shown, apprenticed, owned and resided at the "Overhouse," at Burslem. Of this place, to which I have already alluded, it will now be necessary to my narrative to give some particulars. The Overhouse, which is now the residence of Mr. W. E. Twigg, chief bailiff of Burslem—an office almost tantamount to that of mayor in other places—is a large and somewhat imposing-looking house, opposite to what is now called "Wedgwood Place." It stands back from the street, the grounds being enclosed by a wall where, in Wedgwood's time, wooden railings stood. The "carcase" of the house is, I believe, precisely the same as when occupied by Thomas Wedgwood, but modern windows have been substituted for the old leaden casements, the roof and doorway have been altered, and other changes made, so as to convert it into a residence suited to present requirements.

The "Overhouse Works" are situate at the back and to the side of the house, with entrance in Wedgwood Place, where that place joins the Scotia Road. Since the time when they were occupied by Thomas Wedgwood, of the Churchyard, they have been, of course, much altered, but it is pleasant to know that a considerable part of the buildings,

DOORWAY, OVERHOUSE WORKS.

as they now stand, stood in his day, and that here were produced by him such an amount of earthenware goods as must have helped to secure to his family the handsome competence which they enjoyed. A part, at all events, of the premises now used as pot-works were, I believe, formerly the farm buildings belonging to the Overhouse. They were connected with the house by a doorway in the old brick wall, still remaining, which forms an interesting link between the present and the past. This doorway is shown in the vignette on the preceding page. It is surmounted, as will be seen, by a cleverly carved stone tablet, of remarkably good design, and has evidently been intended to bear an inscription. The Overhouse estate appears for a long time to have belonged to the Wedgwoods. From 1620 to 1657 it was held by Thomas Colclough, who married Catherine, one of the co-heiresses of Thomas Burslem, and sister to the other co-heiress, Margaret, married to Gilbert Wedgwood. Mr. Colclough had an only son, who died without issue, when most of his estates passed to his second cousin, Burslem Wedgwood. Mr. Colclough (who at one time was constable of the Manor of Tunstall) and his wife, Catherine Burslem, resided for many years at the Overhouse, and he is described as its occupier in 1662. In 1678, as appears by the will which I have already given on a preceding page, Thomas Wedgwood, who had married Margaret Shaw, died, seized of the "Upper or Overhouse, with all barns, outhouses, stables, cowhouses, yards, fields, orchards, and gardens thereunto belonging, with the fish-pond and fish, and also the Oxley Crofts, the great Old Field, the little Old Field, the Oxley Croft Meadow, the Kill Yard," &c., along with a considerable estate in land and houses. The Overhouse and kilns, and other appurtenances, he devised to his widow for life, or so long as she remained single, and at her death, to his son John Wedgwood. This John Wedgwood had a daughter, Catherine, who married her relative, Richard Wedgwood. In 1718, Richard Wedgwood, by will, gave to his wife, Catherine (daughter of John Wedgwood), all the messuages, lands, &c., in the holding of Samuel Malkin, with a piece of land, called the "Town Croft," and several closes, called the "Brown Hills," for her life, and after her decease, to his son John, in fee; and to his said wife he gave a *work house*, and one parcel of ground, called the

"Service Yard," for her life, with remainder to his son John. This son, John Wedgwood, was a minor, and died under age, and so never came into possession. Catherine Wedgwood, after the decease of her husband, Richard, married secondly Thomas Bourne, and thirdly Rowland Egerton, Esq., and the Overhouse became their chief residence after the decay of Dale Hall. This lady, usually known as Madam Egerton, died at the Overhouse, at an advanced age, in 1756. Catherine Egerton gave to the parish of Burslem the Communion plate, which is still used, and which bears the inscription recording that it is her gift. The property had already passed to Thomas Wedgwood, brother of Josiah, as heir-at-law of her deceased son, John.

Thomas Wedgwood—who married first Isabel Beech, and had by her two sons, John and Thomas, and three daughters, Catherine, Sarah, and Mary—married secondly Jane Richards, by whom he had issue two sons, William and John, and a daughter, Jane. He died, it appears, in 1772, when the property passed to his son Thomas, who, having married Mary Alsop, had two sons, Thomas and John. He died in 1786, and was succeeded by his son Thomas, who occupied the Overhouse until his death, in 1809, when the property was sold by the trustees under his will to Christopher Robinson, who sold it to John Wood, in whose hands it has remained until recently purchased from his representatives by its present owner, Mr. Challinor.

The "Overhouse Works" were occupied early in the present century by Messrs. Goodfellow and Bathwell, who were succeeded by Mr. Challinor, by whom they were carried on for some years. They next passed into the occupancy of a manufacturer named Pointon, who in turn was, in 1856, succeeded by Messrs. Morgan, Williams, and Co., and Morgan, Wood, and Co., by whom the works were carried on until 1861, when they passed into the hands of the present occupiers, Messrs. Allman, Broughton, and Co. The productions of these works are the ordinary description of earthenware goods, in services of various kinds, and in the usual classes of useful articles. Some of the ware produced is of fine and good quality, and is made to suit the requirements of both home and foreign markets. Like many of the other works in the neighbourhood, much of the goods produced at this establishment are shipped to the United States, Canada, and Sweden, to the requirements of which markets attention is paid in the manufacture. Stoneware jugs are also produced by this firm; and the finer earthenware services, some of which are of good and effective designs, are either plain, printed, enamelled, or gilt. The works give employment to about one hundred and fifty "hands," and these are engaged in producing the ordinary useful classes of wares, no ornamental goods being made by the firm. Those who either at home, or when travelling abroad, notice the printed initials "A. B. & Co.," either with or without the addition of "WEDGWOOD PLACE, BURSLEM," will know, after reading this account, that the crockery which bears it was made at the "Overhouse Works," so long and so intimately connected with the Wedgwood family.

The precarious state of Josiah Wedgwood's health at the time when he was carrying on the Ivy House Works, rendered him incapable for some time of extending his connections so widely as he otherwise would have done; but in the midst of all his distressing ailments he superintended the production of every article, and never allowed himself that proper meed of rest which was so essential to him. His mind, ever active, seemed at this time to spurn the trammels which his bodily afflictions appeared to throw around it, and to rise, phœnix-like, from that fire which would have destroyed hundreds of minds of the ordinary stamp.

He turned his attention not to the making of the ordinary classes of wares which then formed the staple manufactures of the district, though he still, to some degree, produced them, and to no small extent made the tortoiseshell and marble plates which had already gained much celebrity: his principal products at this time were ornamental flower and other vases, with gilt or coloured foliage, mouldings, and handles; jardinieres; white-ware medallions, and other goods of a similar kind. He also made much green-glazed earthenware, and designed and produced some tea-services, in which the different vessels were formed and coloured to represent various fruits and vegetables, as the apple, pine, melon, pear, cauliflower, &c., and these novelties took so well that they soon had an abundant sale. These, like all his other designs and inventions, were speedily caught up by the other potters in the place, and so became a part of the general trade of the district. Some of these pieces which I have seen, and indeed possess, are of great excellence in design, and are well painted in imitation of the fruit sought to be represented.

His connections and reputation rapidly increasing, and his health improving, Josiah Wedgwood soon found it necessary to increase his establishment, and therefore he entered upon fresh premises, not far from the Ivy House; and thus he held at one and the same time three distinct manufactories in his native town.

One of the greatest difficulties he had to contend against was the irregular habits of the workpeople and the consequent want of order in the workrooms. To these matters very little attention had hitherto been given in these manufactories. They might probably be more easily dispensed with in small works, but are essentially requisite when the community becomes too considerable to be always within the compass of the master's eye. "He had to combat in this reform the force of customs that had the authority of ages, but which had tended very much to check improvement, and to injure the morals of the people employed. He made himself acquainted with what had been done in this respect in the great manufactories of other parts that had already been reduced to a state of some discipline. His worthy and ingenious friend, Mr. Boulton, had lately formed his establishment at Soho, near Birmingham, under nearly the same circumstances, and Mr. Wedgwood adopted such parts of his plan as were practicable in a manufactory so dissimilar. The frame and temper of his mind were well suited to such an undertaking. He had now, and retained through life, the habit of a cool and patient investigation of every subject that came before him, and his own previous conviction gave energy to action. His regulations were never introduced, therefore, in a crude or hasty way, but seemed to rise naturally out of the occasion, and stifled opposition by their evident necessity. He felt, too, a sincere and zealous interest in the welfare of his workmen, of which he made them sensible in a thousand ways, and gained over both their judgment and affection to his side. Thus he succeeded in establishing a system of order and management by which, while he held in his own hands the great checks that regulate the general motion, his mind was left at liberty to dwell upon the objects that were to perpetuate the blessing of employment to those he had collected around him, and which have eventually furnished it to many thousands more. He had also other difficulties to encounter, arising from the novelty of his works. The workmanship of the pottery was at that period in a very low state as to style. There were only three professed modellers in the whole manufactory. One of these was brought up under Mr. Wedgwood, at Fenton, and had left him a little before to establish works for himself. The wares he made, however, were all produced for the use of Mr. Wedgwood on an engagement that lasted some years, and they received their last finish at his own manufactory in Burslem. Another of the three was altogether in his employment, and the third was modeller to the country at large.

"The machinery consisted only of the potter's wheel, known from all antiquity, and the common turning lathe, and their tools were little more than a few cutting knives. His manner of working required more nicety and skill than had been used before, and he was not only obliged to instruct his men individually, and to form them upon his own model, but had also their tools to contrive, and new kilns, drying-pans, and other apparatus to construct for the purpose of the new manufacture he introduced from time to time, and for which he had very few resources beyond those of his own mechanical invention. If we consider besides the necessary dependence of his discoveries on experimental chemistry and a knowledge of fossils, which he acquired by his own efforts without any intelligent assistant, we shall perceive him in a state of uncommon labour and fatigue of spirits. He was attached to his profession, he saw very early the improvements it was susceptible of, and he pursued it with a willing mind. His days were spent at the bench with his workmen, instructing them, and generally forming with his own hands the first models of the things he proposed to make; and his evenings were taken up in designing or contriving tools for the purposes of the succeeding day. He possessed a decision of mind very favourable in this situation of difficulty. He began, after contriving anything, by declaring that it must be done let what would stand in the way; and it almost constantly was so in the end, for only a very few things that he undertook were unsuccessful. He contracted at this time a habit of thinking during the night on the difficulties of the day, which generally were surmounted before the return of morning, and he was prepared to go on with his work; but he felt the inconvenience of this custom very much in the advanced part of his life, for if any subject of business took hold of his mind before he went to rest, it was sure to deprive him of sleep the greatest part of the night." Unlike his friend Brindley—who it is said would lie in bed for the day to think over some great scheme—Wedgwood studied in the night, that he might be "up and doing" in the day.

Up to this period the only method—in the few places where even that primitive mode had been adopted, for the workmen generally loitered in and out of the pot-yards as they pleased—for calling the potters to their labours was by sounding a horn. Wedgwood, at the new works he was now entering upon, adopted a better plan, and one which gave a name to the works which will remain with them so long as they are in existence. At this new manufactory he put up a cupola with a bell, which was, as is now the case everywhere, rung to call the workpeople together. This was the first bell put up and used for the purpose in the district, and from this circumstance the Burslem potters, always ready to give to people or places distinctive appellations, got into the habit of calling it the "Bell Bank," or "Bonk," as it was and is more commonly pronounced. Thus the name of the "Bell Works" originated in the same manner as had the distinctive names of "Church Wedgwoods," "Big House Wedgwoods," "Duke Wedgwoods," and a score or two other similar appellations.

The Bell Works, of which, in their present state, I give the accompanying engraving from a sketch recently made by myself, was, at the time when Josiah Wedgwood entered on its occupancy, the property of Mr. John Bourne, an army contractor, in the neighbouring town of Newcastle. From him the property passed to his grandson, Mr. John Adams, of Cobridge, about the year 1771, and in 1847 the estate again passed by will into the hands of its present owner, Mr. Isaac Hitchin, of Alsager. The pot-works were occupied by Josiah Wedgwood, as tenant to Mr. John Bourne, until his removal to Etruria. The next tenant was, I believe, Mr. William Bourne, an earthenware manufacturer, who held them for some years, and was tenant in 1809. Mr. Bourne afterwards entered into partnership with a potter named Cormie, and the works were carried on under the style of "Bourne and Cormie." In 1836, the works having then remained for some time unoccupied, were divided, a portion being taken by Messrs. Beech and Jones as an earthenware manufactory, another portion taken away for the building of the present Independent Chapel, which was erected on its site in the following year; and other parts were let off to various holders for different purposes apart from the pot trade. In 1839, the partnership between Beech and Jones was dissolved, the former gentleman alone continuing to occupy the same portion of the premises, in which

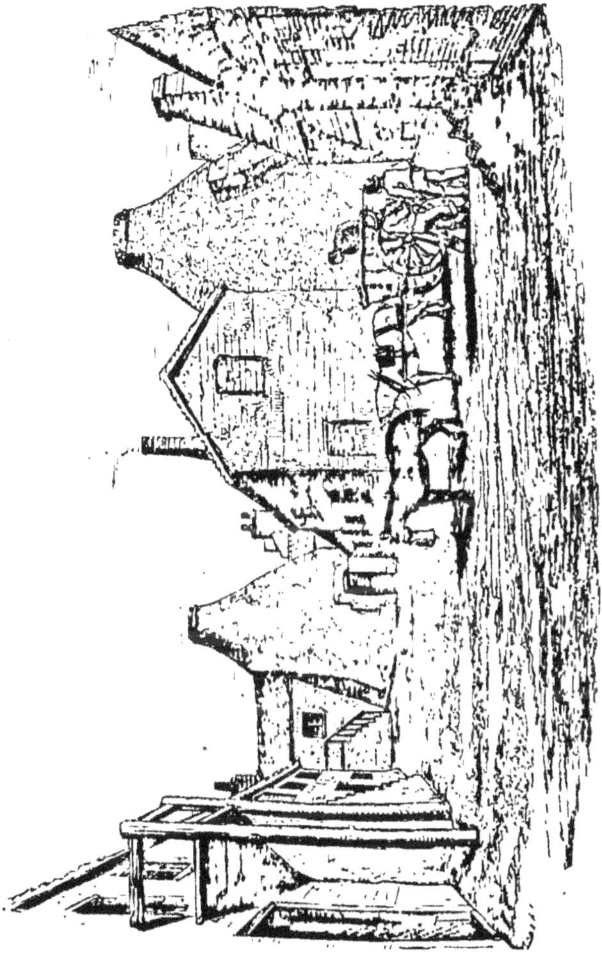

THE "BELL WORKS," BURSLEM.

he produced china and earthenware figures. In 1846, Mr. Beech having increased his business, became tenant of the whole of the remaining premises, with the exception of that part occupied by Mr. Dean's printing-office, &c., and in 1853 took into partnership Mr. Brock, which firm, however, only lasted a couple of years. In 1855 Mr. Brock went out of the concern, and from that date Mr. William Beech carried on the manufactory until his death, which took place in 1864.

The goods produced at the present day at these historically interesting works are the ordinary marketable china and parian chimney ornaments and toys, which are produced in large quantities, both for home sale and for exportation to the United States, the East Indies, the Netherlands, and Australia. In the manufacture of these articles alone, I am given to understand that about a hundred hands are constantly employed at these works. In parian, besides flower-vases and other small ornaments, some tolerably large groups have been produced at this establishment, and among the most recent improvements is an "ivory body," which possesses great softness in appearance, and is capable of being made largely available for ornamental purposes. Unlike the time of Wedgwood, no services of any kind are produced at these once famed works at the present day.

At the Bell work house Josiah Wedgwood turned his attention more especially to the production of the fine and delicate descriptions of earthenware, which soon earned for him the proud distinction of "Queen's Potter." The result of his close and incessant application, and of his endless experiments into the properties of clays, &c., led to the production of this marvellous kind of earthenware, and to the beauty of finish which characterised it, and which is rarely, if ever, equalled at the present day. Well and truthfully has Mr. Gladstone expressed his sense of the beauty, and, at the same time, mechanical nicety for useful purposes, which characterises the "potting" of this earthenware, when he says that the speciality of Wedgwood lay in the uncompromising adaptation of every object to its proper end. Mr. Gladstone says:—

"His most signal and characteristic merit lay, as I have said, in the firmness and fulness of his perception of the true law of what we term industrial art, or in other words, of the application of the higher art to industry: the law which teaches us to aim first at giving to every object the greatest possible degree of fitness and convenience for its purpose, and next at making it the vehicle of the highest degree of beauty, which compatibly with that fitness and convenience it will bear: which does not substitute the secondary for the primary end, but recognises as part of the business the study to harmonise the two. To have a strong grasp of this principle, and to work it out to its results in the details of a vast and varied manufacture, is a praise, high enough for any man, at any time and in any place. But it was higher and more peculiar, as I think, in the case of Wedgwood, than in almost any other case it could be. For that truth of art, which he saw so clearly, and which lies at the root of excellence, was one, of which England, his country, has not usually had a perception at all corresponding in strength and fulness with her other rare endowments. She has long taken a lead among the nations of Europe for the cheapness of her manufactures: not so for their beauty. And if the day shall come when she shall be as eminent in taste as she is in economy of production, my belief is that the result will probably be due to no other single man in so great a degree as to Wedgwood. This part of the subject, however, deserves a somewhat fuller consideration. There are three regions given to man for the exercise of his faculties in the production of objects, or the performance of acts, conducive to civilisation and to the ordinary uses of life. Of these, one is the homely sphere of simple utility. What is done, is done for some purpose of absolute necessity, or of immediate and passing use. What is produced, is produced with an almost exclusive regard to its value in exchange, to the market of the place and day. A dustman, for example, cannot be expected to move with the grace of a fairy; nor can his cart be constructed on the flowing lines of a Greek chariot of war. Not but that, even in this unpromising domain, beauty also has her place. But it is limited, and may for the present purpose be left out of view. Then there is, secondly, the lofty sphere of pure thought and its ministering organs, the sphere of poetry and the highest arts. Here, again, the place of what we term utility is narrow, and the production of the beautiful, in one or other of its innumerable forms, is the supreme, if not the only object.

"Now, I believe it to be undeniable, that in both of these spheres, widely separated as they are, the faculties of Englishmen, and the distinctions of England, have been of the very first order. In the power of economical production, she is at the head of all the nations of the earth. If in the fine arts, in painting for example, she must be content with a second place, yet in poetry, which ranks ever higher than painting (I hope I am not misled by national feeling when I say it), she may fairly challenge all the countries of Christendom, and no one of them, but Italy, can as yet enter into serious competition with the land of Shakspeare. But, for one, I should admit that while thus pre-eminent in the pursuit of pure beauty on the one side, and of unmixed utility on the other, she has been far less fortunate, indeed for the most part she has been decidedly behindhand in that intermediate region where art is brought into contact with industry, and where the pair may wed together. This is a region alike vast and diversified. Upwards, it embraces architecture, an art which, while it affords the noblest scope for grace and grandeur, is also, or rather ought to be, strictly tied down to the purposes of convenience, and has for its chief end to satisfy one of the most imperative and elementary wants of man. Downwards, it extends to a very large proportion of the products of human industry. Some things, indeed, such as scientific instruments for example, are so determined by their purposes to some particular shape, surface, and materials, that even a Wedgwood would find in them little space for the application of his principles. But while all the objects of trade and manufacture admit of fundamental differences in point of fitness and unfitness, probably the major part of them admit of fundamental differences also in point of beauty or of ugliness. Utility is not to be sacrificed for beauty, but they are generally compatible, often positively helpful to each other; and it may be safely asserted, that the periods, when the study of beauty has been neglected, have usually been marked, not by a more successful pursuit of utility, but by a general decline in the energies of man."

And again he most characteristically remarks, "It would be quite unnecessary to dwell on the excellencies of such of the works of Wedgwood as belong to the region of fine art, strictly so called, and are not, in the common sense, commodities for use. To these all the world does justice. Suffice it to say, in general terms, that they may be considered partly as imitations, partly as reproductions of Greek art. As imitations they carry us back to the purest source. As reproductions they are not limited to the province of their originals, but are conceived in the general and free spirit and soaring of that with which they claim relationship. But it is not in happy imitation, it is not in the successful presentation of works of fine art, that, as I conceive, the speciality of Wedgwood really lies. It is in the resuscitation of a principle, the principle of Greek art; it is in the perception and grasp of the unity and comprehensiveness of that principle. That principle, I submit, lies after all in a severe and perfect propriety; in the uncompromising adaptation of every material object to its proper end. If that proper end be the representation of beauty only, then the production of beauty is alone regarded; and none but the highest models of it are accepted. If the proper end be the production of a commodity for use, and perishable, then a plural aim is before the designer and producer. The object must first and foremost be adapted to its use as closely as possible; it must be of material as durable as possible; and while it must be of the most moderate cost, it must receive all the beauty that can be made conducive to, or concordant with, the use. And because this business of harmonising use and beauty, so easy in the works of nature, is so arduous to the frailty of man, it is a business that must be made the object of special and persevering care. To these principles the works of Wedgwood habitually conformed.

"He did not, in his pursuit of beauty, overlook exchangeable value, or practical usefulness. The first he could not overlook, for he had to live by his trade: and it was by the profit derived from the extended sale of his humbler productions that he was enabled to bear the risks and charges of his higher works. Commerce did for him what the King of France did for Sèvres, and the Duke of Cumberland for Chelsea—it found him in funds. And I would venture to say that the lower works of Wedgwood are every whit as much distinguished by the fineness and accuracy of their adaptation to their uses as his higher ones by their successful exhibition of the finest arts. Take for instance his common plates, of the value of, I know not how few, but certainly of a very few pence each. They fit one another as closely as the cards in a pack. At least, I for one have never seen plates that fit like the plates of Wedgwood, and become one solid mass. Such accuracy of form must, I apprehend, render them much more safe in carriage. Of the excellence of these plates we may take it for a proof that they were largely exported to France, if not elsewhere; that they were there printed or painted with buildings or scenes belonging to the country, and then sent out again as national manufactures. Again, take such a jug as he would manufacture for the washhand table of a garret. I have seen these made apparently of the commonest material used in the trade. But instead of being built up, like the usual and much more fashionable jugs of modern manufacture, in such a shape that a crane could not easily get his neck to bend into them, and the water can hardly be poured but without risk of spraining the wrist, they are constructed in a simple capacious form, of flowing curves, broad at the top, and so well poised that a slight and easy movement of the hand discharges the water. A round cheese-holder or dish again generally presents in its upper part a flat space, surrounded by a curved rim; but a cheese-holder of Wedgwood's will make itself known by this—that the flat is so dead a flat, and the curve so marked and bold a curve; thus at once furnishing the eye with a line agreeable and well defined, and affording the utmost available space for the cheese. I feel persuaded that a Wiltshire cheese, if it could speak, would declare itself more comfortable in a dish of Wedgwood's than in any other dish."

In September, 1761, his Majesty George III., who in the previous year had ascended the throne, married the Princess Charlotte of Mecklenburgh Strellitz, and on the occasion of her accouchement in the succeeding year, Wedgwood, having by that time perfected the body and glaze of his fine cream-coloured ware, presented to her Majesty (then of course Queen Charlotte) a caudle and breakfast service of his manufacture, which was most graciously and flatteringly received. This service, which was of course made of the finest and best cream-coloured quality which could be produced, was painted in the highest style of the day by the first artists of the works, Thomas Daniell and Daniel Steele. The ground of this service, which was prepared with all the skill the art would then admit of, was yellow, with raised sprigs of jessamine and other flowers, coloured after nature. The Queen received this tribute of an infant art, and was so pleased with it that she at once expressed a wish to have a complete table service of the same material. Wedgwood submitted patterns for the several pieces, "which were approved with the exception of the plate, which was the common barleycorn pattern, then making by all the salt-glaze manufacturers. Her Majesty objected to the roughness—the *barleycorn-work* as it is called—and therefore this part was made plain; on the edge was left only the bands, marking the compartments; and being approved by her Majesty, the pattern was called *Queen's pattern.*" The ware was at once named by Mr. Wedgwood QUEEN'S WARE, and he received the Queen's commands to call himself by the proud distinction of "Potter to her Majesty." On the service being completed the King gave Wedgwood his immediate patronage by ordering a similar service for himself, but without the bands or ribs. This alteration in pattern was "effected to the entire satisfaction of his Majesty," and some little alterations being made in the forms of some of the other pieces, it was called the "Royal Pattern."

The patronage thus given, and which was continued in the most liberal and gratifying manner, was of incalculable benefit to Wedgwood, to the district around him, and indeed to the whole kingdom, for it opened up a source of wealth to thousands of people, and was the means of extending commerce to a marvellous extent. Orders for the new kind of ware flowed in upon him in a regular and constantly increasing stream, and at prices which were then considered liberal, or even high. It is recorded that at this period he received at the rate of fifteen shillings per dozen for table plates, and for other pieces a proportionate price. The tide of fortune which had thus set in upon him was immensely increased by his subsequent inventions, and ultimately, as will be seen, swept him from his small manufactories at Burslem to the colony he established a few miles off at Etruria. The other most usual form of plate in his Queen's ware, was "the *Bath* or *Trencher*, from its resemblance to the wooden platter;" and this was succeeded by the concave edge, and other varieties.

These successes were not gained without heavy and severe losses, but the mind of Wedgwood overcame them all, as it would have done any amount of obstacles which might have been placed in his way. A most interesting document, written in the reign of George III., which is now before me, thus speaks of some of these difficulties :—

"The uncertain element of fire is the great enemy that the potter has to struggle with all his life. It is more especially formidable to him if he ventures to make vessels of any extraordinary size, such as some of those which are necessary for the use of the dining-table. Hence so few European manufactories of porcelain can be supported in the production of large vessels without the revenues of a prince. Mr. Wedgwood experienced all these vexations when he first began to make this earthenware for the table. Disasters after disasters; the labour and expense of a month destroyed in a few hours; one kiln pulled down and another erected; that, again, found deficient, and to be altered. A fatal mistake removed, another was discovered elsewhere. Thus it was not only after a considerable time, but with very heavy losses, that he accomplished this point, which has bestowed so many benefits on the neighbourhood he lived in, and given such extension to the national commerce. This is the cream-colour, or Queen's ware, now universally used in these kingdoms, and in every part of Europe where it is not shut out by the jealousy of the sovereign. Its introduction was very rapid. Under the auspices of the powerful patroness it had obtained, it found its way at once to the tables of persons of fortune, and was very soon afterwards universally adopted. The other manufacturers immediately took up the making of it, and building on the experience of the inventor, they were enabled to do so without the losses and vexations he had endured.

"This event was very soon followed by a great improvement of the forms of the vessels in use, and the addition of many others that have given taste and conveniency to the economy of the table. This first melioration of the forms in general use belongs exclusively to Mr. Wedgwood, and is a decisive proof that his mind was capable of comprehending whatever had relation to the work he had in hand. The fact is, that the models of everything his manufactory produced were originally formed by himself, with the same ideas of fame and reputation as must possess the mind of every successful artist in more splendid works; and hence it happened that most of his forms were found to be useful studies, and they became patterns not only for the manufacturer in his own way, but for the silversmith and most other workers in metal. They have also been sought for with great eagerness by the conductors of porcelain manufactories on the Continent, and often sent to China as patterns for the manufacturers there. To this last use of them Mr. Wedgwood always thought it right to throw in the way every impediment he could, because the Oriental porcelain, better adapted in its forms to the European table, would very materially injure the sale of English earthenware in many foreign markets, where the former is admitted on low duties, or none at all, and the latter pay very heavy duties.

"About the same time he adapted to the uses of pottery that curious machine the engine-lathe, heretofore employed only in the turning of ivory, wood, or metals. He first became acquainted with the engine-lathe from a large folio volume on the subject in French, which is now perhaps in his library. It was so rare an instrument that the possessor of one in London refused to let him go into the room where it was for a few minutes without paying five guineas.

"By the friendly assistance of Mr. Taylor, of Birmingham, he readily got one of them made at that place, and a person instructed in the manner of using it. The first application he made of this machine was to the red porcelain, which, being of a close texture, and without a glaze, was well suited to receive and retain a sharpness of work; but he also used it to decorate the vases which he made at that time in the green ware, after the antique, and the designs of several ingenious ladies of this country. And it enabled him to introduce so great a variety of new workmanship upon his wares of every species, both for ornament and use, that it may well deserve to constitute an era in the art of pottery, having become so necessary to it that there is scarcely a work without one or more of them."

The Bell Works are situated at the corner of Brick Street

and Queen Street, very near to the new Wedgwood Institution now in course of erection. At the time of which I write, however, Brick Street was not formed, but was a part of the ground belonging to the manufactory, and was, indeed, waste land, covered with "shard rucks," and other unmistakable evidence of the potter's art. Queen Street then, too, was little better than a lane, but was dignified with the name of *Queen* Street, through Wedgwood being now appointed *Queen's* potter, and there making his celebrated *Queen's* ware.

CHAPTER VI.

JOSIAH WEDGWOOD.—DID NOT TAKE OUT PATENTS.—HIS OWN VIEWS CONCERNING THROWING OPEN THE MANUFACTURE.—ENOCH WOOD'S COLLECTION OF POTTERY.—INVENTION OF PRINTING ON EARTHENWARE.—SADLER AND GREEN, OF LIVERPOOL.—NOTICES OF ADAM AND JOHN SADLER, AND OF GUY GREEN.—BADNESS OF THE STAFFORDSHIRE ROADS.—WARES SENT BY PACK-HORSES TO LIVERPOOL.—MR. MAYER'S MUSEUM.—MR. S. C. HALL'S COLLECTION OF WEDGWOOD WARE.—"QUEEN'S WARE."—BURSLEM DIALOGUE.

So liberal-minded, so open in disposition, so devoid of selfish feelings, and so ready to impart to others the knowledge he had gained, was Josiah Wedgwood, that in his "Queen's," or "cream-coloured ware," as in most other matters, he did not secure to himself by patent, as almost every other person would have done, his improvements in the manufacture of earthenware; and thus all the potters in the district immediately, to the utmost of their skill, imitated his ware and his patterns. It is remarkable that of all his inventions only one, and that the least important, was secured to him by patent, as I shall soon have occasion to show. In reference to his Queen's ware, Josiah Wedgwood himself thus writes a few years later on. This remarkable passage I quote from an exceedingly rare paper by himself, in my possession:—

"When Mr. Wedgwood discovered the art of making *Queen's ware*, which employs ten times more people than all the china works in the kingdom, he did not ask for a patent for this important discovery. A patent would greatly have limited its public utility. Instead of *one hundred* manufactories of Queen's ware there would have been *one;* and instead of an exportation to all quarters of the world, a few pretty things would have been made for the amusement of the people of fashion in England. . . . . It is upon these principles, and these only, that he has acted in this business."

A little further on, still speaking of "stone ware, Queen's ware, or porcelain," Wedgwood says—

"It is well known that manufacturers of this kind can only support their credit by continual improvements. It is also well known that there is a competition in these improvements in all parts of Europe. In the last century Burslem, and some other villages in Staffordshire, were famous for making *milk-pans* and *butter-pots*, and by a succession of improvements the manufactory in that neighbourhood has gradually increased in the variety, the quality, and the quantity of its productions, so as to furnish, besides the home consumption, an annual export of useful and ornamental wares, nearly to the amount of *two hundred thousand pounds;* but during all this progress it has had the free range of the country for materials to work upon, to the great advantage of many landowners and of navigators. Queen's ware has already several of the properties of porcelain, but is yet capable of receiving many essential improvements. The public have for some time required and expected them. Innumerable experiments have been made for this purpose," &c.

Of the *early* "Queen's Ware," a specimen, authenticated

as being made at the "Bell Works," is preserved in the Museum of Practical Geology, having previously formed a part of the collection of Mr. Enoch Wood—a collection illustrative of the staple Staffordshire manufacture, which ought never to have been dispersed.* This example, a butter-boat of excellent form, is here engraved.

A few years before this time, Messrs. John Sadler and Guy Green, of Liverpool, had brought out their invention of printing on earthenware tiles, which process had occupied their attention for some years. John Sadler, it appears, from what information has been collected by my friend Mr. Mayer, F.S.A., of Liverpool—who owns one of, if not the, finest private museums in the kingdom, and whose public spirit in the cause of antiquities is beyond all praise—was the son of Adam Sadler, a favourite soldier of the great Duke of Marlborough, and was out with that general in the Low Countries war. Whilst there, he lodged in the house of a printer, and thus obtained an insight into the art of printing. On returning to England on the accession of George I., he left the army in disgust and retired to Ulverstone, where he married a Miss Bibby, who numbered among her acquaintance the daughters of the Earl of Sefton. Through the influence of these ladies he removed to Melling, and afterwards leased a house at Aintree. In this lease he is styled "Adam Sadler, of Melling, gentleman." The taste he had acquired in the Low Countries abiding with him, he shortly afterwards, however, removed to the New Market, Liverpool, where he printed a great number of books—amongst which, being himself an excellent musician, one called "The Muses' Delight" was with him an especial favourite. His son, John Sadler, having learned the art of engraving, on the termination of his apprenticeship bought a house from his father, in Harrington Street, for the nominal sum of five shillings, and in that house, in 1748, commenced business on his own account. Here he married a Miss Elizabeth Parker, daughter of Mr.

* I cannot forbear expressing a profound regret—a regret shared in by all lovers of English fictile Art—that this collection, made long ago, at immense labour and at considerable cost, should have been allowed to be frittered away and destroyed. Some of the examples are now in the Museum at the Mechanics' Institution, Hanley, others are in the Museum of the Athenæum at Stoke, and others again are in the Museum of Practical Geology, London.

Parker, watchmaker, of Seel Street, and soon afterwards became engaged in litigation. Having got together a good business, his fellow-townsmen became jealous of his success, and the corporation attempted to remove him as not being a freeman of Liverpool, and therefore having no right to keep a shop within its boundaries. Disregarding the order of removal, the corporation commenced an action against him, which he successfully defended, and showed that the authorities possessed no power of ejection. This decision was one of great importance to the trading community, and opened the door to numberless people to commence business in the town.

Mr. John Sadler was, according to Mr. Mayer, the first person who applied the art of printing to the ornamentation of pottery, and the story of his discovery is thus told:—Sadler had been in the habit of giving waste and spoiled impressions from his engraved plates to little children, and these they frequently stuck upon pieces of broken pot from the pot-works at Shaw's Brow, for their own amusement and for building dolls' houses with. This circumstance gave him the idea of ornamenting pottery with printed pictures, and, keeping the idea secret, he experimentalised until he had nearly succeeded, when he mentioned the circumstance to Guy Green, who had then recently succeeded Mr. Adam Sadler in his business. Guy Green was a poor boy, who spent what halfpence he could get in buying ballads at Adam Sadler's shop, who, taking a fancy to the boy, who was intelligent beyond his age or his companions, took him into his service and encouraged him in all that was honourable. John Sadler having, as I have said, mentioned his discovery to Guy Green, the two "laid their heads together," conducted joint experiments, and having ultimately succeeded, at length entered into partnership. This done, they determined to apply to the king for a patent; which, however, under the advice of friends, was not done.

The art was first of all turned to good account in the decoration of tiles—"Dutch tiles," as they are usually called;

and the following highly-interesting documents relating to them, which are in the possession of Mr. Mayer, and to whom the antiquarian world is indebted for first making them public, will be read with interest:—

"I, John Sadler, of Liverpoole, in the county of Lancaster, printer, and Guy Green, of Liverpoole, aforesaid, printer, severally maketh oath that on Tuesday, the 27th day of July instant, they, these deponents, without the aid or assistance of any other person or persons, did within the space of six hours, to wit, between the hours of nine in the morning and three in the afternoon of the same day, print upwards of twelve hundred Earthenware tiles of different patterns, at Liverpoole aforesaid, and which, as these deponents have heard and believe, were more in number and better and neater than one hundred skilful pot-painters could have painted in the like space of time, in the common and usual way of painting with a pencil; and these deponents say that they have been upwards of seven years in finding out the method of printing tiles, and in making tryals and experiments for that purpose, which they have now through great pains and expence brought to perfection.

"John Sadler,
"Guy Green.

"Taken and sworn at Liverpoole, in the county of Lancaster, the second day of August, one thousand seven hundred and fifty-six, before William Statham, a Master Extraordinary in Chancery."

"We, Alderman Thomas Shaw and Samuel Gilbody, both of Liverpoole, in the county of Lancaster, clay potters, whose names are hereunto subscribed, do hereby humbly certifye that we are well assured that John Sadler and Guy Green did, at Liverpoole aforesaid, on Tuesday, the 27th day of July last past, within the space of six hours, print upwards of 1,200 earthenware tiles of different colours and patterns, which is upon a moderate computation more than 100 good workmen could have done of the same patterns in the same space of time by the usual painting with the pencil. That we have since burnt the above tiles, and that they are considerably neater than any we have seen pencilled, and may be sold at little more than half the price. We are also assured the said John Sadler and Guy Green have been several years in bringing the art of printing on earthenware to perfection, and we never heard it was done by any other person or persons but themselves. We are also assured that as the Dutch (who import large quantities of tiles into England, Ireland, &c.) may by this improvement be considerably undersold, it cannot fail to be of great advantage to the nation, and to the town of Liverpoole in particular, where the earthenware manufacture is more extensively carried on than in any other town in the kingdom; and for which reasons we hope and do not doubt the above persons will be indulged in their request for a patent, to secure to them the profits that may arise from the above useful and advantageous improvement.

"THOMAS SHAW,
"SAMUEL GILBODY."

"Liverpoole, August 13th, 1756.

"SIR,

"John Sadler, the bearer, and Guy Green, both of this town, have invented a method of printing potters' earthenware tyles for chimneys with surprising expedition. We have seen several of their printed tyles, and are of opinion that they are superior to any done by the pencill, and that this invention will be highly advantageous to the kingdom in generall, and to the town of Liverpoole in particular.

"In consequence of which, and for the encouragement of so useful and ingenious an improvement, we desire the favour of your interest in procuring for them his Majesty's letters patent.

"ELLIS CUNCLIFFE,
"SPENCER STEERS,
"CHARLES GOORE.

"Addressed to Charles Pole, Esq., in London."

In Mr. Mayer's magnificent museum are found, among other invaluable treasures, some enamels on copper bearing impressions from copper-plates transferred on to them, and having the name of "*J. Sadler, Liverp*[t], *Enam*[t]," and other examples of enamels and of earthenware with the names of *Sadler, Sculp.*, or of *Green.* Messrs. Sadler and Green appear to have done a very profitable and excellent business in the printing on pottery. The process was soon found to be as applicable to services and other descriptions of goods as to tiles; and these two enterprising men produced many fine examples of their art, some of which, bearing their names as engravers or enamellers, are still in existence. Josiah Wedgwood, always alive to everything which could tend to improve or render more commercial the productions of his manufactory, although at first opposed to the introduction of this invention, as being, in his opinion, an unsatisfactory and unprofitable substitute for painting, eventually determined to adopt the new style of ornamentation, and arranged with the inventors to decorate such of his Queen's ware as it would be applicable to, by their process.

The work was a troublesome one, and in the then state of the roads—for it must be remembered that this was before the time even of canals in the district, much less of railroads—the communication between Burslem and Liverpool was one of great difficulty. Wedgwood, however, overcame it, and having made the plain body at his works, packed it in waggons and carts, and, I believe, even in the panniers of pack-horses, and sent it to Liverpool, where it was printed by Sadler and Green, and returned to him by the same conveyance, to be, in most cases, finished in his own works.

Adam Sadler died on the 7th of October, 1788, aged eighty-three, and his son John Sadler the 10th of December, 1789, aged sixty-nine, and they were buried at Sefton. Mr. Guy Green continued the business after this date, and printed earthenware for Wedgwood, probably some special patterns only, until as late a date as 1793 or 1794. Examples of Liverpool pottery printed by Sadler and Green, and of Wedgwood's body printed by them, are of uncommon occurrence. In Mr. Mayer's museum, at Liverpool, the best, and indeed only series worthy the name in existence, are to be found. In my own possession, too, are some examples.

Specimens of these early printed goods, bearing Wedgwood's mark, are rare. I select, as an example, a curious teapot, in the possession of Mr. S. C. Hall, F.S.A., which is highly characteristic and interesting.

The teapot bears on one side a remarkably well engraved and sharply printed representation of the quaint subject of the mill to grind old people young again—the kind of curious machine which one recollects in one's boyish days were taken about from fair to fair by strolling mountebanks—and on the

other an oval border of foliage, containing the ballad belonging to the subject, called "The Miller's Maid grinding Old Men Young again." It begins—

"Come, old, decrepid, lame, or blind,
Into my mill to take a grind."

The teapot, which is an excellent specimen of black-printing, is marked WEDGWOOD. In the same superb collection of Wedgwood ware are also other examples of "Queen's ware," among which are some plates with flowers painted in red, in simple and pure taste, and true to nature; a centre and sides with fine figures; and a remarkably elegant and beautifully potted whey jug and cover, formerly in my own collection. In the Museum of Practical Geology is an example of this printing, the design on one side of which is a group at tea—a lady pouring out tea for a gentleman, and on the opposite side the verse:—

"Kindly take this gift of mine,
The gift and giver I hope is thine;
And tho' the value is but small,
A loving Heart is worth it all."

In my own possession are, among other pieces of early

Queen's ware, some marked plates which fit with the mechanical nicety so well pointed out by Mr. Gladstone, and a saucer of a pure cream colour, ornamented with a simple green border of foliage between rich red lines. This saucer bears the impressed mark WEDGWOOD, not at the bottom, but on its side.

The centre and side pieces to which I have just alluded, in Mr. Hall's possession (one of the pieces of which is here

engraved), are among the choicest examples now existing of Wedgwood's Queen's ware. The baskets are beautifully perforated, and are each supported by three exquisite figures on bases. They are of large size, and must have been among the best and most costly productions of the works.

The manufacture of Queen's ware, as I have said, soon became general throughout the district, and numerous manufacturers sprang up around the great centre, Wedgwood, ready to adopt whatever improvements by his great skill and his indomitable perseverance he should from time to time make, and to build their fortunes on the results of his labours. The consequence was that, as we have seen he said, there were one hundred manufactories of Queen's ware instead of one, and ten thousand workmen employed instead of one hundred. At this time Wedgwood bestirred himself to have the roads improved and made more passable for wares; but in this he was met by a strong opposition from the potters, who thought that if the roads were made more passable, their trade would be carried away, and ruin would await them! The roads, however, *were* mended, and the trade of the district has gone on increasing ever since.

In the "Burslem Dialogue," to which I have on a former occasion referred, the following amusing allusion to the state of the roads, and of Wedgwood's plan of sending his Queen's ware to Liverpool to be printed, occurs, and I cannot refrain from giving it as a fitting close to this chapter:—

"*L.*—Oi'd summat t' doo t' get dahn t' L'rpool wi' eawr caart, at th' teyme as oi fust tayd Mester 'Siah Wedgut's wheit ware for t' be printed theer. Yu known as hâe ther wur noo black printin' on ware dun i' Boslem i' thoos deys.

"*T.*—Oi remember 't varry weel. Oi s'pose as 'Siah wur abaht th' same age as thiseln, Rafy, wur he no'?

"*L.*—Ya, oi rek'n he wur tew year yunker til me.

"*T.*—When he started i' bizness fust, he made spewnes, knife hondles, an' smaw crocks, at th' Ivy hahs, close to where we're nah sittin'.

"*L.*—Ay, oi weel remember th' toyme; an' arter that he flitted to th' Bell Workhus, wheer he put up th' bell-coney for t' ring th' men to ther work isted o' blowin' em together wi' a hurn. 'Twur a pity he e'er left Boslum, for he wur th' cob o' th' Wedguts."

Having traced the progress of his works, and followed the career of this remarkable man through another decade of his useful life, I must now close my chapter, reserving for my next the important period down to the time of the building of Etruria.

CHAPTER VII.

MARRIAGE OF JOSIAH WEDGWOOD.—THE WEDGWOODS OF SMALLWOOD.—PEDIGREE SHOWING RELATIONSHIP OF JOSIAH AND SARAH WEDGWOOD.—ACCESSION OF FORTUNE.—THOMAS AND JOHN WEDGWOOD, OF THE "BIG HOUSE."—MOVEMENT FOR BUILDING BURSLEM SCHOOL.—STATE OF THE ROADS IN STAFFORDSHIRE: WEDGWOOD'S PROJECT FOR THEIR IMPROVEMENT—OPPOSITION OF THE POTTERS OF NEWCASTLE.—WEDGWOOD'S VISITS TO LIVERPOOL—ILLNESS THERE.—INTRODUCTION TO THOMAS BENTLEY.—ERROR REGARDING BENTLEY.—MEDALLION OF THOMAS BENTLEY.

In 1764, Josiah Wedgwood, then in his thirty-fourth year, the sole proprietor of an extensive, lucrative, and rapidly increasing manufactory, and enjoying the proud distinction of being "Potter to her Majesty," and of having earned for himself a name and fame which were the envy of all his neighbours, married and brought home his young bride to the Ivy House, at Burslem. The lady who became his wife was his distant—in fact, the magical number of "seven times removed"—cousin, Sarah Wedgwood, the daughter, and eventually sole heiress, of Richard Wedgwood, Esq., of Smallwood, in Cheshire. The marriage was solemnised just a hundred years ago, on the 25th of January, in the year 1764, as will be seen from the following copy of the register of the parish of Astbury, which has been kindly furnished to me by the rector of that place:—

"Astbury Church, Cheshire.

"No. 453.

[All the first part of the register not filled in.]

"Married in this church by License, this twenty-fifth day of

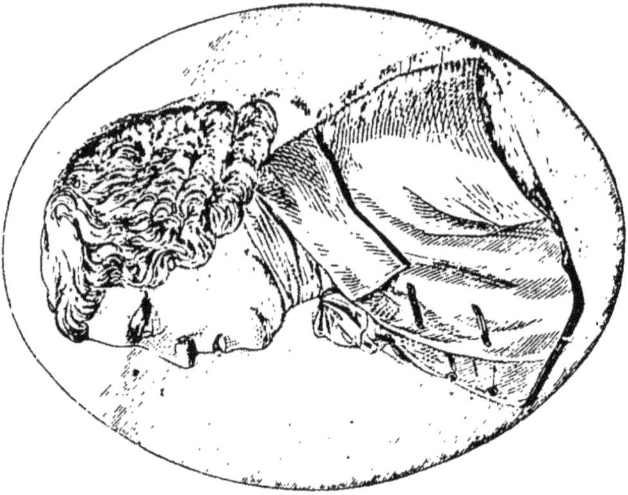

JOSIAH WEDGWOOD.

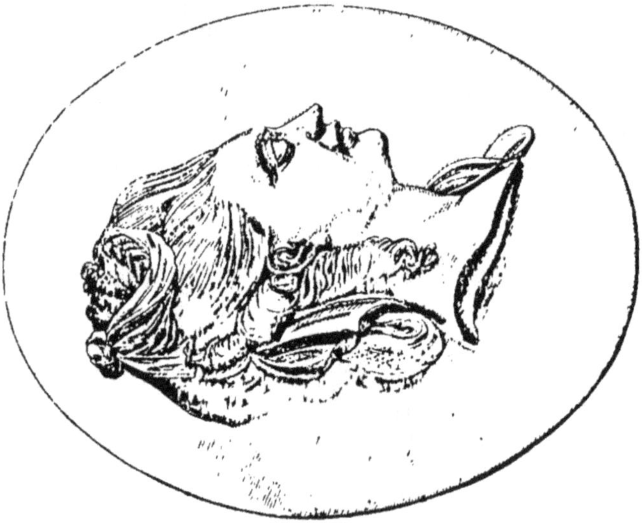

MRS. WEDGWOOD.

[FROM FLAXMAN'S MEDALLIONS.]

January, in the year One Thousand Seven Hundred and Sixty-four, by me,

"JOHN HARDING, *Curate.*

"This marriage was solemnised between us,

"JOS. WEDGWOOD,
"SARAH WEDGWOOD.

"In the presence of
"RD. WEDGWOOD,
"JNO. CLARK."

The Richard Wedgwood, one of the witnesses to the marriage, was, of course, Richard Wedgwood of Smallwood, the father of the bride.

The Wedgwoods of Smallwood were descended from Aaron, the sixth son of Gilbert, from whom also the "Big House" and "Red Lion" families were derived, while Josiah was descended, as I have already shown, from Thomas, the third son of Gilbert, and, therefore, elder brother to Aaron. The simple table on the next page, which I have drawn up, leaving out the collateral branches and descents, will show the relationship that existed between the great Josiah and his bride, and also both his and her descent, through several generations, from the Wedgwoods of Harracles and Leek.

By his marriage Josiah Wedgwood received an accession to his fortune, in the dowry of his wife, who eventually, as sole heiress to her father, and to her brother John, who died without issue in 1774, brought to him the whole of the property of the Smallwood branch of the family. This fortune, I have heard it stated, amounted in the end to no less than £20,000—a magnificent sum in those days, and of incalculable use to a rising, energetic, and judicious manufacturer.

About this period the brothers, Thomas and John Wedgwood, of the "Big House," retired from business, and Josiah made proposals for the purchase of their works and those of the Ivy House, which he then rented under them. This offer, unfortunately for the town, but fortunately for Wedgwood himself, was not accepted. Had the property passed

John Wedgwood, of Dunwood. 1470. = Mary Shaw, heiress of John Shaw, of Harracles.

Richard Wedgwood, of Harracles. = Alice or Jane Sherratt.

John Wedgwood, High Collector of Subsidy, 1563. = Ann, daughter of William Bowyer, of Knypersley.

From whose descendants the Manor of Horton and other property passed to Hollins, and ultimately to Boothby.

Richard Wedgwood, of the Mole, in Biddulph (2nd son). = ...

Gilbert Wedgwood, youngest son, settled in Burslem. = Margaret Burslem, daughter and co-heiress of Thomas Burslem, by Mary Ford, of the Moss.

Joseph. d. s. p.

Burslem Wedgwood = ...

Thomas Wedgwood, 3rd son, ancestor of the "Overhouse" branch. = Margaret Shaw.

William =

Moses =

Aaron Wedgwood, 6th son, ancestor of the "Big House" family = Margaret . . . . .

John Wedgwood = Alice

Catherine, married—
1. Richard Wedgwood.
2. Thomas Bourne.
3. Rowland Egerton.

Thomas Wedgwood, 2nd son, of the Churchyard Works. = Mary Leigh.

Other sons and daughters.

Dr. Thomas Wedgwood and other children. = ...

Aaron Wedgwood = Mary Hollins.

Thomas Wedgwood, eldest son; of the Churchyard Works. = Mary Stringer.

And other sons and daughters.

Richard Wedgwood, of Smallwood. = Susan Irlam.

Other sons and daughters.

Thomas Wedgwood, of the Overhouse, &c., and other children.

JOSIAH WEDGWOOD, youngest son. = SARAH WEDGWOOD, eventually heiress to her father and brother.

John. d. s. p.

Four Sons and four Daughters.

into his hands he would have formed it into an extensive manufactory, which would have been of incalculable benefit to Burslem. As it was, the rejection of the proposal led him to look elsewhere for a site for his manufactory, and ultimately to establish it where it still stands, a lasting monument to his enterprise, his unwearying industry, and his talents, and of the benefits which he conferred on the neighbourhood and on the kingdom at large.

Thomas and John Wedgwood, of the "Big House," were the sons of Aaron Wedgwood, who died in 1743, by his wife, Mary Hollins. This Aaron Wedgwood, who made the white stoneware of the period, was son of Aaron, the sixth son of the Gilbert Wedgwood from whom Josiah and the other Burslem branches were descended. He married Mary Hollins, and it is a remarkable circumstance, which is thus recorded in the parish register, that they were both buried in one grave, and on the same day:—

"Aaron Wedgwood and Mary his wife, both of Burslem, were interred in ye same grave, April 24, 1743."

The tomb of this worthy couple still stands in the churchyard, not far from the north door of the church.

About the year 1740, it is said, the two brothers, Thomas and John Wedgwood, left their father Aaron's employ, "as lead-ore glaze potters, and commenced the manufacture of white stoneware upon their own account; but although very industrious and ingenious workmen (one of them being well skilled in burning or firing the ware, and the other an excellent thrower), they were unsuccessful for a long time, and had actually determined to abandon any further attempt to make the white stoneware, when an accidental circumstance encouraged them to proceed. The water with which they prepared the clay, it seems, became highly saturated with salt, owing to the shard ruck or rubbish from their ovens being placed immediately above their water pool, and which rubbish contained much salt. The rain passing through the shard ruck, dissolved the salt, and carried it into the pool, whence it got into the body of the ware, and, in conjunction with the flint and clay, together with the lime which generally adheres to flint stones, formed a fusible body that arrived at a state of vitrification with a lower degree of heat than was requisite to prepare this body for the salt glaze. This discovery induced them to make another trial with purer water; and in this they succeeded beyond expectation. The Wedgwoods followed up their success with unremitting diligence; and shortly afterwards built a new and commodious manufactory, where they had a supply of good water. This was near the Windmill, invented and erected by the celebrated Brindley for reducing flint stones to a fine powder by grinding them in water, and thereby preventing the pernicious effects upon the health of the men employed in preparing the flint according to the old method, by pounding it by hand in a dry state in a mortar. The fine dust of the flint getting into the lungs produced coughs and consumptions, which frequently proved fatal. This building, censured at the time as having been upon too extensive a scale, was the first earthenware manufactory in the Potteries *not covered with thatch.* In 1750 they erected an excellent and substantial dwelling-house adjoining their manufactory, which so far exceeded the other houses in the Potteries, in point of size and elegance, that it then was, and now is distinguished by the appellation of the '*Big House;*' and in the year 1763 these gentlemen retired from business in the possession of an ample fortune, the just and honourable reward of their industry and integrity."

The "Big House" stands at the corner of Wedgwood Street and Market Place, facing down Swan Square, from which place, and from the Waterloo Road, it forms a conspicuous object. It stands back from the street, with a walled enclosure in front. The old pot-works are at the rear, and are now occupied as builder's premises, by Messrs. Harley and Deane. The property, I believe, still belongs to the Wedgwood family.

Thomas and John Wedgwood, the builders of the Big House, and Aaron Wedgwood, the first maker, with Littler, of china at Longton, being brothers of Richard Wedgwood, of Smallwood, were uncles to Sarah, the wife of the great Josiah.

Thomas was, it appears, born in 1703, and married his cousin Mary, daughter of Dr. Thomas Wedgwood. He died without issue, in 1776, and the following somewhat curious epitaph to his memory—for it is not often that an inscription of "*brother of*" so and so is to be found—is still to be seen on the floor of the vestry:—

"Here lies the body of Thomas, brother of John Wedgwood, who died April 8, 1776, aged 73. Also Mary Wedgwood, wife of the above Thomas Wedgwood, who departed the 6th of July, 1781."

John Wedgwood, who was born in 1705, married Mary Alsop, by whom he had issue, and died in 1779.

At the time of his marriage, and for some time previously, Josiah Wedgwood had, besides the business of his manufactory, been actively engaged in many schemes for the benefit of his native town, for the furtherance of its commercial interest, and for the good of its inhabitants generally. Accordingly, we find him, in 1760, signing a petition to the lords of the manor, praying for a grant of "a small piece of land lying in Burslem, where the Maypole did formerly stand, in order to erect a piece of Building for a Schoole, as there is but one Schoole in the Town, and for want of an other, two parts of the children out of three are put to Work without any learning, by reason the other Schoole is not sufficient to instruct them." To this petition, which went on to say—"so we humbly beg of your Honours that you will be pleas'd to be aiding and assisting in this, and consider that it is a great piece of charity done by your Honours, which will be in memory of you and your posterity for ever, and the prayers of the Poor will always be with you, so we hope your Honours will be agreeable to this charitable request," were appended a number of names, "being the Gentlemen and Freeholders" of the liberty and manor, who "do firmly promise to advance the sums of money following their names, to be applyed in errecting the piece of Building for the use and purpose above mentioned; that is to say, a Schoole for the education of poore children." In this list, Josiah Wedgwood, and his relatives, Burslem and Thomas Wedgwood, appear for the sum of £10 each, being amongst the highest contributors. This scheme was afterwards altered, and from it sprang the present Town Hall and Market of Burslem.

About the same period he had been busying himself in the project for making a turnpike road through the district, which was achieved by the passing of the Act of Parliament a few months before his marriage. The state of the roads at this time may be gleaned from the following extract from the petition of the potters, in 1762; and it is highly creditable to Wedgwood, that in this, as in the case of the schools, of the Grand Trunk Canal (of which I shall have to speak later on), and of every other scheme which could benefit his native town or its surrounding district, or tend to the increase of its trade, he was not only one of the foremost and most strenuous supporters, but was the prime mover. The petition says:—

"In Burslem and its neighbourhood are near one hundred and fifty separate potteries for making various kinds of stone and earthen ware, which together find constant employment and support for near seven thousand people. The ware of these potteries is exported in vast quantities from London, Bristol, Liverpool, Hull, and other seaports, to our several colonies in America and the West Indies, as well as to almost every port in Europe. Great quantities of flint stones are used in making some of the ware, which are brought by sea from different parts of the coast of Liverpool and Hull; and the clay for making the white ware is brought from Devonshire and Cornwall chiefly to Liverpool, the materials from whence are brought by water up the rivers Mersey and Weaver to Winsford, in Cheshire; those from Hull up the Trent to Willington; and from Winsford and Willington the whole are brought by land carriage to Burslem. The ware, when made, is conveyed to Liverpool and Hull in the same manner as the materials are brought from those places.

"Many thousand tons of shipping, and seamen in proportion, which in summer trade to the northern seas, are employed in winter in carrying materials for the Burslem ware; and as much salt is consumed in glazing one species of it as pays annually near £5,000 duty to government. Add to these considerations the prodigious quantity of coal used in the Potteries, and the loading and freight this manufacture constantly supplies as well for land carriage as inland navigation, and it will appear that the manufacturers, sailors, bargemen, carriers, colliers, men employed in the salt works, and others who are supported by the pot trade, amount to a great many thousand people; and every shilling received for ware at foreign markets is so much clear gain to the nation, as not one foreigner is employed in, or any material imported from abroad for, any branch of it; and the trade flourishes so much as to have increased two-thirds within the last fourteen years.

"The potters concerned in this very considerable manufacture, presuming from the above, and many other reasons that might be offered by the pot trade, not unworthy the attention of parliament, have presented a petition for leave to bring in a bill to repair and widen the road from the 'Red Bull' at Lawton, in Cheshire, to Cliff Bank, in Staffordshire, which runs right through the Potteries, and falls at each end into a turnpike road. This road, especially the northern road from Burslem to the 'Red Bull,' is so very narrow, deep, and foundrous, as to be almost impassable for carriages, and in the winter almost for pack-horses; for which reasons the carriages with materials and ware to and from Liverpool, and the salt works in Cheshire, are obliged to go to Newcastle, and from thence to the 'Red Bull,' which is nine miles and a half (whereof three miles and a half, viz., from Burslem to Newcastle, are not turnpike road), instead of five miles, which is the distance from Burslem to the 'Red Bull' by the road prayed to be amended."

In this scheme, as I have before hinted, Wedgwood and his brother manufacturers met with severe opposition, especially from the inhabitants of Newcastle-under-Lyme, who considered that by diverting the traffic into another channel, their town would be ruined, and their trade, especially that of the innkeepers, destroyed. The Act, however, passed with the alteration that it should end at Burslem instead of being continued to Cliff Bank. The formation of this turnpike-road—which has the reputation of being the first in the Potteries—was mainly due to the immense exertions of Wedgwood, who only grew more determined as opposition increased, and eventually carried his point, and thus conferred an incalculable benefit on the neighbourhood, much against its will.

In the course of his own business, as well as upon the schemes of the turnpike-road and canal, Wedgwood had not unfrequently occasion to go to Liverpool, where, indeed, he had already found an important market for his goods. On one of these visits, in consequence of some accidental aggravation of his old complaint, he was laid up for some weeks, and was then under the charge of, I have reason to believe, Dr. Matthew Turner, a man of high intellectual attainments, and an excellent chemist, who resided in John Street, and to whom the merit of the re-discovery of much of the lost art of glass-staining belongs.*

The doctor was an intimate friend of Mr. Thomas Bentley, of Liverpool, a man of superior attainments, of refined taste, and of most agreeable manners and conversational powers, and "pitying the situation of Mr. Wedgwood, a stranger, and so much afflicted, introduced Mr. Bentley to him as a companion, whose intelligence, vivacity, and philanthropy, would quicken the lingering hours of pain." From this acquaintanceship, so accidentally and so strangely brought about, sprung up a lasting friendship, which ripened as time drew on, until it culminated in a partnership, and ended only in the death of Bentley.

And here let me correct a wide-spread error regarding this well-known partner of Josiah Wedgwood's, concerning whom I shall have some particulars to give in another chapter. Ward, in his "History of Stoke-upon-Trent," a

* This clever man, I believe, in conjunction with Mr. Chubbard, executed the south window of St. Anne's Church, Liverpool.

work written at Burslem, Wedgwood's native place, says, speaking of Josiah Wedgwood,—"He took into partnership Mr. Richard Bentley, son of Dr. Bentley, the celebrated critic and Archdeacon of Ely, a man of great ingenuity, taste, and learning, possessing too a large circle of acquaintance among people of rank and science. To him, it is generally understood, Mr. Wedgwood was chiefly indebted for his classical subjects, for which his establishment became so highly celebrated." This statement has been repeated with but little variation, in almost every notice which has yet appeared of Wedgwood or of his productions down to the present time. I am enabled, however, to show that this statement is erroneous, and that not only was Wedgwood's partner not the son of Archdeacon Bentley, the critic, but was not even named Richard. The companion, and afterwards partner, of Josiah Wedgwood was, as will be seen from the fac-simile of his autograph, which

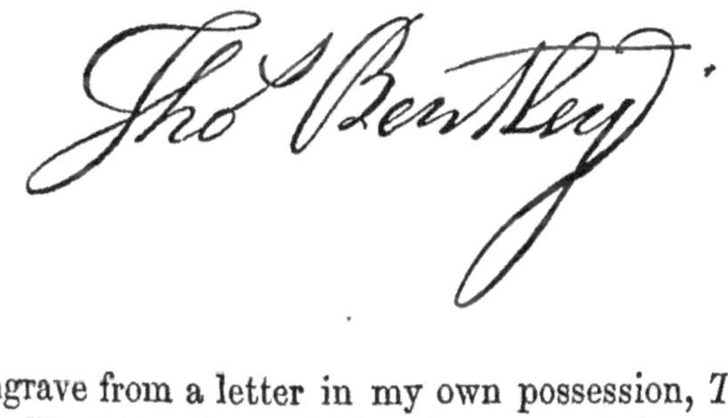

I here engrave from a letter in my own possession, *Thomas* Bentley. The letter from which this autograph is copied, is addressed to "My dear Friend," "Mr. Josiah Wedgwood, at Etruria," &c. In connection with this autograph I give in the following illustration an engraving of the beautiful medallion of Bentley, produced by Wedgwood as a companion, probably, to his own, from an example in my own collection. The bust, it will be seen, is remarkably bold and fine, and must have been the work of an artist of no common order.

In connection with this medallion, it will be interesting

to note that a portrait of Thomas Bentley was painted by Wright, of Derby, and is now preserved at Linley Wood. In

Wright's diary the painting of this portrait is thus entered, under the year 1777 :—" Copy of Mr. Bentley, K.C., £21." Wright also painted a portrait of " Miss Bentley (full), £31 10*s*."

In another chapter I shall show that Thomas Bentley, about whom too little has hitherto been known, and concerning whom so many errors have been perpetuated, was a native of Derbyshire, and a member, doubtless, of the old family of that name long connected with that county.

CHAPTER VIII.

INLAND NAVIGATION.—PROPOSED GRAND TRUNK CANAL.—BRINDLEY'S PLAN.—DUKE OF BRIDGWATER'S CANAL.—MEETING IN FAVOUR OF THE GRAND TRUNK.—JOSIAH WEDGWOOD'S LIBERAL OFFER.—STATE OF THE POTTERY DISTRICT.—WANT OF COMMUNICATION.—PACK-HORSES.—CLAY, FLINT, LEAD, SALT, IRON, ETC.—RICHARD WHITWORTH AND HIS IDEAS.—STATE OF THE PEOPLE IN BURSLEM.—REV. JOHN WESLEY.—HIS FIRST VISIT TO THE POTTERIES.—IS PELTED WHILE PREACHING.—WEDGWOOD CUTS THE FIRST SOD OF THE GRAND TRUNK CANAL.—WONDER EXCITED AT BRINDLEY'S OPERATIONS—WEDGWOOD'S ZEAL WITH REGARD TO THE CANAL.

INLAND navigation, at the period of which I am now writing, was in its veriest infancy; but the advantages which an increased water communication between different towns would give to trade were fully understood by Mr. Wedgwood, whose mind, ever active, grasped the subject in all its bearings, and determined him to bring those advantages to his native place, and to the trade which was its sole support. His mind once made up, nothing was allowed to brook it. Obstacles only increased his determination, and opposition his firmness of purpose. As early as 1755, a scheme had been broached in Liverpool for joining, by means of a canal which should pass through the great towns of Chester, Stafford, Derby, and Nottingham, the rivers Trent and Mersey, and thus connect the important ports of Liverpool on the one hand, and Hull on the other. Surveys were made for this and other schemes, some passing through the "pot district," and others purposely avoiding it.

The progress of the Duke of Bridgwater's canal intensified the interest which had been created in the subject, and at length, in 1762, James Brindley, the prince of engineers, who had been employed in erecting wind flint-mills, corn-mills, engines, &c., in the pot district, and who was successfully carrying out the duke's canal, was engaged to make the survey through Staffordshire. "The schemer," as he was aptly called, had, as early as 1758, made a rough survey of the district, and in the two succeeding years he continued his surveys and mastered the levels necessary on the proposed line of canal. Meetings in support of the proposed scheme were held, and Smeaton as well as Brindley produced their plans; but the project of inland water communication being in its entire infancy, and the duke's canal being unfinished, the projectors left their scheme in abeyance for some time, while they watched with intense anxiety the progress towards completion of the duke's canal. When it was opened, and its success became palpable, the Staffordshire scheme was revived with increased spirit. Wedgwood entered into it with all the ardour and energy of his nature; but at this time rival schemes, unthought of before, sprang up and had to be encountered. Brindley's project was wisely considered to be *the* plan for the district, and to this plan, which was also backed by the Duke of Bridgwater, Josiah Wedgwood gave his firm and lasting adhesion. One of Brindley's letters, written on the 21st of December, 1765, shows how energetically Wedgwood worked in the promotion of this scheme, which became in the end one of the greatest blessings to the district which it ever enjoyed. The following is an extract:—

"On Tusdey Sr Georg sent Nuton in to Manchestr to make what intrest he could for Sir Georg and to gather ye old Navogtors togather to meet Sir Georg at Stoperd to make Head a ganst His grace. I sawe Doctor Seswige who sese Hee wants to see you aboat pamant of His Land in Cheshire. On Wednesday ther was not much transpired, but was so dark I could carse do aneything.

"On Thursday Wadgwood of Burslam came to Dunham and sant for mee and wee dined with Lord Gree & Sir Hare Mainwering and others. Sir Hare cud not ceep His Tamer. Mr. Wedgwood came to seliset Lord Gree in faver of the Staffordshire Canal and stade at Mrs. Latoune all night & I whith him & on frydey sat out to wate on Mr. Edgerton to selesit Him. Hee sase Sparrow and others are indavering to gat ye Land owners consants from Hare Castle to Agden."

On the 30th of the same month (December, 1765) a meeting was held for the furtherance of the scheme, the lord-lieutenant of the county presiding, and being supported by the county and borough members, and others of influence. At this meeting Brindley, in his quiet and simple manner, explained his plans, and having fully shown their feasibility, they were at once adopted, with only some trifling alterations. At this meeting it was determined to apply to Parliament for power to construct the canal, and the question of ways and means was fully discussed. Wedgwood took so prominent a part in the discussion, and was so warm in his support of the scheme, that the chairman, Earl Gower, asked him, it is said somewhat derisively, as he was so forward in pressing the scheme, what was he prepared to embark in it? To this Wedgwood immediately replied, that he would at once subscribe a thousand pounds towards the preliminary expenses and take, I know not how many, shares besides. This liberality, showing an honesty of purpose, and a strong faith in the project, became contagious, and put to the blush many milk-and-water supporters of the scheme who were present. Wedgwood's offer, it would seem, decided the matter; money enough was raised, an Act of Parliament was applied for, and by the middle of the ensuing year, 1766, obtained.

The inhabitants of Burslem and the neighbourhood were so much elated with the news of the result of the meeting, and so rejoiced at the spirit which Wedgwood and others had displayed, that the next evening following the meeting —the last day of the year 1765—they lit a huge bonfire in the town, and round it drank the healths of the promoters of the scheme.

In the preceding chapter I have alluded to the bad state

of the roads in the pottery district, and to the opposition which Wedgwood met in his laudable endeavours for their improvement. The same reason which induced him to promote the improvement of the roads actuated him in his labours to promote the canal. The transit of goods to and fro was heavy, and greatly impeded the rising trade of the county; and it became, in his expansive mind, a matter of absolute necessity that greater means of communication should be provided. As it was, the roads were scarcely passable even in summer to the lumbering old waggons and carts which occasionally jolted along them. They were narrow, with high banks at their sides, always, even in summer, soft and clayey, and full of deep ruts, in which the wheels sank and stuck fast. In winter, even the strings of pack-horses, which did somehow or other manage to drag their weary way along, knee-deep in mud, could scarcely get from place to place, and many a poor brute fell down exhausted, and died on the road, breaking, in falling, the heavy load of crockery it bore on its back.

It must be remembered that some of the essentials of the potter's art had to be brought on the backs of these pack-horses, or by cart and waggon, from great distances, and that by the same means provisions had to be procured and pottery despatched. Although coal was plentiful on the spot, and the commoner clays abundant, flint, one of the essentials of fine wares, and of heavy carriage, had to be brought from the nearest point of water communication, which was at Willington in Derbyshire, to which place, having come by sea to Hull, it was brought up the river Trent. Clays from Cornwall, Devonshire, and Dorsetshire, had to be brought up in like manner from Bewdley, Bridgnorth, Winsford, Cavendish Bridge, and other places, to which it had been brought by water. In the same manner salt and lead had to be conveyed to the district; and thus the restrictions on trade were immense, and there was difficulty in procuring even the common necessaries of food and clothing. Shops, of course, there were none worthy of the name in the pottery district, the people being supplied by itinerant hucksters, chapmen, and packmen from other places. In 1760, Richard Whitworth, of Balcham Grange, wrote:—"There are three pot waggons go from Newcastle and Burslem weekly, through Eccleshall and Newport to Bridgnorth, and carry about eight tons of potware every week, at £3 per ton. The same waggons load back with ten tons of close goods, consisting of white clay, grocery, and iron, at the same price, delivered on their road to Newcastle. Large quantities of potware are conveyed on horses' backs from Burslem and Newcastle to Bridgnorth and Bewdley, for exportation, about one hundred tons yearly, at £2 10*s*. per ton. Two broad-wheel waggons (exclusive of 150 pack-horses) go from Manchester through Stafford weekly, and may be computed to carry 312 tons of cloth and Manchester wares in the year, at £3 10*s*. per ton. The great salt trade that is carried on at Northwich may be computed to send 600 tons yearly along this (proposed) canal, together with Nantwich 400, chiefly carried now on horses' backs at 10*s*. per ton on a medium." So accustomed, however, had the inhabitants of the principal pottery town, Newcastle-under-Lyme, become to this state of things that, as I have already hinted, every scheme for the improvement of the roads and for developing the resources of the district met with dogged and determined opposition. They, in their narrow-mindedness, feared that if the roads were improved, the country opened out with water and other means of communication, the traffic would be taken otherwise than through their good old town, and that therefore their innkeepers and others would lose by the proposed change.

The success of the duke's canal brought forward many opponents to the scheme to which Wedgwood had wedded himself. The promoters of each of these rival schemes had their own interests to serve, and their own selfish ends in view. They were, however, impotent except in delaying the Grand Trunk scheme, and eventually one by one were disposed of. The Duke of Bridgwater threw his influence and interest into the scale of Wedgwood's scheme, and in the end the Act was, as I have said, obtained.

Whitworth, to whose writings I have just alluded, proposed, in order that the pack-horses and other rude modes of conveyance might still be used, that "no main trunk of a canal shall be carried nearer than four miles of any great manufacturing and trading town; which distance from the canal," he says, "would be sufficient to maintain the same number of horses as before." This narrow-minded policy, as in later days has been the case in proposals for railways, was adopted by some towns, and produced their gradual decay and almost ruin. Happily for the pottery district, it contained no "great manufacturing and trading towns," but it possessed public spirit, energy, and perseverance centered in the ever-active brain of Wedgwood and his able coadjutors, and the consequence was that the canal was cut through its very heart, and thus gave its vital trade-streams inlet and outlet, which at once gave it strength, vigour, and nourishment.

It must be remembered that the generality of the people living at that time at Burslem and its surrounding villages were, partly through their isolated position, partly from the want of schools, and partly, it must be confessed, from an innate rudeness, many of them ignorant, low, and brutish in their conduct; but it must be remembered, also, that it was not *these* people who opposed the march of improvement, but their "betters" in a worldly sense—the landowners, innkeepers, and the like. The commoner people, the hardworkers, hailed the proposals with delight, and their joy on the scheme being in a fair way of being successfully carried out culminated in bonfires and other popular demonstrations of satisfaction.

In 1760 John Wesley had for the first time visited Burslem, and in the following highly-interesting extract from his journal he tells how ignorant the poor people there were, and how on one occasion "a clod of earth" was thrown at him while preaching; but he also shows that the "*poor* potters" at Burslem were "more civilised" than "the *better sort* (so-called) at Congleton." The following is an extract:—

"1760, *March 8th.*—Went from Wolverhampton to Burslem (near Newcastle-under-Lyme), a scattered town on the top of a hill, inhabited almost entirely by potters, a multitude of whom assembled at five in the evening. Deep attention sat on every face, though as yet accompanied with deep ignorance; but if the heart be toward God, He will in due time enlighten the understanding.

"—— *Sunday, 9th.*—I preached at eight to near double the number, some quite innocent of thought. Five or six were laughing and talking till I had near done; and one of them threw a clod of earth, which struck me on the side of the head, but it neither disturbed me nor the congregation."

"1761, *March 9th.*—Preached at Burslem at half-past five, in an open place on the top of the hill, to a large and attentive congregation, though it rained almost all the time, and the air was extremely cold. The next morning (being Good Friday) preached at eight, and again in the evening. The cold considerably lessened the congregation—so small are the things which divert mankind from what ought to be the means of their eternal salvation."

"1764, *July 20th.*—It rained all day till seven in the evening, when I began preaching at Burslem. Even the *poor potters* here are a more civilised people than the *better sort* (so called) at Congleton."

The Act of Parliament for the proposed Grand Trunk Canal having been obtained, after constant and unwearied anxiety, the honour of cutting the first sod was wisely accorded to Mr. Wedgwood, its most prominent, most energetic, and most liberal promoter. This important ceremony —important, as it proved to be, not only to the potteries, but to the kingdom at large—was performed with all necessary formalities on the 26th of July, 1766. The first sod was cut by Josiah Wedgwood, on the declivity of Brownhills, on a piece of land within a few yards of the bridge which now crosses the canal. Brindley, the engineer, and many influential persons, were present, and each cut a sod, or wheeled away some earth after Wedgwood had set the good example. In the evening a bonfire was lit in Burslem, a sheep was roasted whole in the market-place, a *feu de joie* was fired in front of Mr. Wedgwood's house, and all the usual demonstrations of joy were indulged in to their hearts' content by the potters of the district.

Thus this important undertaking was fitly inaugurated by the man who had taken the most active part in its promotion, and to whom the neighbourhood was indebted for so many benefits. The history of the progress of this canal, which has been pleasantly and graphically told by Mr. Smiles, would form a pleasing episode in the memoirs of Wedgwood, but it is enough for my present purpose to say that it was carried on with all the energy, and all the tact and skill, of which the truly wonderful nature of Brindley was capable, until his death. For six years he laboured closely and assiduously at it, and after his death, in 1772, the remaining portion of the work was successfully completed by his brother-in-law, John Henshall.

The wonder with which the operations of Brindley, the "Prince of Engineers," especially as regarded his immense cutting of the Harecastle Tunnel, were looked upon by the inhabitants of Burslem, is well told in a letter quoted by Mr. Smiles, dated 1767, and written by an inhabitant of Burslem to a friend in a distant part of the country. It is as follows:—

"Gentlemen,—Come to view our eighth wonder of the world, the subterraneous navigation which is cutting by the great Mr. Brindley, who handles rocks as easily as you would plum pies, and makes the four elements subservient to his will. He is as plain a looking man as one of the boors of the Peak,* or as one of his own carters; but when he speaks, all ears listen, and every mind is filled with wonder at the things he pronounces to be practicable. He has cut a mile through bogs, which he binds up, embanking them with stones which he gets out of other parts of the navigation, besides about a quarter of a mile into the hill Yelden, on the side of which he has a pump worked by water, and a stove, the fire of which sucks through a pipe the damps that

* James Brindley was, it will be remembered, a native of Tunstead, in the High Peak of Derbyshire.

would annoy the men who are cutting towards the centre of the hill. The clay he cuts out serves for bricks to arch the subterraneous part, which we heartily wish to see finished to Wilden Ferry, when we shall be able to send coals and pots to London, and to different parts of the globe."

The zeal which Wedgwood showed in the furtherance of this scheme is thus well expressed in the private manuscript to which I have before had occasion to refer. When he once fairly took up the subject, "business, family, everything, gave place to this important object, for many months in the year 1765. Drawing around him the few that then thought with him on the subject, or were inclined to take an active part, they concerted on the means of gaining friends, and overcoming opposition. At this time the principle itself of the utility of canal navigation was disputed, and if any advantages were admitted, they did not appear to a very powerful class of the people as of sufficient importance to counterbalance the injuries they apprehended to themselves. Here was a great deal of intellectual ground to be cleared, and the contest was not for this or that modification, but whether the thing itself should exist at all. In this struggle Mr. Wedgwood was certainly the foremost and most active person, and for three months, during the progress of the Bill in Parliament, was nearly as much lost to his private connections as though he had been in China. The canal in question was called the Grand Trunk, because it was foreseen that many lesser ones would break out of it, as has since happened. It is upwards of ninety miles in length, joining the Trent about a mile below Cavendish Bridge, in Derbyshire, and terminating in the Duke of Bridgwater's Canal, in Preston Brook, in Cheshire. The internal passage through the hill at Harecastle is an object of great curiosity, being a mile and three quarters in length, and crossing many veins of coal, which are got at a small expense, being thus laid dry, and the canal is greatly benefited by the supply of water. Mr. Brindley began this work on both sides at the same time, and his workmen met in the middle. The contrivances of this great man, by which he executed stupendous works in a short time that seem to have required ages, have been properly noticed in the account of his life in the 'Biographia Britannica,' the materials for which were furnished by Mr. Wedgwood, who lived in habits of intimacy and friendship with him, and ever revered his memory. Mr. Wedgwood was the first treasurer of the canal, and an active member of the committee for making and carrying it on for more than twenty years."

The Grand Trunk Canal was finished by Mr. Henshall, brother-in-law to Brindley, in May, 1777, and was immediately productive of the greatest benefit to the neighbourhood. Trade increased, freight of goods was lowered to about the rate of thirteen shillings per ton, where fifty shillings had before been paid, the despatch and receipt of goods was more rapid and more certain, and the whole district assumed a vitality which has gone on regularly increasing to the present day.

If for no other reason, the part he took in the carrying out to a successful issue the scheme of canal communication, to which undoubtedly the Staffordshire potteries owe their prosperous increase, would fully entitle Josiah Wedgwood to the thanks of his country, and to be ranked among the foremost benefactors of mankind.

CHAPTER IX.

JOSIAH WEDGWOOD TAKES INTO PARTNERSHIP HIS RELATIVE THOMAS WEDGWOOD. — RALPH WEDGWOOD. — HIS POT WORKS IN STAFFORDSHIRE AND YORKSHIRE.—HIS INVENTIONS.—THE POCKET SECRETARY AND THE MANIFOLD WRITER.—INVENTION OF THE ELECTRIC TELEGRAPH.—SCHEME OFFERED TO AND REJECTED BY GOVERNMENT.—JOHN TAYLOR WEDGWOOD, THE LINE ENGRAVER.—HIS WORKS.—JOSIAH WEDGWOOD'S CHEMICAL KNOWLEDGE.—PROCURES CLAYS FROM AMERICA.—ALEXANDER CHISHOLM.—INTRODUCTION OF "BASALTES," OR "EGYPTIAN BLACK" WARE.

HAVING by this time firmly established the manufacture of his staple commodity, "Queen's Ware," and placed its production on a sure and lasting basis, and having by the improvements of the roads, and the construction of the canal, removed the only impediments which seemed to fix a limit to its consumption, from a want of easy and more rapid conveyance of raw materials to, and finished goods from, the pot district, Wedgwood felt that it was time to relieve himself to some extent from the weight of a constant personal supervision. He desired to be more free from this now established branch of his business, in order that he might devote himself more to the study of chemistry, and of clays and other mineral substances, with a view to the production of those higher classes of goods for which his manufactory afterwards became so justly famous. "With this view, and to reward the merit of a worthy man, a relation, Mr. Thomas Wedgwood, who had been some years a faithful and industrious foreman in the manufactory," he entered into partnership with that gentleman, giving him a share of the profit in, with the entire direction of, that branch of the manufactory (the Queen's Ware), and in this position Thomas Wedgwood remained until the time of his death, in 1788.

This Thomas Wedgwood was, I believe, cousin to Josiah, being son of Aaron Wedgwood and his wife Hannah Malkin. He was born, it would appear, in 1734, and was, therefore, four years younger than Josiah. He was a man of high scientific attainments, and has the reputation of being the first inventor of the electric telegraph (afterwards so ably carried out by his son Ralph), and of many other valuable works. He married Elizabeth Taylor, of the Hill, Burslem, and by her had issue, Ralph, of whose descendants more anon; Samuel, who died without issue, at Whitworth; Thomas, who died in New York of yellow fever, also without issue; Aaron, of Liverpool; Abner; and John Taylor Wedgwood, the eminent line engraver, whose works are so justly prized by collectors.

Thomas Wedgwood, the partner of Josiah, of whom I have just spoken, resided at Etruria, after the removal of the works there, and died at that place in 1788, having, it is said, been accidentally drowned.

His eldest son, Ralph Wedgwood (elder brother of the engraver), was three times married—first to Mary Yeomans, of Worcester, by whom he had issue Ralph Wedgwood, of Barnes and Cornhill, still living; secondly, to Sarah Taylor; and thirdly, to Anne Copeland, by each of whom also he had issue. By the latter marriage was his son W. R. Wedgwood, of Greyshot Hall, who has done so much, and so commendably, to establish his father's claim to the invention of the electric telegraph.

Ralph Wedgwood was a man of extraordinary and varied ability, the originator of important scientific inventions, and the author of the "Book of Remembrance," published in 1814, in which the invention of the electric telegraph, under the name of the "fulguri-polygraph," is made known, and its benefits—precisely such as are now reaped by the public—are described. Ralph Wedgwood was born in 1766, and was brought up with his father at Etruria, where he received much valuable aid in chemistry, &c., from Josiah Wedgwood. He afterwards carried on business as a potter, under the style of "Wedgwood & Co.," at the Hill-works, Burslem, but was ruined through losses during the American war. While at the Hill, he prepared and presented to Queen Charlotte some fine examples of his manufacture, on occasion of the restoration of health to the king, which was graciously accepted through the hands of Lord Cremorne. He then removed into Yorkshire, where, having entered into partnership with Messrs. Tomlinson & Seton, of Ferry Bridge, he again commenced business. This engagement, however, was not of long duration, his partners being dissatisfied at the large amount of breakage caused by his experiments and peculiar mode of firing, and he retired from the concern with a thousand pounds awarded as his share of the business. He next removed to Bransford, near Worcester, where he issued prospectuses for teaching chemistry at schools, and thence to London, in 1803, travelling in a carriage of his own constructing, which he describes as "a long coach to get out behind, and on grass-hopper springs, now used by all the mails." This carriage was so extraordinary in its appearance as to be taken for a travelling show. While at Bransford he had been perfecting his many inventions, among which was his celebrated manifold writer, which still maintains its high repute "against all comers." One of his copying schemes, which he called a "Penna-polygraph," that of writing with a number of pens attached to one handle, he found on his arrival in London had already been made by another person. His other plan, proving to be new, he called the "Pocket Secretary," and afterwards the "Manifold Writer;" and on the 7th of October, 1806, after much discouragement and opposition, he took out a patent for this as "an apparatus for producing duplicates of writing." In 1808 he took out a second patent for "an apparatus for producing several original writings or drawings at one and the same time, which I shall call a Pennæpolygraph, or pen and stylographic manifold writer." An "Ærial zone" was also proposed by him, and his invention was laid before the Admiralty, but judging from the following extract from a letter now lying before me, the invention was not considered to be a very feasible one. "The Ærial zone is in proper hands if it is laid before the Admiralty, for there does not seem to be any greater likelihood of its becoming an article of general use, than there is of the ladies leaving off muslin, because some lose their lives every year by its use." *

In 1806, Ralph Wedgwood established himself at Charing Cross, and soon afterwards his whole attention began to be engrossed with his scheme of the electric telegraph, which in the then unsettled state of the kingdom—in midst of war it must be remembered—he considered would be of the utmost importance to the government. In 1814, having perfected his scheme, he submitted his proposal to Lord Castlereagh, and most anxiously awaited the result. His son Ralph having waited on his lordship for a decision as to whether government would accept the plan or not, was informed that "the war being at an end, the old system was sufficient for the country!" The plan, therefore, fell to the ground, until Professor Wheatstone, in happier and more enlightened times again brought the subject forward with such eminent success. The plan, thus brought forward by Ralph Wedgwood in 1814, and of which, as I have stated, he received the first idea from his father, was thus described by him in a pamphlet entitled, "An Address to the Public, on the advantages of a proposed introduction of the Stylographic Principle of writing into general use; and also of an improved species of Telegraphy, calculated for the use of the Public as well as for the Government." The pamphlet is dated May 29th, 1815, and as the question of the merit of invention is one of considerable importance, I gladly give the extract, so as to establish the claim to that merit to a member of the Wedgwood family.

* Letter from Josiah Wedgwood, M.P.

"A modification of the Stylographic principle, proposed for the adoption of parliament, in lieu of telegraphs, viz. :—

"The Fulguri-Polygraph, which admits of writing in several distant places at one and the same time, and by the agency of two persons only.

"This invention is founded on the capacity of electricity to produce motion in the act of acquiring an equilibrium; which motion, by the aid of machinery, is made to distribute matter at the extremities of any given course. And the matter so distributed being variously modified in correspondence with the letters of the alphabet, and communicable in rapid succession at the will of the operator, it is obvious that writing at immense distances hereby becomes practicable, and further, as lines of communication can be multiplied from any given point, and those lines affected by one and the same application of the electric matter, it is evident from hence also that fac-similes of a dispatch, written as for instance in London, may with facility be written also in Plymouth, Dover, Hull, Leith, Liverpool, and Bristol, or any other place, by the same person, and by one and the same act. Whilst this invention proposes to remove the usual impediments and imperfections of telegraphs, it gives the rapidity of lightning to correspondence, when and wherever we wish, and renders null the principal disadvantages of distance to correspondents. Independent of the advantages which this invention offers to government, it is also susceptible of much utility to the public at large; inasmuch as the offices which might be constructed for the purposes of this invention might be let to individuals by the hour, for private uses, by which means the machinery might be at all times fully occupied, and the private uses which could thus be made of this invention might be applied towards refunding the expenses of the institution, and also for increasing the revenue. Innumerable are the instances wherein such an invention may be beneficially applied in this country, more especially at a time when her distinguished situation in the political, commercial, and moral world, has made her the central point of nations, and the great bond of their union. To the seat of her government, therefore, it must be highly desirable to effect the most speedy and certain communication from every quarter of the world, whilst it would at any moment there concentrate instantaneous intelligence of the situation of each and every principal part of the nation, as well as of each and every branch of its various departments."

Ralph Wedgwood from Charing Cross removed successively to Piccadilly, and Southampton Street, Strand, where he continued producing his "Pocket Secretary" in large numbers. Lady Percival had been instrumental in introducing the invention to members of the government and others, and the result was that a profitable business was acquired. The advantages he had thus gained, were, however, lost by his researches concerning the electric telegraph, and in the end his business gradually decayed. He was a man of perhaps too visionary a nature for the ordinary pursuits of life, and was thus led into the speculative ideas rather than the substantialities of worldly existence. Among his schemes was one for the founding of an universal language, over which he held a lengthy and elaborate correspondence with Percy Byshe Shelley and other men of the day. Ralph Wedgwood died at Chelsea in 1837, and I am glad to have been enabled thus briefly to allude to his scientific labours, and to place on record some few particulars of his life.

John Taylor Wedgwood, the line engraver, who received the appointment of "Engraver to H.R.H. the Princess Charlotte, and to Prince Leopold of Saxe Coburg" (the present King of the Belgians), was the youngest brother of Ralph Wedgwood, of whom I have just spoken. He was born in 1782, and spent the whole of his long life in the steady practice of his art. For many years he resided in Paris, but left it at the Revolution of 1830. He was an accurate and most excellent draughtsman as well as engraver, and excelled most in the human figure. In this his intimate knowledge of anatomy, which he had made his constant study, was of immense service. He received the appointment of engraver to the Royal College of Surgeons and to the British Museum; and is said to have been so wrapped up in his art that when not engraving at night he spent his time in making pen and chalk drawings. It is related of him by many who knew him well, that nothing would induce him to engrave anything which he believed to be untruthful. On one occasion he is said to have been applied to, to engrave a portrait of Sir Hudson Lowe from a painting which he thought untruthfully exhibited his somewhat plain features, and he refused the commission because he could not think that the painting was life-like. He engraved, among other exquisite works, an admirable portrait of his deceased relative, the Great Josiah, from Sir Joshua Reynolds' painting. This engraving I have been fortunate enough to secure for my readers, and it will be found as a frontispiece to the present volume. It will be seen to be a remarkably fine work of art, and one in every way worthy not only of himself but of the great man whom it so well represents. Among his other more celebrated works were a fine portrait of Lord Byron, published in Paris, and portraits of the Princess Charlotte and of Prince Leopold, with numberless others which will be well known to print and portrait collectors. John Taylor Wedgwood, who was never married, died in London in the year 1856, aged seventy-four.

With Thomas Wedgwood—himself the improver of some of the wares—as his partner, the "Great Josiah" found himself more at leisure, as I have said, to pursue his experiments and researches. Speaking of these chemical pursuits, the manuscript to which I have before referred says—

"It is not to be wondered at that his mind had a strong direction to this study in connection with chemistry, since he could not but be sensible how entirely the advancement of his views depended upon it, and he had happily acquired a fondness for the pursuit which, independently of the advantages he derived from it, was the source of rational amusement to his latest day. He possessed himself, at considerable expense, of all the minerals in this island, and there were few in other countries whose properties he had not examined. Being once shown a specimen of beautiful white clay, from the country of the Cherokees, in North America, he engaged the person who brought it over to return to that country, and procure him what quantity he could get of it. The fruit of this expedition was, however, only a few tons, which were carried on the backs of mules, from a great distance, to the port of Charlestown, in South Carolina. No clay equal to this in purity has been met with in England, nor perhaps in Europe, except in a few lead mines about Brassington, in Derbyshire, and there only in such small quantities that it cannot be made the basis of a manufactory. In 1792 Colonel Ironsides sent him a specimen of the brown matrix, from the East, which the colonel wrote to be the very clay itself, but herein was set right by Mr. W. in a letter to him. Mr. Wedgwood was well acquainted with the Brassington clay in 1765, and then procured small quantities of it for experiment.*

"By numbering and registering the results of the experiments he was constantly making, he could take up the ideas they furnished at any distant time when occasion required, and by these means he saw in the drawers of his cabinet the employment of his future life, and perhaps of that of his successor. He was thus enabled to keep up the spirit and attraction of his works by a succession of novelties, and his manufactory appeared in a progressive course of improvement. His inventions as they rose had the good fortune to be countenanced by the fashionable world, which secured them a favourable reception with the bulk of mankind. His contemporaries in the pottery (in every instance but one that will be pointed out) soon adopted them, and they became general articles of commerce and public benefit.

"'That the efficacy of causes may have their due influence,' we have known him ever forward to declare that it was alone owing to the munificent protection of his sovereign, and the liberal encouragement of the nobility and gentry of these kingdoms, that he was able to risk the expense of these continual improvements, unparalleled, we believe, in the history of any similar manufactory in Europe.

"Thus honoured and thus prosperous in his humble pot-

* The importance of this material was evidently known to Wedgwood's contemporary, Duesbury, of the Derby china works, who rented some lead mines at the place.

tery, he used to say jocosely, 'his friends threatened him with the statute of lunacy if he should begin to make porcelain.' It was not possible, however, to continue his improvement of earthenware without producing substances that, having most of the genuine and essential properties of porcelain, must necessarily be so classed. But he so profited by the admonition of his friends as to keep himself disengaged from any plan of making the porcelain in common use, so much and often so fatally the ambitious object of so many individuals. His researches marked him out a new and unbeaten track in the same field that was more congenial to his disposition and powers. About this time, the year 1766, he first discovered the art of making the unglazed black porcelain, now so well known in this country, and called it Basaltes, as it has nearly the same properties with the stone of that name. And the first uses that he made of it were to imitate the fine vases of antiquity that he found in Montfaucon's works, and other collections that had then come to his knowledge. He saw the extensive application that might be made of such compact and durable substances as this, and others that he had begun with but not then brought to maturity, in multiplying copies of the fine works of antiquity, as well as those of our own times; and he was not without hopes that the improvement of pottery, by exciting the public attention to the productions of the arts, would lay the foundation of a school of miniature modelling in this country, which had long felt a deficiency of artists in that way. To this end his labours were directed, and it must be allowed that he has done much to promote it; but many objects yet unattained dwelt in his mind's eye, and he used to declare in his later days, that 'he considered the pottery as still in its infancy.'"

The close and constant attention which Wedgwood now gave to the properties of clays and different minerals, and the researches and experiments he prosecuted in chemistry, soon led to the production of a number of different kinds of wares unknown before, and which have gained for him a lasting and honourable fame. He formed an admirable library of chemical works, and carefully noted the results, not only of his own observations and experiments, but of those of others, and he soon became one of the most clever of chemists, as he certainly was one of the most accomplished of the scientific men of his time. I have now lying before me, through the kindness of Mr. Francis and Mr. Godfrey Wedgwood—to whom I have to express my deep obligation for much cordial and valuable assistance throughout my work—three large and thick folio volumes of MS. collections, partly in Josiah Wedgwood's handwriting, but principally in that of his chemist, Alexander Chisholm, on chemicals, metals, and kindred subjects, which show pretty forcibly the great attention which must have been paid to these important matters. In one of these volumes is a long list of scientific books, with the note, "Those marked O are in our collection," which evidently must have been a "collection" of no little importance.

One great result of Wedgwood's labours—indeed, one of the greatest—was the production in 1766 of the fine black ware, which he called "Basaltes" or "Egyptian." In this ware he produced, even in those early days, many fine pieces of work, and of a quality which only his own careful hand could afterwards improve. The other important bodies—the jasper, the white stone, the cane-coloured, and the mortar, &c.,—followed in succession, each producing its beauties, and each being specially adapted for the purposes for which, by his master mind, it had been intended. Each, too, found its imitators among the potters of the district, who, envious of his success, were not slow to follow as closely as might be in his steps. Not one of these varieties of ware did Wedgwood patent, but with that liberality of mind which ever characterised him, he was willing that all who cared to make the bodies he had invented should do so. He was content with the knowledge of his own superiority—a superiority which he ever maintained over all his many competitors.

CHAPTER X.

JOSIAH WEDGWOOD'S INVENTIONS AND DISCOVERIES.—TERRA COTTA.—BASALTES, WHITE PORCELAIN BISCUIT, JASPER, BAMBOO AND MORTAR WARES. — IMITATION AGATE AND MARBLE.—MR. S. C. HALL'S COLLECTION.—WEDGWOOD DETERMINES UPON REMOVING FROM BURSLEM. — PURCHASES THE RIDGE HOUSE ESTATE.—ERECTION OF THE "BLACK WORKS."—TAKES THOMAS BENTLEY INTO PARTNERSHIP.—NOTICE OF THE BENTLEYS.—THE "OCTAGON" CHAPEL AT LIVERPOOL. — WEDGWOOD AND BENTLEY. — "ETRURIA" WORKS. —BUILDING OF ETRURIA HALL.—FOUNDING AND BUILDING OF THE VILLAGE OF ETRURIA.—ETRUSCAN VASES, —SIR WILLIAM HAMILTON.—COUNT CAYLUS.—WEDGWOOD DECLINES TO SECURE HIS INVENTIONS BY PATENT-RIGHT.—TAKES OUT THE ONLY PATENT HE EVER APPLIED FOR.—SPECIFICATION FOR ENCAUSTIC PAINTING, ETC.

THE characteristic properties of the different varieties of wares to which I alluded at the close of the last chapter as having been introduced in rapid succession by Josiah Wedgwood, were thus described by himself; and I cannot, therefore, do better than quote his own words:—

"1. A *terra-cotta;* resembling porphyry, granite, Egyptian pebble, and other beautiful stones of the silicious or crystalline order.

"2. *Basaltes* or black ware; a black porcelain biscuit of nearly the same properties with the natural stone; striking fire with steel, receiving a high polish, serving as a touchstone for metals, resisting all the acids, and bearing without injury a strong fire: stronger, indeed, than the basaltes itself.

"3. *White porcelain biscuit,* of a smooth, wax-like surface, of the same properties with the preceding, except in what depends upon colour.

"4. *Jasper;* a white porcelain biscuit of exquisite beauty and delicacy, possessing the general properties of the basaltes, together with the singular one of receiving through its whole substance, from the admixture of metallic calces with the other materials, the same colours which those calces communicate to glass or enamels in fusion; a property which no other porcelain or earthenware body of ancient or modern composition has been found to possess. This renders it peculiarly fit for making cameos, portraits, and all subjects in bas-relief, as the ground may be of any particular colour, while the raised figures are of a pure white.

"5. *Bamboo,* or cane-coloured biscuit porcelain, of the same nature as No. 3.

"6. A *porcelain biscuit,* remarkable for great hardness, little inferior to that of agate This property, together with its resistance to the strongest acids and corrosives, and its impenetrability by every known liquid, adapts it for mortars and many different kinds of chemical vessels.

"These six distinct species, with the Queen's Ware already mentioned, expanded by the industry and ingenuity of the different manufacturers into an infinity of forms for ornament and use, variously painted and embellished, constitute nearly the whole of the present fine English earthenwares and porcelain, which are now become the source of a very extensive trade, and which, considered as an object of national art, industry, and commerce, may be ranked amongst the most important manufactures of the kingdom."

In the first of these bodies Wedgwood produced some marvellously fine ornamental vases, in imitation of porphyry, granite, various marbles, agates, and other stones, and decorated with medallions, festoons, &c., in white, or gilt. The material was so exceeding hard, that it would bear grinding and working by the lapidary, and took as good and fine a polish as the stone itself. I have in my own possession some small pieces of Wedgwood's producing which have been thus ground and polished, and present as fine a surface as could well be got from the hardest marble.

Some examples of vases in this material are shown in the accompanying woodcut. In this engraving the centre vase, belonging to Mr. Oliver, is a fine example, twelve inches high. It has on its front a medallion of "Cupid Shaving his bow," after Correggio, which, with the heads, &c., is gilt. The other two, one of which has the handles and festoons, and the other the medallion, in white, are from my own

collection, and are excellent and characteristic examples. In the collections of Mr. S. C. Hall, Mr. Mayer, Mr. Marjoribanks, Mr. Rathbone, and others, as well as in different museums, may be seen splendid examples of vases, &c., in this beautiful material.

Of the black ware or basaltes, an infinite variety of goods was in the course of a very few years produced. Of a dense and compact body, hard enough to strike fire when struck on steel, capable of receiving and retaining a high polish, untouched by acid or metal, bearing a much more intense heat than the stone itself, of the deepest and purest colour, and yet having a surface as soft, delicate, and smooth as an infant's flesh, this material was capable of being moulded and used in a variety of ways, and of producing works of the highest and most exquisite order.

A group of examples of this "black ware," which I have selected from the extensive collection of Mr. S. C. Hall, is given in the accompanying engraving; and later on I shall have occasion to speak of other varieties of this truly admir-

able ware, and to again refer to Mr. Hall's collection—a collection which is, unquestionably, one of the finest and most valuable in existence.

In 1766, the same year in which so many other important events connected with Wedgwood took place, he determined upon the purchase of an estate, and the founding of works of a commensurate character with the rapidly increasing extent of his commercial transactions. Foiled in his attempt to purchase the pot-works, &c., at Burslem, and fully impressed with the importance of having his manufactory close to the canal in whose formation he had taken so prominent a part, he fixed his mind upon an estate in the township of Shelton, two miles distant from Burslem, which he considered to be the best adapted of any in the locality.

for this purpose. This estate, called the "Ridge House Estate," lay most advantageously for his projected works, being intersected by the proposed canal, and offering many facilities for his manufacture which others did not possess; and with that quickness of decision which always marked his character, he determined to possess it at any risk. It was at this time in possession of a life tenant, with reversion to a gentleman then in Ireland. To Ireland Mr. Wedgwood at once despatched a trusty and professional friend, who completed the purchase to his entire satisfaction, and, changing the rent into an annuity for the life of the then proprietor, he came into immediate possession. "This land," says the contemporary manuscript from which I have before quoted, "had little to recommend it but conveniency of situation. It was naturally an indifferent soil, and had been neglected for many years. Mr. Wedgwood, now in the new situation of a cultivator of the earth, did not live long in the desert without converting it into a garden; and the taste which he displayed in moulding anew the exterior surface, while he removed its sterility in the disposition of extensive plantations, and laying out the ground for varying the prospects, has a just correspondence with the simplicity and true elegance of his other works. This tract of country, of a cold, clayey nature, seemed before to be despaired of by its inhabitants, who thought it little worth but for the materials it furnished for the manufactories; but since this example, and the making of good roads, it has gradually assumed that smiling aspect which usually accompanies prosperous industry."

Having secured this desirable estate, Wedgwood in the succeeding year, 1767, commenced building the "Black Works," near the canal side. By the "Black Works," I mean, of course, the works intended for the production of the black "basaltes" and ornamental wares. Like Brindley, who cut an underground canal tunnel from his coal pits to the main canal at Harecastle, Wedgwood cut branches into his own pot-works for conveniency of landing the raw materials, and for the despatch of his finished goods to various parts of the kingdom. These "Black Works," in their present state—and it must be mentioned that they are scarcely, if at all, different from the time when they were

THE "BLACK WORKS," ETRURIA.

first erected—are shown, with the branch canal in front, in the accompanying view, which has been specially taken for the purpose.

In the succeeding year, 1768, Josiah Wedgwood, finding more and more that to be successful in his designs it was necessary that he himself should be stationary with his workmen, who possessed no principles of art save such as he was constantly instilling into their minds, determined upon making a change in his establishment, which he soon afterwards happily carried out. Everything in the ornamental portion of his works required the most scrupulous personal attention, for the slightest deviation from the model or drawing of an ornamental vessel would be fatal to its success, and irretrievably mar its beauty. Much also had to be done abroad. To accommodate the ordinary productions of a manufactory to the wants of civil life, there is necessary an intimate knowledge of its customs and manners. To succeed in a profession of art, it is proper to know at least the prevailing taste of the age, the works of contemporaries, and occasionally to sharpen the fancy and skill of the artist by a collision with the talents of others.

Mr. Wedgwood found this employment incompatible with the avocations of his manufactory, though we must not infer from hence that he had any reluctance to go into society. By the habit of never quitting any object till he had completely effected his purpose, by arrangement, and a careful distribution of his time, he never wanted leisure for the service of his friends, and came often to the social circle with an unclouded mind. This was so visible that some of his neighbours, who were witnesses to the progress of his works, expressed their surprise that he should have so much time to spare.

In this situation he opened his views to his friend Mr. Bentley, and proffered to him a partnership in this branch of his manufactory, which was called the *ornamental*, to distinguish it from that of the Queen's ware, which was called the *useful*, and in which Mr. Bentley had no part.

"This gentleman, in taste devoted rather to literature than the drudgery of commerce, of a lively imagination, and a warm and affectionate heart, found in this proposal what at once suited his disposition and gratified his feelings; and thus took place, on the principle of mutual regard, as much as upon those of mutual interest, an intimate union between two deserving men, who, having been inseparable in their subsequent lives, ought not to be separated in any account that may be given of one or the other."

Thomas Bentley was the son of Thomas Bentley, and was born at Scropton, in Derbyshire, on the 1st of January,—New Year's Day,—1730, six months before Josiah Wedgwood first saw light. He was, I believe, brought up at Manchester, and afterwards removed to Liverpool, where, in partnership with a Mr. Boardman, he commenced business as a Manchester warehouseman, under the style of "Bentley and Boardman." In 1766 their names, as Manchester warehousemen, occur in Gore's Directory—the first Directory of Liverpool ever prepared, and now a very scarce and curious work. In 1754 he married, for his first wife, Hannah Oates, of Sheffield, but in the course of a short time became a widower.

In Liverpool Messrs. Bentley and Boardman became agents for Josiah Wedgwood, and this agency continued to be carried on during the time of Bentley's partnership with Wedgwood. The two partners (Bentley and Boardman) lived together in a house in Paradise Street (then the fashionable quarter of Liverpool, and so called from the charms of its situation), since known as the "Cloth Mart," opposite College Lane; and here Mr. Bentley's refined taste and genial habits drew around him an intellectual circle of friends. Dr. Priestley, who then held one of the professorships in the celebrated Warrington Academy (of which academy Bentley was one of the founders), James Brindley, the engineer, John Wyke, "famous for instruments in the watch way," as he is curiously described in the account of his second marriage, in 1768, and one of the founders of the Liverpool Institution, Dr. Turner, an eminent chemist and man of letters, Thomas Chubbard, the portrait painter, Peter Burdett, the engraver, Dr. Clayton, the minister of the Octagon Chapel, and many others, were among his friends and visitors.

In 1757 Thomas Bentley was one of the founders of the Presbyterian Academy at Warrington, which was started on the decay of the famous academies at Findern and Kendal. In the following year, 1758, he was one of the founders of the Liverpool Library; and in 1763 was the originator of a religious society, for whose worship an edifice of octagonal form was erected in Temple Court, and from whence the sect took its curious but appropriate name of "Octagonians." This sect, which was said to be founded for the improvement of religious worship, was, I believe, principally composed of Presbyterians, and had a liturgy specially drawn up for its members. Dr. Clayton, of London, a man of great eminence in his day, was engaged as minister; but the society, after Bentley's removal from Liverpool, seems rapidly to have waned, and in 1776, the chapel was sold. This result was very mortifying to Mr. Bentley, who thus wrote to Mr. Boardman concerning it:—

"I have received a very mortifying letter on the subject of the sale of the Octagon. I cannot understand the principle upon which that institution has been sacrificed, but I am sure if the gentlemen had not been unnecessarily precipitate, and had thought proper to consult their distant friends upon the subject before they had consented to ruin the noblest institution of the kind that has been established, it need not have been given up.

"Considering the pains I have always taken upon this matter, and the many years, I may say, I have spent upon it, I ought in decency to have had some intimation of the state of things before so fatal a determination was made, and especially as I had neither dropped my subscription nor cooled in my affections for that respectable society. But it has been otherwise managed, and at this distance I cannot be active in the matter. I can only lament the loss of an institution favourable to virtue and social worship. . . . . If others who have had much greater benefit from the institution than myself had felt the advantage of it as strongly as I have always done, I am sure it would not have been abandoned."

While Bentley was a resident in Liverpool he was a staunch and unswerving opponent of the slave trade; and this principle, so creditable to him, but so completely at variance with that of the money-making shippers and merchants of those days, made him far from popular. Had he sought *popularity* in the town of his adoption he would have been in favour of the slave trade and of the part which England was taking in the American war; but he chose "the better part;" and taking the enlightened side of religion and humanity, gained for himself, by his pursuits and his principles, a name which is an honour to his country. It is interesting, in connection with this allusion to the slave trade, to remark, that one of the most successful of Wedgwood and Bentley's smaller productions—or, rather, one which took fastest hold on the popular mind—was a small medallion, on which was represented a chained negro kneeling in a supplicating attitude, and having above him the words, "AM I NOT A MAN AND A BROTHER." This medallion was produced of various sizes and in a variety of ways, and has been, in later days, constantly copied in one form or other for purposes of illustration.

In 1768, as I have shown, Thomas Bentley became the partner, after being the Liverpool agent, of Josiah Wedgwood; and from this point the future of his short history—for he lived but twelve years to enjoy his new and useful sphere of life—will be best mixed in with my narrative as it proceeds.

In January, 1768, it appears from one of Wedgwood's letters, in which he discusses the elevation of the "Useful Works," the "Black Works" may probably have been completed, and both the more extensive manufactory and the mansion were soon afterwards commenced, and were so rapidly carried forward that by November the hall was up "plinth high," and in the following year, or 1770, were both finished. Throwing aside its previous name of "Ridge House," Wedgwood, with that refinement of tase and feeling which characterised his every action and thought, named his newly-acquired estate, with its manufactory and hall, "ETRURIA"—a name to which, for purity of taste, beauty of execution, and excellence of body, its productions, under his fostering care, eminently entitled it.

The ETRURIA WORKS were in those days—as, indeed, with but few exceptions, they are now—the most extensive in existence. Planned with the master-mind of Wedgwood, with his practical and practised eye to direct every part, the arrangement of the new manufactory was the most complete of its kind which the world had yet seen: and the world was not long in acknowledging the debt of gratitude which was owing to its founder. No sooner were the works "set in order," and filled with a staff of skilled workmen, than all were fully employed; and it is pleasant to add, that from the day of their opening down to the present hour—in midst of all the many changes which have taken place around them—they remain as they were, fully occupied and fully employed in the production of both the staple branches for which they were founded—the "ornamental ware" and the "useful ware."

The building of the manufactory and the residence for himself was not, however, sufficient for Wedgwood to do. To be comfortable himself, he must know that those around him were comfortable also; to be happy, he must impart happiness to others, even the most lowly of his employés; to sit at ease in his own new home, he must know that those he employed were well and cosily housed. He therefore set about building a village for his workmen and their families, and it is pleasant to add that of late years, since the establishment of locomotives, this village, formed for the workpeople of one establishment, has its station on the main line of the North Staffordshire Railway. The works, which are enclosed in walls on all sides, except where bounded by the canal, which parts them from the lawn of the hall, occupy about seven acres of ground. The village, at its upper end, closely adjoins the manufactory, and consists principally of one long straight street, reaching down to the railway bridge. Etruria contains, I believe, one hundred and twenty-five numbered houses, and about half as many unnumbered ones, and of course a proportionate number of inhabitants, nearly the whole of whom are employed by the Wedgwoods; as were their predecessors—in numberless instances their fathers or grandfathers—by Josiah Wedgwood, its founder and builder. Of its present state, however, I shall have more to say anon.

With Bentley now fairly joined with him in business, Wedgwood had more leisure to apply himself undividedly to his favourite projects for improvement of the Ceramic Arts; and his successes were rapid, as they were varied and surprising. He lost no opportunity of making himself acquainted with specimens of ancient art—Grecian, Roman, or Etruscan—and of studying, not only their forms and decoration, but the composition of their bodies; and collectors and connoisseurs were only too glad to lend him their aid, by entrusting their treasures to his hands. With his great chemical skill, his practical and systematic searchings into the properties of different clays and other materials, his perfect knowledge of the effect of heat in its various degrees, and his almost boundless knowledge of everything relating to his art, and to science generally, he was soon enabled to produce vases comparable with the best period of ancient Etruscan Art.

Of the manner in which he was indebted to Sir William Hamilton's great work, and Sir William to him, the interesting manuscript to which I have more than once alluded in my memoir, says—"We believe that Mr. Wedgwood was the first artist in this country who conceived the design of thus making general the works of long past ages, and he was enabled to carry it into effect by the liberal disposition of the nobility, who opened their cabinets to his use, and permitted him to copy the first specimens of art they had purchased in their travels, with patriotic views. Mr. Bentley, too, situated in London, the great emporium of arts, as of commerce, was very successful in forming other collections, and assisted him in classing them. It will be remembered by many of our contemporaries, that almost all our ideas of taste were borrowed from our neighbours, the French, who, disdaining the study of antiquity, had established a peculiar style, and aspired to the distinctive character of a school of art; till at length, by the unwearied researches and nice discernment of Sir William Hamilton, we were enabled to avail ourselves of a direct application to the fine works of an age when the arts were in so high a state of cultivation, that we must yet despair of excelling, and can but rarely succeed in copying them. Sir William's justly celebrated publication will remain for ever a monument of his patriotism and of his taste; but his labours would not probably have been attended with their full and proper advantages to society, without the aid of Mr. Wedgwood, who diffused the knowledge of these fine models throughout the world, and brought them within the reach of every artist. Those who have given attention to the subject, must feel the difficulty of making a good copy of a fine form, where the slightest deviation destroys the effect. The most minute exactness will not always be sufficient, for some essential thing will escape it unless the artist is capable of comprehending the original intention, is conscious of each beauty as he proceeds, and is warmed with his subject. In addition to these talents others were necessary to a successful imitation of the vases of ancient Etruria, which the industry and energy of Sir William Hamilton had rescued from the oblivion of ages. The art of painting them in durable colours, without the shining appearance of enamel that offends the critical eye, had been lost, it is supposed, ever since the time of Pliny. The ingenious Count Caylus had supplied this desideratum of the moderns in another branch of painting, by the discovery of colours that, applied on canvas by the mediation of wax, made encaustic pictures in the ancient manner. Under the discouraging judgment of all the antiquaries and connoisseurs who spoke upon the subject at that time, and who gave up the art as irretrievable, Wedgwood had the good fortune to produce the same effects in paintings burnt in upon porcelain with a red heat. The colours he made for this purpose had also another advantage; they never spread in the fire, or ran out of the drawing as other enamels must necessarily do, in a greater or less degree, in consequence of their vitrifying and melting upon the piece.

"Mr. Wedgwood was advised by his friends to take out a patent for this discovery, and it was the only one he ever had. He procured it in this instance, not probably with the full consent of his own mind; for at other times when patents have been the subject of conversation among his friends, accompanied with marks of surprise that he did not avail himself of that privilege, he has said that he was content with the advantages he had, and better pleased to see thousands made happy and following him in the same career, than he could be at any exclusive enjoyment."

This principle actuated him throughout the whole of his career, and this and his other noble qualities it is, as well as his intrinsic merit as a producer of wares unapproached for excellence by any other, that has cast such a halo around his memory. The patent of which I have just spoken was granted on the 16th of November, 1769. As it is the only one which he ever applied for, and as, on this ground, as well as for the important matter which it contains, it possesses considerable interest, I here give the specification entire which Wedgwood duly enrolled, after it had been drawn up by himself.

"To all to whom these presents shall come, I, JOSIAH WEDGWOOD, of Burslem, in the County of Stafford, Potter to Her most Excellent Majesty the Queen, send greeting:

"WHEREAS His most Excellent Majesty King George the Third did, by His Letters Patent under the Great Seal of Great Britain, bearing date the Sixteenth day of November, in the tenth year of His reign, give and grant unto me, the said Josiah Wedgwood, His especial licence, that I, the said Josiah Wedgwood, during the term of years therein expressed, should and lawfully might use, exercise, and vend within England, Wales, and town of Berwick-upon-Tweed, my Invention for 'The Purpose of Ornamenting Earthen and Porcelaine Ware with an Encaustic Gold Bronze, together with a peculiar species of Encaustic Painting in Various Colours in Imitation of the Antient Etruscan and Roman Earthenware;' in which said Letters Patent there is contained a provisoe obliging me, the said Josiah Wedgwood, under my hand and seal, to cause a particular description of the nature of my said invention, and how the same is to be performed, to be enrolled in His Majesty's High Court of Chancery within four calendar months after the date of the said recited Letters Patent, as in and by the same (relation being thereunto had) may more fully and at large appear.

"NOW KNOW YE that, in compliance with the said provisoe, I, the said Josiah Wedgwood, do hereby declare that my said invention for the Purpose of Ornamenting Earthen and Porcelaine Ware with an Encaustic Gold Bronze, together with a peculiar species of Encaustic Painting in Various Colours, in Imitation of the Antient Etruscan and Roman Earthenware, is described in the manner following (that is to say):—

"First Process, or Preparation of the Ingredients.

"No. 1. A white Earth from Ayoree, in North America. Calcine this in a red heat about half an hour.

"No. 2. Bronze powder. Dissolve one ounce of pure gold in aqu. rega., precipitate it with copper, then wash the precipitate with hot water till it is sweet or clean from the acid, dry it, and lay it up for use.

"No. 3. Take two ounces of crude antimony livigated, two ounces of tin ashes, and six ounces of white lead; mix them well together, and calcine them in a potter's furnace along with gloss cream-coloured ware.

"No. 4: Take eight ounces of good smalts, one ounce of roasted borax, four ounces of red lead, one ounce of nitre; mix the ingredients well together, and fire them in a crucible in a potter's bisket oven.

"No. 5. Take English copperas or vitriol of iron, calcine it in a moderate red heat about two hours, then wash it in hot water till it is sweet, dry it, and lay it up for use.

"No. 6. White lead.

"No. 7. Flint calcined and ground.

"No. 8. Manganese.

"No. 9. Zaffer.

"No. 10. Copper calcined to blackness.

"Second Process, or Compounding and Mixing the Colours.

"Shineing Black.—A. Three ounces No. 8, three ounces No. 9, three ounces No. 10, eleven ounces No. 6, six ounces of the green F.

"Red.—B. Two ounces No. 1, two ounces No. 3, one ounce No. 5, three ounces No. 6.

"Orange.—C. Two ounces No. 1, fourteen ounces No. 3, half an ounce No. 5, four ounces No. 6.

"Dry Black.—D. One ounce No. 4, two ounces No. 8.

"White.—E. Two ounces No. 1, two ounces No. 6.

"Green.—F. One ounce No. 1, two ounces No. 3, five ounces No. 4.

"Blue.—G. One ounce No. 1, five ounces No. 4.

"Yellow.—H. No. 3 alone.

"THIRD PROCESS, OR APPLICATION OF THE ENCAUSTIC BRONZE AND COLOURS.

"*Application of the Bronze.*

"I. When the vessels are finished ready for burning, and before they are quite dry, grind some of the powder No. 2 in oyl of turpentine, and apply it to the vessels or figures with a spunge or pencil, to imitate bronze in such manner as your fancy directs; polish this powder upon the vessel or figure, and burn it in such a furnace, and to such a degree of heat as is necessary for the ware. After it is burnt, burnish the bronze upon the vessels to what degree you please, and the process is finished.

"*Another method of applying the bronze after the ware is fired Bisket, as some figures or vessels may be too delicate to bear the process* I.

"K. Take four ounces No. 6 and ounce No. 7, grind them well together, spread this very thin with a spunge or pencil over the ware to be bronzed, and fire it till this layer of size is fluxed, which may be done in a potter's furnace; then take the powder No. 2, and apply it to the vessel as before directed; then burn the ware over again till the powder adheres to the size; burnish, &c., as before.

"*Application of the Shineing Black upon Red Vessels in the Manner of the Antique Etruscan Vases.*

"L. Take the colour A, grind it very fine with oyl of turpentine, and with it trace the outlines of the design you intend to have upon the vessel, then fill up the vacant spaces very even, and shade the drapery, &c. Fire the vessels in a heat sufficient to flux the black, and they are finished.

"M. Another method to produce a different effect with the same colour, in the manner of the Etruscans, is to paint the design with black, laid on as dead colouring upon red bisket ware, and to cut up or finish the design with red and other colours, for which purpose the above-mentioned ones are prepared; they must also be ground in oyl of turpentine, and burnt upon the vessels in a muffle or enamel kiln.

"N. Another method to produce in a more expeditious way nearly the effect of the process L. Take the red B or the orange C, and lay in your design with it, as a dead colour upon black bisket vessels, and shade it with the black D, with or without the addition of any of the other colours, firing them upon the vessels as before directed.

"In witness whereof, I, the said Josiah Wedgwood, have hereunto set my hand and seal the thirteenth day of March, one thousand seven hundred and seventy.

"JOSIAH WEDGWOOD. (L.S.)

"And be it remembered, that on the same thirteenth day of March, in the year last above mentioned, the aforesaid Josiah Wedgwood came before our said Lord the King in His Chancery, and acknowledged the Specification, and all and everything therein contained in form above written. And also the Specification aforesaid was stampt according to the tenor of the Statute made in the sixth year of the reign of the late King and Queen William and Mary of England and so forth.

"Inrolled the fourteenth day of March, in the year above written.

"P. HOLFORD."

Examples of the vases made under this patent—which was to secure his invention "for the purpose of ornamenting earthen and porcelain ware with an encaustic gold bronze, together with a peculiar species of encaustic painting in various colours, in imitation of the ancient Etruscan earthenware," to himself—are to be found in many collections, and I shall have more to say of them in my next chapter.

CHAPTER XI.

WEDGWOOD AND BENTLEY.—OPENING OF THE ETRURIA WORKS.—FIRST PRODUCTIONS OF THE WORKS THROWN BY JOSIAH WEDGWOOD WHILE BENTLEY TURNED THE WHEEL.—ETRUSCAN, OR ENCAUSTIC VASES.—ESTABLISHES WORKS AT CHELSEA.—WORKMEN ENGAGED THERE.—FIRST TEAPOT MADE AT ETRURIA.—CHINESE PORTRAIT MODELLER.—AUDIENCE OF THE KING AND QUEEN.—CATHERINE THE GREAT OF RUSSIA.—SERVICE FOR THE GRENOUILLIERE PALACE.—THOMAS BENTLEY'S SECOND MARRIAGE.—THE STAMFORD AND CROMPTON FAMILIES.—WEDGWOOD AND BENTLEY'S FIRST CATALOGUE.—BLACK AND WHITE MEDALLIONS.—INTRODUCTION OF "JASPER WARE."—DECLARATION OF NOBLE PRINCIPLES.—THE. WEDGWOOD INKSTAND.—EYE CUPS AND CLOSET PANS.—LETTER FROM JOSIAH WEDGWOOD TO HIS COUSIN THOMAS.

In 1769 the works at Etruria were opened, and on the 13th of June in that year the first productions of the manufactory were thrown. On that day might have been seen gathered together in one of the rooms of the "Black Works" such a group of persons as would have made a painter's heart glad—such as would have been a fit subject for the painter of the orrery and the air-pump* to have revelled in, and such as I hope yet to see treated by a "master hand." Here sat the great Josiah Wedgwood—great in fame, great in reputation, great in worldly goods, but greater far in mind and intellect, and in nobleness of character—at the potter's bench, his bare arms encircling the ball of pliant clay, while his busy fingers and practised eye formed it into classic shape; and there stood his partner, Thomas Bentley, at the potter's wheel, which he turned with a care suited to the auspicious occasion and to the requirements of his great

* Wright, of Derby.

chief. Standing by, no doubt, and watching with pleasureable anxiety the progress of the work, were Mrs. Wedgwood and many friends; while on the board in front of the "father of potters" would be ranged the urns as he produced them.

The vases thus formed, of Etruscan shape, went through all the subsequent processes of baking, &c., and were ultimately painted in the purest Etruscan style, with figures, and each piece bore this appropriate inscription :—

JUNE XIII. MDCCLXIX.
ONE OF THE FIRST DAY'S PRODUCTIONS
AT
ETRURIA, IN STAFFORDSHIRE,
BY
WEDGWOOD AND BENTLEY.
ARTES ETRURIÆ RENASCUNTER.

Three of these vases—the historical interest attaching to which it is impossible to overrate—are in the possession of Mr. Francis Wedgwood, of Barlaston, through whose courtesy I am enabled to engrave two of them for my readers. These two are shown in the engraving on the following page, from sketches recently made by myself, and I have so arranged them as to show the inscription on one vase, and a group of figures on the other. The body, "Basaltes," is hard, of a slightly bluish tinge, with the surface, of course, like the original Etruscan, black. On this the figures and inscriptions are painted in red. The vases are respectively ten inches, and ten and a half inches, in height. Each one bears a group—differing from the others—of Hercules and his companions in the garden of the Hesperides, on its front; and beneath, the appropriate inscription of

ARTES ETRURIÆ RENASCUNTER.

On the opposite side of each is the inscription given above, and around the lid and upper portion are characteristic and elegant borders. Each vase is labelled, in Josiah Wedgwood's own handwriting, "Part of Plate 129, vol. i. of Hamilton's Antiq. Hercules and his Companions in the Garden of the Hesperides."

Similar vases to these, it is recorded, were deposited under the foundation of one of the wings of Etruria Hall.

Like every other production of the inimitable Wedgwood, these Etruscan vases—the "peculiar species of encaustic painting in various colours, in imitation of the ancient Etruscan and Roman earthenware" which is spoken of in his specification—soon "took" amazingly with the wealthy and influential classes, and produced a taste for the antique

which before did not exist. When they thus became called for in large quantities by the public, it was judged best to have them painted in the neighbourhood of London, where a number of ingenious artists, such as would be required, might more easily be assembled together, and where this species of classical decoration, so entirely in consonance with his taste, might be carried on under the immediate superintendence of Mr. Bentley, whose residence had been fixed in London for the purpose of managing the business there. Accordingly works were established at Chelsea—the locality, doubtless, being fixed upon as being near the then famous Chelsea China Works, where painters would be more easily procured; and I am fortunate in being able, from a document in my possession, to show the names of a portion, at all events, of the artists who were employed there in the month of October, 1770. The document is very fragmentary and imperfect, but, so far as remains, is as follows. The year 1770, it must be borne in mind, was the very year when the Chelsea China Works passed by purchase into the hands of Duesbury, the owner of the Derby China Works, and where, of course, the now much-sought-for "Derby-Chelsea" porcelain was produced.*

Cash paid at Chelsea for Wages.		On J. W.'s Acct.	On W. & B.'s Acct.
1770.		£ *s.* *d.*	£ *s.* *d.*
Oct. 6.	John Lawrence, 6 days..	0 5 3	0 5 3
	Timothy Roberts, 6 days		0 12 0
,, 5.	James Bakewell, 6 days . .	0 16 0	
	Thos. Blomeley's Bill ..	1 0 5	
	Thos. Hutchings, 6 days		1 6 0
	William Roberts, 4 days	0 4 4	
	Nathl. Cooper, 6 days..	0 16 0	
	William Shuter's Bill ..		0 8 0
	Thomas Simcock, 6 days	0 16 0	
	Ralph Wilcocks, 6 days.		
	Mrs. ditto 6 days.		
	John Winstanley, 6 days	0 13 0	
,, 6.	Thomas Barrett,† 5 days	0 7 0	
	Thomas Green, 6 days.		
	Miss Edwards, 6 days.		
	Miss Parkes,‡ 6 days.		
	Mr. Rhodes		
	Ditto for Joe.		
	Ditto for Will.		
	Ditto for Unwin.		

* For an account of these works see *Art-Journal* for January, 1862, and February and April, 1863.

† Or Barnett. ‡ Or Parker.

How long the establishment at Chelsea was continued, I do not know; but painting was done in London for Wedgwood to a late date. In a letter now lying before me, dated February 27th, 1795—the month following Josiah Wedgwood's death—while speaking of painters and enamellers on porcelain, the writer says, "I believe Wedgwood's men here do not get less than 26*s.* or 28*s.* per week."

I have before explained that the partnership of Wedgwood and Bentley had reference only to the *ornamented*, not to the *useful* ware; and it will be seen in the above account, that although the workmen at Chelsea were employed on both branches, the amounts paid them in wages were distinguished as on "Josiah Wedgwood's account," and as on "Wedgwood and Bentley's account." Thus, for instance, John Lawrence, for the week ending October 6th, is paid for six days' work, at 1*s.* 9*d.* a-day, of which 5*s.* 3*d.* is charged to "J. W.," and the other 5*s.* 3*d.* to "W. & B."

An immense number of these Etruscan vases, pateræ, &c., were sold both at home and on the Continent, "where there is scarcely any museum without specimens of them. As this material is undoubtedly as durable as that of the original vases, we may reasonably predict that these too will find their way to very remote posterity, and illustrate the history of our era. Some few of them (and only a few, on account of the expense) were finished with all the art that the age was capable of, and will convey no unfavourable idea of the state of the arts at this time. It may with truth be said that the body is *far more* durable than the antique. It is basaltic, and has this great advantage over the antiques, that whereas they are of a tender, brittle body, this is the hardest body made. It is as durable as mortar material, which is the most durable that any product of clay can be made to arrive at."

At Etruria is preserved a small teapot, of red ware, of what is usually called the "crab-stock pattern," which bears a written label, stating that it is "the first teapot at Josiah Wedgwood's, made by Josiah Wedgwood himself." This piece I show on the accompanying engraving, not because I place credence in the statement, but because it is interesting to note that an example with such a memorandum attached

to it is preserved at the works. I ought to mention that the original spout has been replaced by one of metal.

Mr. Bentley seems to have busied himself, as did also Wedgwood, in seeking out all the talent which could be rendered available for the purposes of the manufactory, and in getting together, by loan or purchase, impressions of intaglios, bas-reliefs, and other specimens of ancient art. And in all this the partners were well and liberally seconded by people of every rank, who appear to have been only too glad to place at their disposal the treasures of their cabinets.

In 1769, on the 4th of November, Bentley thus writes in one of his interesting letters from London:—

"We have been so much taken up of late with fine articles and fine things that I have not had a moment to spare, and am in debt to everybody. We are every day finding out some ingenious man or curious piece of workmanship, all which we endeavour to make subservient to the improvement of our taste or the perfection of our manufacture. I have not time to name the things that we have seen; but one great curiosity I cannot omit, with which we have been highly entertained—I mean a Chinese portrait modeller, lately arrived from Canton; one of those artists who make the mandarin figures that are brought to England, a pair of which you may remember to have seen at Mr. Walley's shop. He intends to stay here some years, is in the Chinese dress, makes portraits (small busts in clay, which he colours), and produces very striking likenesses, with great expedition. I have paid him three visits, and had a good deal of conversation with him, for he speaks some English, and is a good-natured, sensible man, very mild in his temper and gentle in his motions. His dresses are chiefly of satin. I have seen him in crimson and in black. The India figures upon the fans are very just resemblances of the originals. His complexion is very swarthy, but the eyelashes almost always in motion. His arms are very slender, like those of a delicate woman, and his fingers very long; all his limbs extremely supple; his hair is cut off before, and he has a long plaited tail hanging down to the bottom of his back. He has been with the King and Queen, who are much pleased with him, and he is to take the portraits of the royal infantry. I have not time to be more particular now, but he is far the greatest curiosity I have seen. He has ten guineas a-piece for his portraits which are very small."

The patronage of the King and Queen continued to be accorded to Wedgwood in all his new inventions; and this fostering care of his arts was of endless and incalculable benefit to him. On the 15th of December, 1770, dating from *Chelsea*, where their branch works then were, as I have shown, Bentley wrote:—

"Last Monday Mr. Wedgwood and I had the honour of a long audience of their Majesties at the Queen's palace, to present some bas-reliefs her Majesty had ordered, and to show some new improvements, with which they were well pleased. They expressed in the most obliging and condescending manner their attention to our manufacture, and entered very freely into conversation on the further improvement of it, and on many other subjects. The King is well acquainted with business, and with the characters of the principal manufacturers, merchants, and artists; and seems to have the success of all our manufactures much at heart, and to understand the importance of them. The Queen has more sensibility, true politeness, engaging affability, and sweetness of temper, than any great lady I ever had the honour of speaking to."

Wedgwood was about this time honoured by receiving from the Empress Catherine of Russia a commission of extraordinary magnitude. He was directed to make a very large service of Queen's ware for her Majesty's use, and to "paint in black enamel upon each piece a different view of the palaces, seats of the nobility, and other remarkable places in this kingdom. Upon every piece there was also to be painted the image of a green toad or frog, as is elsewhere stated. He was very unwilling to disfigure the service with this reptile, but was told it was not to be dispensed with, because the ware was intended for the use of a palace that bore its name. The idea of such a service was well worthy the mind of a sovereign, but the undertaking seemed a great one for the powers of an individual manufacturer. The number of views necessary, to avoid a repetition of the same subjects, was about twelve hundred, and a great proportion of them were original sketches. He spent three years in making the collection and painting the views upon the pieces of this service, with all the correctness of design and drawing that is necessary to a good picture. The Empress, we have been told, was entirely satisfied with the execution of this work; and no doubt it conveyed to her mind a pretty just sentiment of our national splendour, ingenuity, and character."

A number of very ingenious artists having been got together for completing this service, Mr. Wedgwood was very unwilling to part with them, and "determined to try whether works of such expense would succeed upon his wares, and with this view he continued to employ them some time afterwards. It is believed, however, that their productions of this kind, though unexceptionable in point of merit, have never found a purchaser, even when offered at the exact price that the artists were paid for the painting. The matter was still EARTHENWARE; and was neglected when its modest simple garb was changed for the plumes which seemed more properly to belong to its superior—*porcelain.* This was not the only occasion that brought so mortifying a reflection to the mind of our potter, and induced him to defer many designs till, by improving the quality of his Queen's ware, he should make it less inferior to its rival."

When the Russian service was completed, in 1774, it was exhibited in London, and caused quite a "sensation" among people of taste. Thus Mrs. Delaney, in a letter to Mrs. Port, 1774, says:—

"I am just returned from viewing the Wedgwood ware that is to be sent to the Empress of Russia. It consists, I believe, of as many pieces as there are days in the year, if not hours. They are displayed at a house in Greek Street, Soho, called Portland House. There are three rooms below, and two above, filled with it, laid out on tables; everything that can be wanted to serve a dinner. The ground, the common ware, pale brimstone, the drawings in purple, the borders a wreath of leaves, the middle of each piece a particular view of all the remarkable places in the King's dominions, neatly executed. I suppose it will come to a princely price: it is well for the manufacturer, which I am glad of, as his ingenuity and industry deserve encouragement."

This magnificent service the Empress showed with pride to Lord Malmesbury when he visited the Grenouillière Palace, in 1795.*

In 1772 Thomas Bentley married for his second wife Mary Stamford, of Derby, a lady in every way suited to his taste, and with whom he lived a most happy, though short life. The marriage of Mr. Bentley took place at All Saints' Church, Derby, on the 22nd of June, as will be seen from the following extract from the register of that parish. It will be noticed that in this register he is again described as "of Chelsea," the place where the branch works had been established:—

"Thomas Bentley, of Chelsea, in Middlesex, gentleman and widower, and Mary Stamford, of this parish, spinster, were married in this church by Licence, the Twenty-second day of June, in the

* A cup and saucer of this "Empress's pattern" is preserved in the splendid museum of Mr. Joseph Mayer, of Liverpool.

year of our Lord One Thousand Seven Hundred and Seventy-two, by me,

"JOSH. WINTER. Min^r.

"This marriage was solemnised between us,

"THOMAS BENTLEY.
"MARY STAMFORD.

"In the presence of
"THOMAS STAMFORD,
"MARTHA STAMFORD."

The Stamfords were a family of considerable standing in Derby, and the half-brother of Mrs. Bentley, Thomas Stamford the younger, was mayor of that borough in 1769. Thomas Stamford, the father of Mrs. Bentley, was twice married, she being the issue of the second marriage. His son Thomas was also twice married; by his first wife he had no children, but by his second—who was Sarah, the eldest daughter of John Crompton, of Chorley Hall, of the wide-spread and prosperous family of Crompton, to which Samuel Crompton, "the inventor," Sir Charles Crompton, the present respected judge, and the families still resident in Derby, in Lancashire, and in Yorkshire, belong—he had two daughters, one of whom was married to James Caldwell, Esq., of Linley Wood, Staffordshire, and was the mother of the gifted and popular authoress of "Emilia Wyndham," and many other works—Mrs. Marsh Caldwell.

In 1773 Messrs. Wedgwood and Bentley, whose London warehouse was in Great Newport Street, issued their first catalogue of goods; and as this edition is of excessive rarity, I transcribe its title-page in full for the purpose of comparing it later on with succeeding editions. It is called

"A Catalogue of Cameos, Intaglios, Medals, and Bas-reliefs, with a general account of Vases and other ornaments after the antique; made by Wedgwood and Bentley, and sold at their rooms in Great Newport Street, London.

"'Quoniam et sic gentes nobilitantur.'
"PLIN., lib. XXXV., *De vasis fictilibus.*

"London: printed in the year MDCCLXXIII., and sold by Cadel, in the Strand; Robson, New Bond Street; and Parker, printseller, Cornhill."

This catalogue, which is of much smaller size than the later editions, contains sixty pages, inclusive of introduction, &c., and is so curious as to be well worth reprinting entire. From the introductory portion I make the following important quotation, for the purpose of enabling collectors to arrive at a correct idea of the dates of the production of the various wares for which Wedgwood became so celebrated:—

"The proprietors of this manufactory have been encouraged by the generous attention of the nobility and connoisseurs to their first essays to give it all the extent and improvement they were able, and with constant application and great expense they have now produced a considerable variety of ornaments in different kinds, the merit of which they humbly submit to the judgment of those who are best skilled in these subjects.

"The variety of new articles which many of their respectable friends have not seen, and multitudes of persons of curiosity and taste in the works of art have never heard of, render some account or catalogue of them desirable, and even necessary: but many of the articles, and especially the vases, being of such a nature as not to admit of satisfactory and clear descriptions, several parts of this catalogue can only give a slight and general enumeration of the classes, without descending to particulars.

"We shall, however, hope to make the general enumeration sufficiently intelligible, and descend to particulars where the nature of the subjects admits of it.

"To give an idea of the *nature* and *variety* of the productions of our ornamental works, it will be necessary to point out and describe the various *compositions* of which the forms, &c., are made, and to distinguish and arrange the several productions in suitable *classes*.

'The *compositions*, or bodies, of which the ornamental pieces are made, may be divided into the following branches:—

"I. A composition of *terra-cotta*, resembling porphyry, lapis lazuli, jasper, and other beautiful stones, of the vitrescent or crystalline class.

"II. A fine *black porcelain*, having nearly the same properties as the *basaltes*, resisting the attacks of acids, being a touchstone to copper, silver, and gold, and equal in hardness to agate or porphyry.

"III. A fine white biscuit ware, or *terra-cotta*, polished and unpolished."

By this it will be seen that the only three varieties of ware introduced up to 1773 were the "terra-cotta resembling porphyry, lapis lazuli, jasper, and other beautiful stones, of the vitrescent or crystalline class," such as the imitation porphyry, marble, and other vases, were composed of; the "fine black porcelain, or *basaltes*," so largely used for vases, figures, medallions, and other ornamental purposes, as well as for teapots, &c.; and the "white biscuit ware, or terra-cotta," used both in combination with other materials in the production of vases, medallions, and other decorative pieces, and separately for the manufacture of stands and other ornamental goods. The combination of these two latter bodies will be called to mind by collectors, perhaps, more

easily with regard to medallions than otherwise. In these the oval of the plaque was frequently made of the black "basaltes," and the bust of the white jasper, or terra-cotta. The effect of this, which is most striking and pleasing, is shown in the accompanying illustration.

Another pleasing combination is seen on a small but beautifully engine-turned cup, also in my own collection, where the cup itself is of black and the stand of white. This piece is marked on its under side—

WEDGWOOD
& BENTLEY.

In 1773-4 the *fourth* description of ware which I have enumerated in my last chapter was invented and introduced by Wedgwood, and for the first time makes its appearance in the "Catalogue," in the second edition, published in 1774, where it is thus described:—

"IV. A fine white *terra-cotta*, of great beauty and delicacy, proper for cameos, portraits, and bas-reliefs.

This was the first appearance of what afterwards, as I shall show, became, by constant attention and improvement, the most beautiful of all Wedgwood's productions—the "Jasper ware." It will be perceived that at this date (1774) it was simply spoken of as a "fine white terra-cotta," and that it remained for later years to produce it with its splendid blue and other coloured grounds, with raised white figures and ornaments.

The entry in this catalogue, it will thus be seen, fixes the introduction of this splendid body to 1773-4. In the latest catalogue (1787) this variety, which then had attained its highest perfection, is described at greater length as—

"IV. Jasper—a white porcelain *bisqué* of exquisite beauty and delicacy, possessing the general properties of the basaltes, together with that of receiving colours through its whole substance, in a manner which no other *body*, ancient or modern, has been known to do. This renders it peculiarly fit for cameos, portaits, and all subjects in bas-relief, as the ground may be made of any colour throughout, without paint or enamel, and the raised figures of a pure white."

Of the productions in this ware Wedgwood thus wrote:— "As these are my latest, I hope they will be found to be my most approved, works. Verbal descriptions could give but an imperfect idea of the delicacy of the materials, the execution of the artist, or the general effect, and I must therefore beg leave to refer those who wish for information in these respects to a view of the articles themselves."

Acting upon Wedgwood's excellent advice, although not in strict chronological order, I "refer those" of my readers "who wish for information in these respects, to a view of the articles themselves," in the accompanying engraving of a group of jasper ware, selected from the magnificent collection of Mr. S. C. Hall, to which I have before referred. The group exhibits a few of the many highly characteristic

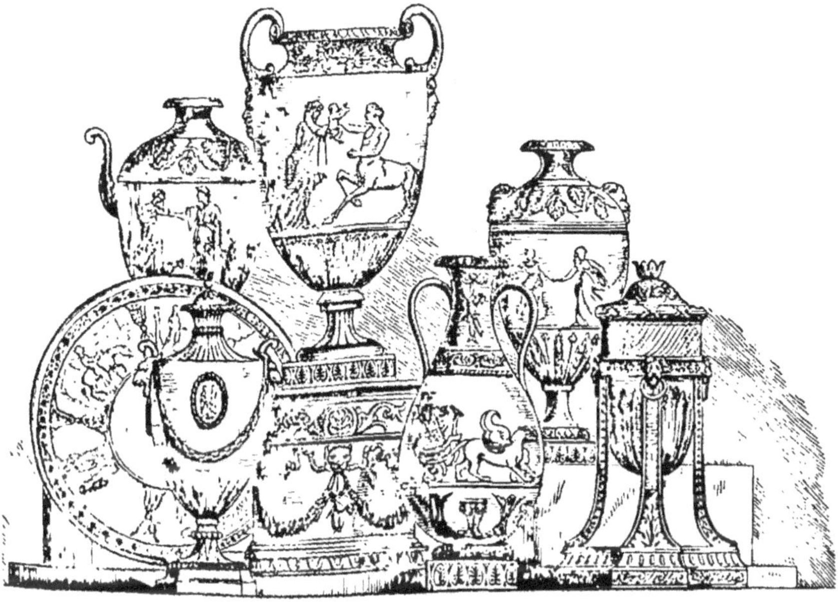

and exquisite examples which have been got together at great cost, and with much judgment and skill, by Mr. Hall.

A further notice of this jasper ware will follow in its proper place, later on in this memoir, when I shall enumerate some of the principal varieties of goods which were produced in it.

In 1774, I have stated, a second edition of their catalogue was issued by Wedgwood and Bentley; and in the same year a third edition of the catalogue translated into the French language, was also issued. In the succeeding year (1775) a re-issue (still called the second edition) of the English catalogue made its appearance, consequent on the change of the

London warehouse from Great Newport Street * to Greek Street, Soho. The re-issue of this second edition is peculiarly interesting, as fixing the introduction of one or two objects for which Wedgwood became famous. At the end of the pamphlet is an addition of six pages, containing an engraving (W. Darling, *sc.*, Newport Street) and an explanation of his newly-invented inkstands and eye-cups; and with a "conclusion" which, from its manly and noble principle, deserves to be perpetuated, and which, therefore, I here give:—

"The proprietors of this manufactory hope it will appear to all those who may have been pleased to attend to its progress, that ever since its establishment it has been continually *improving* both in the variety and in the perfection of its productions.

"A competition for *cheapness*, and not for *excellence of workmanship*, is the most frequent and certain cause of the rapid decay and entire destruction of arts and manufactures.

"The desire of selling much in a little time, without respect to the *taste* or *quality* of the goods, leads manufacturers and merchants to ruin the reputation of the articles which they manufacture and deal in; and whilst those who buy for the sake of a fallacious saving prefer mediocrity to excellence, it will be impossible for manufacturers either to improve or keep up the quality of their works.

"This observation is equally applicable to manufacturers and to the productions of the Fine Arts; but the degradation is more fatal to the latter than the former, for tho' an ordinary piece of goods, for common use, is always dearer than the best of the kind, yet an ordinary and tasteless piece of ornament is not only *dear* at any price, but absolutely *useless* and *ridiculous*.

"All works of art must bear a price in proportion to the skill, the taste, the time, the expence, and the risque attending the invention and execution of them. Those pieces that for these reasons bear the highest price, and which those who are not accustomed to consider the real difficulty and expence of making *fine things* are apt to call *dear*, are, when justly estimated, the *cheapest* articles that can be purchased; and such as are generally attended with much less profit to the artist than those that everybody calls *cheap*.

---

* The warehouse was at the corner of Great Newport Street, facing Long Acre.

"There is another mistake that gentlemen who are not acquainted with the particular difficulties of an art are apt to fall into. They frequently observe that a handsome thing may be made as cheap as an ugly one. A moment's reflection would rectify this opinion.

"The most successful artists know that they can turn out ten ugly and defective things for one that is beautiful and perfect in its kind. Even suppose the artist has the true idea of the kind of beauty at which he aims; how many lame and unsuccessful efforts does he make in his design, and every part of it, before he can please himself? And suppose one piece is well composed and tolerably finished, as in vases and encaustic paintings, for instance, where every succeeding vase, and every picture, is made not in a Mould or by a Stamp, but separately by the Hand, with the same attention and diligence as the first, how difficult must it be to preserve the beauty of the first model?

"It is so difficult that without the constant attention of the master's eye, such variations are frequently made in the form and taste of the work, even while the model is before the workman, as totally change and degrade the character of the piece.

"*Beautiful forms* and *compositions* are not to be made by chance, and they never were made nor can be made in any kind at a small expence; but the proprietors of this manufactory have the satisfaction of knowing, by a careful comparison, that the prices of many of their ornaments are *much lower*, and of all of them *as low* as those of any other ornamental works in Europe, of equal quality and risque, notwithstanding the high price of labour in England, and they are determined rather to give up the making of any article than to degrade it. They do not manufacture for those who estimate works of ornament by their *magnitude*, and who would buy pictures at *so much a foot*. They have been happy in the encouragement and support of many illustrious persons who judge of the works of art by better principles; and so long as they have the honour of being thus patronised, they will endeavour to support and improve the quality and taste of their manufactures."

This admirable and noble principle it was which actuated Wedgwood throughout his career, and which enabled him to produce so many, and such exquisite, specimens of art; and this principle it was which made him so scrupulously careful that none but the most perfect examples should leave his manufactory.

The inkstand to which I have alluded—to which Mr. Gladstone has, for simplicity of construction and efficiency in use, paid so well-merited a tribute—was, then, invented by Wedgwood in 1775, and it is pleasant to know that besides being cared for in the "cabinets of the curious," it is still to be found in use in many places, and is constantly used in the very room, and at the same desk, at which the Great Josiah sat at Etruria.

The "Eye-cups," made of the composition imitating various pebbles, and "sold at one shilling a-piece," were also introduced in the same year, as were also closet pans.

The following letter, addressed by Josiah Wedgwood to his cousin and partner, Thomas Wedgwood, at Etruria, and dated "London, 20th March, 1775," is so full of practical information, and is so highly characteristic of Wedgwood's scrupulous care in all the details of his art, that I cannot better close this chapter than by giving it to my readers:—

"London, 20th March, 1775.

"Dear Cousin,

"I have your good letter of the 17th, and thank you for it.

"The service for Mr. Scott will be sent from hence on Friday or Monday next; and hope he will be pleas'd with the dispatch we shall be able to use in this Commission.

"Messrs. Rabone and Co.'s order with green flowers is finish'd, and waits his orders; but are we to let him know, or will you do it?

"The small pattern boxes shall be sent with the next goods. And with respect to the Cisterns for the Water Closets, I hope they may be made when properly understood, as the Sale for them will, in all probability, be very considerable, and the purchasers will be willing to pay a very good price for them—from 4 to 6 guineas apiece.

"They now give 8 or 10 guineas for marble cisterns, and do not order these of our ware for cheapness, but because they will be *sweeter* than marble ones. You may make them an inch thick, or more if you please; for the architects do not care how thick they are.

"The pipes you mention are not to be made. The plugs sent with the model are meant only to shew that there are to be holes in the Cisterns to fit Cocks or Lead Pipes of the size of the plugs sent. They had not any notion of our Clay shrinking, and therefore sent those wood pegs for us to make the holes with; and where there is any shouldering in the pegs (as I think there is in some of them), the holes should have the same sort of shouldering as that peg would make by thrusting it into the Cistern when made.

"Another thing is necessary for you to observe respecting the wood model sent. It was intended as a *core*, or *model*, for us to form the vessel upon, and they want to have the cisterns, when finish'd, to be of the same shape and size on the inside as the model is on the outside. For, as I mention'd above, they had no idea of our clay shrinking, and so thought, if they furnish'd us with a model to work our clay upon of the size they wanted it, that w[d] be an unerring rule for us. But they are not nice in respect to the size; for half an inch, or even an inch, larger or less than the model will do.

"I think the best method of making your mould will be to chop and make their model rough on the outside, and then coat it with plaister, making the coat as thick as you think will be sufficient to allow for shrinking—that is, if you think it will shrink 4 inches, then you coat it 2 inches thick, taking care to preserve the form of the vessel. And you must likewise allow for shrinking in the size of the holes; for the pegs sent with the model are the real size of the cocks which are made for these cisterns.

"I shall be glad if what I have said above may sufficiently explain this matter to you. I should have wrote this sooner, but expected to have been with you in time for the execution of this order.

"Messrs. B and F's* bills shall be discounted here another time.

"I should have sent some glass, but have had some difference with the man about the price; however, I intend to send some on Friday; and in the meantime I wish Joseph Unwin would buy some Cullet † for them to go on with.

---

* "B and F" would probably be Messrs. Boulton & Fothergill, of the Soho Works, Birmingham, with whom Wedgwood was in many ways connected.

† *Cullett* is broken glass, which was much bought and used by potters.

"We have an order from the Duke of Athol for a Dinner and Dessert, Tea and Coffee service, enamel'd, all of which are to be plain, except 12 teacups and sars, unhandled, about the size of the drawing on the other side.* We sh[d] be glad to have a few doz[ns] by the next waggon, as we have only a month from this time allow'd us to get them done.

"I have had a letter from Mr. Green, but not satisfactory, and I intend to write to him again.

"The American affairs will not be settled at present. Our Rulers seem determined to try an experiment upon the Continent; and a very ruinous one I am afraid it will prove. All we can do seems to be to wait, though it must be with considerable anxiety, the very important and interesting event.

"Be so good to give my respects to all friends, and tell Mr. Cox we have just now rec[d] a pair of brown pebble (say jasper) vase candlesticks in No. 81: the best pebble we ever had, and we wish to have more of them—8 or 10 doz. of Candlesticks, and other vases, as soon as may be.

"I am, Dear Cousin,

"Yrs affectionately,

"JOS. WEDGWOOD."

---

* The "drawing on the other side" is a slight pencil sketch, by Josiah Wedgwood, showing the diameter of the cup to be 3½ inches, and its height 2 inches.

CHAPTER XII.

WILLIAM COOKWORTHY DISCOVERS THE USE OF CORNISH CLAY AND CORNISH STONE.—MEMOIR OF COOKWORTHY.—HIS ACCOUNT OF HIS DISCOVERIES.—ESTABLISHES WORKS AT PLYMOUTH.—PLYMOUTH CHINA.—TAKES OUT A PATENT. SUCCESS OF THE WORKS.—EMPLOYS ARTISTS FROM SEVRES AND DRESDEN.—DECLINE OF THE WORKS.—ASSIGNMENT TO RICHARD CHAMPION, OF BRISTOL.—REMOVAL OF THE CHINA WORKS FROM PLYMOUTH TO BRISTOL.—ACT OF PARLIAMENT FOR EXTENDING TERM OF PATENT RIGHT.

In 1755, Richard Champion, of Bristol, having in the previous year become possessed of the patent of William Cookworthy, of Plymouth, for the making of china, applied on the 22nd of February, by petition to parliament, for an extension of the term of patent right in the use of the raw materials—the Cornish stone and clay, and the manufacture of porcelain. To this application Wedgwood, on behalf of himself and the potters of Staffordshire, made an energetic and determined opposition, with, however, but partial success. This being the case, and the matter being one of vital importance not only to himself but to potters generally, resulting, in fact, in the first introduction of the manufacture of china into Staffordshire, and being the first discovery of the use of Cornish clay and stone in the potter's art, renders some account of Cookworthy and his discoveries necessary in this place.

William Cookworthy was born at Kingsbridge, not many miles from Plymouth, on the 12th of April, 1705, his parents being William and Edith Cookworthy, who were Quakers. His father was a weaver, and died leaving his family but ill provided for, in 1718. Thus young Cookworthy, at the age of thirteen, and with six younger brothers and sisters—for he was the eldest of the family of seven—was left fatherless. His mother entered upon her heavy task of providing for and maintaining her large family with true courage, and appears to have succeeded in working out a good position for them all. She betook herself to dress-making, and as her little daughters grew old enough to handle the needle, they were taught to aid her, and thus she maintained them in comparative comfort. In the following spring, at the age of fourteen, young Cookworthy was apprenticed to a chemist in London, named Bevans; but his mother's means being too scanty to admit of his being sent to the metropolis in any other way, he was compelled to walk there on foot. This task, no light one in those days, a hundred and fifty years ago, or now, for a boy of fourteen, he successfully accomplished.

His apprenticeship he appears to have passed with extreme credit, and on its termination returned into Devonshire, not only with the good opinion, but with the co-operation of his late master, and commenced business in Nutt-street, Plymouth, as wholesale chemist and druggist, under the name of Bevans and Cookworthy. Here he gradually worked his way forward, and became one of the little knot of intelligent men who in those days met regularly together at each other's houses, of whom Cookworthy, Dr. Huxham, Dr. Mudge, and the elder Northcote were amongst the most celebrated. Here he brought his mother to live under his roof, and she became by her excellent and charitable character a general favourite among the leading people of the place, and was looked up to with great respect by the lower classes whom she benefited. In 1735 Cookworthy married a young Quaker lady of Somersetshire, named Berry. This lady, to whom he seems to have been most deeply attached, lived only ten years after their marriage, and left him with five little daughters, and Cookworthy remained a widower for the remaining thirty-five years of his life.

In 1745 his attention seems first to have been seriously directed to experimenting in the manufacture of porcelain—at all events, in this year the first allusion to the matter which is made in his letters and papers occurs, and this only casually.

At this time the business was still carried on under the style of "Bevans and Cookworthy." The death of his wife, in 1745, entirely took away his attention from business, and his researches into china clays were thrown aside. He retired into seclusion at Looe, in Cornwall, where he remained for several months, and, on his return to business, took his brother Philip, who, it appears, had lately returned from abroad, into partnership, and carried it on, with him, under the style of "William Cookworthy & Co." This arrangement enabled Cookworthy to devote his time to the scientific part of the business, and to the prosecution of his researches, while his brother took the commercial management of the concern. Left thus more to the bent of his scientific inclinations, he pursued his inquiries relative to the manufacture of porcelain, and lost no opportunity of searching into and experimenting upon the properties of the different natural productions of Cornwall; and it is related of him that, in his journeys into that county, he has passed many nights sitting up with the managers of mines, obtaining information on matters connected with mines and their products. In the course of these visits he first became acquainted with the supposed wonderful properties of the "Divining Rod," or "Dowsing Rod," as it was called by the Cornish miners, in the discovery of ore of various kinds. In the magic properties of this rod he was an ardent believer, and he wrote an elaborate dissertation upon its uses, which has been published.

His journeys into Cornwall, however, were productive of much more important results than the fabulous properties of the divining rod, for it was in these journeys that he succeeded in discovering, after much anxious inquiry and research, the materials for the manufacture of genuine porcelain. The information given him by the American in 1745 had never been lost sight of, and he prosecuted inquiries wherever he went. After many searchings and experiments, he at length discovered the two materials, first in Tregonnin Hill, in Germo parish; next in the parish of St. Stephen's; and again at Boconnoc, the family seat of Thomas Pitt, Lord Camelford. There is a kind of traditionary belief that he first found the stone he was anxious to discover in the tower of St. Columb Church, which is built of stone from St. Stephen's, and which thus led him to the spot where it was to be procured. At this time he lodged at Carlogges, in St. Stephen's parish, with a Mr. Yelland, and was in the habit of going about the neighbourhood with his "dowsing rod," in search of mineral treasures. This discovery would probably be about 1754 or 1755.

Having made this important discovery, Cookworthy appears to have determined at once to carry out his intention of making porcelain, and to secure the material to himself. To this end he went to London to see the proprietors of the land, and to arrange for the royalty of the materials. In this he succeeded; and ultimately Lord Camelford joined him in the manufacture of china, and, as appears from a letter of that nobleman to Polwhele, the historian of Cornwall, the two expended about three thousand pounds in prosecuting the work.

Of this discovery, so interesting and important to all engaged in the potters' art, and which ultimately led to immense commercial results, Cookworthy has left the following account. The importance of the subject—a subject which for a long time engrossed the Wedgwoods—will warrant the length of the extract:—

"It is now near twenty years since I discovered that the ingredients used by the Chinese in the composition of their porcelain, were to be got, in immense quantities, in the county of Cornwall; and as I have since that time, by abundance of experiments, clearly proved this to the entire satisfaction of many ingenious men, I was willing this discovery might be preserved to posterity, if I should not live to carry it into a manufacture; and with this view, I have thought proper to put in writing, in a summary way, all I have discovered about this matter.

"The account of the materials used by the Chinese is very justly given by the Jesuit missionaries, as well as their manner of preparing and mixing them into the china-ware paste. They observe, the Chinese have two sorts of bodies for porcelain; one prepared with Petunse and Caulin, the other with Petunse and Wha She or Soapy Rock. The Petunse they describe to be prepared from a quarry stone of a particular kind, by beating it in stamping-mills, and washing off and settling the parts which are beaten fine. This ingredient gives the ware transparency and mellowness, and is used for glazing it. The stone of this Petunse is a species of the granite, or, as we in the west call it, the moor-stone.

"I first discovered it in the parish of Germo, in a hill called Tregonnin Hill; the whole country in depth is of this stone. It reaches, east and west, from Breag to Germo, and, north and south, from Tregonnin Hill to the sea. From the cliffs some of this stone hath been brought to Plymouth, where it was used in the casemates of the garrison; but I think the best quarries are in Tregonnin Hill. The stone is compounded of small pellucid gravel, and a whitish matter, which, indeed, is Caulin petrified; and as the Caulin of Tregonnin Hill hath abundance of mica in it, this stone hath them also. If the stone is taken a fathom or two from the surface, where the rock is quite solid, it is stained with abundance of greenish spots, which are very apparent when it is wetted. This is a circumstance noted by the Jesuits, who observe that the stones which have the most of this quality are the most proper for the preparation of the glaze; and I believe this remark is just, as I know that they are the most easily vitrifiable, and that a vein of this kind in Tregonnin Hill is so much so that it makes an excellent glaze without the addition of vitrescent ingredients. If a small crucible is filled up with this stone, or a piece of it put in it, and exposed to the most violent fire of a good wind furnace for an hour, the stone will be melted into a beautiful mass; all its impurities will be discharged, one part of it will be almost of a limpid transparency, and the other appear in spots as white as snow. The former is the gravel, the other the Caulin, reduced by fire to purity. If the fire is not continued long enough to effect this, the upper part and middle of the mass will be of a dirty colour, and the bottom and parts of the sides fine.

Q 2

"CAULIN.

"This material, in the Chinese way of speaking, constitutes the bones, as the Petunse does the flesh, of china-ware. It is a white talcy earth, found in our granite countries, both in the counties of Devon and Cornwall. It lies in different depths beneath the surface. Sometimes there shall be a fathom or more of earth above it, and at other times two or three feet. It is found in the sides of hills, and in valleys; in the sides, where, following the course of the hills, the surface sinks, or is concave, and seldom, I believe, or never where it swells, or is convex. By what I have observed, it is by no means a regular stratum, but is rather in bunches or heaps, the regular continuance of which is frequently interrupted by gravel and other matters. At times there are veins of it among the solid rocks, when it is constantly very pure from gravel. I have a piece by me of this kind, very fine.

"There are inexhaustible stores of this Caulin in the two western counties. The use it's commonly put to is in mending the tin furnaces and the fireplaces of the fire-engines, for which 'tis very proper. The sort I have chiefly tried is what is got from the side of Tregonnin Hill, where there are several pits of it. As the stone hath a pretty large quantity of Caulin in it, so the Caulin hath a large mixture of the same sort of gravel as enters into the composition of the stone. It contains, besides, mica in abundance.

"In order to prepare the Caulin for porcelain, nothing more is necessary but pouring a large quantity of water on it, so that it may not, when dissolved, be of so thick a consistence as to suspend the mica. Let it settle about ten minutes, and pour off the dissolved clay into another vessel. Let it settle, pour off the water, and dry it. I would observe here, that care ought to be taken about the water used in washing off both the Petunse and Caulin. It ought to be pure, without any metallic or calcareous mixture. Our rivers in the west afford excellent water for this purpose, as they arise, the most of them, and run through a granite country. The Caulin of Tregonnin Hill is very unvitrifiable, and exceedingly apt to take stains from the fire. I know no way to keep it clean but the following:—Form it into cakes of the thickness of two or three crown pieces, and beat some of the stone to a very coarse powder; cover the bottom of the crucible with this powder; then put in a cake of the Caulin; cover this the thickness of one-third of an inch with the powder of stone; fill the crucible in this way, ending with a layer of the stone; cover the crucible, and treat it as in the process for melting the stone before described. If the stone is burned to purity, the Caulin will be as white as snow; if but partially calcined, so far as the stone is pure, the Caulin will be so; and when that is of a dirty colour, the Caulin will be of the same hue.

"I have lately discovered that, in the neighbourhood of the parish of St. Stephen's, in Cornwall, there are immense quantities both of the Petunse stone and the Caulin, and which, I believe, may be more commodiously and advantageously wrought than those of Tregonnin Hill, as, by the experiments I have made on them, they produce a much whiter body, and do not shrink so much, by far, in baking, nor take stains so readily from the fire. Tregonnin Hill is about a mile from Godolphin House, between Helston and Penzance. St. Stephen's lies between Truro, St. Austel, and St. Columb; and the parish of Dennis, the next to St. Stephen's, I believe, hath both the ingredients in plenty in it. I know of two quarries of the stone—one is just above St. Stephen's, the other is called Caluggus, somewhat more than a mile from it, and appears to be the finer stone.

"Having given this sketch of the natural history of the materials, 'tis needless to say much about the composition. Pottery being at present in great perfection in England, our potters'-mills prepare the Petunse much better than stamping mills, and excuse one from the trouble of washing it off, it being fit to be used as it comes from the mill. I would further observe that the mills should be made of the Petunse granite, it being obvious that, in grinding, some of the mill-stones must wear off and mix with the Petunse. If those stones should be of a nature disagreeable to the body, this mixture must, in some degree, be hurtful to it; whereas, whatever wears off from mill-stones of the same stone, cannot be so in the least degree. I have generally mixed about equal parts of the washed Caulin and Petunse for the composition of the body, which, when burnt, is very white, and sufficiently transparent. The Caulin of St. Stephen's burns to a degree of transparency without the addition of Petunse. The materials from this place make a body much whiter than the Asiatic, and, I think, full as white as the ancient china-ware, or that of Dresden.

"The stones I have hitherto used for glazing are those with the green spots of Tregonnin Hill. These, barely ground fine, make a good glaze. If 'tis wanted softer, vitrescent materials must be added. The best I have tried are those said to be used by the Chinese, viz., lime and fern-ashes, prepared as follows:—The lime is to be slaked by water, and sifted. One part of this, by measure, is to be mixed with twice its quantity of fern-ashes, and calcined together in an iron pot, the fire to be raised till the matter is red hot. It should not melt, and for that reason should be kept continually stirred. When it sinks in the pot, and grows of a light ash colour, 'tis done. It then must be levigated in the potter's mill to perfect smoothness. It may be used in proportion of one part to ten, and so on to fifteen or twenty of the stone, as shall be found necessary. We found one to fifteen of the stone a very suitable proportion. Our manner of mixing was to dilute both the stones and the ashes to a proper degree for dipping, and then to mix them as above. On mixing, the whole grows thicker. If 'tis too thick for dipping, more water must be added. Our method of dipping was just the same as is used by the delft-ware people. We first baked our ware to a soft biscuit, which would suck, then painted it with blue, and dipped them with the same ease; and the glazing grows hard and dry, as soon as it does in the delft-ware. Large vessels may be dipped raw, as the Chinese are said to do it. But the proper thickness of the glaze is not so easily distinguished this way, as when the ware is biscuited; for, the raw body being of the same colour and consistence with the glaze, when the latter is dry, 'tis hardly possible to determine the limits of either; a thing very easy to be done when the body is hardened by biscuiting. Our china-ware makers in general deny it to be possible to glaze on a raw body or soft biscuit. And so it is with their glaze; which, abounding in lead and other fluxing materials, melts soon and runs thin, and, melting before the body closes, penetrates it, and is lost in the body, whereas our stone is almost as hard to melt as the body is to close; and, not melting thin, neither runs nor penetrates the body. I insist on the truth of this observation, and 'tis necessary to be insisted on, as scarcely any of our potters, misled by too slavish dependence on their own too partial experience, will allow it. I have said above that the Jesuits observe that the Chinese paint and glaze their ware on the raw body. I know this can be done, for I have done it; and so may any one else who pleases to try it. I have now by me the bottom of a Chinese punch-bowl, which was plainly glazed, when it was raw, or a soft biscuit; for the ware wants a great deal of being burnt, it being of the colour of coarse whited-brown paper. But the same body, when exposed to a proper degree of fire, turns to a china-ware of a very good colour—a demonstration that it had not, as our ware in England hath, the great fire before the glaze was laid on. I don't point out the advantages of painting and glazing on a soft biscuit, as they are very obvious to any one, ever so little used to pottery.

"In regard to burning, I have to remark, that by all the experiments we have made, the north of England kilns, where the fire is applied in mouths on the outside of the kilns, and the fuel is coal, will not do for our body, at least when it is composed of the materials of Tregonnin Hill.

"In those kilns especially, when bags are used, there is no passage of air through the middle of the kiln; and a vapour, in spite of all the care that can be taken, will either transpire through the bags, or be reflected from the crown, which will smoke and spoil our ware, though it doth not appear to affect other compositions. How true this remark may be, with regard to the St. Stephen's materials, I cannot determine, as they have not yet been tried in a kiln. The only furnace or kiln which we have tried with any degree of success, is the kiln used by the potters who make brown stone. It is called the 36-hole kiln. Wood is the fuel used in it. They burn billets before and under it, where there is an oven or arch pierced by 36 holes, through which the flame ascends into the chamber which contains the ware, and goes out at as many holes of the same dimensions in the crown of the furnace. The safeguards at bottom stand on knobs of clay, which won't melt, about two inches square, and two inches and a half or three inches high; by which means more of the holes are stopped by the bottoms of the safeguard, but the air and flame freely ascend, and play round every safeguard; by which means those tingeing vapours, which have given us so much trouble, are kept in continual motion upward, and hindered from penetrating and staining the ware.

"Experience must determine the best form and way of using this kiln. 'Tis the only desideratum wanting to the bringing of the manufacture of porcelain, equal to any in the world, to perfection in England.

"Caulin pipe-clay and a coarse unvitrifiable sand make excellent safeguards."

The experiments on the Cornish materials having been perfectly successful, Cookworthy established himself as a china manufacturer at Plymouth, where the buildings still exist, and are known by the name of the "China House."

In these works Cookworthy prosecuted his new art with

great success, and was soon enabled to enter the market with English-made hard-paste china, composed of native materials alone. The early examples are, as is natural to expect, very coarse, rough, and inferior, but they evidence, nevertheless, considerable skill in mixing, though not so much, perhaps, in firing. And they are also remarkable for their clumsiness, as well as for their bad colour, their uneven glazing, and their being almost invariably disfigured by fire cracks, usually at the bottom.

As on the earliest productions of all the old china works, the decorations on the Plymouth examples are invariably blue; the blue at first being of a heavy, dull, blackish

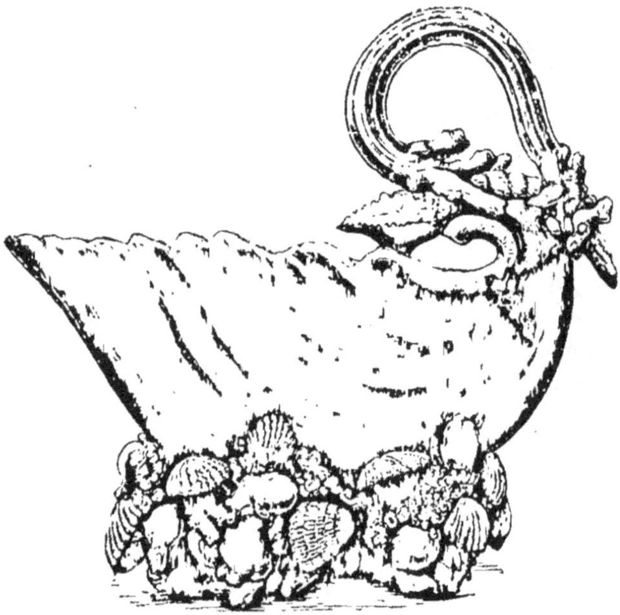

shade, but gradually improving, until, on some specimens which I have seen, it had attained a clear brilliance. Cookworthy, being an experienced chemist, paid considerable attention to the producing of a good blue, and was the first who succeeded in this country in manufacturing cobalt blue direct from the ore. Before this time the colour was prepared by grinding foreign imported zaffres with slab and muller; but after a series of experiments he succeeded in producing a fine and excellent blue from the cobalt ore, and prepared it by a better process. It is said that Cookworthy himself painted some of the earlier blue and white productions of his manufactory, and this is not at all improbable. The white porcelain of Plymouth is one of its notable features, for in it some remarkably fine works exist in different collections. These mostly consist of salt-cellars, pickle-cups, and toilet-pieces, formed of shells and corals, beautifully, indeed exquisitely, modelled from nature. The shells and corals, and other marine objects which compose these pieces, are remarkably true to nature, and their

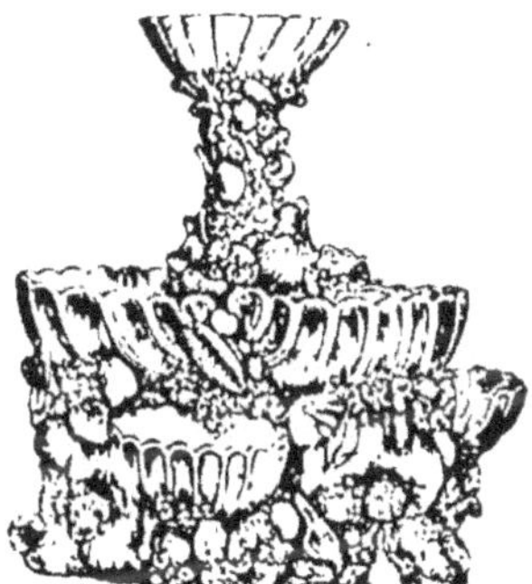

arrangement in groups is very artistic and good, as will be seen in the accompanying engravings.

In 1768 Cookworthy took out a patent for the manufacture of a "kind of porcelain newly invented by me, composed of moor-stone or growan, and growan clay." The patent was dated the 17th of March, 1768, and contained the usual proviso that full specification should be lodged and enrolled within four months of that date, which was duly done.*

Cookworthy, who determined to make his porcelain equal to that of Sèvres and Dresden, both in body, which he himself mixed, and in ornamentation, for which he procured

* For this specification, and a full account of the Plymouth China Works, see the *Art-Journal* for September, 1863.

the services of such artists as were available, engaged a Mon. Saqui, or Soqui, from Sèvres, who was a man of rare talent as a painter and enameller, and to whose hands, and those of Henry Bone, a native of Plymouth, who was apprenticed to Cookworthy, and afterwards became very celebrated, the best painted specimens may be ascribed.

The ware made at Plymouth consisted of dinner-services, tea and coffee services, mugs and jugs, vases, trinket and toilet stands, busts, single figures and groups, animals, "Madonnas" and other figures after foreign models, candlesticks with birds, flowers, &c., &c. The mug here shown, engraved from a specimen in my own collection, is an excellent example of the higher, and, of course, later, productions of Cookworthy's manufactory, and is, I believe, painted by Saqui. The tea-pot, also from my collection, is beautifully painted with groups of flowers, in pink.

On the next engraving is shown one of a pair of vases and covers, sixteen inches high, in the possession of Mr. Francis Fry, F.S.A., which is marked with the usual sign in red.

However beautiful and satisfactory the productions of the Plymouth works might be as *china*, they were not, it would appear, remunerative *commercially*. Coal, which was abundant in Staffordshire, and in other localities, was entirely wanting at Plymouth, and the "firing" of the kilns had to be done with wood. The clay and the stone Cookworthy had within easy distance, but coal was wanting;

this material was difficult and expensive to make, and therefore he was unable to keep pace with other manufactories, and to compete with them. Add to this that he was far

from being a young man —being then in his seventieth year —it is not surprising that he should determine on giving up the works, especially when Lord Camelford, who was one of his partners, says between two and three thousand pounds had been sunk in their prosecution.

On the 6th of May, 1774, therefore, William Cookworthy, for considerations set forth in the deed of assignment, sold the business and patent-right to Richard Champion, merchant, of Bristol, a connection of Cookworthy's who had been connected pecuniarily with the works at Plymouth, and they were transferred to that city.

The deed of assignment of the patent rights, &c., from Cookworthy to Champion, is dated May 6th, 1774, and among other "considerations" it was covenanted that whatever the amount of value of the raw material (the Cornish clay and stone which Cookworthy had discovered and brought into use) Champion used in the course of a year, an equal amount of money should be paid to Cookworthy. Thus if, in the course of a year, Champion paid £1000 for material in Cornwall, he would also have to pay another £1000 to Cookworthy for the privilege of using it, thus doubling the price of the material from that at which Cookworthy had himself worked it. Having thus become proprietor of the concern which had been carried on jointly by Cookworthy, Lord Camelford, and himself (and probably others), Champion at once established them near to his own residence in Castle Green, Bristol, and on the 22nd of the following February (1775), presented a petition to the House of Commons, praying for the term of patent right to be enlarged for a further period of fourteen years to himself. His petition was referred to a committee, which began its sittings on the 28th of April. By this time he had prepared and produced some specimens of china made at his works, for examination by the committee. The result of his application was the ultimate passing of an Act of Parliament, by which the patent was accordingly enlarged. This Act was passed in 1775 (15 Geo. III., cap. 52), and is entitled "An Act for enlarging the term of Letters Patent granted by his present Majesty to William Cookworthy, of Plymouth, Chymist, for the sole use and exercise of a discovery of certain materials for making Porcelain, in order to enable Richard Champion, of Bristol, merchant (to whom the said Letters Patent have been assigned), to carry the said discovery into effectual execution for the benefit of the public." *

* For this Act see the *Art-Journal* for November, 1863.

CHAPTER XIII.

JOSIAH WEDGWOOD'S OPPOSITION IN PARLIAMENT TO THE EXTENSION OF CHAMPION'S PATENT.—"MEMORIAL" OF WEDGWOOD AND OTHERS.—CHAMPION'S "REPLY."—JOSIAH WEDGWOOD ISSUES HIS "REMARKS."—WEDGWOOD'S "REASONS" FOR OPPOSING THE ACT.—"CASE OF THE POTTERS."—THE BILL PASSES THE HOUSE OF COMMONS.—AMENDED BY THE LORDS.—PASSING OF THE ACT.—EXAMPLES OF CHAMPION'S BRISTOL CHINA.—DECAY OF THE WORKS.—CHAMPION SELLS HIS PATENT RIGHT TO A COMPANY IN STAFFORDSHIRE.

I HAVE stated in my last chapter that Richard Champion, having applied to Parliament for an extension of the term of his patent-right, such petition was referred to a select committee of the House. Immediately this was done, Josiah Wedgwood, ever alive to the interests of the potters, saw that the extension would be injurious, and resolved upon giving the scheme his determined opposition. He therefore, ostensibly on behalf of the potters of Staffordshire, but really at first alone, opposed the petition with his usual zeal and energy. He therefore presented a "Memorial" to the House, of which the following is a copy :—

"A Petition being presented to the Honourable House of Commons by Mr. *Champion*, of *Bristol*, Merchant, praying for an Extension of a Patent granted by his Majesty, *March* 17th, 1768, to *William Cookworthy*, Chemist, for the Sole Use of certain Materials for making Porcelain; and reciting that the said *William Cookworthy* had assigned all his Right and Interest in the said Letters Patents to the Petitioner.—*Josiah Wedgwood*, in behalf of himself and the Manufacturers of Earthen-ware in *Staffordshire*, begs Leave to represent :—

"That the Manufacture of Earthenware, in that county, has

of late received many essential improvements, and is continually advancing to higher Degrees of perfection.

"That the further Improvement of the Manufactury must depend upon the Application and *free Use* of the various Raw Materials that are the Natural Products of this Country.

"That the Raw Materials now secured for a limited Time to the Petitioner, may at the Expiration of the Patent assigned to him, be of great Use to enable the Potters, throughout Great Britain, to improve their Manufactures into the finest Porcelain; and thereby produce a Branch of Commerce of more national Importance than any of this Kind hitherto established.

"The Case of the ingenious Mr. *Watt*, and the Extension of his Patent, having been urged in Favour of Mr. *Champion's* Application for the like Indulgence, it may be proper to observe that the Cases are far from being similar,—Mr. *Watt* being the *original Inventor* of the Machine for which his Patent was granted, and Mr. *Champion* the *purchaser only* of the unexpired Term of a Patent granted to another Man, who does not appear to have any Interest in this Application.

"The Petitioner, therefore, *not being the original Discoverer*, and having *purchased* the remaining Term of the Patent at a *proportionate Price*, can have no Right to expect a further Extension of a Monopoly injurious to the Community at large, which neither the Ingenious Discoverer nor Purchaser, for want, perhaps, of Skill and Experience in this particular Business, have been able during the Space of Seven Years, already elapsed, to bring to any useful Degree of Perfection.

"But supposing the Petitioner, as he alledges, has now brought this Discovery to Perfection,* it may surely be presumed that the remaining Seven Years will give him such an Opportunity of reimbursing himself, and so great an Advantage over any persons who may Succeed him at the end of that Term, as must render the Extension or the Monopoly both unnecessary and unreasonable."

To this memorial of Josiah Wedgwood's, Champion presented the following honourable reply † :—

"When Mr. Champion presented a petition to the Honourable House of Commons, praying the aid of Parliament for a prolonga-

* See the Petition presented to the House the 22nd of February.

† "A Reply to Mr. Wedgwood's Memorial relative to Mr. Champion's Application for a Bill to prolong his Patent for making Porcelain."

tion of the term granted by the Patent for making porcelain, he built his hopes of success on two circumstances: the first, the apparent utility resulting from such a manufacture carried to a perfection equal to that of the Dresden and Asiatic. The second circumstance on which he grounded his expectation was the sense which he hoped the House would entertain of the justice of compensating, by some reasonable privilege, the great labour, expense, and risque which had been incurred, not only in the invention of the material and composition, but in the improvement of this important manufacture. He was also almost certain that no person whatsoever in this kingdom could, on a supposition of their being prejudiced in their rights in a similar property, have had any cause of complaint, or pretence to interfere with him, or to oppose the prayer of his petition.

"Mr. Champion however finds, with some surprise, that Mr. Wedgwood, who has never hitherto undertaken any similar manufacture, conceives himself likely to be injured by the indulgence which Mr. Champion has solicited. He has accordingly printed a memorial containing his reasons against the granting the prayer of Mr. Champion's petition, and is now actually gone in person into Staffordshire in order to solicit others to prefer a petition to Parliament against Mr. Champion's Bill.

"Before Mr. Champion replies to Mr. Wedgwood's observations or complaints, he begs leave to remark on the time when Mr. Wedgwood introduces them. Mr. Champion presented his petition to the Honourable House of Commons on the twenty-second day of February. The committee to which that petition was referred did not sit until the twenty-eighth day of April, during which time Mr. Wedgwood neither made any public application against Mr. Champion, or gave him any sort of private information of intended opposition. Neither did any manufacturers in Staffordshire or elsewhere express any uneasiness or make any complaint of Mr. Champion's application, though it is not improbable that Mr. Wedgwood's journey thither may be productive of both.

"Mr. Champion forbore to bring forward his petition before the committee until he had prepared such specimens of his manufacture as might give the committee the most striking proofs of the truths of his allegations, and this could not be done sooner in a manufacture so very lately, and with such incredible difficulty, brought to its present perfection. He trusts that the specimens which he has produced in various kinds will show that he has been usefully employed, and merits the public protection.

"Mr. Wedgwood is pleased to represent his memorial on behalf of himself and the manufacturers of earthenware in Staffordshire. Mr. Champion says, as has been already hinted, that Mr. Wedgwood had not any authority from such manufacturers, or any others, to make any representations in their behalf.

"Mr. Champion most cheerfully joins in the general praise which is given to Mr. Wedgwood for the many improvements which he has made in the Staffordshire earthenware, and the great pains and assiduity with which he has pursued them. He richly deserves the large fortune he has made from these improvements. But should he not be content with the rewards he has met with, and not have the avidity to grasp at a manufacture which another has been at as great pains as Mr. Wedgwood has employed in his own, to establish?—a manufacture entirely original in this kingdom, and which all nations in Europe have been desirous to obtain?

"Mr. Wedgwood says the application and free use of the raw materials of this country will make a great improvement in the manufacture of Staffordshire earthenware. Mr. Champion has no objection to the use which the potters of Staffordshire may make of his or any other raw materials, provided earthenware only, as distinguished by that title, is made from it. He wants to interfere with no manufacture whatever, and is content to insert any clause to confine him to the invention which he possesses, and which he has improved. He is contented that Mr. Wedgwood, and every manufacturer, should reap the fruit of their labour; all he asks is, such a protection for his own as the legislature in its wisdom shall think it merits.

"Mr. Wedgwood's remark on the difference of merit betwixt Mr. Watt and Mr. Champion is ungenerous and unjust: ungenerous, as Mr. Champion has not, or does not, compare himself to Mr. Watt; he has not even mentioned his name in any of his applications. His business is not with comparative or similar merits; it is his duty to prove the merit of his own manufacture, for which he solicits the encouragement of the legislature. He hopes that the specimens which he has produced before the committee are incontrovertible evidences of it. The remark is unjust, because he has been many years concerned in this undertaking: nearly from the time the patent was granted to Mr. Cookworthy, in whose name it continued till assigned over to Mr. Champion. To deny the advantage of any part of Mr. Cookworthy's merits to his assignee is to deny that advantage to Mr. Cookworthy himself. One part of the benefit of every work, from whence profit may be derived, is the power of assignment; and if, in fact, the manufacture could not be completed, nor the inventor, of course, derive any profit from it, without the expense, care, and perseverance of the assignee and once partner, the merit of that assignee, who both completes the manufacture and rewards the discoverer, is equal in equity to that of the discoverer himself—equal in every respect, except the honour that attends original genius and power of invention.

"Mr. Champion can assert with truth that his hazard and expense was many times greater than those of the original inventor. Mr. Champion mentions this without the least disparagement to the worthy gentleman, who is his particular friend; he gives him all the merit which was due to so great a discovery; he deserves it, for finding out the means of a manufacture which will, in all probability, be a very great advantage to this country; but yet Mr. Champion claims the merit of supporting the work, and, when the inventor declined the undertaking himself, with his time, his labour, and his fortune, improved it from a very imperfect to an almost perfect manufacture; and he hopes soon, with proper encouragement, to one altogether perfect.

"What regards the original discoverer is, in some measure, answered in the foregoing paragraph; but the original discoverer is not without a reward. Mr. Champion at this moment allows him, and is bound to his heirs, &c., in a profit equal to the first cost of the raw material, and, as Mr. Champion's manufactory is encouraged, must increase to a very great degree.

"Nor is Mr. Wedgwood more excusable for his implication that a want of skill prevented the work being brought earlier to perfection. Undoubtedly the difficulty arose from a want of skill in working these new materials. This is a profound as well as civil remark of Mr. Wedgwood's; but that skill was to be acquired only by care and expense, and that care and expense are Mr. Champion's merits. Mr. Champion pretends to no other knowledge as a potter than what he has acquired in the progress of this manufacture, his profession of a merchant not putting more in his power; but he had the experience of Mr. Cooksworthy, the inventor, one of the most able chemists in this kingdom, to whom the public is indebted for many useful discoveries; he had the experience of the manager of his works, a person bred in the Potteries, and thoroughly conversant in manufactures of this kind; the workmen he employed were brought up to the branch, and he has spared no expense in encouraging foreign artificers.

"But Mr. Champion, as a further answer to Mr. Wedgwood's implication of want of skill, begs leave to observe that the *Dresden* manufacture (like this, a native clay), which has been established so great a number of years, was long before it attained perfection, and even now it has not that exact proportion of shape which the Chinese manufacture possesses. The *Austrian* manufacture (also a native clay) was twenty-five years before it attained any degree of perfection, and then only by accidental aid of the Dresden workmen who were dispersed during the late war. The work in *Brandenburgh* is nothing more than the Dresden materials, wrought by workmen removed hither from that city, the Brandenburgh work having no clay of its own territory. Mr. Champion is surprised that Mr. Wedgwood can find no cause but one, which he chooses to blame, why a new manufacture, upon a principle never before tried in England, should not have attained perfection in a shorter space than the very short space of seven years.

"As to Mr. Wedgwood's calculation of the profits sufficient to recompense the ingenuity, and repay the trouble and expense of others, Mr. Champion submits it to a discerning and encouraging legislature, whether a seven years' sale is likely to repay a seven years' unproductive, experimental, and chargeable labour, as well as the future improvement to grow from new endeavours? Until Mr. Champion was able to make this porcelain in quantities to supply a market, it was rather an object of curiosity than a manufacture for national benefit.

"There is one branch of the manufacture, the *blue and white*, upon which he has just entered—this branch is likely to be the most generally useful of any: but the giving a blue colour under the glaze, on so hard a material as he uses, has been found full of difficulty. This object he has pursued at a great expense by means of a foreign artificer; and he can now venture to assert that he shall bring that to perfection which has been found so difficult in Europe in native clay.

"If the various difficulties which have attended his work from its beginning could have been foreseen, this patent ought not to have been applied for at so early a period. The time in which profit was to be expected has necessarily been laid out in experiment. It was thought that when the principle was found the work was done; but the perfecting a chemical discovery into a merchantable commodity has been found a troublesome and a tedious work. It is therefore presumed that the legislature will distinguish between the over-sanguine hopes, in point of time, of an invention which, however, has at length succeeded, and those visionary projects which deceive for ever. Upon the whole, Mr. Champion humbly rests his pretensions to the protection of the legislature upon three grounds—that he has been almost from the beginning concerned in the work which has cost so much labour and expense; that he now allows the inventor a certain and increasing recompense, though the carrying that invention to an actual merchantable manufacture was entirely his own work; that the potteries of china-ware in most other countries in Europe have been at the charge of sovereign princes. It has been immediately so in France, Austria, Dresden, and Brandenburgh; in Italy they have been under the care of great noblemen. In this original work, Mr. Champion claims the principal share of supporting, improving, and carrying into execution a manufacture so much admired in China and Japan, and now first attempted in Britain, in capacity of resisting the greatest heat, equal to the Asiatic and Dresden."

Josiah Wedgwood answered this "Reply" of Champion's by a paper of Remarks.* In these he said:—

"It would be very unbecoming in Mr. Wedgwood to take up much of the valuable time of the honourable members of the House of Commons, who may be pleased to attend to the subject of his Memorial, in remarking upon several reflections that Mr. Champion has thrown out, which do not at all affect the merit of the question. But it is necessary to observe that Mr. Wedgwood has all his life been concerned in the manufacture and improvement of various branches of pottery and porcelain; that he has long had an ambition to carry these manufactures to the highest pitch of perfection they will admit of; and that so far from having any personal interest in opposing Mr. Champion, it would evidently have been his interest to have accepted of some of the obliging proposals that have been made to him by Mr. Champion and his friends, and to have said nothing more upon the subject; but Mr. Wedgwood is so fully convinced of the great injury that would be done to the landed, manufacturing, and commercial interests of this nation by extending the term of Mr. Champion's monopoly of raw materials, of which there are immense quantities in the kingdom, and confining the use of them to one or a few hands, that he thought it a duty of moral obligation to take the sense of his neighbours upon the subject, and

* "Remarks upon Mr. Champion's Reply to Mr. Wedgwood's Memorial on behalf of himself and the Potters in Staffordshire."

to give up to the manufactory at large all advantages he might have secured to himself. It is upon these principles, and these alone, that he has acted in this business, and therefore he humbly presumes he does not merit the censure of *avidity* in grasping at other men's manufactures, though he thinks that himself and all manufacturers should be protected in the *free use* of all raw materials that are not invented by men, but are the natural productions of the earth. When Mr. Wedgwood discovered the art of making *Queen's Ware*, which employs ten times more people than all the china works in the kingdom, he did not ask for a patent for this important discovery. A patent would greatly have limited its public utility. Instead of *one hundred manufactories* of Queen's Ware, there would have been *one;* and instead of an exportation to all parts of the world, a few pretty things would have been made for the amusement of the people of fashion in England. It will be the same with the use of the materials in question: if they are not only confined to the use of one person or manufactory, by patent, for fourteen years, but that patent be extended for twenty or thirty years longer, so long may they be the means of supporting *one* trifling manufactory; but if the materials are left free for general use, and Mr. Champion is in the possession of the result of all his experiments and real discoveries with respect to the art of manufacturing these raw materials into porcelain, no essential part of which has been revealed by him to the public, either in his specifications or otherwise, then there is reason to expect a very large and extensive manufactory of porcelain will be established in various parts of this kingdom, to the great benefit of the public, without any injury to Mr. Champion."

Wedgwood continued his "remarks" by replying that Mr. Champion's offer of inserting a clause to allow the potters the free use of the raw material in all kinds of earthenware, restricting its use in porcelain only to himself, was a useless concession, because Champion had failed to define the difference between earthenware and porcelain, and had failed to impart the secret of his manufacture to the public, either by his specifications or otherwise. "How then," he asked, "are the Staffordshire potters to use the growan stone and growan clay for the improvement of their finer stone and earthenwares, without producing such a manufacture as may in Westminster Hall be deemed porcelain?" He also said that, judging from Mr. Champion's own words, Cookworthy's patent "ought not to have been applied for at so early a period;" it was evident that the "patent was taken out for a discovery of the art of making true porcelain before it *was* made; and if the discovery has been since made, there can have been no specification of it; it has not been revealed to the public; it is in Mr. Champion's own possession, and being *unknown*, it is presumed the right to practise it cannot be confirmed or extended by Act of Parliament, which ought to have some clear ground to go upon." The patent, he says, has evidently been considered as a privilege to the patentee, "for the sole right of *making experiments* upon materials which many persons have thought would make good porcelain, and on which experiments have been prosecuted by several successive sets of operators many years before the date of the patent." He contended that it would be an "egregious injury to the public" to continue the patent to one person who was no original discoverer, who was only just commencing the commonest and most useful part of his business with the aid of a foreign artificer, in the hope that a discovery might at some future time be made. He considered that if the raw materials were thrown open to all, "a variety of experienced hands would probably produce more advantage to the nation in a few years than they would ever do when confined to one manufactory, however skilful the director might be," and that the extension of the patent securing the monopoly "would be a precedent of the most dangerous nature, contrary to policy, and of general inconvenience," and therefore he "humbly hopes the legislature will not grant the prayer of Mr. Champion's petition."

In addition to the "Memorial" and the "Remarks" already spoken of as a part of the zealous opposition which Wedgwood made to the proposed extension, he issued a sheet of "Reasons why the extension of the term of Mr. Cookworthy's patent, by authority of Parliament, would be injurious to many landowners, to the manufacturers of earthenware, and to the public." In addition to this, he made out and presented a "Case of the manufacturers of earthenware in Staffordshire," setting forth the advantages that would be derived from throwing open the use of the raw materials, and the disadvantages which an extension of the monopoly would entail, not only on the manufacturers, but on the public at large.

These "reasons" are so ingenious, and the "case" so carefully made out, that I give them to my readers entire, as I am, I believe, the first to bring them into notice in connection with any account of the porcelain works of this kingdom. The following are the "reasons" why the extension of the term of Mr. Cookworthy's patent, by authority of Parliament, would be injurious to landowners, to the manufacturers of earthenware, and to the public:—

"It would be injurious to the *landowners*, because by means of this monopoly materials of great value would be locked up within the bowels of the earth, and the owners be deprived of the power of disposing of them; for the present patentee and his assigns have contracted with *one gentleman* that he shall sell these materials only to *them*, and that they shall purchase such materials only from *him*, during the term of *ninety-nine* years.

"It would be injurious to the *manufacturers* of earthenware; because, notwithstanding the mechanical part of their manufactory, their execution, their forms, their painting, &c., are equal, if not superior, to those of any other country, yet the *body* of their ware stands in great need of improvement, both in colour and texture; because the public begin to require and expect such improvement; because without such improvement the sale of their manufactures will probably decline in favour of foreign manufacturers, who may not be deprived of the use of the materials that their countries produce—for the consideration in this case is not whether one manufacturer or manufactory shall be supported against another, but whether the earthenware manufactories of *Great Britain* shall be supported in their improvements against those of every other country in the world; because the materials in question are the most proper of any that have been found in this island for the improvement of the manufactures of earthenware; and because *no line has been drawn, or can be drawn*, with sufficient distinctness, between earthenware and porcelain, and especially between earthenware and the various kinds of this patent porcelain, to render it safe for any potter to make use of these materials in his works.

"The extension of this monopoly would be injurious to the *public*, by preventing the employment of a great number of vessels in the coasting trade in bringing the raw materials from the places where they would be dug out of the earth, to the different parts of this island where they would be manufactured.

"This extension would also be injurious to the public because it would prevent our manufactures of earthenware from being *improved in their quality* and *increased in their quantity and value* to the amount of many hundred thousand pounds *per annum*.

"And lastly, it would be injurious to the public by preventing a very great increase of our exports, *which must infallibly take place* when the body of our earthenwares shall come to be improved so as to bear a proportion to the beauty of their forms and the excellence of their workmanship.

"Upon the whole, would it not be unreasonable to extend the term of a monopoly in favour of an individual to the prejudice of ten thousand industrious manufacturers, when the individual can have no merit with the public, as he has made no discovery to them?"

"The Case of the Manufacturers of Earthenware in Staffordshire," as drawn up by Wedgwood, to which I have referred, is as follows:—

"The potters, and other persons depending upon the pottery in *Staffordshire*, beg leave humbly to represent that Nature has provided this island with immense quantities of materials proper for the improvement of their manufactures; that such materials have been known and used twenty or thirty years ago; and that many experiments were made upon them by various operators, with various degrees of success.

"That porcelain was made of these materials, and publicly sold before the year 1768.

"That in March, 1768, *Mr. Cookworthy*, of *Plymouth*, took out a patent for the sole use of the materials in question, called in the patent moor-stone or growan, and growan clay, for the making of porcelain, which is defined to have a fine colour and a lucid grain, and likewise to be as infusible as the Asiatic.

"That *Mr. Cookworthy* contracted, as the condition upon which he held the privilege of his monopoly, that he would make a full and true specification of the art by which he converted these materials into porcelain; and that he entirely failed in fulfilling this obligation.

"For in the pretended specification which he made, he omitted to describe the *principal operations* in which his art or discovery consisted, having neither exhibited the proportions in which the materials were to be mixed to produce the *body* or the *glaze*, nor the art of *burning* the *ware*, which he knew to be the *most difficult* and important part of the discovery.

"That the company concerned in the porcelain manufactory at *Plymouth*, established under the authority of this patent, contracted with one gentleman, in whose lands these materials are found, that he should sell the materials only to them, and that they should purchase materials from no other person, during the term of ninety-nine years.

"That nevertheless there are great quantities of such materials in other estates in *Cornwall* and *Devonshire*, and probably in many other parts of this island.

"That in the year 1774 *Mr. Cookworthy* assigned over his patent right to *Mr. Champion*, of *Bristol*, who now applies to Parliament for an extension of this monopoly, seven years before the expiration of the patent, which assignment was made upon condition that *Mr. Cookworthy* should receive for ninety-nine years from *Mr. Champion* as large a sum every year as should be paid to the proprietor for the raw material, hereby levying a tax of 100 per cent. upon them.

"That *Mr Champion* in his petition sets forth that he has brought this discovery to perfection; and that in a paper he has published, entitled *A Reply, &c.*, he says that if the various difficulties which have attended this work from the beginning could have been foreseen, *this patent ought not to have been applied for at so early a period;* that is, in plain English, the patent was taken out for the discovery of an art before the discovery was made by the patentee. And if the discovery has been made since, there has been no specification of it; it has not been recorded for the public benefit; it is in *Mr. Champion's* own possession; it is kept from the public for his own private emolument: and the *nature* of it being *unknown*, it is humbly presumed such a pretended discovery can neither entitle the patentee nor the petitioner to the extension of a monopoly injurious to many thousands of industrious manufacturers in various parts of the kingdom.

"And in the same paper in which we find the above curious confession, *Mr. Champion* acknowledges that even at *this time* he has just entered upon the commonest and most useful branch of this manufactory, which he has pursued at a great expense by means of a *foreign artificer*, and can *now* venture to assert that he *shall* bring it to perfection. And in the space of seven years yet to come of his patent, and fourteen years' further indulgence which he expects from Parliament, one would hope some discovery might be made; but would it not be an egregious injury to the public, an unheard of and unprecedented discouragement to many manufacturers who have great and acknowledged merit with the public, to continue to *one person* who, in *this instance*, has no *public merit*, the monopoly of earth and stones that Nature has furnished this country with in immense quantities, which are necessary to the support and improvement of one of the most valuable manufactures in the kingdom?

"*Mr. Champion* says, in the Reply referred to above, he 'has no objection to the use which the potters of *Staffordshire* may make of his or any other raw materials, provided earthenware only, as distinguished by that title, is made from them. He wants to interfere with no manufactory whatsoever, and is content to insert any clause to *confine* him to the invention which he possesses, and which he has improved,' &c.

"If *Mr. Champion* had accurately defined the *nature* of his own invention; if he had described the proportions of his material necessary to make the body of his ware; if he had also specified the proportions of his materials necessary to produce his glaze, as every mechanical inventor who takes out a patent is obliged to specify the nature of the machine by which he produces his effect; if *Mr. Champion* could have drawn a *distinct line* between the *various kinds of earthenware and porcelain* that have been made, and are now made in this kingdom, and *his porcelain*, a clause might have been formed to have confined him to the invention which he says he possesses, and to have prevented him from *interrupting the progress of other men's improvements*, which he may think proper to call imitations of his porcelain; but, as he has not chosen to do the former, nor been able to do the latter, no manufacturer of stoneware, Queen's ware, or porcelain, can with safety improve the present state of his manufacture.

"It is well known that manufactures of this kind can only support their credit by continual improvements. It is also well known that there is a *competition* in these improvements through all *parts of Europe*. In the last century *Burslem*, and some other villages in

Staffordshire, were famous for making *milk pans* and *butter pots*, and, by a succession of improvements, the manufactory in that neighbourhood has gradually increased in the variety, the quality, and the quantity of its productions, so as to furnish, beside the home consumption, an annual export of useful and ornamental wares, nearly to the amount of *two hundred thousand* pounds; but during all this progress, it has had the free range of the country for materials to work upon, to the great advantage of many landowners and of navigation.

"*Queen's* ware has already several of the properties of porcelain, but is yet capable of receiving many essential improvements. The public have for some time *required* and expected them. Innumerable experiments have been made for this purpose. There are immense quantities of materials in the kingdom that would answer this end; but they are locked up by a monopoly in the bowels of the earth, useless to the *landowners*, useless to the *manufacturers*, useless to the public; and one person is petitioning the legislature, in effect, to stop all the improvements in earthenware and porcelain in this kingdom but his own.

"For the next step, and the only step the manufacturers can take to improve their wares, will be deemed an invasion of this *vague* and *incomprehensible* patent.

"The manufacturers of earthenware are justly alarmed at the prospect of extending the term of the patent, because, without improvements, the sale of their manufactures *must certainly decline* in favour of *foreign manufacturers*, who may not be deprived of the *free use of the materials their countries produce;* for the consideration in this case is not whether one manufacturer or manufactory shall be supported against another, but whether the earthenware and porcelain manufactories of *Great Britain* shall be supported, in their improvements, against those of every other country in the world. Upon the whole, the petitioners against the Bill humbly presume this monopoly will appear to be *contrary to good policy*, highly *injurious* to the public, and *generally inconvenient;* that the extension of the monopoly, supposing any patent to be valid, would be greater *increasing the injury;* that the bill now depending is not only calculated to *extend*, but to *confirm* it, and therefore they humbly hope it will not be suffered to pass into a law."

Despite all this opposition to his petition by Wedgwood, as the representative of the potters, and by the members of parliament for the county of Stafford, and others who had been moved by the exertions of Wedgwood and his friends, the Bill passed the House of Commons, and was sent up to the Lords without amendment. The "case" just given, along with extracts from the Bill, with comments, showing, among other things, that the passing of the Act, as originally framed, conferred the full benefits of Cookworthy's patent on Champion, without compelling him to enroll anew any specification of his process of manufacture, was printed for circulation among the members of the Upper House. With reference to this important point, it was shown that Cookworthy, having enrolled his specification, and having afterwards assigned the patent right to Champion, the Bill enacted that all and every the powers, liberties, privileges, authorities, and advantages which in and by the said letters patent were originally granted to the said William Cookworthy, shall be held, exercised, and enjoyed by the said Richard Champion for the present term of fourteen years, granted by the said letters patent, and after the expiration thereof, for the further term of fourteen years, in as full, ample, and beneficial a manner as the said Richard Champion could have held the same in case the said letters patent had originally been granted to him. The view of the Bill is manifestly to confirm to Mr. Champion the letters patent for the present term of fourteen years, as well as to grant him fourteen years more. Had it been intended only to *enlarge* the term, and that the letters patent should have stood upon their own ground, such words of confirmation would not have been necessary; or if they had been thought so, they should have been succeeded by words to the effect following:—"*Subject, nevertheless, to the same provisos, conditions, limitations, and agreements, as the said William Cookworthy held and enjoyed the same before the date of the said assignment.*" But these being omitted, and the Bill having stated that the "said William Cookworthy had described the nature of his said invention and the manner in which the same is to be performed," it is evident that the design of the Bill is not only to confirm absolutely the letters patent, and consequently the monopoly of these materials for the present term of fourteen years, but also to grant it to him for fourteen years more; and the Act is to have this operation, even though the letters patent may be void by the discovery not being a new invention, according to the statute of James I., or by Mr. Cookworthy's not having conformed to the terms and conditions of the letters patent, by having described and ascertained the nature of the said invention, and the manner in which the same is to be performed. That the making of porcelain is not a new invention is too evident to need any proof; that the letters patent are not within the intent of the statute is manifest by a cursory perusal of it. That Mr. Cookworthy has not described and ascertained the nature of this invention and the manner in which the same is to be performed (unless the discovery of the materials can alone be deemed so), will appear by what he has been pleased to call his specification. But it will appear in evidence that even the discovery of the materials was not, at the time of granting the letters patent to Mr. Cookworthy, "new and his own," but that they were at that time, and had been long before, applied to the uses of pottery.

"Is it therefore reasonable that Parliament should confirm to Mr. Champion the present term of fourteen years, and also grant him fourteen years more in a monopoly of an immense quantity of materials, the natural products of the earth, for the making of porcelain, which no person is to *imitate or resemble;* but also virtually the sole privilege of vending and disposing of these materials at what price and in what manner he thinks proper? For no person can use them in any respect but they will produce (if not the same effect) an effect that will *resemble* what he may call his patent porcelain; and it is not to conceive how he can be deprived of the exclusive right of selling as well of using these materials if the Bill now depending should pass into a law."

The presenting these papers to the Lords produced more effect, it would seem, than the efforts in a similar direction had apparently done in the Commons. The consequence was, that "Lord Gower and some other noble lords, having fully informed themselves of the facts upon which the merits of the case depended, and having considered the subject with a degree of attention proportioned to its importance, saw clearly the injurious nature of the Bill, and were determined to oppose it." This determination brought on a conference between the two noble lords who took the most active part for and against the Bill, and the result was the introduction of two clauses, the first making it imperative on Champion to enrol anew his specification of both body and glaze within the usual period of four months. The second, throwing open the use of the raw materials to potters for any purpose except the manufacture of porcelain, was as follows:—

"Provided, also, that nothing in this Act contained shall be construed to hinder or prevent any potter or potters, or any other person or persons, from making use of any such raw materials, or any mixture or mixtures thereof (except such mixture of raw materials, and in such proportions, as are described in the specification hereinbefore directed to be enrolled), anything in this Act to the contrary notwithstanding."

The Act being obtained, the specification dated the 12th of September, 1755, was duly enrolled on the 15th of the same month.

Armed with his new Act of Parliament, by which he was empowered to enjoy nearly twenty-two years' patent right, Champion spared no pains and no expense to make the productions of his works as good as possible; and that he succeeded in producing a magnificent body and a remarkably fine glaze, and in turning out some truly exquisite specimens of fictile art, both in design, in potting, in modelling, and in painting, is fully evident by examples still remaining in the hands of some fortunate possessors. As I have already given examples of some of the productions of the Plymouth works, my readers, I doubt not, will be glad to have them supplemented by one or two of Champion's make.

The commoner description of goods, the blue and white ware, seem to have been, very naturally, considered by Champion to be the branch most likely to pay him, commercially, and this he at one time cultivated to a greater extent than any other. The patterns in many cases being almost identical with those of Worcester and other places —which, of course, arose from the fact of the different works copying from the same original Oriental models—the ware made by Champion is sometimes apt to be appropriated by collectors to that manufactory. It may, however, easily be distinguished by those who are conversant with the peculiarities of its make.

In blue and white, Champion produced dinner, tea, and coffee services, toilet pieces, jugs, mugs, and all the varieties of goods usually made at that period. The blue is generally of good colour, and the painting quite equal to that of other manufactories. Some of these pieces are embossed, and of really excellent workmanship. A good deal of the blue and white ware was marked with the usual cross, but it appears more than probable that the greatest part of this kind of goods passed out of the works unmarked.

Another characteristic class of goods made by Champion

was the imitation of the most common Chinese patterns, examples of which, from my own collection, are shown in the accompanying engraving of a saucer and a teapot.

One of the choicest examples of the highest class of Bristol art existing at the present day, is the tea-service of which the cup and saucer engraved below forms a part, the cup and saucer now being in my own collection. This example is also highly important as showing the perfection to which the manufacture of porcelain had been brought at the time of the transfer of the works from Cookworthy to Champion—the service having been made in 1774-5, within a very few months after the establishment of the works in Bristol. It

was made to the order of Edmund Burke, while the contested election for Bristol was going on, as a present to Mr. and Mrs. Smith, who were his warm friends and zealous supporters, and whose guest he was. The decorations are of the most chaste and elaborate design, and of the most delicate workmanship, and the pieces profusely and massively gilt in both dead and burnished gold.

Another notable and beautiful feature of the Bristol works was the production of plaques, bouquets of flowers, wreaths, and armorial bearings, in biscuit. Of these, two examples, belonging to Mr. Lucas and Mr. Baller, are shown on the following page, as is also a large vase.

Despite the energy of himself, the skill of his workmen, and the beauty of the ware produced at his manufactory, Richard Champion's hopes of permanently establishing an art in Bristol, which should not only be an honourable and useful, but a remunerative one, proved fallacious, and in

little more than two years from his obtaining the Act of

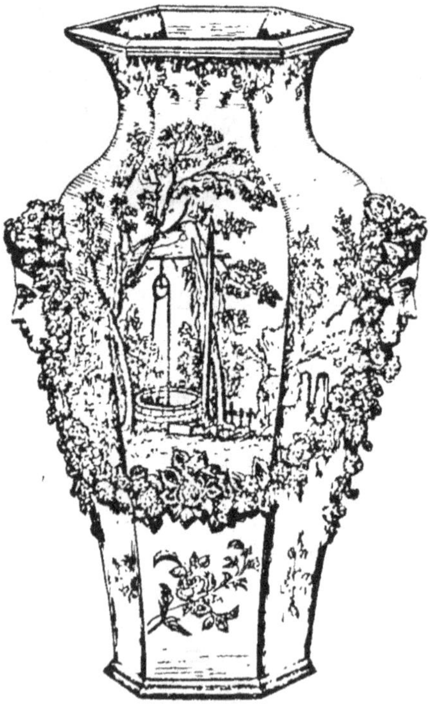

Parliament, he sold his patent right to a company of Staffordshire potters, who continued the manufacture at New Hall for some time, when the ordinary soft-paste china, which had previously been tried by Champion, was allowed to supersede it. Thus the works at Bristol were brought to a close, and the manufacture of porcelain was lost to the locality. Champion himself is said to have removed for a time into Staffordshire, and to have remained there until the year 1782.

CHAPTER XIV.

INTRODUCTION OF THE MANUFACTURE OF CHINA INTO STAFFORDSHIRE. — WILLIAM LITTLER AND AARON WEDGWOOD. — CHAMPION'S PATENT BOUGHT BY A COMPANY. — WORKS ESTABLISHED AT TUNSTALL.—REMOVED TO SHELTON.—NEW HALL WORKS. — SAMUEL HOLLINS; ANTHONY KEELING; JOHN TURNER; JACOB WARBURTON, AND OTHERS.—EXAMPLES OF NEW HALL CHINA.—JOSIAH WEDGWOOD ENTERS INTO PARTNERSHIP WITH MR. CARTHEW FOR WORKING CORNISH STONE.—THOMAS BENTLEY VISITS PARIS.—WEDGWOOD AND BENTLEY'S DUTCH AND FRENCH CATALOGUES. —JOHN FLAXMAN.—DEATH OF THOMAS BENTLEY.—HIS MONUMENT AT CHISWICK.—PROPOSED INSCRIPTIONS TO HIS MEMORY.

At the time when experiments were being made in various parts of the kingdom, and when works were successfully carried on at Chelsea, at Worcester, at Derby, and at many other places, Staffordshire, long the great seat of the potter's art, as I have shown, had made no progress in the manufacture of china, and its production remained a sealed book to manufacturers in that county. It is true that one of its sons had made experiments about the middle of last century, and had produced some tolerably good pieces of ware, but no other attempt had been made to introduce this important manufacture into the locality which is now its principal seat. The potter to whom I allude was William Littler, the brother-in-law and partner of Aaron Wedgwood, of whom I have before spoken, who, it seems, like many other pioneers of science and manufacture, sacrificed his patrimony in the cause, and found himself later in life rich in experience, but poor in worldly goods. To this gentleman, too, is ascribed the honour of first using the fluid glaze by immersion, which was afterwards so much improved upon by Enoch Booth. Despite Littler's attempts, however, Staffordshire produced no china until 1777 or 1778, when the Bristol patent right was, as I have shown, transferred to the company which afterwards commenced the New Hall works at Shelton. The company consisted of six persons, viz., Samuel Hollins, of Shelton, Anthony Keeling, of Tunstall, John Turner, of Lane End, Peter (or Jacob) Warburton, of Hot Lane, William Clowes, of Port Hill, and Charles Bagnall, of Shelton. Of these six persons—all men of good standing and of large experience—a few words will no doubt be interesting and useful to my readers.

Samuel Hollins, a maker of the fine red-ware teapots, &c., from the clay at Bradwell, previously worked by the brothers Elers, was of Shelton, and was the son of Mr. Hollins, of the Upper Green, Hanley. He was an excellent practical potter, and made many improvements in his art.

Anthony Keeling, of Tunstall, was son-in-law of the celebrated potter, Enoch Booth, having married his daughter Ann. Keeling succeeded Enoch Booth in his business, which he carried on successfully for many years, and retired on a small independence to Liverpool, where he died.

John Turner, first of Stoke, and then of Lane End, father of Messrs. John and William Turner, was one of the most clever and successful potters Staffordshire ever produced, but one about whom little has been written. Many of his productions in black and in jasper, &c., are quite equal to those of Wedgwood, and, indeed, are often mistaken for the work of that great man. Mr. Turner's cream ware, too, as well as his stone ware, of which his jugs are best known to collectors, rank high in excellence both of design and manipulation. In 1762 Mr. Turner commenced manufacturing at Lane End, and made many improvements in the art, and by the discovery of a vein of fine clay at Green Dock, was enabled successfully to compete not only with other potters, but with Wedgwood himself. Mr. Turner is stated to have been deputed, with Wedgwood, by the Staffordshire potters, to oppose the extension of the patent to Champion.

Jacob Warburton, of Hot Lane, a man highly respected by every class, and who lived until the year 1826, was born in 1740, and passed his long and useful life as a potter, in which art he rose to considerable eminence in his early years in connection with his father and brothers, and later on his own account, and, in partnership with others, in the New Hall Works. He was the "last member of the old school of potters, the early friend and contemporary of the 'father of the Potteries,' Josiah Wedgwood, with whom he was for many years in the habit of confidential intercourse and friendship. Numerous are the benefits which the public derived from the united exertions of the talents and abilities of these two venerated characters, on every point connected with the local interest and prosperity of the Staffordshire Potteries."

William Clowes, of Port Hill, was a gentleman of property, and was, I have reason to believe, only a sleeping partner in the concern.

Charles Bagnall, of Shelton, was a potter of considerable experience, who had previously been with Joshua Heath. The family has been connected with Staffordshire for many generations.

The company thus formed commenced operations at the works of one of the partners, Anthony Keeling, at Tunstall, the pottery formerly belonging, as just stated, to his father-in-law, the well-known potter, Enoch Booth. Tunstall at this period was a mere small street, or rather roadway, with only a few houses—probably not many more than a score—scattered about it and the lanes leading to Chatterley and Red Street. To this spot, the forerunner of the present large and important town, Cookworthy's patent was brought, and here, with the experienced potters who had become its purchasers, and under the management of Champion, who had produced such exquisite specimens of Art at Bristol, and who had been induced, as a part of the arrangement, to superintend the manufacture, the first pieces of china made in Staffordshire, with the exception of the trial pieces of Littler, before spoken of, were produced. Some disagreements having arisen, Turner and Keeling withdrew from the concern, and the remaining partners removed their works to a house in Shelton, known as "Shelton Hall," afterwards the "New Hall," in contradistinction to the "Old Hall," celebrated as being the birthplace of Elijah Fenton, the poet.

About the time of the withdrawal of Keeling and Turner from the partnership, and the removal of the works from Tunstall to Shelton, Richard Champion received, through Burke, then in office, whom he had materially assisted in his election for Bristol, as spoken of in the preceding chapter, and who had patronised his manufacture in that city, the appointment of Deputy Paymaster of the Forces. On receiving this appointment, in 1782, Champion, it appears, immediately left Staffordshire. The ministry soon afterwards being dissolved, however, Champion was of necessity thrown out of office, and soon afterwards sailed for America. He settled, it seems, at Camden, South Carolina, and died there in 1787.

The company next took for manager Mr. John Daniel, who afterwards became a partner in the concern. A considerable quantity of china was produced, but the most extensive and profitable branch of the New Hall business was the making and vending of the glaze called "composition," made by the company of the materials to whose use they had the exclusive right. This "composition," made from the ingredients given in the specification, was supplied by the New Hall firm to the potters of the neighbourhood, and even sent to other localities, to a large extent, and at a highly remunerative price.

The ware made at these works was precisely similar in body and glaze to that of Bristol, to which, from the fact of some of the same artists being employed, it bears also a marked resemblance in ornamentation. In 1796 the patent, which had been enjoyed successively by Cookworthy, Champion, and the Staffordshire company, for a period of twenty-eight years, expired; but the company continued to make the hard paste china, and to supply "composition" (many potters finding it more convenient still to purchase instead of make that essential) to other manufacturers.

Hard paste porcelain, on the system of the patent, continued to be made at New Hall until about the year 1810 or

1812, when the bone paste, which had been gradually making its way in the distritc, finally superseded it, and the company

continued their works on the newer system. In 1825, the entire stock of the concern, which had for a short time been carried on for the firm by a person named Tittensor, was sold off, and the manufacture of china, of any description, entirely ceased at New Hall.. The engravings on the preceding page show some of the "hard paste" china made at these works, from examples principally in my own collection.

Thus, the introduction of the manufacture of "china ware"—a manufacture which has grown and increased to an enormous extent in the district—into Staffordshire, was made mainly through the exertions of Josiah Wedgwood, in throwing open the use of the raw materials from Devonshire and Cornwall. As soon as the use of these materials, the Cornish clay and Cornish stone, was, by Act of Parliament, on the concession of Champion, thrown open to the manufacturers of earthenware, Wedgwood availed himself of the fruit of his opposition by immediately entering into partnership with Mr. Carthew, of St. Austell, in Cornwall, for the working of the mines of Cornish stone, and for the supply of the materials to other manufactories besides his own.

These mines were worked by Wedgwood to the time ot his death, and after his decease were continued, for at all events some years, by his successors. I have in my own possession a letter, dated "Etruria, May 27, 1795"—a few months after the death of the great Josiah—and signed "Josiah Wedgwood and Byerley," which, as it gives the price of Cornish clay and stone at that period, is particularly interesting. The following is an extract:—

"We beg leave to acquaint you that we now possess and are working the Cornish clay and stone mines that for twenty years have been known under the name of Wedgwood and Carthew's.

"We can speak very decidedly from our own experience of the quality of these materials, which are certainly equal to any of the kind. If you should be in want of any, we shall be very glad to serve you.

"The clay will be four guineas per ton in London, Bristol, or Liverpool, the casks included. Wt. 112 lbs. to the cwt. in 4 casks of 5 cwt. each.

"The stone 30*s*. per ton at the same places—120 lbs. to the cwt."

Having thus obtained the use of the Cornish stone and clay for himself and brother potters, Wedgwood introduced them into his manufactory with marked success, as is particularly evident in his glazes, and in the body of his earthenware.

In 1776 Thomas Bentley visited Paris, being away from his London duties for seven weeks. His journey was "professedly a journey of expense and amusement, without much attention to business," but he nevertheless contrived to mix up business conveniently with it, and to return richer in decorative ideas, and in impressions of gems, &c., from different cabinets. And here it may not be out of place to say that in this same year,—the year in which he writes, "We have Mr., Mrs., and Miss Wedgwood, with their servants, with Miss Oates [I presume sister to his first wife, Hannah Oates] and Miss Stamford [sister to the then Mrs. Bentley], in the house, besides five clerks and our own servants; so that I have constant fears lest my good governess should be laid up, though I take the best care I can of her," —Mr. Bentley, jointly with his friend the Rev. David Williams, one of the founders of a congregation on principles consonant with Mr. Bentley's feelings, at Chelsea, published a "Liturgy on the Universal Principles of Morality and Religion." This establishment at Chelsea would appear, probably, to have been formed on somewhat similar principles to that of the "Octagonians" at Liverpool.

In 1777 Wedgwood and Bentley issued a fourth edition of their catalogue; and in the succeeding year they again published it translated into the Dutch language. A copy of this remarkably scarce publication, issued at Amsterdam in this year, 1778, is in my own possession, and is particularly interesting in many respects. By its title-page it appears that the agent was Lambert Van Veldhuysen. The goods being to be sold by "Wedgwood en Bentley, en verkogt in hun Magazyn, in de Groote Nieuwpoort-Straat te Londen, en by Lambertus Van Veldhuysen, Alleen in de Zeven Provintien, in's Konigs Waapen, le Amsterdam." In the following year, 1779, a sixth edition of the French catalogue, and a fifth of the English one, were published. This latter is interesting as being the last edition issued by Wedgwood and Bentley. In it only the four varieties of bodies are named, showing clearly that the "Bamboo" and the "Mortar" bodies were of later invention. The "Jasper" was then, too, apparently still in its infancy, and is not described as in the later catalogue, to which I shall have occasion yet to refer.

Somewhat before this period—but I cannot speak with certainty to the year—Wedgwood and Bentley engaged the services of John Flaxman, then a young and unknown man, and to his fostering care, to no inconsiderable extent, did the great sculptor owe his name and his imperishable fame. It was the employment he received from Wedgwood which for years "kept the wolf from his door," and enabled him to live while he worked his way up in art. It was this employment which enabled him to earn money to take a home for himself, and to plant in it that blessing and joy of his life, his wife, Ann Denman, and which also helped him on to lay by money to visit Rome, and study the works of the great masters. It would be highly interesting to compile a list of all the groups, and medallions, and bas-reliefs of one kind or other which Flaxman produced for Wedgwood. A complete list of this kind, however, there is little hope of getting together. So far as may be done I purpose doing at a future time. For the present I shall content myself with the pleasure of giving my readers, a little later on in the present chapter, copies of some of Flaxman's original bills for models and drawings, which will be of no inconsiderable service to collectors of Wedgwood ware.

In 1780, on the 26th of November, Thomas Bentley, the friend and partner of Josiah Wedgwood, died at his residence at Turnham Green, near London, and his burial is thus recorded in the parish register of Chiswick, where he was interred on the 2nd of December—

"Burials, 1780.
"Thomas Bentley. December 2nd, in the Church."

In the *St. James's Chronicle* the following brief but telling notice of his death appeared:—"Died, on Sunday, at his house on Turnham Green, Mr. Bentley, in partnership with Mr. Wedgwood. For his uncommon ingenuity, for his fine taste in the Arts, his amiable character in private life, and his ardent zeal for the prosperity of his country, he was justly admired, and will long be most seriously regretted by all who had the pleasure of knowing so excellent a character."

Mr. Bentley was buried, as I have already stated, at Chiswick, where a tablet was erected to his memory. This monument, the joint production of Stuart, who published the well-known splendid work on Athens, and Scheemakers, the artist who executed the monument to Shakspeare, in Westminster Abbey, exhibiting a sarcophagus, with medallion of Bentley, and boys holding inverted torches, bears the following touching and admirable inscription:—

THOMAS BENTLEY,
Born at Scrapton, in Derbyshire, Jan. 1st, 1730.
He married Hannah Oates, of Sheffield, in the Year 1754:
Mary Stamford, of Derby, in the Year 1772,
who survived to mourn her loss.
He Died Nov. 26th, 1780.
Blessed with an elevated and comprehensive understanding,
Informed in variety of science;
He possessed
A warm and brilliant imagination,
A pure and elegant taste;
His extensive abilities,
Guided by the most expansive philanthropy,
were employed
In forming and executing plans for the public good:
He thought
With the freedom of a philosopher.
He acted
With the integrity of a virtuous citizen.

The monument bears the names "Stuart Inv[t]. Scheemaker Sculpt."

It is pleasant to add to this inscription two other epitaphs on Mr. Bentley—the one written by Mr. Rasbotham and the other by Dr. Percival, which were communicated to me, not long before his lamented death, by the late Dr. James Markland, F.S.A., of Bath, whose literary and antiquarian labours are so well known. The epitaphs, which have never till now appeared in print, speak volumes as to the character of the man whom Wedgwood chose as his friend and partner. They are as follows :—

AN EPITAPH ON MR. BENTLEY, BY MR. RASBOTHAM.*

Sacred to the Memory
of
THOMAS BENTLEY,
late of
Turnham Green,
in
this Parish.

Reader,
If thou hast a taste formed to relish the Elegancies
of the Politer Arts;
If a mind unwarped by prejudice, and steady in
the pursuit of Truth;
If a soul capable of the most extensive benevolence,
warm in its friendships, and susceptible of the endearments of conjugal affection;
here pause a moment!
The real Critic,
The Philosopher,
The Man—The Friend—The Husband,
Beneath this lies buried.
He died in the year of his age.

* Dorning Rasbotham, Esq., a magistrate, "distinguished for his probity, sound judgment, and juridicial skill."—*Works of Thomas Percival, Esq., M.D.*, vol ii. 290.

AN EPITAPH BY THOMAS PERCIVAL, M.D.

To
Commemorate distinguished merit
and
Prolong the influence of bright Example,
This Tablet
is inscribed to
THOMAS BENTLEY, ESQ.,
Whose inventive genius,
Elegant Taste,
and capacious understanding
were directed,
in their various exertions, by
Genuine Patriotism,
and
Universal Philanthropy.
Art
owes to him the revival of
Antique Beauty;
Commerce
the extension of
Inland Navigation;
and
Science
Its true application to
Human Life and Manners:
In the meridian of his
reputation, usefulness, and prosperity,
lamented by the public,
Praised, wept, and honoured by the friends
His Attic converse
gladdened and improved,
He died, aged 50,
Nov. 26, A.D. 1780.

Mr. Bentley died childless. By his first wife I believe he had one infant, which died in its first year; by his second marriage he had none. And thus his name, as well as his pure and refined taste, his brilliant intellect, and his blameless and philanthropic life, died with him. Mrs. Bentley, who survived her husband many years, after a time it appears removed to Gower Street, where she died.

In 1781, consequent on the death of Thomas Bentley, the

London stock, so far as related to the partnership of Messrs. Wedgwood and Bentley, was sold at Christie's, the sale occupying twelve days.

And here, at the close of Bentley's life, let me introduce one or two of his letters, to show the care he bestowed on the details of the business in which he had become a partner, and the easy style of his correspondence. The first letter I shall give is a most interesting one, from its allusions to medallions, to the Empress of Russia's service, and other matters, and I therefore give it entire. It is addressed "To Mr. Josiah Wedgwood, at Etruria, near Newcastle, Staffordshire."

"London, July 30, 1774.

MY DR. FRIEND,

"I have rec^{d} from Mr. Hodgson 20 India Bonds, which with Interest & Premium due upon them, amount to £2070 15*s*. 11*d*., and have given him a Receipt for them on your Account. He says they are very safe security for 3 pr. Ct.

"We have now almost no Company, & are busy arranging Things in our New House, & winding up the Bottoms of the Russian Service, which I hope will be all finish'd about the latter end of next Week.

"I have very great Satisfaction in seeing all our Medallions, Bas-reliefs, &c., before me at once, a Sight I never could gratify myself with before. They can now be seen by others; & I shall now be able to tell what we have, & what we want, in a few Minutes.

"This, I should think, must considerably promote the Sale of them.

"I shall give you a List of what we want to compleat the Sets, &c., & I can now correct some Errors, and fill up Vacancies in the Catalogue against another Edition.

"CLASS 1.

"Mr. Wood writes for these Things; but we want a great many good Bracelets, when you have setled your Composition.

"CLASS 2.

"No. 1.—Continence of Scipio.—I know you wait for the Book, which I will send down with ye other Books at Chelsea.

"I shall give you no more wants out of this Class at present, as we have not quite finish'd the Arrangement.

"Class 3.

"No. 1.—Hesiod, Black in a Gem Frame.
2.—Homer, do.
3.—Aristodemus, King of Messina.—Wanting in two Sets.
11.—Pithagoras.
18.—Socrates.
20.—Aristippus. The Names or Numbers on the Backs.

"When you make these, I think you may make two or three Compleat Sets—in Gem Frames, Black, at 18*d.*, and 2 or 3 sets unframed, at 1*s.* If your Moulds do not agree with our Catalogue, I shou'd be glad to know in what respect, & which are deficient, that we may correct the Catalogue. I only doubt y^r having any Mould for the Head call'd Aristodemus; tho' you once had such a One.

"Class 4.

"We have never a compleat Set of the Roman History. We shou'd have half a dozen Sets made at once. The last is sold that was compleat. Please to take Care to send *compleat* Setts.

"Class the 5th

"I propose calling *Heads of illustrious Greeks & Romans.* Cyrus & Lysimachus, from Class XI., will be transfer'd to this.

"You may make all the Heads in this Class, with or without Frames, in Black. 2 or 3 Sets.

"Class ye 6.

"There are several Deficiencies in most of the Sizes of ye 12 Cæsars; but we have not got them all together yet.

"We want several Sets framed at 1*s.* 6*d.* & 3*s.*, in Gem Frames, in Black. Please to Number them *carefully* at the Back, according to the Catalogue. Many of the Heads have been number'd & mark'd wrong.

"Class 7.

"We have few of these; but this Class is so incompleat, it may be as well to defer a while making them.

"Class the 8th.

"We only want the following:—No. 27, Caius; 108, Adrian 2d; 133, Leo 8th; 138, Boniface 7th; 156, Benedict 10th; 160, Hildebrand; 249, Innocent 13th; 250, Benedict 13th; 251, Clement 12; 252, Benedict 14; 84, In° 6th. Perhaps you have Moulds for some of these. Please to let us know which you really want; for we have had a great many from you since we were informed you had no more.

"CLASS ye 9th.

"We may have two or three Setts of these as soon as you please.

"Class 10th & 11th, with the Acc^t of Stores I defer, as we are going to take an Account of Stock.

"Severall of the Things mention'd above we want to compleat our Sets for the Rooms. With respect to the rest, we shall be more particular when we have got all our Affairs in a narrower Compass.

"Mr. Hodgson informs Us, Cutler, Perryman, & Co., at Naples, are very safe.

"Dr. Jebb has been with Us twice. For several Days Mrs. Bentley had no Pulse in One Arm, & very little in the other. She cou'd get no sleep in the Night, & was extremely low, so as often only to be relieved with a Flood of Tears. She is considerably better, & has some Pulse this Morning; and I hope the Doctor's Cordials, & kitchen Physick—for he orders her to live well—will soon restore her to Health & Spirits. Our Love to Mrs. W.

"I am always yrs. most affy.,

"THOS. BENTLEY."

" . . . . . to send immediately, or as soon as possible, . . . Sets of the 8 Small Statues in fine white jasper and . . in Black, without Frames, and some Sets of the Medallions, Cupid shaving his Bow, Diamede, &c., about 8, or as many as there are in a Set of the full relief; but not the Poor slender flat Lady coming out of a Bath. These will be wanted immediately; & we shou'd be glad to have some of them by the Coach, with some of those that were modell'd here, that Hackwood has been finishing. Pray make us a Pair of Herculaneum Nymphs, without Frames, out of the Moulds you have, as well & *as soon* as you can, and then Massey, or any of the Men that want Work, may be repairing them. Dr. Franklin, a Dozen or two very good, with Frames, both black & white. Fine Cleopatra's Heads, white, a dozen or two, 3*s*. 6*d*. each.

"We want a match for Dr. Franklin, but do not stay for that. Send some as soon as possible. Your Carriers disappoint Us sadly.

Socrates & Pittarus, in Pairs. Be good now, & let us have these Things as soon as possible.

"Mr. Wedgwood desires his Duty to his good Lady. He is well, but extremely busy. A delightful Sale of Fossils is come to our relief, & will keep him here a while longer.

"All our respects to Mrs. Wedgwood & the good Family.

"Yrs. &c.,

"T. B."

"On the other side my Dr. Friend will receive the Copy of an order from Mr. Westmacot, Architect, for a Chimney Piece, for Sr. Geo. Warren, which he desires may be executed with all possible dispatch: The Tablets & Blocks, the small Statues & Heads, are all to be in *white*, to be grounded with pale blue or laylock colour. In the Dimensions you will be as exact as possible; & I suppose it wou'd be better they shou'd be a little larger than a little less, as they are to go into Rabits."

"Wanted for Mr. Westmacot, with all possible dispatch.

	Ft.	Ins. Ins.	
1 White square Tablet	1	$6\frac{3}{4}$ by $8\frac{1}{8}$	
2 White oval Blocks		$4\frac{3}{4}$ by 3	
2 White square Do.		$5\frac{1}{8}$ by $4\frac{1}{8}$	
Messalina & another Empress to match her		$1\frac{3}{4}$ by $1\frac{1}{4}$	oval in white.
Faustina & Do. Do. .		$2\frac{1}{10}$ by $1\frac{1}{2}$	Do.
Basso Releivos, the Set of eight white Statues .		$3\frac{1}{2}$ by $2\frac{1}{2}$	
2 Do. Hercules & Lion & Diomede with ye Pal.		$3\frac{3}{8}$ by $2\frac{1}{2}$	White.
2 Do. Cupid shaving his Bow and sacrificing Fig.		3 by $2\frac{1}{4}$	Do. Althea.
Apollo, Sappho, Poppea, & Apulius . . .		$1\frac{7}{8}$ by $1\frac{5}{8}$	Do. 4 heads all of a size."

CHAPTER XV.

JOHN FLAXMAN—HIS CONNECTION WITH JOSIAH WEDGWOOD. —ORIGINAL BILLS AND LETTERS OF FLAXMAN'S.—MODE OF REDUCING MEDALLIONS, ETC., BY FIRING.—FLAXMAN'S MEDALLION PORTRAITS—HIS BAS-RELIEFS—HIS DESIGNS FOR SET OF CHESSMEN.—MR. MARJORIBANK'S COLLECTION. —FRIEZES AND PLAQUES.—FLAXMAN'S MODELS IN WAX. —JOSIAH WEDGWOOD ELECTED F.R.S.—SIR JOSHUA REYNOLDS PAINTS PORTRAITS OF JOSIAH AND MRS. WEDGWOOD. —WRIGHT OF DERBY.—WEDGWOOD INVENTS A THERMOMETER FOR MEASURING HEAT.—CHAMBER OF COMMERCE. —INVENTION OF "JASPER DIP."

I HAVE spoken in the last chapter of Flaxman's connection with Wedgwood. I am fortunately enabled, in connection with this interesting part of the memoir of the great Josiah, to introduce here, in their chronological place, some original bills of Flaxman's, which are extremely important and valuable as showing the prices then paid to that afterwards great artist, and as enabling, so far as they go, collectors to know which pieces were really the productions of his master mind. And here let me say that it is a fixed belief—a belief in which I fully share—that Flaxman for a time modelled at Etruria, in one of the rooms shown in the view just given of the Black Works. The prices paid to him as a young man, it will be seen, were really handsome and liberal, when the time and other matters are considered.

I have thought it well to illustrate, to some extent, these important and highly interesting bills, which I have the gratification of being the first to make public, so as to enable my readers to authenticate such examples as may be in their collections. The first bill, now before me, is as follows:—

Mr. Wedgenwood to J. Flaxman

1782.		£	s.	d.
April 28.	Moulding a Turin	0	18	0
83.	Moulding a Bust of Mr. & Mrs. Siddons .	1	11	6
Sept. 6.	A Cast of a Fragment by Phidias . .	0	10	6
		3	0	0

Receiv'd in full by John Flaxman

Succeeding this in point of date, the following interesting letter, written in October, 1782, from Wardour Street, where Flaxman had only a short time before removed from his father's house, and to which he had only then taken home his young and loving bride—written, too, it will be remembered, soon after the time when the bachelor president of the Academy, Sir Joshua Reynolds, had said to him, "So, Flaxman, I am told you are married; if so, sir, I tell you, you are ruined for an artist!"—will be read with much interest:—

"Oct. 28th, 1782, Wardour Street,

"Sir,

"According to the desire you expressed in the last letter you favoured me with, I have designed some groups of children proper for bas-reliefs to decorate the sides of tea-pots. No. 1 & 2 are intended to go intirely round a tea-pot of a flat shape, except where the handle and spout interrupt them. I have therefore made separate stories for each side; the first is 'Blind Man's Buff,' the second is the 'Game of Marbles,' 3 & 4 are the 'Triumph of Cupid,' to be disposed in a similar manner on the sides of round & upright tea-pots. When you return the sketches to be modelled from, be pleased to give instructions concerning the size and other necessary particulars. Mrs. Flaxman presents her respects to Mrs. & Miss Wedgwood and yourself.

"And I have the honour to remain, Sir,
"Your obliged Servant,
"JOHN FLAXMAN."

The designs for groups for the teapots here spoken of by Flaxman were modelled, and no doubt will be familiar to some collectors. The same groups were also introduced into other pieces, of various sizes. And here let me say a word or two on a matter of great interest to collectors, but on which, unfortunately, not having the practical knowledge of the potter's art, they possess but very scanty information.

I have often heard it remarked what an enormous cost it must have been to produce models of the same group in so many different sizes, from seven or eight, or even more, inches in height, down to the most minute and exquisite little gem of three quarters or half an inch in height; and I have heard the remark, from those who had carefully examined them, repeatedly made, of how marvellous it was that in producing so many separate models of the same subject, such strict and unerring fidelity should have been preserved in all their details. This reduction, my readers will be glad to learn, is produced by the action of fire, and this—one of the wonderful properties of heat, with all of which in their effect on the form, size, colour, &c., the successful potter must be thoroughly acquainted—is one of the nicest and most careful operations which the master eye of the producer has to accomplish.

The properties of different clays in their shrinking, no less than in their combinations for the production of different bodies and varieties of colours, have to be understood thoroughly by the manufacturer, who has to proportion the degrees of heat to which his wares must be subjected to produce the desired result. For instance, if a piece—no matter what—is required to be of a certain size when finished, the model for it has to be made of a larger size, to allow for shrinking, proportionate to the body and to the degree of heat to which it has to be subjected. When the model, I will suppose of a bas-relief, has been made, a mould is taken from it, and into this matrix, when dried, the prepared clay is pressed. If the original model was, say eight inches in height, its counterpart in soft clay, thus produced, would be precisely the same. This, in passing through the oven, would in some instances, according to the composition of the body, and the heat to which it was subjected, shrink as much as one-eighth; so that what went into the kiln in a soft state of eight inches would come out hardened only seven inches in height, and being shrunk bodily, its entire proportions and its minutest details would be reduced alike. Another mould being taken from this, and a clay squeeze from the matrix of seven inches being again subjected to the same heat, the second perfect piece would come out of the kiln measuring only six inches and an eighth—and so on; each time a reduction is made, the proportion of loss of one-eighth of its then size being preserved. It will thus be seen that with care and experience reductions to almost any size may be procured.

The next bill of Flaxman's, which I have the good fortune to produce through the courtesy of Messrs. Wedgwood, is one of great importance, being a statement of accounts from July 11th, 1783, the year after his marriage, down to August 10th, 1787, the time when he and his true helpmate set off to Rome to study the great masters, and to prove to Reynolds and the world "that wedlock is for a man's good rather than for his harm."

MR. WEDGWOOD,

TO J. FLAXMAN, JUN.

1783.		£	s.	d.
July 11.	Two Drawings of Crests, an Owl & a Griffin's Head	0	3	0
	A portrait of Mr Herschel . . .	2	2	0
	A ——— Dr Buchan . . .	2	2	0
Oct. 12.	A ——— an officer from a print, for a ring	2	12	6

		£	s.	d.
1783.				
Oct. 12.	A drawing of a Crest, Cap of Liberty & a flame	0	1	0
„ 30.	A figure of a Fool for Chess	1	5	0
Dec. 13.	A drawing of the Shield, Crest, and Arms of Sir N. Nugent	0	2	6
„ 18.	Grinding the edges of six snuff boxes for the Spanish Ambassador	0	15	0
1784.				
Jany. 24.	A model in wax of Captain Cook	2	2	0
Feby. 3.	A ——— of Dr Johnson	2	2	0
	A print of the Dr for assistance in the model	0	2	6
Mar. 21.	A bas-relief of boys in wax	11	0	6
	A portrait of C. Jenkinson, Esq.	2	2	0
..	Two drawings for the Manufacturer's Arms	0	15	0
	A third for the Manufacturer's Arms	0	5	0
Dec. 31.	Three days employed in drawing bas-relief vases, Chess Men, &c.	3	3	0
„ 12.	A bas relief in Wax of Veturia & Volumnia entreating Coriolanus	9	9	0
Jan. 14.	A portrait of Govr. Hastings	3	3	0
Mar. 8.	A drawing of Chess Men	6	6	0
	An Outline for a Lamp & Stand	0	10	6
	Cutting the curved sides of two ornamental friezes parallel 3 days & half	0	9	7½
April 29.	A drawing of a Chimney piece	0	10	6
July 23.	A ditto from that in Mr. Wedgwood's show-room, & several mouldings drawn at large	1	1	0
Aug. 8th.	A mason's time taking down a Chimney piece	0	2	0
	A labourer at do. do.	0	1	3
	A drawing of an Arm & Olive branch	0	2	0
Novr. 23.	A model of the King of Sweden	2	2	0
Decr.	Mr & Mrs Meermans portraits	5	5	0
Decr. 18.	Four patterns for Steel frogs	0	10	0
1787.				
Jan. 16.	A model of Peace preventing Mars from bursting the door of Janus's Temple	15	15	0
	A packing case	0	1	0
	Drawing of an Oak branch for the border of a plate	0	3	0
March 26.	A model of Mercury uniting the hands of England & France	13	13	0

1787.		£	s.	d.
March 26.	A packing case	0	1	6
	A drawing of a Cypher R. H. and Bloody Hand	0	2	0
June 1.	A model of the Queen of Portugal	3	3	0
„ 11.	A marble Chimney piece containing 5 ft. 11 in. at £1 18 0 per foot	11	4	0
	Masonry & polishing	18	0	0
	Carving	6	0	0
	A marble Chimney piece containing 5 ft. 3 in.	9	19	6
	Masonry and polishing	21	4	0
	Twenty-four Tinned Cramps	0	12	0
	Seven packing cases, 7*s.* 6*d*.. 7*s.* 11*d.*, 7*s.* 2*d.*, 6*s.* 9*d.*, 5*s.* 6*d.*, 7*s.* 6*d.*, 8*s.* 1*d.*	2	8	5
	Nails	0	2	10
	Packing three days	0	10	6
	Cart to the Inn	0	6	0
	Toll, porter, & booking	0	1	9
		£163	11	4½
	Taking down a Chimney piece.	0	5	3
	Cutting Tiles	0	5	0
	Cases for the chimney piece	0	19	6½
Augst. 10.	A bas-relief of Hercules in the Hesperian Garden	23	0	0
		£188	4	2
	Cr	116	11	9
		£71	14	5

Received on account of this Bill

1785.		£	s.	d.
March 22.		25	0	0
Augt. 10.		25	0	0
1787.				
July 10.		50	0	0
Aug. 10.		10	0	0
	By amount of Goods	6	11	9
		£116	11	9

It would appear from this account that the famous group of "Hercules in the Hesperian Garden" was the last pro-

MRS. MEERMAN.

MRS. SIDDONS.

MR. MEERMAN.

HERSCHELL.

C. JENKINSON.

THE QUEEN OF PORTUGAL.

KING OF SWEDEN.

DR. BUCHAN.

duction of Flaxman for Wedgwood, it having been delivered on the 10th of August, 1787—I presume immediately previous to his departure for Rome, down to which period this bill was a general statement of accounts, and more than probably the last which passed between them. It appears that in July and August in that year, Flaxman had received two sums of £50 and £10 on account, and that there was still due to him a balance of £71 14*s.* 5*d.*, making altogether a sum of £113 14*s.* 5*d.* received by him in that autumn—a nice little amount to help the frugal couple in the arrangements for, and the expenses of, their journey to Italy.

In illustration of this bill I give engravings of some of Flaxman's productions contained in its items. Of the medallions therein charged, I give those of Herschell,

Buchan, Jenkinson, the King of Sweden, the Queen of Portugal, Mr. and Mrs. Meerman, and Mrs. Siddons. These form a remarkably characteristic and interesting series of the works of this great artist. Of bas-reliefs, for use in various ways, I also give engravings of the exquisite compositions of "Peace preventing Mars from bursting the Door of Janus's Temple," for which Flaxman was paid fifteen guineas, and

"Mercury uniting the Hands of England and France," for which he received thirteen guineas.

The "drawings for the manufacturer's arms" I take to have been drawings of the arms of Wedgwood for a seal, and I am gratified in being able here to introduce an engraving of those arms as they appear on a seal of the celebrated "basaltes," now in possession of Mr. W. R. Wedgwood. The arms of Wedgwood are:—*gules*, four

mullets of five points and a canton, *argent*. The shield on this pretty little seal is highly interesting, as showing these arms with the same borne on an escutcheon of pretence; showing that the bearing was that of Josiah Wedgwood, with that of his wife, Sarah, daughter and heiress of Richard Wedgwood, on the escutcheon.

I give a copy, with the dark sepia background removed, also of his exquisite drawing of the chessmen, preserved at Etruria, for which drawing he charged six guineas in the bill just given. The drawing is of marvellous beauty and finish, and bears the name of *I. Flaxman, inv^t et delin^t*. Of these chessmen I shall have more to say later on. The "Figure of a Fool for Chess," charged in Flaxman's bill at £1 5*s*., will be seen in the lower row, the second figure from the castle in the centre, to the spectator's left.

Supplementary to Flaxman's statement of account just given, I print the following "little bill" for work done by a mason, I presume, in setting up two of the fine marble chimney pieces with Wedgwood's medallions inlaid, which were then so fashionable:—

Jos. Wedgwood to Mr. Flaxman.

1787.	£	*s.*	*d.*
Time, 27 days, at 4*s*.	5	0	0
Board and Lodging	1	15	6
J. W.'s share of washing and expenses . .	1	8	6
	£8	11	6

Sep. 25, 1787. By Cash, £8 11*s*. 6*d*.

Robert Wilson.

This bill is endorsed "Mr. Flaxman's bill for setting up 2 chimney pieces, Sept., 1787."

In the possession of Mr. Dudley Coutts Marjoribanks, M.P., who is the fortunate owner of a splendid and valuable

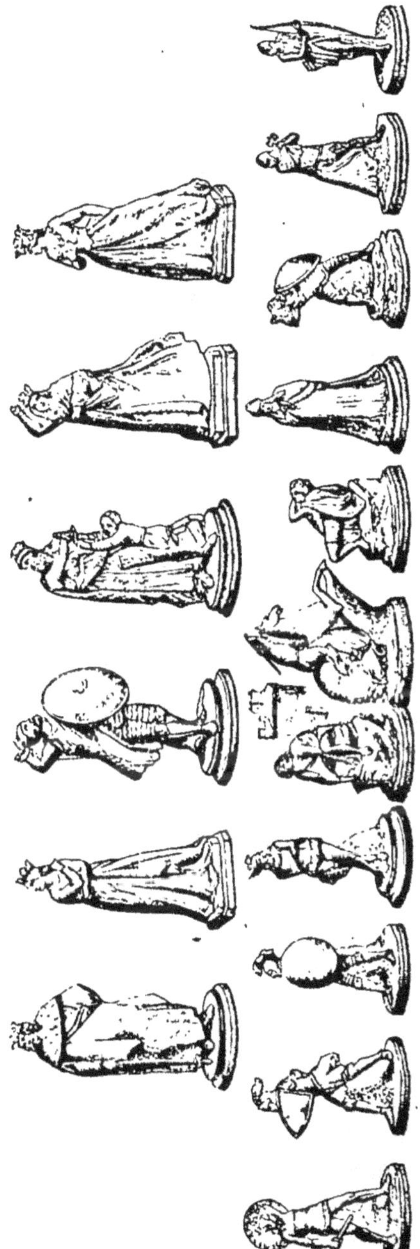

FLAXMAN'S CHESSMEN.

collection of Wedgwood ware, are thirty-two of the original models in wax, on slate, of bas-reliefs by Flaxman and other artists, Italian and French, made for Wedgwood. This series of models passed into the hands of Mr. Marjoribanks a few years ago by purchase, from one branch of the Wedgwood family. Amongst these are the "Death of Adonis," the "Departure of Achilles," and a number of other similar

classical subjects, besides bacchanalian and other groups. Portions of one of these models for a plaque (19 inches long by 10 inches in height) of cupids, with masks and ivy above, are shown on the engravings on this and two following pages. They are exquisitely, but at the same time powerfully, modelled in red wax on a slab of slate. In Mr. Marjoribanks' possession are also a pair of beautifully-designed crocus jardinieres, of a delicate and lovely pink and white, on which these very figures are introduced.

At Etruria some of Flaxman's original models in wax,

on slabs of slate, are also still preserved. One of these is the "Mercury uniting the Hands of England and France," of which I have just spoken. The original wax models of some of Flaxman's chessmen are also still in being, though, unfortunately, in a very fragmentary and dilapidated condition.* At Etruria also are original wax models by Lady Temple and others, and innumerable models, moulds, and

impressions of gems, intaglios, seals, medals, and every conceivable variety of ornament that could assist the great mind of the master in the arrangement of his designs, and in extending the advantages of his manufacture.

While speaking of Mr. Marjoribanks and his collection of

* These exquisitely beautiful figures are modelled in white wax, the "cores," or "strengtheners," being of twisted wire. They are, as a matter of course, of a somewhat larger size than the jasper figures, so as to allow for shrinking by fire.

the original models, it may be well to take the opportunity of saying a word or two on his collection of Wedgwood ware in general. At his seat at Guisachan, Inverness-shire, that gentleman has devoted two rooms to the works of the great potter, in which the walls, bookcases, and other pieces of furniture are decorated with plaques, medallions, &c., inlaid with great taste. His collection contains many choice examples of the different wares produced by Wedgwood,

including among the jaspers, the celebrated "Dancing Nymphs," the "Head of Medusa," from Sir William Hamilton's original, the "Muses with Apollo," the "Fall of Phaeton," the "Infant Academy," after Sir Joshua Reynolds, "The Graces erecting the Statue of Cupid," "Diana visiting Endymion," from the Capitol at Rome, and many fine vases, including a rare pegasus vase in peach-green, 18¼ inches high, and a pair of magnificent black and white vases, with signs of the zodiac, and triumphal pagan procession, 21 inches high, including pedestals, &c.

In 1782 (May 9th and 16th) Josiah Wedgwood communicated to the Royal Society an account of "an attempt to make a Thermometer for measuring the higher degrees of Heat, from a red-heat up to the strongest that vessels made of clay can support," and this learned paper was afterwards translated, not only into the French, but into the Dutch language. In the same month (May 30, 1782) he was proposed as a Fellow of the Royal Society. His election took place on the 16th of January, 1783, and he was admitted on the 13th of February.

In this year Sir Joshua Reynolds painted the well-known portrait of Wedgwood, and also one of Mrs. Wedgwood. The sittings, as appears by Sir Joshua's own pocket memorandum book, were in May of that year. This portrait of Josiah Wedgwood has been engraved, first by W. Holman in 1787, and secondly by John Taylor Wedgwood in 1841. It has also been repeatedly copied in wood for illustration of fugitive notices. The portrait of Mrs. Wedgwood has not, I believe, been engraved. The engraving by John Taylor Wedgwood will be found as the frontispiece to my present work.

Wedgwood, besides being a good judge of painting, was a cordial and liberal friend of art. Wright, of Derby, received commissions from him for several paintings, among which were the following:—"A Moonlight Scene with the Lady in Comus," the "Maid of Corinth," "Penelope unravelling the web—Moonlight,"* and a fine portrait of Sir Richard Arkwright,† with, I believe, others. It is sad to

* The subject of this picture, as a companion to the "Maid of Corinth," was evidently, from the following extract from a letter from Wright to his friend Hayley, the poet, chosen by the latter. Wright says:—"Mr. Wedgwood approves of your subject of Penelope as a companion to the Maid of Corinth."

† This portrait now hangs in the Royal Exchange at Manchester, where I saw it during the present summer. It bears the following

know that, after the death of the "great Josiah," these pictures, being consigned to the care of some one, were lost to the family.

In 1783 Mr. Wedgwood communicated to the Royal Society "Some Experiments on the Ochra Friabilis Nigro Fusca of Da Costa (Hist. Fos., p. 102), and called by the miners in Derbyshire *Black Wadd*;" which, like the former, was printed in the "Philosophical Transactions." At the same time Wedgwood exhibited to the Society several specimens of the products of these experiments.

Continuing, in midst of all his manufacturing operations, and his experiments in other branches of philosophy, his researches into heat, Wedgwood, in 1784, communicated to the Royal Society (printed in the Philosophical Transactions), "An attempt to compare and connect the Thermometer for strong fire with common mercurial ones;" and this he supplemented two years later by "additional observations on a Thermometer for measuring the higher degrees of heat." His observations on thermometers were also published respectively as pamphlets, in the French and in the Dutch languages.

In 1785 a "Chamber of Manufacturers" (or Chamber of Commerce) was established in London "to watch over their interests at large, as one aggregate." The meeting at which this "Chamber of Manufacturers" was established was presided over by Sir Herbert Mackworth. The first point of importance which this chamber had to consider—and which it considered immediately on its formation—was the then all-engrossing subject of the commercial negotiations with Ireland as to the admittance of Irish linens into Great Britain duty free, without a corresponding admittance of

inscription:—"This portrait, painted for the late Josiah Wedgwood, Esquire, by 'Wright, of Derby,' was presented to the Committee of the Manchester Royal Exchange by Edmund Buckley, Esquire, to be placed in the Publick Room, as a memorial to his fellow-citizens of one who, by his important discoveries and persevering energy, mainly contributed to the great extension and success of Cotton Spinning. June, 1853."

British goods on the same terms into that country. A Committee of the Chamber was formed, of which it would appear Josiah Wedgwood was chairman. At all events, the minutes, now lying before me, of the special committee, are signed by him on its behalf.

In this year, 1785, Wedgwood, ever inventing and ever improving, introduced a "jasper dip," in which the clay vessels were "dipped," and so received a coating of jasper instead of being formed of that body throughout. This improvement, being made, was adopted for the whole, with but occasional exceptions, of the jasper goods, and has continued to be used to the present time. Its adoption rendered an increase in the price of the finished goods necessary, and the amount of that increase is seen by the following extract from correspondence of 1785:—"The new jasper, white within, will be the only sort made in future; but as the workmanship is nearly double, the price must be raised. I think it must be about 20 per cent. Nov. 21, 1785."

Collectors will, from this fact, be able to know that, as a general rule, vases made of jasper body throughout were made before 1785, while those white inside were of subsequent production, down to the year 1858, when "solid jasper" body again began to be used, and is still made.

Having now brought down my history to an important period—the introduction of the "jasper dip"—I close my chapter, to resume the narrative in my next with the circumstances attending the food riots at Etruria.

CHAPTER XVI.

FOOD RIOTS AT ETRURIA.—BOAT-LOAD OF PROVISIONS SEIZED. —MILITARY CALLED OUT.—RINGLEADERS SEIZED AND CONDEMNED.—EXECUTION OF BARLOW AT STAFFORD.—CONTEMPORARY ACCOUNT OF THE RIOTS.—JOSIAH WEDGWOOD'S "ADDRESS TO THE YOUNG INHABITANTS OF THE POTTERIES."—SALE OF THE DUCHESS OF PORTLAND'S COLLECTION OF ANTIQUITIES.—THE BARBERINI OR PORTLAND VASE.—WEDGWOOD'S DETERMINATION TO POSSESS AND COPY THE VASE.—ARRANGEMENT WITH THE DUKE OF PORTLAND.—FIFTY COPIES PRODUCED.—JOSIAH WEDGWOOD ELECTED F.S.A.—PUBLICATION OF THE SIXTH EDITION OF HIS CATALOGUE.—"BAMBOO OR CANE-COLOURED BISQUÉ PORCELAIN," AND "MORTAR WARE" INTRODUCED.—DEATH OF THOMAS WEDGWOOD.—CLAY FROM NEW SOUTH WALES.—COMMEMORATIVE MEDALLION. —DARWIN'S BOTANIC GARDEN.—WEDGWOOD TAKES HIS SONS INTO PARTNERSHIP.—THOMAS BYERLEY BECOMES A PARTNER.—MEMOIR OF BYERLEY AND HIS FAMILY.—TREATY WITH SAXONY.—ESTABLISHMENT OF A NATIONAL GALLERY OF SCULPTURE.

In the year 1783, an unfortunate occurrence took place at Etruria, which caused intense anxiety to Josiah Wedgwood. It will be remembered that, consequent on the disastrous American war, trade became stagnant, there was a dearth of provisions, and "food riots" of a fearful character took place in various districts. Etruria, the newly formed, well conducted, and usually peaceable colony of potters, unfortunately became the scene of one of the wildest and most daring of these risings of a starving people. The proceedings are thus well described by Ward:—"A boat laden with flour and cheese had stopped at the wharf near the manufactory,* and the cargo was intended to have been there delivered for consumption in the Potteries; but by a sudden determination of the owners, the boat was directed to proceed forward to Manchester. Information was given by some parties to the provision dealers in Hanley and Shelton, and by them to their anxious customers; the people were led to believe that a design was formed further to enhance the scarcity and price. A large number of them collected together, and hastened down to Etruria, determined to arrest the progress of the boat; but before they got there she had proceeded onward towards her destination. They followed and overtook her at Longport, where they seized her, and brought her back to Etruria. They then took out the flour and cheese, and sold it at a reduced price, paying over the proceeds, however, to the master of the boat. A second boat laden with provisions, which had come up to the locks, was also seized by them, and the cargo disposed of in like manner. There was then stationed at Newcastle a company of the Welsh Fusileers, which, with a detachment of Staffordshire militia, under the command of Major Sneyd, who happened to be at Keel at the time, were marched to Etruria during these riotous proceedings in order to quell them. The Major, with much humanity, harangued the mob on the wickedness and danger of their conduct; but they had become daring and insolent. Two magistrates were on the spot; the riot act was read; and, at the end of an hour's grace, the Major was under the necessity of proceeding to disperse them by force. On the order being given to the military to charge, the rioters fled in all directions; two of them, who had been noticed as their leaders or most daring abettors, were immediately afterwards arrested, and committed to Stafford gaol for trial. Their names were Stephen Barlow and Joseph Boulton, and they were charged with the capital

* Wedgwood's works at Etruria, the wharf being on the canal already at some length spoken of, and which had not long previously been opened.

offence at the assizes, which were held within a few days afterwards. Barlow was convicted and left for execution; and notwithstanding great exertions were made to save his life, he suffered the extreme penalty of the law. The Government were alarmed at the popular disposition to tumult; and poor Barlow became a victim rather to the public safety than to the heinousness of his crime."

From a contemporary account—a letter from Newcastle-under-Lyme, published in the *Derby Mercury* of March 20, 1783, which I for the first time here reprint—the following interesting particulars are gleaned:—

"The people in the pottery and neighbourhood of this town are in a state of absolute anarchy. On Friday last a boat-load of flour and cheese, going up the navigation to Manchester, was seized by a mob of about 400 persons. They opened the hatches, kept possession of it all night, and on Saturday proceeded to sell the flour, &c., at their own prices. An express had been sent to Lichfield to obtain some of the Militia who were stationed there to come to our relief. Two companies were accordingly dispatched; and Mr. Inge, Dr. Faulkner, and Major Sneyd, with the utmost politeness and alacrity, came here. On Saturday afternoon, there happening to be a company of the Carnarvonshire Militia in town, on their route homewards, the commanding-officer, in the most obliging manner, complied with the request of the magistrates to assist them in case of need. The magistrates, military, and many of the most respectable inhabitants of this town, immediately went down to Etruria, near Mr. Wedgwood's manufactory (where the mob still kept the boat), determined to quell and disperse them. The military were kept at some distance from the spot, in order that an opportunity might be given to reason with the persons assembled; and the magistrates and others had the satisfaction of seeing that in a short time they yielded to reason; and, being promised all the assistance that the law could give against the forestallers and others that kept up the markets, and that a subscription would be entered into to obviate the present scarcity as far as they could, they agreed to disperse, provided the boat was not removed.

"But on Monday they assembled again in greater numbers, and sent deputies to the magistrates with a written requisition of what they would have done; in fine, they grew so ill-behaved, that, though there was a very liberal subscription entered into, they had all the assurances of redress and other assistance that the magistrates, the gentlemen present, and their masters could give them, they would not disperse without the boat was fully delivered to them on the instant, that the flour might be sold there. The magistrates not choosing, out of humanity, to go to extremities, by which there would have been much bloodshed, thought it best to comply; and so the mob are now selling the flour at their own prices; but, at the same time, the gentlemen are determined to prosecute the ringleaders to the utmost rigour of the law. Two of the ringleaders are taken and committed to Stafford Gaol."

The following paragraphs relating to the fate of one of the ringleaders, Barlow, are from the same paper:—

"On Saturday the assizes ended at Stafford, when the following persons received sentence of death—viz., Mary Baker, for stealing from the shop of Thos. Heveningham eight yards of printed linen cloth; John Crutchley, for stealing two cows, the property of Sarah Biddulph; James Bagley, for stealing thirteen sheep, the property of E. Cartwright; Wm. Faulkner, for stealing two sheep, the property of C. Adams; John Shepherd, for assaulting and wounding John Holmes, and robbing him of a watch and six shillings; also Stephen Barlow, for assembling with a number of other persons in a riotous manner at Etruria (Barlow was hanged on Monday); Thomas Smith and William Smith, for stealing a fork and a quantity of oats; and James Poole, for assaulting Um. Watson, to be transported to Africa for seven years; likewise Ralph Udale, for breaking into the shop of Henry Kniveton and stealing fustians, &c., was sent to the Thames for four years.

"On Monday last, agreeable to the above sentence, Stephen Barlow was executed at Stafford for rioting, &c. He was attended to the tree by a body of militia. The fate of this unhappy man (who is cut off almost instantly), it is hoped, will be a warning to those deluded people who thus daringly assemble in defiance of the law against rioting, which is a capital offence."

To the peaceable, kindly, gentle, and liberal disposition of Wedgwood, nothing could be more painful than this disorder, happening in his own locality, and by people of his own calling, among whom he had lived throughout his whole life. He immediately wrote and published, in form of a pamphlet, which he distributed through the district,

"An Address to the Young Inhabitants of the Potteries, by Josiah Wedgwood, F.R.S.," in which he calmly considered the grievance of the people, and reasoned with them on their lawless and mischievous course of proceedings. Of this pamphlet, which is now of excessive rarity, I possess a copy. It was "printed at Newcastle, by J. Smith," and is dated "Etruria, 27th March, 1783." This admirable address, which, for kindliness, manly and fatherly feeling, and strict integrity of principle, has seldom been equalled, is here for the first time reproduced.

"Etruria, 27th March, 1783.

"My young Friends,

"The very serious events which have just now taken place amongst us must alarm every one who has any regard for the welfare of his country, or good wishes towards the deluded people themselves who were concerned in the late riots; but young minds like yours receive stronger impressions, and are more affected with such uncommon appearances than older people. At the same time, for want of that experience which should accompany riper years, you are more likely to be misled in judging of the part you ought to take when such violent measures are in agitation. This difficulty of knowing what to decide upon, and the danger of judging and acting wrong, are greatly increased, not only by the unsettled state of the mind in the midst of riot and tumult, but more particularly by seeing your friends, your relations, perhaps even your parents—to whom you have always looked up for advice and direction—taking the most active part in these disturbances.

"I therefore address myself particularly to you, because when you are placed in these unhappy circumstances, seeing those who have fed and protected you from your infancy very forward in promoting such disorders, it is not to be wondered at that you should approve their actions and be prepared yourselves to follow their example upon any future occasion. But though this may be the frame and temper of your minds at the present moment, whilst you believe that the conduct of your friends has been right, yet, if I am happy enough to convince you that, notwithstanding such appearances, they have been mistaken, I have little doubt, from the general good disposition of youth, but that you will change your sentiments and acknowledge that the late tumultuous proceedings were contrary to their own and your real interests. It is of the last importance to you, who are just entering into life, to think upon this subject with great seriousness.

"The evils complained of, and which it is pretended the tumults were to remedy, are, if I am rightly informed—

"1. The dearness of provisions.

"2. The great number of dealers in those provisions.

"3. That no relief is given to the poor by their rich neighbours unless the former rise in a body to demand it.

"With respect to the first evil (*the dearness of provisions*), it is admitted that provisions are dear; but before any censure or abuse is on this account offered to people who may be as innocent as ourselves, we ought first to inquire if the hand of Providence is not visible—to all who will see it—in this dispensation; and surely that consideration may be sufficient to stop the most daring man, and induce him to bear with becoming patience his share of the public calamity, and submit quietly to the will of Heaven, lest he be found fighting against his Maker. Let us then coolly examine into the causes of this scarcity of provisions, and how we can best alleviate a distress which no human power may be able entirely to remove.

"It is well known the weather was so unfavourable the last season, that the farmer with difficulty got his seed into the ground; and the following cold and the almost continual rains rendered the crops so small as scarcely to pay him for that seed and his own labour. We all know, likewise, that the harvest was so late and so wet that nearly half of that small crop was spoiled before it could be got into the barn. What can we expect from the farmer in these circumstances? He must raise the price of the produce of his lands, or he can neither maintain his family nor pay his rents—that is, he must be ruined. Is it reasonable, then, to expect, when the seasons have been so unfavourable, and the earth has not yielded her wonted supply of corn and other provisions, that the farmer only should suffer, and the manufacturer shield himself by violence from bearing his share of the public calamity?

"It is an unhappy circumstance that there should, in times of scarcity especially, be such an unreasonable antipathy between the growers and consumers of provisions, that one party will scarcely hear a word in favour of the other without accusing him who offers it of too much partiality. But as there is such a natural connection between them that one cannot subsist without the other, it would be very desirable to have these prejudices removed; and it must argue a want of fairness in us if we do not consider the farmers' situation in this case as though it were our own. For these reasons

I shall make no apology for saying a word or two more in their behalf.

"The farmer must be supposed to enter upon his useful employment with the same views as the tradesman does upon his business. He means to provide a comfortable subsistence for himself and his family, and surely every labourer is worthy of his hire; but if he is compelled to sell the produce of his farm at the same price when the badness of the season prevents him from getting more than half the usual crop from his land, though he pays for getting it the same or a greater expense than he does when the seasons are more plentiful, his case would be hard indeed! No person would be found to till the land upon those unreasonable conditions; and would not the consequences of the ground lying untilled be felt by us as soon and as severely as by the farmer?

"Let me now intreat you to look back for a moment, and reflect coolly upon the late violent proceedings. Can you think that they were the likeliest means of relieving you under your present distress? Will riot and tumult, accompanied with acts of injustice, incline Providence to be more bountiful to us in the next season? Or will the forcibly seizing upon provisions brought to our markets induce the farmers to supply them better in the future? You cannot think it will. These certainly are not the proper means to redress the grievances complained of. And as the corn grown in our neighbourhood is not at all sufficient for our wants, we should at least permit those who supply us with this and other necessaries of life from distant parts to do it with safety to their persons and properties. It is, indeed, happy for them and us that we live under the same equal laws, which must and will protect both from the violence offered by either. I say the laws MUST *protect us both;* for if it was not so, there would be an end of all government—an end of the State. No man could be secure in the enjoyment of the fruits of his labour for a single day. No man, therefore, would labour; but the stronger would rob and murder the weaker, till the kingdom was filled with rapine and violence, and every man afraid to meet his neighbour. The land would be untilled; for who would plough and sow without the hopes of reaping for himself, and being protected in his property? Famine and its companion, pestilence, must follow, and sweep the miserable remains of the people who had not murdered one another into an untimely grave, the kingdom itself falling a prey to some foreign invader.

"These, my friends and neighbours, would be the inevitable consequences of such proceedings as have lately happened amongst us, if our forefathers had not wisely provided means of putting a stop to them. If you do not know what those means are, I will inform you in so few words as I am able. When the justices of the peace, or other civil magistrates, are informed of a riot, it is their indispensable duty to use all lawful means for putting the speediest end to it. For which purpose they are authorised to press into this service every man or body of men they find necessary—soldiers as well as others; and when the soldiers are so engaged in the assistance of the civil magistrate, it is not the War Office, as some have erroneously supposed, that has a power to give the soldiers orders respecting their firing—not even the officers themselves belonging to the regiments called in; but the power is by our excellent Constitution given to the civil magistrates: 'tis they, and they alone, who have the whole authority in these cases; they must give the word of command to the military officers, and then the officers that *word of command* to the men.

"Such were the wise and necessary regulations established by our forefathers, and I wish you seriously to think of them, that you may be convinced of the folly, as well with respect to yourselves as the public, of resisting that power in the first instance which must in the end prevail. If any one doubts of this, I call upon him to name a time or place, in this or any other civilised nation, where a tumultuous rising of the people, obstinately refusing to disperse, has not been quelled either by the civil or military powers of the State. It is, indeed, impossible, from the nature of things, that it should be otherwise; for if order and obedience of the laws could not be restored, there must be an end of that community.

"And here I cannot help observing that if you consider the behaviour of the magistrates and the military officers upon the late unhappy occasion—how they bore every insult and abuse, and could not be provoked to order the military to fire, by which great numbers must have fallen, and many of you now be mourning the loss of your parents, brothers, and friends, but left the guilty persons to the quiet decision of that law against which they had offended—I am sure you must think their moderation and humanity deserving of the highest praise.

"I would now open to your view the means which we are taking to alleviate the distresses arising from this scarcity of provisions.

"The most obvious and effectual is the opening of our seaports for the importation of foreign grain, which will give effect to the subscriptions now raising for your relief; for unless a real plenty can be introduced into the market, it is vain to expect that the prices can become low. The benefit of this measure has already been felt in several parts of the kingdom, and will unavoidably reach us in a little time; but ours being one of the most inland counties, we cannot so soon receive all the advantages of it as those who are situated near the ports. An impatience natural to people under any immediate distress, induces them to think that the relief which does not come in the moment will never reach them. Accordingly, I do not wonder to hear it asked, '*What shall we be benefited by the importation of corn? The dealers will still contrive to keep up the price, and starve the poor.*' I should be sorry indeed if this was likely to be the case; but you may depend upon the contrary. Nor is it in their power to do it. Provisions will rise and fall in their price according to their quality (either from our own crop, or imported from foreign parts) as naturally as water finds its level. And though this price or market value may be disturbed for awhile by combination where the dealers are too few, yet experience—our surest guide—has shown that this cannot be lasting: the risk and expense are too great. For if corn is kept in large quantities together, it requires to be frequently turned and aired, or it will soon be spoil'd; now, the expense of doing this, the interest of money lying dead, and the risk of fresh importations rendering the market still lower, whilst the dealer is hoarding up to make it higher, must always prevent the corn from being thus kept up to any considerable degree. Some, indeed, have formerly attempted this iniquitous measure; but they suffered severely by it, and will take care how they burn their fingers again.

"The system of canal navigation which runs through the midland part of the country, and completes a communication by water between the four capital seaports of this kingdom, must be of great service in keeping provisions at a less price than they otherwise would be in a situation like ours, where corn is not grown sufficient for the consumption; this it does by conveying corn from the ports or other places, where it is plentiful, to those parts where there is a scarcity, at one-fourth of the price of land carriage, besides lessening the number of horses so greatly, for upon the canal one horse will draw as many tons as forty can do by land, and each horse consumes as much provisions as would maintain six men, I believe more, but I cannot just now find the calculation made upon another occasion; so that each boat upon the canal, reckoned at one-half its burden only, saves to the public daily the provisions of twenty horses, or one hundred and twenty men, and this must have its good effects, though they are not of a nature to strike the common observer so forcibly as many others do of much less importance.

"That these were some of the principal objects in the first planning of the canals I can from my own knowledge assure you, and Parliament was so sensible of the great benefits which the public would receive from these works, that by the same Act in which they gave leave to make them, it was declared felony for any one wilfully to injure or destroy the canals or the works belonging to them.*

"I can therefore no otherwise account for what I have heard was threatened on the late occasion, to *destroy our canal and let out the water*, than from the common frailty of human nature, that when the passions are uppermost, a man shall take revenge upon objects which have no relation to the subject in dispute, and even abuse his best friends if they happen to be nearest to him. I may perhaps be told that in the instance alluded to provisions were carrying *out* of the country by the canal, and not *into* it. The simple fact is, that they were passing *through it*, being the produce of distant counties (Norfolk and Suffolk), and were passing along the canal to Manchester, to be sold there for the support of a numerous body of manufacturers like ourselves, and they were *passing by us* only because corn was dearer there than here, for otherwise we cannot suppose that the dealer would have carried it forty miles farther, to sell it at the same price he might have had with us; and upon a change of circumstances, the next boat of flour or corn would, for the same reason, have been sold *amongst us*; but neither the one nor the other could have come into this country from such distant parts by any other than *water carriage*. Some, I am told, have been weak enough to believe themselves, and to persuade others, that the corn was to be exported to foreign parts while it was so

* The words of the Act are:—" If any person or persons shall wilfully, maliciously, and to the prejudice of the said navigation, break, throw down, damage, or destroy, any banks or other works, to be erected or made, by virtue of this Act, or do any other wilful hurt or mischief, to obstruct, hinder, or prevent the carrying on, compleating, supporting, and maintaining the said intended navigation, such person or persons shall be adjudged guilty of FELONY; and every such felon shall be subject and liable to the like pains and penalties as in cases of felony. And the Court before whom such person and persons shall be tried and convicted, shall have power to TRANSPORT, &c., every such felon, in like manner as other felons."

much wanted amongst our own poor at home. Now you have already been made acquainted that our ports are opened for the importation of foreign corn, and that considerable quantities are actually brought to us by that means. The merchants who buy this corn at foreign markets, bring it to England by a long sea-voyage, and many other expenses attend its importation, besides which they must have an allowance for their profits in trade. They must therefore buy it much lower there than they can afford to sell it in London or any other port; add to this the expenses of carriage from such port to the inland parts of the kingdom, to our own county in particular, and we may fairly conclude that a bushel of foreign corn, if sold for nine shillings here, did not originally cost more than five or six when first purchased abroad. How, then, can it for a moment be supposed that any dealer would send corn from hence, where he could sell it for nine shillings a bushel, to the foreign markets, where, after the additional expense of sending it thither, it would not be sold for more than five or six? The idea is too ridiculous to need any other refutation than this plain statement of facts; but nothing is too absurd to be believed when men's passions overpower their reason.

"Add to the foregoing considerations that, peace being now restored, we may expect that trade and commerce will flourish anew. We have already experienced a very considerable increase of the demand for our manufacture, which will enable masters to give out over-work to their servants, and thereby increase their wages, to the better support of them and their families.

"After thus mentioning what is doing for you by others, if I ask you whether there is not something which you can do for yourselves, it must occur to you that youth is a time in which something should be saved for future contingencies; and if a married man can maintain a wife and four or five children, with no more than you do or may earn, who have only yourselves to provide for, surely some small weekly saving may be made, which, I can promise you, you will afterwards find the comfort of when you marry and have a house to furnish, and other things to provide for a wife and growing family. I know some who have tried this experiment, and do not repent it now; and others I know (would to God the numbers were fewer!) who by too frequently visiting public houses, wakes, and other places where time and money is wasted, have acquired habits in their youth which entail poverty and distress on those who have the misfortune to depend upon their support in future life.

"What I have to say upon the second complaint, '*the great*

number of dealers in provisions,' will take up but little of your time, the case appearing to me too plain to be easily mistaken. The universal opinion of merchants and commercial men, formed upon long experience, is, that the more dealers there are in any particular article, the cheaper that article will be sold, because every dealer considers all others in the same profession as rivals, and will naturally endeavour to gain as much custom to himself as possible, which cannot otherwise be done than either by *underselling* the rest, by giving *longer credit*, or by procuring a *better commodity*—all which are in favour of the buyer. This is certainly the case in general; and I think, if you examine any one particular instance, it will confirm you in this opinion. In this examination we cannot perhaps begin more properly than with the publicans, who retail out drink, as the hucksters do meat, to their respective customers. Let us consider what would be the case if there was only one publican instead of twenty or more, which there are in some of our villages. He would soon be sensible of his importance, that he was the only vendor of liquors in your district, and that you must come to his house when you mean to indulge in that way; and can you think he would be likely to give you *stronger ale* or *larger measure*, or permit you to be *longer in his debt*, because you were obliged to make use of his house, having no other to go to? Surely the contrary would be more likely to happen.

"And if your butcher and baker were placed in the same situation, without a rival in business, would not the like happen with them? I must confess that I think all three, nay, that every retailer of meat, drink, or clothes would be more likely to raise than lower the price of the articles they deal in, upon diminishing their numbers, and thereby destroying that competition and rivalry which is the buyer's best security for a plentiful and reasonable market; and why the hucksters should be excepted—why they would not, like other dealers, raise the price of their goods upon their numbers being lessened, I own I cannot conceive. There may be some circumstances in this case with which I am unacquainted; and if so, I would gladly learn them.

"Perhaps it may be thought best that there should be no hucksters or retailers of provisions at all, but the consumers should buy all they want, and at all times, from the hands of the farmer only. This may seem desirable, and to a certain degree it may, and actually does take place; but, to extend this connection between the farmer and consumer to such a length as to render the retailer useless to the poor housekeeper—in supplying his immediate wants, or giving him a little credit when necessary—is absolutely impracticable, as every one must perceive, upon considering the subject with sufficient attention.

"It is, I know, made a matter of complaint that these dealers meet the farmers on the road, with their butter, their eggs, fowls, &c., and buy them up before they reach market. It is very probable that they do so. But if this is a real grievance, do not make it worse by an ill-judged attempt to remedy it. Do not think that *diminishing the number* of these dealers would cure it: for consider, if you had only one dealer instead of ten, he would probably become ten times as rich, and ten times as able to forestall the markets, as those you now have; and might not content himself with meeting the farmers' baskets in the lanes near here, where you may do the like if you please: he might go himself, or send his agents, to the farm-houses at any distance, and thereby injure you much more than the petty dealers now complained of have it in their power to do.

"If the huckster's profits are thought too large, let us examine the particular circumstances of a number of other trades with which we are acquainted; and if from thence we can form a reasonable conjecture of what their respective profits ought to be—and if we find they are in fact what we have from such circumstances supposed them—it will throw some light upon this matter.

"In general, the professions or trades which require an expensive education or a large capital, or where the articles they deal in are liable to spoil or grow out of fashion, and in which, after all, the return is small,—in these professions the profits upon the sale must necessarily be high; and so we find them to be in apothecaries, toymen, &c. On the other hand, where very little education is required, where even an apprenticeship is not necessary, where a small capital is sufficient, where the articles are in constant and most general use, and in no danger of going out of fashion, where the return is quick, and the article bought in with little trouble, and as readily disposed of again,—it will appear at first sight that upon a business so circumstanced the profits cannot be large; and that if they were so at any particular time, the interference of their neighbours, who could almost any of them begin such a business as this, would soon regulate and bring them to their proper level. Do I need to tell you that this is the case with the hucksters? or do I need to say another word of the improbability of their injuring you *by their numbers*, when those very numbers are your best security against such injury?

"The business of the publican may at first sight seem to be an exception to the above general rule; because, though his capital is not required to be great, and the commodities he deals in have a quick sale, and do not grow out of fashion, his profits, nevertheless, must appear high, if we judge from the price he sells them at compared with the quantity of food sold for the same money. Compare a *glass of brandy*, for instance, with a *twopenny loaf;* or a gallon of his unwholesome liquors, retailed out at the enormous price of *twelve or fourteen shillings*, with a gallon of milk, which is real and nourishing food, sold by the farmer for *fourpence.* But this business will be found to have very great drawbacks, not commonly attended to, particularly his losses by unpaid debts, from the poverty, sickness, and death of his most constant customers—to all which evils they are more liable than other men. The supposed high profit, therefore, of this business is fallacious, as many have found, to their mortification and ruin.

"To return to the dealers in provisions: if they are found to abuse the trust reposed in them, and to cheat the poor people by false weights and measures, they ought to be punished severely. You have it in your power easily to detect the imposition by weighing after them; and I offer, for one, to take any trouble or expense upon myself in bringing such base offenders to the most public justice, and examplary punishment; and protecting the poor from any injury they may apprehend from the hucksters, to whom they may perhaps be indebted.

"The other complaint which has come to my knowledge is, *that no relief is given to the poor* by their rich neighbours, *unless the former rise in a body to demand it.*

"If this complaint is well founded—if the grievances on account of the high prices of provisions have been too great to be supported, and the sufferers have taken proper methods to make their case known, and to solicit relief in a quiet and peaceable manner from the magistrates, or those of their neighbours who were able to give it, and have been refused a proper attention to their complaints, I shall readily join with them in blaming the conduct of such magistrates or neighbours very much, and am willing to take my own share, whatever it may be, of such blame and censure; as I do not mean in this address to be an advocate either for them or myself in whatever we may have done wrong; nor is anything further from my intention than to bear hard upon the poor workman, in this or any other instance. But the fact is that I have not heard of such applications to my neighbours; and having had none made to myself, I must conclude till better informed that recourse was had to violent measures at first, before any legal and proper applications were made for redress of the grievances complained of. But, however this may have been (for it will avail nothing to enter into a dispute upon the subject at this time), let me now beg of you who are approaching to manhood, and who, by your future behaviour, must stamp the character of the potters of the rising generation; let me entreat you, as you value your own reputation and happiness, and the welfare of your country, never to harbour a thought of following the fatal example which has been set you by men who have so greatly mistaken their own and your real interests. But when you labour under any real grievances, make your case known in a peaceable manner to some magistrate near you, or to your employers, who are best acquainted with your situation; and I have not a doubt of your meeting in this way with a speedy and effectual redress, which it would be impossible to procure for yourselves by the measures you have lately seen pursued, or any illegal ones whatever.

"Before I take my leave, I would request you to ask your parents for a description of the district we inhabit when they first knew it; and they will tell you that the inhabitants bore all the marks of poverty to a much greater degree than they do now. Their houses were miserable huts; the lands poorly cultivated, and yielded little of value for the food of man or beast; and these disadvantages, with roads almost impassable, might be said to have cut off our part of the country from the rest of the world, besides rendering it not very comfortable to ourselves. Compare this picture, which I know to be a true one, with the present state of the same country. The workmen earning near double their former wages; their houses mostly new and comfortable; and the lands, roads, and every other circumstance bearing evident marks of the most pleasing and rapid improvements. From whence, and from what cause, has this happy change taken place? You will be beforehand with me in acknowledging a truth too evident to be denied by any one. Industry has been the parent of this happy change. A well-directed and long-continued series of industrious exertions, both in masters and servants, has so changed for the better the face of our country, its buildings, lands, roads, and—notwithstanding the present unfavourable appearances—I must say, the manners and deportment of its inhabitants too, as to attract notice and admiration of countries which had scarcely heard of us before; and how far these improvements may still be carried on, by the same laudable means which have brought us thus far, has been one of the most pleasing contemplations of my life. How mortifying, then, is it to have this fair prospect endangered by one rash act! How ill a return is it to those gentlemen, who by their protection of, and attention to, the interests of this manufactory, have contributed greatly to its advancement; and more especially to the noble person who, as lord lieutenant of the county, is particularly interested in its peace and good order, and who has on every occasion stood up the powerful patron of our infant trade!

"If, after the mention of a name which has every claim to your respectful attention, I may say a word of one who has so little as myself, I can very truly assure you of my sorrow, who, for more than twenty years past, in public and in private, on every proper occasion, have represented the Staffordshire potters as the most orderly body of manufacturers in the kingdom: that this fair and well-earned character should be rendered suspicious, and my mouth so stopped upon this pleasing subject, by the wickedness of a few, and the credulity of many, in too easily believing and following their blind guides into the late mischiefs. But I place my hopes, with some good degree of confidence, in the rising generation; being persuaded that they will, by their better conduct, make atonement for this unhappy, this unwise slip of their fathers.

"Do not, however, mistake me; for though the anxiety and concern of mind I am under may lead me to express myself strongly upon this occasion, I am far from meaning to say that people who for an age past have been generally well behaved and orderly, shall, for a single deviation from this line of conduct, entirely lose their character, and be deemed incapable of a return to that course of well regulated behaviour which had before gained for them so much reputation. Far from it: I am persuaded that your fathers will show, by some proper means, that they are recovered from that unhappy fit of phrensy, under the influence of which they were hurried into acts that in their cooler moments they must condemn; and if the magistracy, to whose care the peace and good order of the country is entrusted, can be convinced that this is really and truly the case, it will be the likeliest means to have the hand of justice stayed and contented with one unfortunate victim, that those unhappy persons whose just apprehensions have obliged them to leave their homes may return again to the support and comfort of their families.

"Permit me one word more, to assure you that the earnest wishes I feel for your welfare, and the peace and good order of our neighbourhood, have been my only inducement to address you upon this occasion; and that if, in pursuit of these objects, I have found it necessary to blame the conduct of those whom nature bids you to love and reverence, I have done it with reluctance, as it is far more pleasing for me to bestow praise than blame upon my neighbours."

The "Address" met with universal approval, and had the desired effect of restoring peace and order in the district. In Mr. Hall's possession is a letter from Josiah Wedgwood, dated "Etruria, 12th May, 1783," in which is an interesting allusion to this pamphlet, as follows:—"Dear Sir,—I am much obliged to you for your partiality to my pamphlet, which was written solely with a view to produce good order and satisfaction among the young and unthinking part of my neighbourhood. . . . . Your much obliged and affectionate friend, and humble servant, JOSIAH WEDGWOOD."

In April, 1786, the magnificent collection of antiquities and articles of vertu belonging to the late Duchess of Portland (Margaret Cavendish, daughter and heiress of Edward Harley, second Earl of Oxford), who died in the July of the previous year, were sold by Messrs. Skinner and Co. In this sale was included that unique and truly magnificent work of ancient art, the "Barberini Vase," so called from having belonged to the famous Barberini family at Rome, from whom it came, by purchase, to Sir William Hamilton, who sold it to her Grace, when it received the name by which it has since been universally known, of the "Portland Vase." This gem of ancient art, Wedgwood determined to possess, that he might carefully examine, study, and, if possible, reproduce in all its exquisite beauty. He attended the sale, and contested the purchase with the then Duke of Portland (son of the late duchess). I have before said that one of his great characteristics was a determination of mind and a fixedness of purpose in whatever he undertook, that was not to be moved; but only strengthened, by opposition. Thus it was over the Barberini Vase. He had determined to examine and reproduce it, and he was not to be diverted from his purpose by a few or many pounds, or by having for his opponent a wealthy duke, the son of its late owner. So he bid on to upwards of a thousand pounds, until, it is related, the duke, stepping across the room to him, asked his object in wishing to possess the vase. On learning his object, the duke offered, if Wedgwood would give over bidding and permit him to become its purchaser, to place it in his hands, and allow him to keep it sufficiently long to reproduce and do what he required. This arrangement being as frankly accepted as it was offered, the duke became the purchaser of the vase for £1,029, and Wedgwood took with him the priceless gem. The price paid for this vase has been variously stated from £1,000 to £1,800. Wedgwood himself says, in his treatise, "The Duke of Portland purchased the vase for about 1,000 guineas, and, thanks to this nobleman's zeal for the Fine Arts, I was soon enabled to accomplish my anxious desire, by his Grace's readiness to afford me the means of making a copy." In a priced copy of the catalogue, the sum of £1,029 is put against the vase, and this being "about 1,000 guineas," as Wedgwood says, may probably have been the correct sum. The duke kept his word liberally, and Wedgwood never lost an opportunity of speaking in high terms of his Grace's consideration. "I cannot," he writes in 1787, "sufficiently express my obligation to his Grace the Duke of Portland for entrusting this inestimable jewel to my care, and continuing it so long—*more than twelve months*—in my hands, without which it would have been impossible to do any tolerable justice to this rare work of art. I have now some reason to flatter myself with the hope of producing, in a short time, a copy which will not be unworthy the public notice."

This copy was in due time produced, and as a *chef-d'œuvre* of modern ceramic art was perfectly unrivalled. Wedgwood produced fifty copies, which were subscribed for at fifty guineas each; but it is said that the sum thus realised (£2,500) fell far short of his actual outlay in making them. One of the first fifty is still in the possession of Mr. Francis Wedgwood, at Barlaston; another is in the possession of Mr. Marjoribanks, at Guisachan, and others are preserved in different collections, while the public have the opportunity of examining one in Mr. Mayer's magnificent museum at Liverpool. The body used for this vase was black jasper, a body used on but few other occasions. The figures were worked up and cut, to the utmost degree of sharpness and finish, by the seal and gem engraver, and thus the beauty of the original was well preserved.

It may be useful to note, that the original moulds are still in existence, and that "Portland Vases" from them are still produced by the Messrs. Wedgwood, both with a black and with a deep blue ground, and are much and deservedly admired.

The month following the sale of the Portland Vase, Josiah Wedgwood was elected a Fellow of the Society of Antiquaries,—his election taking place on the 4th of May, 1786. He never, however, made any communication to the Society, although he published an elaborate dissertation on the Portland Vase.

The following letter, addressed to Mr. Eden, who became Lord Auckland, contains some very interesting particulars concerning Wedgwood's progress in copying the Portland Vase, and of the difficulty he experienced in getting his cameos modelled :—

"Etruria, 5th July, 1789.

"Dear Sir,—I had once flattered myself with the expectation of Your Excellency's arriving in England so soon, as to prevent a letter's finding you upon the Continent, but am now told from too good authority, from the palace, that there is no probability of your leaving Spain for some time. I was very sorry to hear this news, and should have been much more so, if I had not been told at the same time that Mrs. Eden's health was much mended. This circumstance will, I well know, make Your Excellency's stay less irksome, and reconcile you to almost any hardships which the service of your country may impose upon you. I hope and trust the good news of Mrs. Eden's amendment will be confirmed, that we shall soon have the pleasure to hear of her perfect recovery, and that your friends in England will have the additional satisfaction of welcoming you and your good family to your native country, much sooner than you may now perhaps expect. I need not say what true pleasure this will give to them, and few I am sure can enjoy it more than myself. Immediately on the receipt of your Excellency's good letter, of the 25th of March, I despatched a small parcel of Restoration medallions to meet you at Paris, just to show you what we are doing here, despairing of their being in time to find you at Madrid;—and there they will now rest till the occasion is grown old, though it will never be forgotten in this country. I have the pleasure to tell you that the ladies are still so good as to continue my cameos in fashion; and in order to merit this favour as far as I am able, I endeavour to introduce all the novelty, and as much good work as I can procure for their subjects. I employ several modellers constantly in Rome, and get what I can from Paris, and am very happy when I can have anything done by our own artists in England; but my works are too small and delicate for them, so that little assistance can be obtained in England, except what is done under my own eye at Etruria. You will perhaps wonder at your not having heard something of the Barberini Vase. I was always very sensible of the difficulty of attempting to copy so exquisite a piece of workmanship; but in the progress of the undertaking difficulties have occurred which nothing but practice could have discovered to me. The prospect, however, brightens before me, and, after having made several defective copies, I think I begin to see my way to the final completion of it. I shall take the liberty of troubling your Excellency with a further account of my progress in this great work—for such you must permit me to call it—as I advance nearer to the end. My son has been at home near six months. He is now on a tour of discovery in his own country—Wales, the West of England, as far as the Land's End—along with a Mr. Hawkins, an excellent mineralogist, of Cornwall, with whom he became acquainted abroad—otherwise, he would gladly have embraced this opportunity of thanking you for your friendly notice of him. What an interesting situation the affairs of France have lately been in! One day we are told that an express is arrived from the Duke of Dorset, with an account that the King was deposed. The next post (the last) tells us that the nobles, the clergy, and the commons, are happily united; that the King and Queen have shown themselves to their subjects, who were happy and contented; that the English constitution will, in all appearance, soon be established there; and that France may, from the 29th of June, say, what she never could say before, that liberty is established, property assured, and the constitution fixed. Politicians here say, that *we* shall have no cause to rejoice at this revolution; for that if the French become a free people like ourselves, they will immediately apply themselves to the extension of manufactures, and soon become more formidable rivals to us than it was possible for them to do under a despotic government. For my own part, I should be very glad to see so near neighbours partake of the same blessing with ourselves, and indeed should rejoice to see English liberty and security spread over the face of the earth, without being over-anxious about the effects they might have upon our manufactures or commerce; for I should be very loth to believe that an event so happy for mankind in general could be injurious to us in particular. I beg your pardon for this launch into politics, and have done.—I have the honour to be, most respectfully, your Excellency's most obliged and faithful humble servant,

"Jos. Wedgwood."

In 1787, the sixth edition of the Catalogue was published, with the following title:—

"Catalogue of Cameos, Intaglios, Medals, Bas-reliefs, Busts, and small Statues: with a general account of Tablets, Vases, Ecritoires, and other ornamental and useful articles. The whole formed in different kinds of Porcelain and Terra Cotta, chiefly after the antique, and the finest models of modern artists. By Josiah Wedgwood, F.R.S. and A.S., Potter to Her Majesty, and to his Royal Highness the Duke of York and Albany. Sold at his rooms in Greek Street, Soho, London, and at his manufactory in Staffordshire. The Sixth Edition with additions. Etruria, 1787."

This Catalogue occupies seventy-four closely printed octavo pages, the lists of subjects being mostly printed in double columns. In it, besides the four bodies described in the former editions, and which I have already spoken of, the other two of his famed inventions are introduced, thus showing that they date subsequently to the others. These are the "Bamboo" and the "Mortar" bodies, which are thus described by their inventor:—

"V.—*Bamboo*, or cane-coloured bisqué porcelain, of the same nature with the porcelain No. 3.

"VI.—A porcelain bisqué of extreme *hardness*, little inferior to that of Agate. This property, together with its resistance to the strongest acids and corrosives, and its impenetrability by every known species of liquids, adapts it happily for mortars and different kinds of chemical vessels."

Of the "bamboo, or cane-coloured" ware, specimens exist in most collections, and "Wedgwood Mortars" are, of course, known universally to chemists, and are to be found in every good household.

In 1788, on the 20th of October, Thomas Wedgwood, the relative and partner (so far as the "useful ware" was concerned) of Josiah, died, and thus he was left, as he had begun, sole proprietor of the great establishment he had founded. In this same year another edition of the French catalogue was issued.

In 1789 a beautiful emblematical medallion, shown on the accompanying engraving, from an example in Mr. Hall's col-

lection, was produced by Josiah Wedgwood. It is said to have been executed in clay brought from New South Wales, commemorative of that then important event. Of this clay Wedgwood, in 1790, communicated an account to the Royal Society, which appears in the "Philosophical Transactions" as an "Analysis of a Mineral Substance from New South Wales." This medal possesses an additional interest from the fact of its having been copied, with alterations to adapt it to that country, by the French potters of Sèvres. In Mr. Hall's possession is one of these curious and interesting pieces. On it the charming figure of Commerce has had her anchor and ship taken away, and has been converted into a figure with a very different meaning, holding in her hand the cap of Liberty; and a pedestal has been introduced, on which hangs the French shield of three fleurs-de-lis—"marking the time of its execution before the royal arms were abolished, but after Louis XVI. had adopted the cap of liberty."

Of the Etruria medallion Dr. Darwin, in his "Botanic Garden," thus speaks:—

"Gnomes! as you now dissect with hammers fine
The granite rock, the nodul'd flint calcine;
Grind with strong arm the circling chertz betwixt,
Your pure ka-o-lins and pe-tun-tses mixt;
O'er each red sagger's burning cave preside,
The keen-eyed Fine-nymphs blazing by your side;
And pleased on WEDGWOOD ray your partial smile,
A new *Etruria* decks Britannia's isle.
Charm'd by your touch, the flint liquescent pours
Through finer sieves, and falls in whiter showers;
Charm'd by your touch, the kneady clay refines,
The biscuit hardens, the enamel shines;
Each nicer mould a softer feature drinks,
The bold cameo speaks, the soft intaglio thinks.
"To call the pearly drops from Pity's eye,
Or stay Despair's disanimating sigh,
Whether, O friend of Art! the gem you mould,
Rich with new taste, with ancient virtue bold,
Form the poor fetter'd SLAVE on bended knee,
From Britain's sons imploring to be free;
Or with fair HOPE the brightening scenes improve,
And cheer the dreary wastes at Sydney-cove;
Or bid mortality rejoice and mourn
O'er the fine forms on Portland's mystic urn."

To this Darwin appended a note, to say he "alluded to two cameos of Mr. Wedgwood's manufacture: one of a Slave in chains, of which he distributed many hundreds to excite the humane to attend to and assist in the abolition of the detestable traffic in human creatures; and the other a cameo of Hope, attended by Peace and Art and Labour, which was made of clay brought from Botany Bay, to which place he sent many of them, to show the inhabitants what their materials would do, and to encourage their industry." The first of the cameos thus alluded to will be familiar to collectors. It represents a chained slave kneeling, and with hands clasped, and bears the touching appeal, "Am I not a man and a brother?" The second one, which is represented on the engraving on page 311, is more scarce. A representation of it appears in Stockdale's edition of Philips' "Expedition to Botany Bay," and also in the quarto edition of Darwin's "Botanic Garden."

In 1790 the first fifty copies of the Portland Vase were issued, and in the same year Josiah Wedgwood published his "Dissertation on the Portland Vase," in which he detailed the results of his observations on the processes employed in its manufacture, and explained his views as to the design of the groups of figures which surround it.

To the faithfulness and beauty of the copies of the Portland Vase, Sir Joseph Banks, the President of the Royal Society, Sir Joshua Reynolds, the President of the Royal Academy, and other *savans*, gave unqualified testimony. The latter, dating "Leicester Fields, 15th June, 1790," said, "I have compared the copy of the Portland Vase by Mr. Wedgwood with the original, and I can venture to declare it to be a correct and faithful imitation, both in regard to the general effect and the most minute detail of the parts.—J. Reynolds."

On the 18th January, 1790, Josiah Wedgwood took into partnership his three sons, John, Josiah, and Thomas, and his nephew, Thomas Byerley, the style of the firm being that of "Josiah Wedgwood, Sons, and Byerley." The latter had, I believe, by the terms of agreement, one eighth part as his share in the partnership, which he continued to hold until his death in 1810. The following are the official letters issued by the firm on this occasion:—

"Etrurie, ce 18 Janvier, 1790.

"M ——

"La Lettre à la quelle nous avons l'honneur de joindre la presente, vous fait part du changement qui a eu lieu aujourdhui dans la raison de cette Manufacture, et dont nous vous prions de prendre notte.

"Appuyés de l'experience et des conseils de notre Sr Josiah Wedgwood, nous pouvons avec confiance vous assurer que cette manufacture sera conduite avec la même integrité & le même esprit de perfection qui l'ont jusqu'à ce jour caracterisé:—C'est sur ces principes que se fondent nos esperances dans la continuation de vos bontés, que nous tâcherons de meriter par notre zêle et nos soins dans l'administration de vos interets, toutes les fois que vous daignerez nous honorer de votre confiance.

"Nous avons l'honneur d'etre très parfaitement.

"M ——,

"Vos très humble & très obeissants Serviteurs,

La signature de votre très humb. Serv^r^ Josiah Wedgwood.	
La signature de votre très humb. Serv^r^ John Wedgwood.	Josiah Wedgwood, Fils & Byerley.
La signature de votre très humb. Serv^r^ Josiah Wedgwood Fils.	
La signature de votre très humb. Serv^r^ Thomas Wedgwood.	Josiah Wedgwood, Fils & Byerley.
La signature de votre très humb. Serv^r^ Thomas Byerley.	

"P.S.—La marque Wedgwood qu'on a toujours misé sur les productions de cette Manufacture, y sera continuée sans aucune addition."

"Etrurie, ce 18 Janvier, 1790.

"M ——

"Après avoir pendant près de quarante Ans donné l'attention la plus suivie à une mauufacture que j'ai eu le bonheur d'etablir et de voir fleurir même au de lá de mon attente; le desir de jouir un peu de cette aisance & de cette tranquilité si necessaire dans un age avancé, meriteroit peutêtre votre indulgence, mais des considerations plus puissantes m'ont engagé de former le nouvel arrangement dont actuellement j'ai l'honneur de vous faire part.

"J'ai de fils parvenus à cet age, & proprement disposés pour s'occuper des affaires, et un neveu qui a depuis longtems géré les affaires de mon magazin à Londres, à mon entiere satisfaction. Ils se sont proposés de reunir tous leurs efforts pour suivre les diverses branches de cette manufacture, & se promettent de perseverer avec diligence dans le chemin que je leur ai tracé, your les porter à une plus grande perfection.

"C'est pourquoi que je les ai associé dans mon commerce sous la raison de JOSIAH WEDGWOOD, FILS & BYERLEY.

"Permettez moi de saisir cette occasion pour vous temoigner ma gratitude pour toutes les bontés dont vous avez bien voulu me combler: Je vous en demande la continuation pour ce nouvel etablissement, vous assurant d'avance de tous leurs efforts pour meriter votre amitié & votre confiance.

"J'ai l'honneur d'être avec la plus grande consideration.

"M ———, votre très humb. & très obt. Serv."

Thomas Byerley, the relative and now partner of Josiah Wedgwood, was born in 1745, in, I believe, the neighbourhood of Welchpool, where his father; who was a commissioner of excise, resided. Mr. Byerley, senior, who was a descendant of the Byerleys of Byerley Hall, Yorkshire, and of the county of Durham, and married Margaret Wedgwood, sister to the great Josiah, died when his son was only about ten or eleven years of age; and Mrs. Byerley also died early. The young man spent some years in America, where he was successful, but at the commencement of the war he returned to England, and was for some time with his relatives, the Wedgwoods, at Burslem, with whom he gained a knowledge of the potter's art. He was much noticed by his uncle, Josiah Wedgwood, who took him, during the time of "Wedgwood and Bentley," into his establishment, and eventually, as I have shown, admitted him into partnership.

Of Thomas Byerley I introduce, in the engraving on the following page, a portrait, from a medallion produced as a companion, I presume, to those of Josiah and Mrs. Wedgwood, and of Thomas Bentley, of whom I have already given engravings.

It is somewhat curious that both of Josiah Wedgwood's partners—Thomas Bentley and Thomas Byerley—should have married their wives from Derby, but so it was. Mr.

Bentley married, as I have shown, Miss Stamford, of that town, and Mr. Byerley married Frances, third daughter of Mr. John Bruckfield, of Kirk Ireton and Derby, a lady possessed of every domestic virtue, and of the purest and most refined tastes. By her, who survived him many years, he had a family of five sons and eight daughters, more than one of whom have been distinguished in the literary world. They were as follows:—Josiah (so named after the great

potter), who was a magistrate and merchant at St. Mary's, on the Gambia, where he died; Thomas, who, while in the East India Company's service, was commander of a fort, and died of fever in India, at the age of twenty-three; John, who died at Malta; Francis Bruckfield, who, at the early age of eighteen, died on board ship while returning home from Jamaica; Samuel, now living in Indiana, where he is settled and has a family; Frances, married to Mr. William Parkes, of the Marble Yard, Warwick, and afterwards of London (Mrs. Parkes was the authoress of "Domestic Duties," and other works), and was the mother of the present Dr. Parkes, of London, whose writings are so well known among the profession, and related also to the present gifted writer, "Bessie Parkes," whose name is so well known to readers; Maria, who died unmarried; Sarah, who also died unmarried; Anne, married to Mr. Samuel Coltman, late of Leicester and of Thornbridge, Derbyshire, and is the only surviving daughter of Mr. Byerley; Jane Margaret, who died unmarried; Elizabeth, married to Mr. Lowndes, of Liverpool; Catherine, married (as second wife) to Dr. Anthony Todd Thomson, President of the Royal Physical Society of Edinburgh, and authoress of many highly popular stories; and Charlotte Octavia, who died young and unmarried. Mr. Byerley was a man of great business capabilities, of scrupulous exactness, and of unwearied industry; and both during his residence in London, where he managed the London business, and at Etruria, he took a very active and useful part in the management of the commercial part of the concern.

In the beginning of the year 1792 a treaty with Saxony, somewhat on the same principle as the existing one with France, for the importation of their china into this country, and of our earthenware into Saxony, was proposed, and the earthenware and china manufacturers of this country were invited to meet the Privy Council to give information as to their respective trades, and the effect the treaty would have upon them. This treaty was said by the china makers to have been promoted by Mr. Wedgwood. A letter, written at the time, of the 12th of March, 1792, the day before the china manufacturers met the Privy Council, in my possession, says—

"I find the business may be a very serious one as it is respecting a treaty of commerce for the importation of Saxon and other china, much upon the same principle as the treaty with France, which, if it takes place, will be very injurious to the china manufacturers of this country. I believe this is a business brought forward by Mr. Wedgwood for the importation of his pottery; it will be greatly in his favour."

And another, written on the 14th of March, immediately after the Privy Council meeting, gives the following interesting account of the business:—

"When we waited on the lords yesterday at the Privy Council the purport of the business was as follows. My Lord Hawksbury began in saying that an offer had been made from Saxony to admitt our pottery into their country, providing we woud allow the importation of their porcelain here at a certain duty of about 12 per cent. The first question his lordship asked was, wether such a treaty woud affect the manufactorys here? Our answer was, it weud be very injurious, and that we had already felt the very bad effect of the French treaty. Second question was, wether we exported any goods to France since the treaty, or any before? The answer was, no. Third question was, wether our trade had diminis[d] or increased since the treaty? The answer was, the returns at present was nearly the same, but had not the treaty took place with France, the returns woud a been very much enlarged. The last question was, how many people did we think there was employed in the different manufactorys. Mr. Flight gave in, I think, about 110, and Turner's partner 107, besides painters & gilders, which might together make near 200, besides the gilders in town employ[d] on their wares; I gave in about 130. After all this my Lord Hawksbury said he had nothing more to say on the business at present. I am very much afraid that this treaty will take place, and I shoud suppose Mr. Wedgwood has been the principal promoter of it, for most undoubtedly it will be a very advantageous thing to the whole of the Staffordshire ware manufacturers; and when the lords come to see the many thousands of people that are employed in their works, I am afraid the few hundreds that are in the china works will have but little weight. I think it a great hardship on the china makers that the potters shoud come under the same description. I shoud suppose something more will be said on the business very soon. Wether it is ment to be brought through the House or no I cannot tell."

The treaty having been concluded, produced, despite the

croakings of the china manufacturers, good instead of evil commercial results, and in its promotion the far-seeing and deeply-thinking Josiah Wedgwood acted as he always did, for the good of *all.*

In this same year, 1792, it is related that Wedgwood made a liberal offer towards establishing a national gallery of sculpture, &c. Professor Cockerell, when examined before a committee of the House of Commons, on the establishing of Schools of Art, in 1836, thus spoke of this offer of Wedgwood's:—"I beg leave to mention an anecdote of the late Mr. Wedgwood, related to me by Mr. Cumberland, of Bristol, who wrote a pamphlet in 1792, recommending a national gallery of sculpture, casts, &c., viz., that Mr. Wedgwood made a tender of £1,000 in aid of such an institution. I beg further to state, that I have found Wedgwood's works esteemed in all parts of Europe, and placed in the more precious collections of this description of works."

In June, 1793, a change took place in the Etruria firm, caused by the retirement of Mr. John Wedgwood. The firm thereafter consisted of Josiah Wedgwood, Josiah Wedgwood, jun., and Thomas Byerley, and was carried on under the style of "Josiah Wedgwood, Son, and Byerley," until the death of the great and good man in eighteen months afterwards.

CHAPTER XVII.

JASPER WARE.—TURNER'S PRODUCTIONS.—WEDGWOOD'S INVENTIONS AND DISCOVERIES.—EXAMPLES OF JASPER.—MR. HALL'S COLLECTION.—MR. GLADSTONE'S COLLECTION.—DEJEUNE SERVICE.—JASPER BEADS.—CLASSES OF WEDGWOOD'S PRODUCTIONS.—INTAGLIOS AND MEDALLIONS.—SEALS, BRACELETS, ETC.—PORTRAIT MEDALLIONS.—BAS-RELIEFS AND PLAQUES.—BLACK WARE, OR "BASALTES."—BUSTS AND STATUES.—LAMPS AND CANDELABRA.—TEA AND COFFEE EQUIPAGES.—FLOWER AND ROOT POTS.—VASES.—SEPULCHRAL URNS.—ETRUSCAN VASES.—INK-STANDS, MORTARS, ETC.—STUBBS, THE "ANIMAL PAINTER."—THERMOMETERS FOR MEASURING HEAT.

AND now, before the eventful and useful life of Wedgwood, which I have so far traced through its various phases, fairly draws to its close, let me pause to give some few notices of his beautiful productions, as promised in my last chapter, and to add a few words to what I have already said on some of the more noted examples which have come under my notice. And here, too, let me make my final quotation—final, because it is the last which was written—from the original manuscript memoir, to which I have so often had occasion to refer in this my biography of the "great Josiah." I quote it because it refers to the jasper ware, about which, especially, I am about to speak. "These events," says the narrative, "were succeeded by a discovery of very considerable importance to the plastic art, and which occurred to Mr. W. in the course of his experiments. This was the making of white porcelain bisque, susceptible of receiving colours throughout its whole substance, but more especially of being stained with the fine mazarine blue, which was one of the early characteristics of the Saxon porcelain. The mineral from whence this colour is obtained is said to be guarded with so much jealousy in Saxony, that conveying it out of the country is made a capital offence. This porcelain is called jasper, from its resemblances in properties to that stone; and this property of receiving colours, which no other body, either ancient or modern, has been known to do, renders it peculiarly fit for cameos, portraits, and all subjects in bas-relief, as the ground may be made of any colour throughout, and the raised figures of a pure white.

"He possessed this valuable secret about twelve years before anything of the same kind was done by another, notwithstanding that he lived in the midst of a great number of ingenious men engaged in the same pursuits with himself. The first nearly similar effect was produced by an intelligent neighbour,* with a material different from that employed by Mr. Wedgwood; and afterwards, through *an incident* partly accidental, and partly proceeding from treachery, the whole discovery was laid open to several others; but the directors of the principal manufactories of porcelain on the Continent have not yet, as we believe, succeeded in producing this species, although it has been an object of extreme solicitude among them. The bas-reliefs which he finished at this time, partly after the subjects upon the Etruscan vases, and partly from the engravings which he found in different authors, were frequently inlaid into marble for chimney-pieces, and used to ornament girandoles, and in some instances abroad they were set in panels of coaches. Commissions for these and his other productions were often received from foreign princes, and artists have even been sent to make collections of them, to be conveyed to Rome, and there fitted up.

"The bamboo, or cane-coloured porcelain, is another of the inventions of Mr. Wedgwood, which was soon and very well imitated by other makers, and, while it adds variety to

* Turner.

the productions of these useful manufactories, has tended considerably to extend their general commerce.

"He had the good fortune, too, to be of some service to science and experimental philosophy, by making a porcelain bisqué of a hardness nearly equal to that of agate, which, together with its property of resisting the strongest acids and corrosives, and its impenetrability to every known species of liquid, adapts it admirably for mortars and different kinds of chemical vessels. In the foregoing projects, which we have only described generally, but which, in the detailed operations, must have occupied a very great portion of his time and of his thoughts, Mr. Wedgwood never lost sight of the Queen's ware, the first-fruit of his genius, and certainly the best, in point of pecuniary benefits to himself, and of general prosperity. If he had been impelled to the ardent pursuit in which we have seen him engaged by mere sordid motives, he would have found here a resting-place—everything in this one discovery to gratify his wishes; for a matter so suited and so essential to the conveniences of life must necessarily have an immense consumption, and from these results all its advantages. This can never happen, in any comparative degree, to works of mere art and fancy, always accompanied with great expense, employing a much smaller number of persons, and not uniformly returning even the original cost.

"He was continually enlarging the number of useful vessels made of that ware, and several times completely changed his models, in order to keep up the vigour of this branch of his business. He fancied, from the general predilection for porcelain, that if, by an alteration in its colour, he could bring it nearer to that appearance, it would be an improvement acceptable to his patrons. He invented for this purpose a whiter glaze with a tint of blue, now generally known in the manufactory by the name of China glaze; and to introduce this ware, he modelled an entirely new pattern with raised borders, in imitation of shell-work. These borders, or rather edges, he stained with a rich blue colour, laid on under the glaze, in the manner that the oriental porcelain is done; and this was the first time the same art was practised upon earthenware. He was disappointed, however, in its success, for those who were in the habit of buying his wares considered it as an imitation of something better, and they preferred the Queen's ware, which had no pretensions of that kind, but stood on its own merits. It became, however, a very considerable branch of pottery, and in general use. His enterprising and ingenious

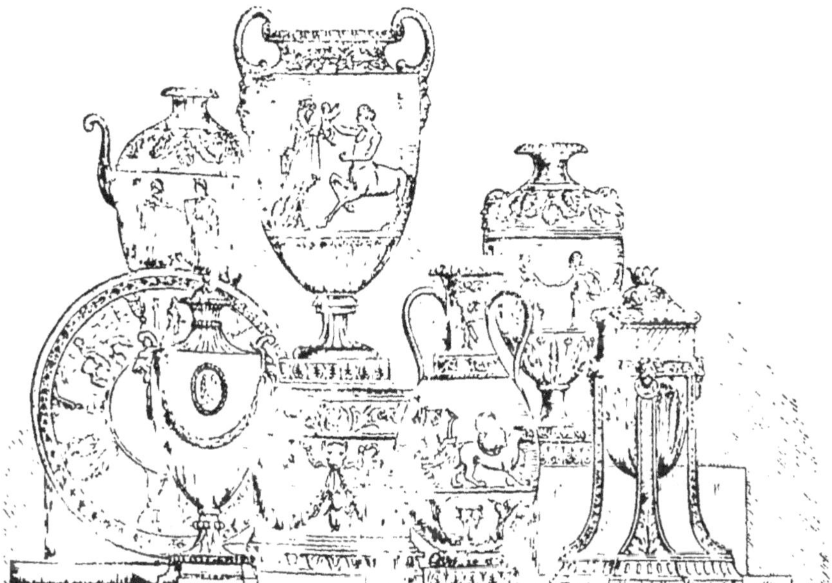

neighbours did not abandon the idea, as he was obliged to do, but improved upon it, covering almost the whole of the surface of their ware with oriental designs in blue; and it now is seen to rival in external appearance the wares of China itself, for which it is substituted among the great body of the people.

"This improvement of the common ware was in some measure owing to the introduction of materials which an attempt had at first been made to preclude the very useful body of manufacturers of earthenware from making any use of."

I have already given, in a former chapter, an engraving, re-introduced on the preceding page, of a fine group of jasper vases belonging to Mr. Hall, and have spoken of the peculiar properties and beauties of that material. It will only be necessary to add to those examples of vases one whose date is well authenticated. The vase shown on the accompanying

engraving belongs to Mr. Benson Rathbone, of Liverpool, who is the fortunate possessor of many beautiful examples of fictile art, among which is an interesting Queen's ware jelly mould, with centre or core painted with groups of flowers, so as to be seen through the transparent jelly. This remarkably interesting piece is marked WEDGWOOD in large capitals on the centre or core, and on the mould the same name in smaller capitals, with the figures 10. A similar one may be seen in Mr. Mayer's museum. The vase here engraved, which is twelve inches in height, was purchased at Etruria by Mr. Reynolds, of Bristol, in 1785-6, as a wedding present to the grandmother of its present owner. In Mr. Rathbone's possession, among other highly interesting examples, is also a charming flower-vase, of a later period, formed of blue and white perpendicular bands, interlaced with plaits of straw.

The next engraving is a representation of an elegant example of Wedgwood ware, but of a larger and more costly kind. It is a simple but very chaste *déjeuné* service, belonging to the Right Hon. W. E. Gladstone, M.P., Her Majesty's Chancellor of the Exchequer, to whom I have pleasure in expressing my obligations for the use of his collection, and for other acts of kindly courtesy. Of this *déjeuné* service Mr. Gladstone says, in his "Wedgwood: an Address:"—I have a *déjeuner*, nearly slate-coloured, of the ware which, I believe, is called jasper ware. This seems to me a perfect model of workmanship and taste. The tray is a short oval, extremely light, with a surface as soft as an infant's flesh to the touch, and having for ornament a scroll of white ribbon, very graceful in its folds, and shaded with partial transparency. The detached pieces have a

ribbed surface, and a similar scroll reappears; while for their principal ornament they are dotted with white quatrefoils. These quatrefoils are delicately adjusted in size to the varying circumferences, and are executed both with a true feeling of nature and with a precision that would scarcely be discredit to a jeweller."

Mr. Gladstone possesses a fine collection of English and foreign fictile art, including besides this service a portion of a Queen's ware dessert service, of the plain escallop shell pattern, with leaves effectively drawn, and specimens of red ware, as well as imitation of agate, porphyry, and other specimens of Wedgwood's manufacture of different periods.

The accompanying illustration shows two patterns of one of the most minute and most exquisitely beautiful of the productions to which the jasper ware was applied—viz., beads for the neck and for bracelets. Those here exhibited

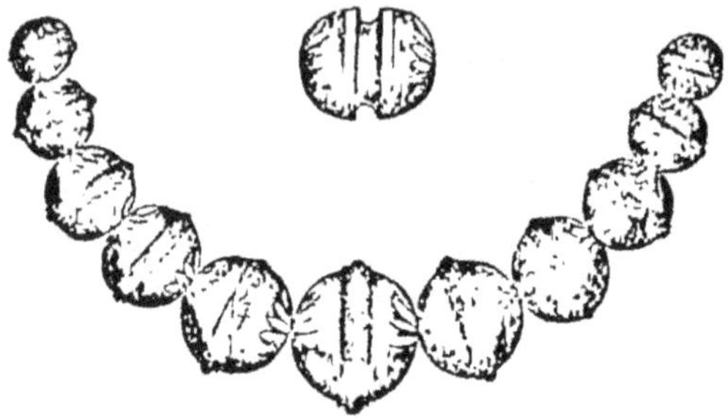

are engraved from examples in the possession of my friend Dr. Davis, F.S.A., and others are to be seen in various collections. The body is the blue, or other coloured jasper, and the foliage and ornaments are raised in white.

One notable feature of the jasper ware, besides those of its extreme beauty and its many remarkable properties, is its applicability to such a variety of, and such widely different, articles. From the lofty pedestaled vase down to the minutest bead, scarcely larger than a pea; from the bold and massive frieze down to the most delicate ear-drop; and from the large inlaid plaque of the chimney-piece down to the most exquisitely and almost microscopically decorated settings for jewellery,—the jasper possessed, and possesses (for it is still made), greater capability and adaptability than any other ware which has ever been, or apparently can be, invented. It is well, perhaps, to say a few words on these different varieties of goods produced by Wedgwood, that the uninitiated as well as collectors may know something of the extent to which this branch of ornamental art was carried by its great master.

Wedgwood divided his *ornamental* productions into twenty

classes. The First Class comprised intaglios and medallions "accurately taken from antique gems, and from the finest models that can be procured from modern artists." In 1787, in this class alone, no less than 1,032 separate designs had been issued. This class was subdivided into two sections; the first embracing "cameos, which are made either in jasper with different coloured grounds, for ornamental purposes, or in white porcelain *bisqué*, at a very moderate price, for those who wish to form mythological or historical cabinets;" the section being again subdivided under the heads of "Egyptian mythology," "Grecian and Roman mythology," "sacrifices," "heads of ancient philosophers, poets, and orators," "Sovereigns of Macedonia," "fabulous age of the Greeks," "War of Troy," "Roman History," "Masks, Chimeras," &c., "Illustrious Moderns," and "Miscellaneous;" and the second "Intaglios," also subdivided under different heads. "The intaglios," Wedgwood says, "take a good polish, and, when polished, have exactly the effect of fine black basaltes or jasper. Another method has been discovered of adding very considerably to their beauty, by making the intaglio part black, and the flat surface blue and highly polished, by which means they are made to imitate the black and blue onyx (or niccolo) with great exactness, and become equally ornamental for rings as for seals. They are likewise made and polished in imitation of various coloured agates and other stones, and in cyphers, with the letters of one colour and the ground of another. The correct sharpness and superior hardness of these intaglios have now been sufficiently ascertained by experience."

Most of the subjects in these sections were produced as seals, as well as of various sizes and forms for rings, bracelets, brooches, &c. The seals were principally made with shanks, to hang to the watch chain, or double-sided for setting as "swivel seals." Those made with shanks were highly polished, so as to require no mounting; and examples are to be found in most collections. In seals, besides classical and other groups, heads of celebrated personages, armorial bearings, &c., Wedgwood produced a complete double set of cyphers, "one consisting of all the combinations of *two* letters, and the other of all the *single* letters, which last," he says, "are now much used, especially for notes."

Portraits of individuals were also cleverly produced in seals, as well as in medallions, &c.; and it is interesting to be enabled to give my readers the cost at which such objects were made. A portrait of the individual would be modelled in wax, by Flaxman, or Hackwood, or some other artist employed by Wedgwood, in the same manner as those I have already spoken of and engraved in connection with Flaxman's bills. The cost of this model in wax, made from the life, would be, to the party himself, from three to five guineas, according to the size. From this a mould would be taken, as I have already described, and finished cameos produced, of proper size for brooches, at 7*s.* 6*d.* each; for rings or seals, at 5*s.* each; and as medallions, at 10*s.* 6*d.* each. As the same wax model would, of course, as I have explained, serve for all these various sizes (the reductions being produced by successive firings), and as not less than ten copies were made in any one way, it will be seen that the total cost to the customer of ten six-inch medallions of his or her portrait, including the original wax model, would be ten guineas, and for rings, &c., five-and-a-half guineas. The following is Josiah Wedgwood's notice respecting these cameo portraits :—

"It may be proper in this place to observe, that if gentlemen or ladies choose to have models of themselves, families, or friends, made in wax, or cut in stones of proper sizes for seals, rings, lockets, or bracelets, they may have as many durable copies of those models as they please, either in cameo or intaglio, for any of the above purposes, at a moderate expense; and this nation is at present happy in the possession of several artists of distinguished merit, as engravers and modellers, who are capable of executing these fine works with great delicacy and precision. If the nobility and gentry should please to encourage this design, they will not only procure for themselves *everlasting portraits*, but have the pleasure of giving life and vigour to the arts of modelling and engraving. The art of making *durable copies* at a small expense will thus promote the art of *making* originals, and future ages may view the productions of the age of George the Third with the same veneration that we now behold those of *Alexander* and *Augustus*.

"Nothing can contribute more effectually to diffuse a good taste through the arts than the power of multiplying copies of fine things in materials fit to be applied for ornaments, by which means the public eye is instructed, good and bad works are nicely discriminated, and all arts receive improvement. Nor can there be a surer way of rendering any exquisite piece possessed by an individual famous, without diminishing the value of the original; for the more copies there are of any works, as of the *Venus de Medicis*, for instance, the more celebrated the original will be, and the more honour derived to the possessor. Everybody wishes to see the original of a beautiful copy.

"A model of a portrait in wax, when it is of a proper size for a seal, ring, or bracelet, will cost about *three guineas*, and of a portrait from three to six inches in diameter, *three*, *four*, or *five guineas*. Any number of copies of *cameos* for rings, in jasper, with coloured grounds, not fewer than ten, are made at 5*s*. each. Any number of *cameos* for bracelets in the jasper, with coloured grounds, at 7*s*. 6*d*. each. Any number of *portraits* in the same material, from three to six inches diameter, not fewer than ten, at 10*s*. 6*d*. each."

Examples of these medallion portraits have already been given.

The Second Class into which Josiah Wedgwood divided his productions was "bas-reliefs, medallions, tablets," &c.; and of these he produced about three hundred distinct designs of groups, &c., many of them of the most exquisite character, and of faultless workmanship.

"The articles of this class," says Wedgwood, "have employed some of the best artists in Europe, and it has been a work of much time and attention, as well as expense, to bring it to its present state. It is still receiving continual additions, not only from *artists* in our own and other countries, but likewise from the *amateurs* and *patrons* of the arts. I have lately been enabled to enrich it with some charming groups, which Lady Diana Beauclerk and Lady Templetoun, whose exquisite taste is universally acknowledged, have honoured me with the liberty of copying from their designs. The Portland Vase, late Barberini, for the acquisition of which to this country the artists are so much obliged to their well-known benefactor, Sir William Hamilton, will furnish a noble addition, and I cannot sufficiently express my obligation to his Grace the Duke of Portland, for entrusting this inestimable jewel to my care, and continuing it so long—more than twelve months—in my hands, without which it would have been impossible to do any tolerable justice to this rare work of art. I have now some reason to flatter myself with the hope of producing, in a short time, a copy which will not be unworthy the public notice. I wish likewise to pay my grateful acknowledgments to the Marquis of Lansdowne, for the liberty of taking moulds from a suite of dancing nymphs, and other beautiful figures, modelled in Italy from the paintings found in Herculaneum, and to the Duke of Marlborough, for a cast from the exquisite gem in His Grace's collection, the Marriage of Cupid and Psyche. The Herculaneum figures are all executed in the basaltes, and only three or four of them have as yet been adapted to the jasper of two colours; the Marlborough gem has been made in the jasper composition for some time, but not till very lately in the degree of perfection I wished for. I am likewise under particular obligations to Lady Margaret Fordyce, Lady Anne Lindsey, Mrs. Montague, Mrs. Crew, and Miss Emma Crew, to his Grace the Duke of Montague, Lord Besborough, Sir Watkin Williams Wynne, Sir Joshua Reynolds, Sir William Chambers, Mr. West, Mr. Astle, and many others of the nobility, connoisseurs, and principal artists of this kingdom, for their kind and valuable assistance in bringing these works to that degree of perfection, and that notice with the public, which they at present possess. With such ample and liberal assistance, I may, perhaps, be allowed to hope that the articles of this class may with propriety have a place among the finest ornaments which the arts of the present age have produced, and that no cameos, medallions, or bas-reliefs, of equal beauty, magnitude, and durability, or so highly finished, have ever before been offered to the public. These bas-reliefs, chiefly in the jasper of two colours, are applied as cabinet pictures, or for ornamenting cabinets, book-cases, writing tables, in the composition of a great variety of chimney-pieces, and other ornamental works. With what *effect* they are thus applied, may be seen in the houses of many of the first nobility and gentry in the kingdom."

It is pleasant to be able to state that in some of "the houses of the first nobility and gentry"—as at Kedleston Hall, the seat of Lord Scarsdale, for instance—chimney-pieces, decorated with these beautiful plaques in Wedgwood's own time, are still to be seen in all their original beauty.

The THIRD CLASS consisted of medallions, &c., of kings, queens, and illustrious persons, "of Asia, Egypt, and Greece," a series which, in 1787, consisted of more than one hundred heads. CLASS FOUR, "the ancient Roman history, from the foundation of the city to the end of the Consular government, including the age of Augustus, in a regular series of sixty medals, from Dassier, at one guinea the set, or singly at sixpence each." CLASS FIVE, heads of illustrious Romans, of which about forty were produced. CLASS SIX, the twelve Cæsars, which were produced in four different sizes, and their empresses, which were produced in one size only. CLASS SEVEN, "sequel of emperors, from Nerva to Constantine the Great, inclusive," a series of fifty-two medallions. CLASS EIGHT, the heads of the popes, a series of two hundred and fifty-three medallions, "at sixpence a-piece singly, or at threepence a-piece to those who take the set." CLASS NINE, a series of a hundred heads of kings and queens of England and France, which were sold in sets only, either in or out of cabinets; and CLASS TEN, "heads of illustrious moderns;" this series had at that time extended to about two hundred and thirty heads, which were made both in black basaltes and in blue and white jasper, and of various sizes, their prices varying "from one shilling a-piece to a guinea, with and without frames of the same composition; but most of them, in one colour and without frames, are sold at one shilling each."

Of the medallions in these highly interesting and important classes, Josiah Wedgwood wrote in 1787:—

"The peculiar fitness of these fine porcelains for rendering exact and durable copies of medallions, heads, &c, at a moderate price, has induced the proprietor to aim at regular *biographical suites* of distinguished characters, in different ages and nations, for the illustration of that pleasing and instructive branch of history; and with this view he has been at a considerable expense in collecting, repairing, modelling, and arranging portraits of illustrious men, both of ancient and modern times. The present class contains those of Greece, Egypt, and the neighbouring states, in chronological order. The four following classes exhibit a complete series of the Roman history, from the foundation of Rome to the removal of the seat of empire to Constantinople. The thread of history is continued in the next two classes by a set of the popes, and of all the kings and queens of England and France; and the more recent periods of history are illustrated in the succeeding one by a considerable number of princes, statesmen, philosophers, poets, artists, and other eminent men, down to the present time. These portraits are made both in the basaltes and in the jasper with coloured grounds; they are sold either with or without their cabinets. Their general size is *two inches by one and three quarters*, unless where otherwise expressed."

Wedgwood's next class (ELEVEN), which he headed "busts, small statues, boys, animals," &c., was a very important one, and included many of his most extraordinary works. These are the large busts of distinguished persons, which now are so rare and so much sought after. Of his productions in this class the great master wrote as follows, and his opinions on the production of popular copies of fine works of Art were so correct, that they will be read with pleasure and profit at the present time.

"The black basaltes having the appearance of antique bronze, and so nearly agreeing in properties with the basaltes of the Egyptians, is excellently adapted for busts, sphynxes, small statues, &c.; and it is certainly an object of importance to preserve in such *durable* materials as many as possible of the fine works, both of antiquity and the present age, for after time has destroyed even marbles and bronzes, as well as pictures, these copies will remain, and will transmit the productions of genius and the portraits of illustrious men to the most distant times.

"Those who duly consider the influence of the *fine arts* on the *human mind*, will not think it a small benefit to the world to diffuse their productions as wide, and to preserve them as long, as possible.

The multiplying of copies of fine works in beautiful and durable materials, must obviously have the same effect in respect to the arts, as the invention of printing has upon literature and the sciences; by their means the principal productions of both kinds will be for ever preserved, and will effectually prevent the return of ignorant and barbarous ages.

"Nor have the artists themselves anything to fear from this multiplication of copies. Whatever awakens and keeps alive the attention of the public to the production of the arts—and nothing can be more effectual for that purpose than the diffusion of *copies of fine works*—must ultimately be advantageous to the artist who is capable of producing *fine originals;* for this general attention, in whatever country it is sufficiently excited, will always produce *amateurs* who, not contented with copies which every one may procure, will be ambitious of possessing fine originals, that copies from them may be multiplied and diffused to the credit of the possessor, and the emolument as well as credit of the original artist. On these considerations the proprietor has, at a very considerable expense, extended the subjects of this class, and endeavoured to give them all the perfection in his power, and he hopes the articles in the following list will be found not unworthy the notice of those who have been pleased to honour this difficult and expensive undertaking with their generous patronage. A small assortment of the figures is now made in the jasper of two colours, the effect of which is new and pleasing.

"The proprietor is ambitious of preserving in these materials the distinguished characters of the present times, either by making their *busts* in basaltes, or their *portraits* in bas-relief, in the jasper with coloured grounds, and he begs leave to observe to those who may honour him with models or moulds for this purpose, that if the models be made in clay, they either should be burnt to enable them to bear carriage, or plaster moulds taken from them in their soft state, which will answer equally well; but that neither clay models nor plasters are to be oiled; they should be a fifth part larger than the figure required. These models, casts, or moulds may be safely sent from any distance, and they may be returned if desired."

In this durable material, the "black basaltes," busts of M. Aurelius Antoninus, Lord Chatham, Zeno, Plato, Epicurus, Junius Brutus, Marcus Brutus, Pindar, Homer, Cornelius de Witt, and John de Witt were produced, of the extraordinary size of twenty-five inches in height, while about eighty other busts were produced, of various sizes, from twenty-two down to four inches in height. In the same material was also made a fine series of more than forty statues, animals, sphynxes, &c. Of the latter an example

will be seen on the accompanying engraving of a group of black ware belonging to Mr. Hall.

The next class (Class Twelve) embraced various kinds of lamps and candelabra, which were made both in the variegated pebble and black basaltes, in tripods with three lights, and other antique forms. Some were also made in jasper of two colours, "adapted to Argand's patent lamp, the brilliant light of which being thrown upon the bas-reliefs, has a singular and beautiful effect. They all bear the flame perfectly well." The prices of the lamps were from "two shillings a-piece to five guineas," and the candelabra from one guinea to four or five guineas a pair. These were never made to a great extent, and are now scarce, and much sought after by collectors.

Class Thirteen was a very important division in the productions of Wedgwood's establishment. It comprised tea and coffee equipages of every variety of shape and style of decoration. In this class the teapots, coffee-pots, chocolates, sugar dishes, cream ewers, with cabinet cups and saucers, and all the articles of the tea-table and *déjeuné,* were made in the "bamboo" and "basaltes," both plain and enriched with Grecian and Etruscan ornaments. They were likewise made in jasper of two colours, "polished within (not glazed) like the natural stone, ornamented with bas-reliefs, and very highly finished," and of truly exquisite beauty. In the catalogue issued by Josiah Wedgwood in 1787, is an aquatint plate printed in colours, of one of these beautiful cups, in which the artist (I have reason to believe Francis Eginton)* has sought to show the transparency of

the thin jasper. This cup, with the addition of the gilding from a fragment of one of these very choice pieces in my own collection, I show on the accompanying engraving. The material is the finest and most delicate jasper, the body of intense hardness, the surface truly, as Mr. Glad-

* Some particulars regarding Eginton and his works will be given later on.

stone has so well expressed it, "soft as an infant's flesh to the touch," and the decoration and workmanship of marvellous beauty and finish. In Mr. Hall's collection are, among other rare examples of tea and coffee-cups, &c., a choice coffee-cup of black jasper, white inside, with white rims, white wreaths, and a blue and white cameo in front; a bamboo or cane-coloured embossed teapot and stand, with raised red border and classical groups, and many other notable specimens; and in my own possession, as well as in the hands of most collectors, are examples of bamboo and various coloured jasper services.

The next class—Class Fourteen—consisted of "flower-pots and root-pots," which Wedgwood thus described:—

"Of *root-pots*, as well for bulbous as other roots, and of flower-pots and *bouquetiers*, there is a great variety, both in respect to pattern and colour, and the prices vary accordingly. The flower and root-pots are from sixpence a-piece to seven shillings and sixpence. Some of the bulbous root-pots are finished higher, with bas-reliefs, enamelling, &c., and the prices are in proportion. The ornamental, or vase flower-pots, are from one shilling to eighteen shillings, or more."

Class Fifteen comprised the "ornamental vases of antique form, in the 'terra-cotta,' resembling agate, jasper, porphyry, and other variegated stones of the crystalline kind," of which I have already at some length spoken. These vases he describes as being—

"Adapted for ornamenting chimney-pieces, cabinets, book-cases, &c. They are from 6 to 18 or 20 inches high. The prices from 7*s*. 6*d*. to two or three guineas, according to their size and the manner in which they are finished, with or without handles, bas-reliefs, gilding, draperies, festoons, medallions, &c. They are generally sold in *pairs*, or in sets of *three*, *five*, or *seven* pieces. The sets of five pieces are from about two guineas to five or six guineas the set."

Class Sixteen included the "antique vases of black porcelain, or artificial basaltes, highly finished, with bas-relief ornaments," &c., which I have already described. Of this species of vase a large number of forms, chiefly Grecian or Etruscan, were produced, and at prices at which it would make a collector's heart glad to meet with them now. The sizes were "from three or four inches high to more than two feet, the prices from 7*s.* 6*d.* a piece to three or four guineas, exclusive of the very large ones, and those which consist of several parts. The sets of five, for chimney-pieces, are from two guineas to six or eight guineas a set." While speaking of the productions in this class, it may be well to note one use to which these black basaltes vases were put, which will probably be unknown to my readers. It is that they were used for monumental purposes. At Ashley Church, for instance, in 1770, a monument to William Viscount Chetwynd was erected, "the top part of which is a niche with a circular head, and within it is placed a large Egyptian black urn, which was made at Etruria in the time of the late Josiah Wedgwood."

CLASS SEVENTEEN was composed of vases, pateras, tablets, &c., with encaustic paintings, Etruscan and Grecian. Of these vases I have already spoken, and it is therefore only necessary here to say that they were produced of various sizes, from six inches up to twenty inches in height, at prices varying from one to ten or twelve guineas each. Tablets for chimney-pieces, for cabinets, and for inlaying, were also enriched in the same manner as the vases, with encaustic painting, and produced an admirable and striking effect. They were made of every size, from that suitable for a bracelet to eighteen or twenty inches in diameter. "Some have been made," writes Wedgwood, "for that excellent artist, Mr. Stubbs,* so large as thirty-six inches; and his

* Stubbs, the famous painter of horses, &c., was employed to a considerable extent by Mr. Wedgwood in designing and decorating; and a large painting by him—a family group, representing Josiah Wedgwood and Mrs. Wedgwood seated under a tree in the grounds of Etruria, with their family, some on horseback, and others grouped with a child's carriage, with Woolstanton Church, &c., in the distance—hangs in the dining-room at Barlaston.

exquisite enamels upon them after nature, which have been repeatedly exhibited in the Royal Academy, are evidences of the species and value of the enamel paintings that may be produced upon these tablets."

To CLASS EIGHTEEN belonged the magnificent vases, tripods, and other ornaments, in jasper, with coloured grounds and white bas-reliefs, of which I have so often spoken, and of which a selection of examples has been engraved from Mr. Hall's collection, and from that of Mr. Rathbone, &c. Their prices Wedgwood stated to be "nearly the same as those of the high-finished vases with encaustic painting." Of these vases an immense variety was produced, and examples of different degrees of excellence and rarity are to be found in every collection.

The next class (NINETEEN) was devoted to "inkstands, paint-chests, eye-cups, mortars, and chemical vessels," of some of which I have already spoken. The most notable ink-stand, described by Josiah Wedgwood as his own invention, is the plain one I have before alluded to, and of which I give the following account from the Catalogue, and also a copy of one of the descriptive papers drawn up in the French language, by Wedgwood himself, and its accompanying diagram, from the original paper in my own collection.

"Different kinds of ink-vessels and inkstands" says the Catalogue, "have been made at this manufactory; but the following is presumed to be the best and most convenient that has ever yet been brought into use.

A A, the ink cistern, filled with ink up to F.

B, pen tubes, close at bottom.

C, a small opening into the cistern, stopped with an air-tight plug.

D, a conical tube, communicating at bottom with the cistern, and in which the ink rises only to E, being kept down while the aperture C is stopped by the pressure of the atmosphere.

"When the cistern is to be filled, take out the plug C, and pour in ink till it rises nearly to the top, D and F. The plug being then returned into its place, the ink in the cavity D E may be taken out; or on standing for a few hours, it will subside of itself to E, especially if warmed a little before the plug is put in.

"The advantages of this inkstand are, that the form of the tube D E, through which the pen is dipped, prevents the soiling of the pen and fingers; that the narrow end of this tube, below E, pre-

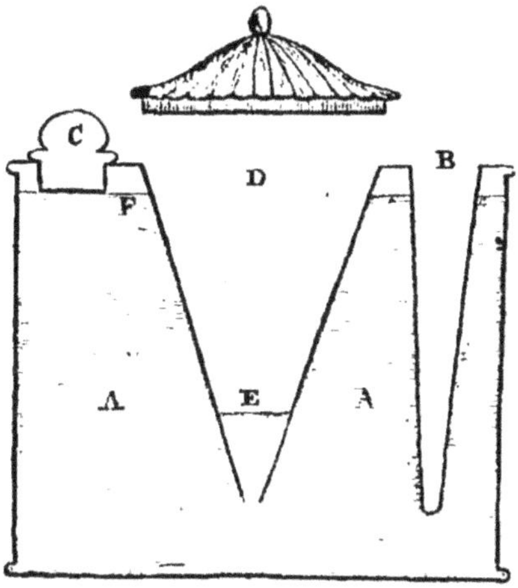

vents the pen from striking the bottom; that the ink comes in contact with the air only in the small space E, by which means it is prevented from evaporating, growing thick, and spoiling, as it does in all the common inkstands, where a large surface is unavoidably exposed to the air; that the sediment which the ink may deposit on standing, will settle chiefly on the broad part of the bottom, under the main body of ink, not where the pen is dipped, as the ink is there in small quantity, and continually supplied with the fine part from above; that the vessel being made of the fine compost black basaltes, is neither corroded by the ink nor absorbs it, nor injures its colour, as the metals used for these purposes do; and that it admits of being finished, in point of workmanship, with the highest degree of accuracy.

"These inkstands are sold separately, as represented in the above plate, or with sand boxes, wafer boxes, &c., forming various kinds of useful and ornamental ecritoires, as well in the jasper of two colours, as in the basaltes. The prices are from Sixpence, rising according to the sizes, forms, and workmanship, to Two Guineas."

The French advertisement to which I have alluded is as

follows, and it has the same diagram as the one just introduced : —

"DES ECRITOIRES EN PORCELAINE NOIRE, FABRIQUÉES PAR MESSRS. WEDGWOOD ET BENTLEY.

"De parmi tout le grand Nombre des Ecritoires et d'Encriers qu'on a inventé jusqu'ici, celle, qui est representé dans la Figure ci-dessus, est la meilleure et la plus commode: et comme elle est d'une Invention tout neuve, il en faut une Description.

"EXPLICATION DE LA FIGURE.

"A A. La Citerne, remplie d'Encre jusqu'à F.

"B. Des Tuyaux pour les Plumes, qui sont fermées en bas, ce qui empêche qu'il n'y entre point d'Air.

"Une petite Ouverture, qui va à la Citerne, avec un Bouchon très serré.

"D. Un Cone, par où l'on remplit la Citerne, en tirant premierement le Bouchon à C.

"On verse l'Encre dans le Cone, jusqu'à ce qu'il soit plein, après quoi on remet le Bouchon dans sa Place ; puis, en vuide l'Encre hors du Cone, soit en versant ou par un Eponge, aussi bas que E, alors l'Encre restera dans la Citerne, à la Hauteur de F, et agira en Fontaine ; la Plume puisant l'Encre par le Cone D, au Point E.

"*Les Avantages et Proprietês de ces Ecritoires.*

"L'Ouverture graduelle du Cone fait, qu'on n'est pas sujêt de se salir les Doigts, ou la Plume, comme on fait avec les autres très communes.

"Le Bout du Cone etant etroit, previent que la Plume ne grâte contre le Fond.

"La Surface de l'Encre n'est pas exposée à l'Air, autrement qu'au petit Point E, ce qui en previent l'Evaporation, et l'empêche de se gâter en s'épaissant, comme il arrive dans tous les Encriers communs, ou il y a une grande Surface necessairement exposée à l'Air.

"Ce qui recommande ces Ecritoires encore davantage, est, qu'ils sont composés d'un Jaspe ou Porcelaine Noire, très fine et bien lié, qui n'est jamais corrodé par l'Encre, et ne l'absorbe point : aussi ils se laissent finir et achever avec la dernier delicatesse ; comme on en finit constamment un grand Nombre, qui meritent bien d'être placés armi les plus beaux Productions de l'Art.

"Les Encriers se vendent separament, comme ils sont representés dans l'Estampe ci-dessus; ou bien avec des Sabliers, Oubliers, &c. forment plusieurs Especes des Ecritoires, tant utiles qu'embellies des Ornemens: les Prix sont de Six Sols, en montant graduellement selon la Beauté de l'Ouvrage, leur Grandeur, et les Formes, jusqu'à environ Huit Chelins la Piece.

"Messrs. WEDGWOOD et BENTLEY prennent la Liberté de recommander à Messrs. les Marchands étrangers qui voudroient bien acheter de leurs Ouvrages, d'adresser les Ordres à leurs Correspondens ordinaires en Angleterre; car la grande Attention que leur Manufacture demande constamment, et leur Situation, rendent les Soins des Commissions, et d'une Correspondence étrangere et extensive, extremement difficile."

Truly elegant inkstands were made in jasper and other materials. One of the most beautiful is shown in the accom-

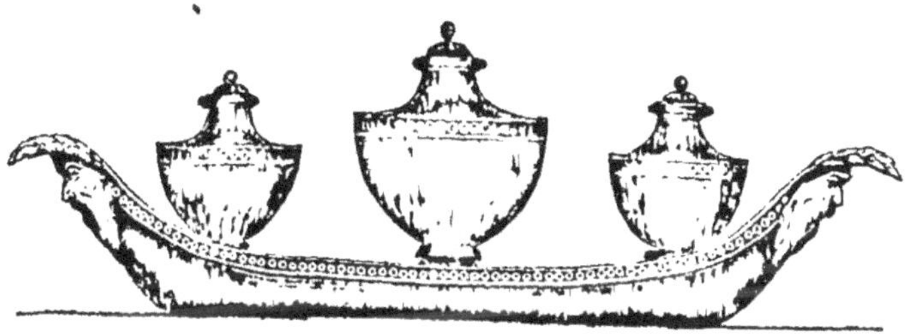

panying engraving, drawn from an inkstand in Mr. Hall's possession. The other articles in this class are thus spoken of by Mr. Wedgwood:—

"The 'Paint-chests' contain sets of large and small vessels, and neat pallets, for the use of those who paint in water-colours; they are sold from five shillings to half a guinea. The EYE-CUPS, for bathing the eyes, are made of the compositions imitating variegated pebbles, &c. The MORTARS, of various forms and sizes, from *two* to *thirteen* inches in diameter, outside measure, and from *one and a half* to *ten* in the clear, are made in the hard porcelain, No. 6; a material far superior to all those in common use for these purposes, and nearly equal to agate. The excellence of these mortars for chemical and other curious uses is already well known, and their valuable properties render them equally desirable for the purposes of the apothecary and the housekeeper. MARBLE mortars are *soft* in comparison with these, and a very considerable quantity of the substance of the marble is abraded and mixed with all powders of the hard kind that are ground in them; they are corroded and dissolved by all acids, and hence, besides altering the nature of any acid liquor put into them, by imparting to it as much of their substance as the quantity of acid requires for its saturation, the surface of the marble itself is rendered rough and cavernulous, and on that account still more liable to be abraded, and very difficult to be made clean. Oils of all kinds are imbibed by them, so that whatever follows an oily substance in such a mortar must partake of the smell and taste of the oil. METALLINE mortars are dissolved or corroded not only by acids, but by all saline substances, by simple moisture, and by the air; and some experiments lately published by Mr. Blizard have given grounds to apprehend that even *dry* substances of the mere *earthy* kind, *void of saline matter*, and of no great *hardness*, will receive, by being powdered in brass or bell-metal mortars, though perfectly clean, a coppery impregnation, sufficient to manifest itself in the common chemical trials, and perhaps not altogether innocent in medicines or in aliments. From all these imperfections the PORCELAIN mortars are free; and their price is sufficiently moderate to admit of their general use. This compact, hard porcelain is excellently adapted also for evaporating pans, digesting vessels, basons, filtering funnels, syphons, tubes—such as Dr. Priestly uses in some of his experiments instead of gun barrels—retorts, and many other vessels for chemical uses, which I have made for my friends, of different forms and magnitudes, and with some variations in the composition itself, according to the views for which they were wanted. If in this department I should be happy enough to contribute anything towards facilitating chemical experiments, by supplying vessels more serviceable or more commodious for particular uses than are commonly to be met with, my utmost wishes with respect to these articles will be gratified."

The last class (CLASS TWENTY) into which Josiah Wedgwood divided his productions was "thermometers for measuring strong fire, or the degree of heat above ignition." The principle on which these thermometers (accounts of which had been, as I have stated, read before the Royal Society) were constructed, was that of the shrinking of earthly bodies of the argillaceous order by heat—the diminution of their bulk being in proportion to the degrees of heat to which they are subjected. The following is Wedgwood's own account of this important invention:—

"*Thermometers for Measuring Strong Fire, or the Degrees of Heat above Ignition.*

"To those who are conversant in experimental inquiries, or in the operations of manufactures and arts that are carried on by fire, it is unnecessary to mention the importance of a thermometer by which the force of fire in furnaces of every kind may be accurately measured and appreciated, in the same denominations as the lower degrees of heat are by the common thermometers.

"Such an instrument I have now the satisfaction of offering to the public. As the thermometer itself is accompanied with a pamphlet explaining its construction and use, and as the results of my experiments, both respecting its construction and the comparison of its scale with that of Fahrenheit's continued, have been honoured with a place in the Transactions of the Royal Society,* it will here be sufficient just to mention the general principles on which it is founded, viz.:—that earthy bodies of the *argillaceous* order have their bulk *diminished by fire* in proportion to the degree of heat they are made to undergo; and that, consequently, the *contraction* of this species of matter affords as true a measure for strong fire as the *expansion* of mercury or spirit of wine does for the lower degrees of heat; but with this difference, that the contraction of the argillaceous mass is a *permanent* effect; so that the degree of heat is not here determined by a single transient observation made in the fire itself, but its measure is preserved, and is to be examined when grown cold, or at any future time.

"The argillaceous matter is formed into equal small pieces, called thermometer pieces; and one of these, which may be conceived as the detached bulb of a thermometer, is put into the fire that is to be measured, either in a little case made for that purpose, or in the same vessel with the subject matter of the operation.

"A gauge, consisting of two rules fixed on a flat plate, a little nearer together at one end than the other, so as to include between them a long converging canal, divided on the side, serves for discovering minute variations in the bulk of the pieces. A raw piece will just enter to 0 at the wider end of the canal: after it has been in the fire, if it be gently slid along till it is stopped by the convergency of the sides, the degree at which it stops will be the measure of its diminution, and, consequently, of the heat which it has undergone.

"As the accuracy of the scale of the common thermometer

* Phil. Transact., vols. lxxii., lxxiv., lxxvii.

depends upon the perfect equality of the bore of the tube from one end to the other, so the accuracy of this gauge depends upon the perfect straightness of its sides; and the difficulty of obtaining this essential condition necessarily occasions a considerable enhancement of the price. I have now happily succeeded in making gauges of the hard species of porcelain more perfect than those I can generally procure in brass: the porcelain ones have the advantage of not being susceptible of any bruise or derangement; they may be broken, but they cannot, in this respect, deceive."

The account of this invention, which had been read before the Royal Society, was issued in pamphlet form, in different languages; a copy translated into the Dutch language* is in my possession.

Besides these twenty classes of goods manufactured by Wedgwood, and which were, it will have been seen, principally ornamented varieties, he announced at the end of his catalogue that "the QUEEN'S WARE of Mr. Wedgwood's manufacture, with various improvements in the table and dessert services, tea equipages, &c., continues to be sold as usual at his warehouse in Greek Street, Soho, and at no other place in London." This was in 1787, and the same ware has continued to be regularly made down to our own day. About this time (1785), along with others, Wedgwood's name found its way into some of the political lampoons and squibs which the wits of the day threw off unmercifully at the leading men of the government. One of these, alluding to spittoons and other vessels bearing the head of William Pitt, is to be found in the "Asylum for Fugitive Pieces"—a strange collection of these lampoons, which had been got together by John Almon—where it forms part of "an irregular ode," said to be "by Edward Lord Thurlow, Lord High Chancellor of Great Britain"—

* Beschreibung und Gebrauch eines Thermometers die Höhern grade der Hitz zu Messen, von der rothen Hitze an bis zu der allerstärcksten welche irdene Gefässe ertragen konnen. Von Josias Wedgwood," &c. &c. &c. "London: Bey J. Young, MDCCLXXXVI."

"Lo! *Wedgwood*, too, waves his PITT-*pots* on high!
Lo! he points where the bottoms, yet dry,
The Visage Immaculate bear!
Be Wedgwood d——d, and double d——d his ware."

"I am told that a scoundrel of a potter, one *Mr. Wedgwood*, is making 10,000 *spitting-pots*, and other vile utensils, with a figure of Mr. Pitt in the bottom; round the head is to be a motto—

'We will spit
On Mr. Pitt;'

and other such d——d rhymes suited to the uses of the different vessels."

Of the universal repute in which this ware — the "Queen's," or usual earthenware of Wedgwood's manufacture —was held, numberless instances could be given, but it is unnecessary to do so. I may, however, just quote two little passages to show the opinion which was held of the excellence of its quality, and the way in which it made its way to remote quarters of the globe. The first is from the Travels of M. St. Fond, Professor of Geology in the Museum of Natural History, in Paris, in 1799, who wrote—

"Its excellent workmanship; its solidity; the advantage which it possesses of withstanding the action of the fire; its fine glaze, impenetrable to acids; the beauty, convenience, and variety of its forms, and its moderate price, have created a commerce so active, and so universal, that in travelling from Paris to St. Petersburg, from Amsterdam to the farthest point of Sweden, one is served at every inn from English earthenware. The same fine article adorns the tables of Spain, Portugal, and Italy; it provides the cargoes of ships to the East Indies, the West Indies, and America."

In Hamilton's "Voyage Round the World," 1793, the author says—

"It was a pleasing and flattering sight to an Englishman at this remotest corner of the globe, to see that Wedgwood's stone ware, and Birmingham goods, had found their way into the shops of Coupang" (East Indies).

CHAPTER XVIII.

CHINA MANUFACTURE.—JONATHAN WEDGWOOD.—AGREEMENT WITH WILLIAM DUESBURY, OF THE DERBY CHINA WORKS.—ABNER WEDGWOOD.—CHINA MADE FROM GUANO.—ENOCH WEDGWOOD.—FRANCIS EGINTON, INVENTOR OF POLYGRAPHIC PICTURES.—MUG GIVEN HIM BY JOSIAH WEDGWOOD.—MATTHEW BOULTON, OF THE SOHO WORKS.—LETTERS OF EGINTON.—THE "EARLY PHOTOGRAPHS."—LETTER OF BOULTON, OBJECTING TO A PENSION FOR EGINTON.—EGINTON'S WORKS IN STAINED GLASS.—WILLIAM RAPHAEL EGINTON.—LETTER OF JOSIAH WEDGWOOD.—ETRUSCAN VASE AND FRENCH PIE.

It is an interesting feature in the annals of the Wedgwoods, that although its head and chief, the "Great Josiah," was not at any time a maker of china ware, other members of that family were, during his lifetime, connected practically with it, and that his sons, as I shall shortly show, afterwards embarked in the trade.

I have shown that Aaron Wedgwood, in conjunction with his brother-in-law, Littler, was one of the, indeed *the* earliest maker of china in the pottery district. Another member of the family, a Jonathan Wedgwood, also was a "China or Porcelain Repairer or Thrower" in the latter half of last century, and was connected with William Duesbury in the Derby China Works, as will be seen by the following copy of the draft of agreement from the original document in my possession. The agreement, it will be seen, was for an engagement for the term of three years, at the weekly wages of fourteen shillings, out of which

Wedgwood was to "find and provide for himself, meat drink, washing, lodging, and apparrel:"—

"ARTICLES of Agreement indented, made, concluded, and agreed upon the second Day of December, in the year of our Lord one thousand seven hundred and Seventy-two: Between JONATHAN WEDGWOOD, of the Borough of Derby, China or Porcelain Repairer or Thrower, of the one part; and WM. DUESBURY, of the same place, China or Porcelain Manufacturer, of the other part, as follows: First, the said Jonathan Wedgwood, for the Consideration hereafter mentioned, doth hereby for himself Covenant, promise, and agree to and with the said Wm. Duesbury, his Executors and Administrators, as his and their Covenant Servant, and diligently and faithfully shall serve them with his whole abilities and services, according to the best and utmost of his skill and knowledge will exercise and employ himself in the arts of Repairing or Throwing China or Porcelain Ware, for the said Wm. Duesbury, his Executors and Administrators, for the most profit, benifit, and Advantage that he, the said Jonathan Wedgwood, can; and shall and will keep the secrets of the said Wm. Duesbury, his Executors and Administrators, Relateing to the said business, and be just and true to the said Wm. Duesbury, his Executors and Administrators, in all Matters and things; and also that the said Jonathan Wedgwood will find and provide for himself Meat, Drink, Washing, Lodging, and Apparrel, and all other necessary's, during the said term of three years, to commence from the day of the date hereof; and in consideration of the premisescs, and of the Several Matters and things by the said Jonathan Wedgwood to be done and performed, as aforesaid, he, the said Wm. Duesbury, doth for himself, his executors and administrators, Covenant, promise, and agree to and with the said Jonathan Wedgwood, that he, the said Wm. Duesbury, his executors and administrators, shall and will well and truely pay or cause to be paid unto the said Jonathan Wedgwood weekley, and every week during the said term of Three years, for every whole week thereof which the said Jonathan Wedgwood shall work, according to the usual hours of Repairing at the said Wm. Duesbury's Manufactory, in Derby aforesaid, the Sum of fourteen shillings of Lawfull Money of Great Britain; but if the said Jonathan Wedgwood shall at any time during the said term, by Sickness or any other Inevitable accident, be rendered unable to repair China or Porcelain-ware for the said Wm. Duesbury, his Executors or Administrators, at the said Manufactory, or shall wilfully decline or neglect so to do, then, and in either of the said cases, the said Wm. Duesbury, his executors and administrators, shall and will only pay to the said Jonathan Wedgwood, in proportion and after the rate aforesaid, for such part and so much of every week as he shall actually Repair for the said Wm. Duesbury, his Executors and Administrators, as aforesaid: and for the true performance of all and every the Articles, Covenants, and agreements aforesaid, Each of the said Parties bindeth himself to the other in the Penal sum of Fifty pounds firmly by these presents. In Witness whereof the said Parties have hereunto set their hands and seals the day and Year first before written.

Sealed and deliver'd in the presence of (Not signed.)

How long this Jonathan Wedgwood was connected with the Derby China Works I have not, as yet, been able to ascertain, but it is probable that he continued in Derby for some years. At all events I find by the registers of St. Alkmund's church, in that town, that a Jonathan Wedgwood, on the 12th of November, 1785—thirteen years after the date of the above draft of agreement—was married to Mary Stenson; and three years before this time, September 22nd, 1782, Abijah Tyrrell had married Amy Wedgwood, both of that parish. I have reason to believe that the Jonathan Wedgwood whose agreement I have given, was born at Ellenborough in 1735; that he migrated to Burslem, where, by his wife Sarah Wedgwood, one of his children was born in 1757, and that the Jonathan and Amy, whose marriages I have just noted at Derby, were his son and daughter.

Of late years it is well to note that a member of the Wedgwood family—a family of inventors and of practical and philosophical minds—discovered a mode of making china ware from guano. Of this highly interesting ware an example, a fine bowl, is preserved in Mr. Mayer's museum. It bears the following inscription :—" Manufactured by Saml. Alcock & Co., from Guano prepared by Abner Wedgwood, from whom the idea emanated. Staffordshire Potteries, 1854."

So far as my knowledge goes, these instances, and that of Etruria, to which I shall yet have occasion to refer, are all which have occurred in which the Wedgwoods have been practical makers of china ware. With earthenware as I have shown, nearly every member of the family, until late years, has apparently been connected, and at the present day, besides the, establishment at Etruria, the representative of another branch of the family, Mr. Enoch Wedgwood, has a large manufactory at Tunstall, where he employs six or seven hundred hands, and does a large home, as well as to some extent a foreign, trade.

In my last chapter I spoke of Francis Eginton, and it will be well here to give my readers some little information concerning him, as his, like that of many other deserving men, has hitherto been a "neglected biography." Francis Eginton was a man of great ability as an artist, and his productions were much esteemed in his own day, as, indeed, they are now. His acquaintance with Josiah Wedgwood was productive, it is believed, of some improvements in the colours and in the body of wares, which his intimate know-

ledge of chemistry, of colours, and ot fire, made him capable of experimenting upon.

On the accompanying engraving is represented a remarkably fine black-ware mug of Wedgwood's make, which possesses considerable interest. It was given by Josiah Wedgwood to Francis Eginton, and has remained in the family from that day until within the last few months, when it passed through my own hands into those of my friend Mr. Lucas, in whose collection I am pleased to have placed so interesting an example. The mug, which holds two quarts, and is 7⅝ inches in height, and 5½ inches in diameter, is said to have been subjected to several experiments to test its firmness by Wedgwood and Eginton. One of these experiments was that of boiling the vessel in milk, and I can quite understand why this should have been done, for it is well known to all old housekeepers that nothing is so good for preserving the colour and beauty of Egyptian black-ware as skimmed milk.

Eginton was, it appears, the inventor (about the year 1773 it is said) of that curious process by which pictures were mechanically reproduced at the close of last century, and which has of late made so much noise in the scientific world. The process is said to be closely allied to photography, and examples having been discovered among the old papers at Soho, Birmingham, and placed in the Museum of Patents, at South Kensington, have been brought under the notice of the Photographic Society, and produced much discussion at its meeting. What the process adopted by Eginton, who was in the employ of Matthew Boulton, of the Soho Works, was, is at present a mystery; the books which he left, and which contained his recipes, &c., having been abstracted from the family, and lost. The process was called "Polygraphic," and the pictures were said to be produced "by Chymical and Mechanical process," and consisted of copies of paintings by different artists—West, Kauffman, Reynolds, Rubens, &c. The following copy of an invoice from Eginton to Boulton, will show the kinds of subjects produced by this process, whose peculiarities it is not necessary to inquire into here:—

Handsworth, April 15th, 1791.

Mr. BOULTON,

Bt of FR. EGINTON, for Order, S. W. L.

	£	s.	d.
One Square Mechanical Painting from West—Venus and Adonis	1	5	0
One ditto from ditto—Cephalus and Procris .	1	5	0
One ditto, from Angelica Kauffman—Penelope .	1	1	0
One ditto ditto ditto—Calipso	1	1	0
16 *oval pictures in form of Medalions, viz.:—*			
One old man from Sir Joshua Reynolds . .	0	15	0
One Eastern Lady, from Bertalotzi . . .	0	15	0
One Vestal, from ditto	0	10	6
One Patience, from Angelica Kauffman . .	0	10	6
One Religion, from ditto	0	12	0
One Hope, from Rubens	0	12	0
One Shakspear's Tomb, from Angelica . .	0	12	0
One Flora	0	7	6
One Diana	0	7	6
One Dancing Nymph	0	7	6
One Ditto	0	7	6
One Bacante	0	7	6
One ditto	0	7	6
One Apollo	0	7	6
One Una, from Angelica	0	7	6
One Oliver and Orlanda	0	7	6
	£12	6	6
Finish from the dead Colour and retouching Tragedy and Comedy Heads and Melpomony, 15*s.*; and Thalia, 15*s.* Figures 4 in all, 7*s.* 6*d.*	1	1	0
	£13	7	6

"SIR,—In the above I have conform'd to the Order as near as the very low prices to which I was limeted would permit. Some alterations I have been obliged to make on that ac^{t}, particularly in the four historical square ones, which should have been, according to order, from 15*s.* to 20*s.*; instead of which you will find one pair from West at 25*s.* each, and one pair from Angelica at 21*s.* each, which were the lowest Historical Pictures I could send. The 16 Oval or Medalion formed Pictures are of different sizes; and altho' some of them are something higher priced than what was fixed, others are lower, so that upon the average they will be nearly the price at which they were ordered.

"I hope they will meet y^{r}
"approbation, and
"am, Sir,
"Your ob^{t} Ser^{t},
"FR. EGINTON."

Josiah Wedgwood, the friend of Boulton and of Eginton, the warm patron of art, and the encourager of every useful invention, purchased some of these pictures, as will be seen by the following interesting letter:—

"W'hampton, Septr. 22nd, 1781.

"MR. HODGES.

"SIR,—After considering the great risk you run, in sending the picture by the Coach, with the uncertainty even of its being dry against the time fixed, I conclude it of much less consequence that I should bestow a few days more in rendering the Picture I am now at work on equal to the original, than to have one totally spoiled in the carriage, and the intention of the whole order frustrated thereby. I have therefore sent you the Original, as a companion to the other; and you may depend on having the remaining picture returned to you equal to either of the former, and I shall have the satisfaction of compleating my part of the order in due time. If these pictures are not sent away till Monday, there should be some white of egg given to the Time and Cupid, as it is scarcely dry enough to bear the carriage.

"Please, if you can, to return by the bearer the Time and Cupid which is to be painted for Mr. Boulton, with the Circle of the Graces breaking Cupid's bow, for Mr. Wedgwood.

"I am, Sir, Your obt. St.,
"JOSH. BARNEY."

"Mr. Jo^{N} HODGES, Soho."

Eginton's process was so successful, and was so highly approved by people of taste, that interest was made to get him an annual pension from Government in acknowledgment of his services. Boulton, however, not much to his credit, put a veto on the movement, and thus prevented a fitting and gratifying recognition of his talents from being made. Thus says Mr. Boulton—

Copy of a Letter to the Right Honourable the Earl of Dartmouth.

"My Lord,—A few days ago I received a letter from Sir John Dalrymple, dated Dublin, May 27, in which he surprises me by saying, 'I have written to Sir Gray Cooper to have a pension of £20 per annum for Mr. Eginton; so, if there is any stop, write me of it to Scotland, and I will get it set to rights, as I know nothing but inattention can stop it.'

"As I think I cannot with propriety write to Sir Gray Cooper upon that matter, not having the honour of being known to him, and as I have never mentioned the subject to him, or any person besides your Lordship, I hope therefore to be pardoned for thus troubling you with my sentiments and wishes.

"In the first place, I wish to have an entire stop put to the pension; because Mr. Eginton hath no claim nor expectations. I pay him by the year; and, consequently, he is already paid by me for all the three or four months spent in that business; and as to an overplus reward for his secrecy, I know how to do that more effectually, and with more prudence, than giving him annually £20, which will only serve to keep up the remembrance of that business, and therefore it is impolitical.

"Besides, it might perhaps be injurious to me, as such a pension would tend to make him more independent of me and my manufacture.

"His attachment to me, his knowing that no use hath been made of the things, the obligation he is under to me, and his own natural caution and prudence, renders me firmly persuaded that the scheme will die away in his memory, or at least will never be mentioned.

"If any body is entitled to any pecuniary reward in this business, it is myself; because I have not only bestowed some time upon it, but have actually expended in money between one and two hundred pounds, as I can readily convince your Lordship when I have the honour of seeing you at Soho; and although I was induced by [ ] to believe that I was working at the request and under the authority of a noble Lord (whose wisdom and virtue I revere), yet I never intended making any charge to Government of my expenses or for my trouble.

"All that I have now to request of your Lordship is that a negative be put upon the pension.

"My Lord, your Lordship's most dutiful, most obliged, and most faithful humble Servant,

"M. B."

Francis Eginton was, too, a clever artist in stained glass, and brought that art to great perfection. Amongst his principal works—"the first of any consequence" being executed in 1784—were arms of the knights of the Garter on the windows on the stalls in St. George's Chapel, Windsor; some fine windows in Wanstead Church, Essex; a large representation of the "Good Samaritan" in the private chapel of the Archbishop of Armagh, and another in the chapel of the Bishop of Derry; a remarkably fine window in St. Paul's Church, Birmingham; memorial and other windows in Babworth Church, Nottinghamshire; Aston Church, near Birmingham; Hatton, Warwickshire; Shuckburgh Church, in the same county; Pepplewick, Nottinghamshire; Barr and Bromley Regis, Staffordshire; Stannor, Berkshire; Earthing and Llangollen, Denbighshire; Shrivenham and Frome, Somersetshire; St. Martin's Outwich, London; Tewkesbury Abbey Church, and many other places. Besides these, some of Francis Eginton's principal works were the large window over the altar of Salisbury Cathedral, representing the Resurrection, after a design by Sir Joshua Reynolds, but which has since been removed to make room for memorial windows to Dean Lear; the west and several other windows in the same cathedral; the east and other windows of Lichfield Cathedral (1795); the windows of Merton College Chapel, Oxford (in 1794); windows in the Mausoleum at Brocklesby, in the chapel at Wardour Castle, in the chapel at Pain's Hill, in the banqueting-room and other rooms at Arundel Castle, at Sundorn Castle, and at Fonthill, the charming art-seat of William Beckford.

Francis Eginton had a son Francis, who was also, like his father, a clever engraver. He had also another son, William Raphael Eginton, who inherited his father's talents as a glass stainer, and produced many exquisite, indeed matchless, works. His son was my late friend, Harvey Eginton, the architect, who did so much and so well towards restoring and preserving the magnificent Guesten Hall, at Worcester, which has of late years been ruthlessly destroyed. Two daughters of William Raphael Eginton survive, the youngest of whom inherits to the fullest extent the exquisite taste, the ability, and the artistic excellence of her family.

If proof of the love which Josiah Wedgwood felt for his art, and of the pride and satisfaction with which he stored some of his successful works, were wanting, it would abundantly be found in the following interesting and characteristic letter written by him in 1789:—

"Etruria, 16th October, 1789.

"I do not know what to say about parting with the fine Etruscan vase. It is the most perfect and complete piece I ever made—quite a chef-d'œuvre; but then you will say, how can it be placed more honourably than in the cabinet of a king? No one can be more sensible of the honour done to me and to my manufacture in the present instance; but notwithstanding the advantageous change this favourite piece would experience, I cannot help feeling a pang at the thoughts of parting with it, as I am certain I shall never make, or perhaps see, the like again. I will consult my son Jos., who is from home this evening, and will let you know the result in my next.

"I will try to get a French pye made, and take a mould from it; but ten to one it will be so old-fashioned made here, that it will not be liked.

"The original order for St. Andrew's Cross did not mention any hole to be made, for I looked at it myself. "Adieu."

The body of which the imitation "French pies" were made was the "Bamboo" ware. Of this same body were made those wonderful and elegant achievements of fictile art, open-work baskets, which were considered to be among the most choice of Wedgwood's productions. The body was well calculated, both by its lightness, its colour, and other characteristics, to carry out deception, and to make the

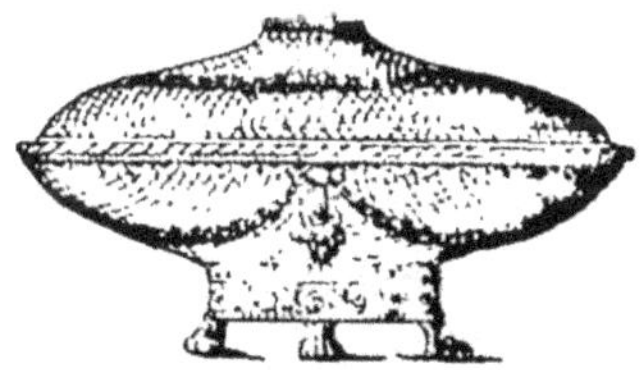

plainer patterns pass for real wicker-work of the finest quality. The example here engraved is in the museum at Hanley. It is an open-work basket and cover, of peculiar but remarkably graceful form—a form difficult to produce, and is ornamented with festoons and wreaths of flowers.

CHAPTER XIX.

JOSIAH WEDGWOOD.—HIS LAST ILLNESS AND DEATH.—ETRURIA HALL.—BURIAL AT STOKE.—MONODY BY REV. W. FERNYHOUGH.—WEDGWOOD'S MONUMENT AT STOKE-UPON-TRENT.—OBITUARY NOTICES.

I HAVE already, before this digression, brought my narrative down to the middle of the year 1793. In the following year Josiah Wedgwood was seized with his last illness, and on the 3rd of January, 1795, breathed his last.

From the time when he first—at that early age already spoken of—turned the lumbering potter's wheel in that old, old room at the churchyard at Burslem, to the time when he lay on his death-bed in that fine mansion, Etruria Hall—built on his own estate, and reared at his own cost—the proprietor of the largest pottery manufactory in the world, and looked up to by people of every class—his mind had ever been active, ever rising above his bodily ailments, ever seeking out fresh scientific truths, and ever busying itself to benefit his fellow-men; and in the midst of his most successful labours—after reaping to the full the reward of his industry, his toil, and his research—that mind which had by its working been the support of thousands of his fellow-creatures, and from which there are few who do not at the present day derive benefit in some way or other, died out but with his life, and left him resting from his worldly toil.

On the 3rd of January, 1795, Josiah Wedgwood died, and on the 6th his remains were interred in the parish church of St. Peter, Stoke-upon-Trent, as shown by the following extract from the parish register :—

"Burials in 1795.
Jany. 6th, Josiah Wedgwood, of Etruria ;"

the entry being in the handwriting of "William Fernyhough, minister of Stoke-upon-Trent," by whom it is

ETRURIA HALL.

attested. This clergyman, a man of rare talent, impressed with the solemnity of the death of so great and good a man, wrote the following

"MONODY ON THE LATE JOSIAH WEDGWOOD, ESQ., F.R.S., F.S.A.

"The plaintive Muse o'er WEDGWOOD'S mournful bier
Heaves the sad sigh and drops the pearly tear;
'Tis Nature's voice, and hearts that swell with grief,
In these rude numbers seeks some kind relief;

He needs no verse in artful language drest,
Where well-earn'd fame will live in ev'ry breast.
Dear friend of men, thy philanthropic mind
Felt daily for the miseries of thy kind;
Thy liberal hand ten thousand blessings spread,
And oft supplied the hungry poor with bread.
When wintry winds with hollow murmurs blew,
And fleecy snow in circling eddies flew,
In this rough season of the rolling year
The sigh of sorrow met thy tender ear;
The shivering limbs were cover'd from the cold,
The orphan succour'd and relieved the old;—
These bending o'er the grave shall weeping show
The striking marks of unaffected woe.
No common loss afflicts our throbbing hearts,
A nation feels when such a man departs.
Say ye, who near his favoured mansion dwell,
How truly good he was, for ye can tell;
Say how his active mind with genius fired,
Display those arts which all the world admired:
Those fine turn'd models, where at once we spy
That just proportion which attracts the eye;
Nor Greece nor Rome stands matchless now in fame,
While Wedgwood's genius bears an equal claim.
Ye sons of Art! with me his death deplore!
Your Father—friend, and Patron is no more:
Whose fostering hand made modest merit live,
And busy commerce all around him thrive.
Such the true Patriot who improves the hours,
And for his country's weal employs his powers.
While pension'd peers inactive dream'd away
In dull stupidity life's fleeting day,
His soul superior ranged the fictile field,
Where heavenly science sweet instruction yield,
Traced classic ground, and from Italian shores,
With skill unrivall'd drew the choicest stores.
Such the true patriot, from whose gates each day
A crowd of healthy workmen make their way,
Whose rare productions foreign courts demand,
And while they praise, enrich his native land.
View his ETRURIA, late a barren waste,
Now high in culture and adorn'd with taste;
The pine, the beech, their ample branches spread,
And the tall poplar rears his pointed head;
The broad canal here winds his watery way
Through the long vale with native beauties gay."

The illness which ended in the death of Josiah Wedgwood was a very painful one. Of this illness Mrs. Byerley, the

widow of his nephew and partner, Thomas Byerley, who was at the time living near Etruria, wrote :—

"He was seized with a dreadful pain in his face and teeth. A medical man was sent for, and as he had long been a friend of the family, he could not restrain his feelings. He perceived a slough or mortification had began in the mouth; he told the wife, and ordered immediately an eminent physician to be sent for from a distant county. He applyed what he thought best till the medical friend arrived, and then everything was resorted to, which kept this great good man in existence three weeks, but he then died—a *poor* man would not have lived more than three days."

In the chancel of St. Peter's Church, Stoke-upon-Trent, close by the pulpit, is a large and imposing-looking tablet to the memory of this great man, of which I give an engraving on the preceding page.

The monument consists of a plain slab of black marble, bearing an inscription tablet of white marble, on which rest a Portland vase and an Etruscan vase. These are surmounted by a finely-sculptured three-quarter head of Wedgwood, in white marble, in a circular medallion. The monument bears the following excellent and appropriate inscription:—

Sacred to the Memory of
JOSIAH WEDGWOOD, F.R.S. & S.A.,
Of Etruria, in this County,
Born in August, 1730, died January 3rd, 1795,
Who converted a rude and inconsiderable manufacture into an elegant art and an important part of national Commerce.
By these services to his country he acquired an ample fortune,
Which he blamelessly and reasonably enjoyed,
And generously dispensed for the reward of merit and the relief of misfortune.
His mind was inventive and original, yet perfectly sober and well regulated;
His character was decisive and commanding, without rashness or arrogance;
His probity was inflexible, his kindness unwearied;
His manners simple and dignified, and the cheerfulness of his temper was the natural reward of the activity of his pure and useful life.
He was most loved by those who knew him best,
And he has left indelible impressions of affection and veneration on the minds of his family, who have erected this monument to his memory.

Having brought down my narrative to the close of the useful and busy life of the great potter, it is well that I should, at the same time, close this chapter. In doing so, I feel that I cannot do better than quote the words of the obituary notice which appeared in the *Gentleman's Magazine* at the time of his death, and also the words of one well able to judge of his excellencies as a man. The writer of the first says—

"Died, at Etruria, in Staffordshire, aged sixty-four, Josiah Wedgwood, Esq., F.R. and A. SS.; to whose indefatigable labours is owing the establishment of a manufacture that has opened a new scene of extensive commerce, before unknown to this or any other country. It is unnecessary to say that this alludes to the Pottery of Staffordshire, which, by the united efforts of Mr. Wedgwood, and his late partner, Mr. Bentley, has been carried to a degree of perfection, both in the line of utility and ornament, that leaves all works, ancient or modern, far behind.

"Mr. Wedgwood was the younger son of a potter, but derived little or no property from his father, whose possessions consisted chiefly of a small entailed estate, which descended to the eldest son. He was the maker of his own fortune, and his country has been benefited in a proportion not to be calculated. His many discoveries of new species of earthen wares and porcelains, his studied forms and chaste style of decoration, and the correctness and judgment with which all his works were executed under his own eye, and by artists, for the most part, of his own forming, have turned the current in this branch of commerce; for, before his time, England imported the finer earthen wares: but, for more than twenty years past, she has exported them to a very great annual amount, the whole of which is drawn from the earth, and from the industry of the inhabitants; while the national taste has been improved, and its reputation raised in foreign countries. His inventions have prodigiously increased the number of persons employed in the potteries, and in the traffic and transport of their materials from distant parts of the kingdom: and this class of manufacturers is also indebted to him for much mechanical contrivance and arrangement in their operations; his private manufactory having had, for thirty years and upwards, all the efficacy of a public work of experiment. Neither was he unknown in the walks of philosophy. His communications to the Royal Society show a mind enlightened by science, and contributed to procure him the esteem of scientific men at home and throughout Europe. His invention of a thermometer for measuring the higher degrees of heat employed in the various arts, is of the highest importance to their promotion, and will add celebrity to his name. At an early period of his life, seeing the impossibility of extending considerably the manufactory he was engaged in on the spot which gave him birth, without the advantages of inland navigation, he was the proposer of the Grand Trunk Canal, and the chief agent in obtaining the Act of Parliament for making it, against the prejudices of the landed interest, which at that time stood very high, and but just before had been with great difficulty evercome in another quarter by all the powerful influence of a noble duke, whose canal was at that time but lately finished. Having acquired a large fortune, his purse was always open to the calls of charity, and to the support of every institution for the public good. To his relations, friends, and neighbours, he was endeared by his many private virtues; and his loss will be deeply and long deplored by all who had the pleasure of knowing them intimately, and by the numerous objects to whom his benevolence was extended: and he will be regretted by his country as the able and zealous supporter of her commerce, and the steady patron of every valuable interest of society."

The opinion of one who knew him well is as follows:—

"Mr. Wedgwood, for many years prior to his death, in the virtuous exercise of benevolence enjoyed the highest luxury, the most delightful pleasure in which the human mind can participate. Each Martinmas he sent to certain persons in Shelton, Cobridge, and Burslem, for a list of the names, and a full statement of the peculiar circumstances, of poor persons in each liberty likely to require assistance during the winter; and for supplying them with comfortable bedding, clothing, coals, and some food, he always furnished adequate funds. His purse was ever open to the calls of charity, to the amelioration of misery, and the patronage of every philanthropic institution; and his name will go down to posterity with the highest claims on their gratitude for being a true friend to mankind. He had intrinsic merit on a true basis, and needs no tralatitious ascription of excellence. He was a truly industrious potter; he followed the openings of business suggested by the different experiments of himself and other potters; he pushed every successful trial to a considerable extent; and his success in business enabled him to employ and remunerate the best workmen, whose utmost ability was constantly excited and directed by his enlarging knowledge. Thus he raised himself to the acme of his art, and the public were amazed that a person with so contracted an education, and so little of any advantage over his fellows, had thus been eminently successful as the founder of his own fortune and fame (immortal as the art of pottery), and in raising himself among the benefactors of man and the princes of the people."

CHAPTER XX.

JOSIAH WEDGWOOD.—MEDALLION PORTRAITS OF HIM BY FLAXMAN AND OTHERS.—MEDALLION OF MRS. WEDGWOOD.—MACCARONI HEAD-DRESSES.—COSTUME OF THE PERIOD.—SATIRES ON THE PREVAILING MODE.—NETWORK BAGS FOR THE HEAD.—HEADS NOT DRESSED FOR NINE WEEKS.—SIR JOSHUA REYNOLDS' PORTRAIT OF WEDGWOOD.—STUBBS' FAMILY PICTURE OF THE WEDGWOODS.—FASHION OF WEARING HUGE CAPS.—STATUE OF WEDGWOOD.—FONTANA'S BUST.—BUST ON THE MONUMENT AT STOKE.

AND here, at the close of his useful and eventful life, a few words may be well introduced concerning the different portraits of Josiah Wedgwood which have been executed. And, first, with regard to the medallions which have been produced in Wedgwood's own matchless jasper ware. Of these medallions I have the good fortune to be enabled to bring under my readers' notice, for the first time, four different varieties. Of these two have not, I believe, before been either engraved or described, and will, therefore, be welcome additions to the data I am giving to collectors.

The first of these medallions of which I shall speak, is one of Flaxman's happiest relief-portraits, and is shown on the accompanying engraving. In it Wedgwood is represented, as will be seen, in the fashionable dress of the period, with bag wig, lace frill, and collarless coat. This I take to have been one of the earliest of the medallion portraits of Wedgwood, and it is one which is but little known to collectors. The "bag" of the wig on this medallion is small, when compared with what was worn by those who were in the "height of fashion" in those days, and which caused one of the writers of the time to say, "At present,

such unmerciful ones are worn, that a little man's shoulders are perfectly covered with black satin."

When fashion had changed, when the bag wig was discarded, and the coat assumed its deep collar, the next medallion was evidently prepared, and bore the admirable profile which I engrave on the next page. The few years that had intervened, too, had, besides changing the fashion of the garments and of the hair, deepened the features of the great man, and given to them even a more solid thoughtfulness and an air of greater kindliness and benevolence than they had before. The figure, too, had grown proportionately, and had become more portly; and all these points were caught by the quick eye, and presented in the new medallion by the almost magically manipulative fingers of Flaxman. This medallion, which is the one best

known to collectors, is still produced by Messrs. Wedgwood in their finest jasper ware. The two profiles which I have just given have been engraved to illustrate Mr. Gladstone's "Wedgwood: An Address."* And I have to express my obligations to Mr. Murray for his courtesy in giving me the free use of these two admirable engravings.

* London: John Murray, Albemarle Street, 1863.

The next medallion of which I give an illustration is undoubtedly of an earlier date than the last; it is of great rarity, and has never before been engraved. The accompanying illustration is drawn from an example in the possession of my friend, Dr. Barnard Davis; and a similar one may be seen in Mr. Mayer's museum, Liverpool. On this, Wedgwood is represented in a bag wig, frilled shirt, and collared coat, and an ermine mantle is thrown over the lower

part of the bust. This medallion I feel disposed, and not without reason, to believe to have been the work of Hackwood, a clever modeller, who was employed by Wedgwood, and produced a large number of portraits and bas-reliefs.

Another medallion of a different size, and of totally different character, is the one shown on the engraving on the following page. Like the last one, this striking and admirable profile portrait of Wedgwood has never before been engraved or noticed by any writer, and I am much gratified at being the means of bringing it and the previous one into notice. The portrait in this instance consists simply of the head, without any drapery or ornament of any kind. It is remarkably well and boldly modelled, and is of very great rarity.

While speaking of the medallions, it would be unpardonable not to say a word or two about the exquisite model of Mrs. Wedgwood which was executed as a fitting companion

to that of her husband. This medallion represents Mrs. Wedgwood in one of the fashionable head-dresses of her day. Her hair is dressed in the "maccaroni" style, but of much less dimensions, and more simply elegant, than was worn by most ladies of fashion. The head-dress consisted of a pile of tow and pads, supported frequently with a frame-work of wire, over which false hair was arranged and hung with gauze, in folds, ribbons of every gay colour, feathers, flowers, and strings of pearls. The extraordinary size of the head-dresses of the period when Mrs. Wedgwood's medallion was modelled, and for a few years previous to that time, was a constant and fruitful source of amusement to the satirical writers of the day, and many droll stories were told concerning them. One writer says, speaking of the enormous size of the heads of the ladies, "It is not very long since that part of their sweet bodies used to be bound so tight, and trimmed so amazingly snug, that they appeared like a pin's head on the top of a knitting-needle; but they have now so far exceeded the golden mean in the contrary extreme, that our fine ladies remind me of an apple stuck on the point of a small skewer." Another writer jocosely says:—

"Give Chloe a bushel of horse-hair and wool,
Of paste and pomatum a pound;
Ten yards of gay ribbon to deck her sweet skull,
And gauze to encompass it round.

"Of all the bright colours the rainbow displays,
Be those ribbons which hang on her head;
Be her flounces adapted to make the folks gaze,
And about the whole work be they spread.

"Let her gown be tucked up to the hip on each side,
Shoes too high for to walk or to jump," &c.

And then, after describing other artificial means of adding to the figure, concludes—

"Thus finished in taste, while on Chloe you gaze,
You may take the dear charmer for life;
But never undress her, for, out of her stays,
You'll find you have lost half your wife!"

Ladies' heads, when dressed in the height of fashion, were not to be disturbed for some time. The process of building up the immense structure was a tedious and expensive one, and the head had to be preserved with great care. So much care, indeed, was sometimes taken, that ladies provided themselves with a net-bag, which enveloped the whole head, including the face, and fastened round the neck. These they put on when they went to what was supposed to be rest, but which, in reality, must have been torture, and were propped and bolstered up with the utmost care to prevent the structure being damaged. "False locks to supply deficiency of native hair, pomatum in profusion, greasy wool to bolster up the adopted locks, and grey powder to conceal dust," were said to be the characteristics of the prevailing fashion, and these being unopened for a long time together, could not have been very healthful additions to a lady's head. One of the writers makes a hair-dresser ask a lady "how long it was since her head had been opened and repaired?" She answered, "Not above nine weeks!" To which he replied, "that that was as long as a head could well go in summer; and that, therefore, it was proper to deliver it now, as it began to be a little *hasardé.*"

Mrs. Wedgwood's hair and head-dress, it will be seen by the accompanying engraving, were, in comparison with the monstrosities then in vogue, particularly simple, graceful, and elegant. The toupee is formed of the hair brushed up from the forehead: close curls fit to the side of the head, and a loose one beneath the ear. On the top of the head the back-hair is brought up and plaited, and graceful folds of gauze are lightly and negligently arranged.

Of original paintings of Josiah Wedgwood I am only aware of three. The first is the fine and well-known portrait by Sir Joshua Reynolds, from which the engraving by John Taylor Wedgwood, prefixed to this volume, is taken. This fine portrait was also engraved, of a large size, in 1787, by W. Halman. It has also been engraved by S. W. Reynolds, and has been copied in reduced form in a variety of ways.

The next is a fine, large, family picture, which hangs in the dining-room of Mr. Francis Wedgwood's mansion at Barlaston. This painting is by Stubbs, the celebrated animal painter, and represents a part of the grounds at Etruria, with the great potter and his family introduced

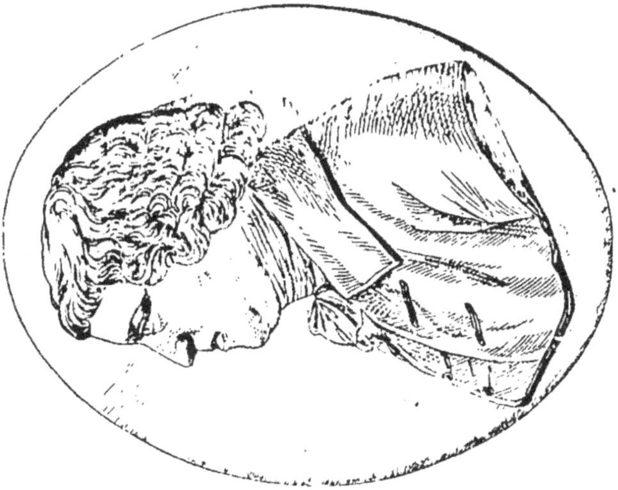

JOSIAH WEDGWOOD.

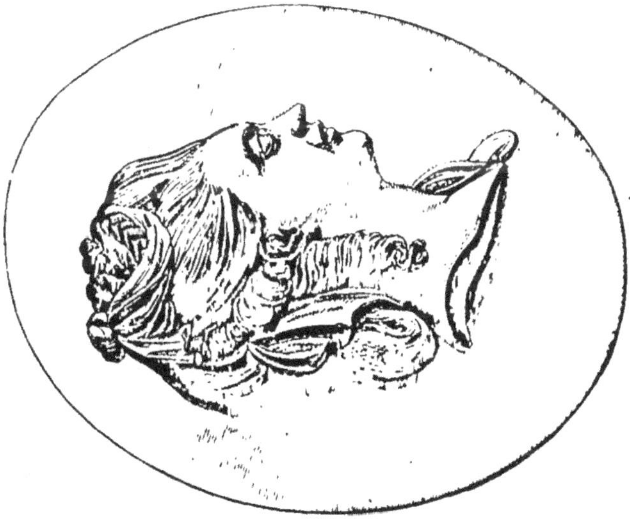

MRS. WEDGWOOD.

[FROM FLAXMAN'S MEDALLIONS.]

in a group. Josiah Wedgwood and his amiable wife are represented in the characteristic costume of the period, seated in a garden, beneath a large tree. Wedgwood is habited in a coat with deep collar, same as in the medallion; one of the old-fashioned waistcoats reaching over the hips; knee-breeches, stockings, and shoes, with large buckles. By the side of Wedgwood is a small stand, on which lies a paper. Mrs. Wedgwood, who is holding out her hand to one of the little children, who is drawing a child's carriage, containing two young children, wears one of the immense caps, about two feet in height, which were necessary to cover the monstrous piles of tow and pomatum which I have already spoken of as forming the ladies' fashionable head-dresses of that time. Of these caps it was said—

"The pride of our females all bound'ry exceeds;
'Tis now quite the fashion to wear double heads.
Approaching this town to disburse heavenly treasure,
I passed by a head that would fill a strike measure;
If I'd had that measure but close to my side,
I then should have had the experiment tried.
By sins a man's said to be cover'd all o'er
With bruises and many a putrefied sore,
From the sole of his foot to his crown they aspire—
But the sins of a woman rise *half a yard higher!*"

The eldest child, Susannah, afterwards wife of Dr. Darwin, of Shrewsbury, is represented on horseback, as are her three brothers, John, Josiah, and Thomas.* The little girl I have spoken of as drawing a child's carriage, is Catherine, and the two little ones who are seated in the carriage are Sarah and Mary Anne, the two youngest members of the family.

The third of these is "an enamel as large as life," painted by George Stubbs. It is a fine three-quarter head, in bag-wig and grey collarless coat, and is, I apprehend, of about the same period as the earlier medallions. From this painting a tinted stipple-print was engraved by George Townley Stubbs, and published by him on February 10th,

* Richard, the second son, having died in 1782, is of course not included in this family picture.

1795, the month following the death of Wedgwood. This print is now rare.

Turning from painting to sculpture, the admirable bust of Josiah Wedgwood, on his monument at Stoke-upon-Trent, remains to be noticed. This bust, which is a three-quarter faced portrait, will be seen represented on the accompanying

engraving. It is sculptured in white marble, and is evidently an admirable and truthful likeness.

Of later sculptured representations of the "father of potters," the most notable are, undoubtedly, the memorial statue, by Gibson, which has been erected at Stoke, and the splendid bust, by Fontana, which has been liberally presented, by Mr. Mayer, to the new Wedgwood Memorial Institute at Burslem.

CHAPTER XXI.

CHILDREN OF JOSIAH WEDGWOOD AND THEIR ALLIANCES—THEIR DESCENDANTS.—DARWIN'S "ORIGIN OF SPECIES." —JOHN WEDGWOOD.—LETTER OF JOSIAH WEDGWOOD.—THOMAS WEDGWOOD. — SAMUEL TAYLOR COLERIDGE—GENEROUS HELP ACCORDED TO HIM BY THE BROTHERS WEDGWOOD.—THOMAS WEDGWOOD'S RESEARCHES INTO THE PROPERTIES OF LIGHT.—DISCOVERS PHOTOGRAPHY.—SIR HUMPHREY DAVY.—JOSIAH WEDGWOOD THE SECOND.—WAR WITH FRANCE: MARBLES USED AS BULLETS.—THOMAS BYERLEY.—DEATH OF THOMAS BYERLEY—CHANGE IN THE FIRM.—MANUFACTURE OF CHINA AT ETRURIA.—STONE CHINA.—DEATH OF MRS. WEDGWOOD.—JOHN BOYLE BECOMES A PARTNER.—ROBERT BROWN TAKEN IN PARTNERSHIP.—MARKS USED ON WEDGWOOD WARE.—"WEDGWOOD AND CO."—INJUNCTION AGAINST MESSRS. W. SMITH AND OTHERS, OF STOCKTON.

On the 3rd of January, 1795, as I have stated, Josiah Wedgwood died. By this wife, of whom I have before spoken, he had a family of eight children. The eldest child, Susannah, baptised at Burslem, on the 2nd of January, 1765, married Dr. Robert Darwin, of Shrewsbury, son of the celebrated Dr. Erasmus Darwin, of Derby (and half-brother to Sir Francis Darwin, M.D., of Breadsall Priory, and Sydnope, Darley Dale, both in Derbyshire), by his first wife, Mary Howard, of Lichfield, and was the mother, along with other sons and daughters, of Charles Darwin, author of the "Origin of Species," &c. The second child of Josiah Wedgwood was John, baptised at Burslem, April 2nd, 1766. He was of Seabridge, and married Louisa Jane, daughter of Mr. John Bartlett Allen, of Criselly, Pembrokeshire, and by her had four sons and three daughters, viz., the Rev. John Allen Wedgwood; Lieut.-Colonel Thomas Josiah Wedgwood, who married Anne Maria, daughter of Admiral Sir C. Tyler; Charles, who died without issue; the Rev. Robert Wedgwood, who married Frances, daughter of the Rev. Offley Crewe; Sarah Elizabeth; Caroline Louisa Jane; and Jessie, who married her cousin, Henry Allen Wedgwood. The third of Josiah Wedgwood's children was Richard Wedgwood, who was born in 1767, and died in 1782. The fourth was Josiah Wedgwood, one of the first two members of parliament for the borough of Stoke-upon Trent. Mr. Wedgwood, who was of Maer Hall, married Elizabeth Allen, sister to Louisa Jane, wife to his brother John, and daughter of Mr. John Bartlett Allen, of Criselly, Pembrokeshire, and by her had four sons and five daughters, viz., first, Josiah Wedgwood (the third of that name), who married his cousin Caroline Elizabeth, daughter of Dr. Darwin, of Shrewsbury, and had issue; second, Henry Allen Wedgwood, barrister-at-law, who married his cousin Jessie, daughter of John Wedgwood, of Seabridge; third, Francis Wedgwood, of Etruria and Barlaston, the present highly respected head of the Etruria firm, who married Frances, daughter of the Rev. J. P. Mosley, of Rolleston Rectory, and has issue three sons, two of whom, Godfrey and Clement, are in partnership with their father—and four daughters; fourth, Hensleigh Wedgwood, barrister-at-law, of London, who married Elizabeth, daughter of the Right Hon. Sir James Mackintosh, the historian, and has issue; fifth, Sarah Elizabeth; sixth, Mary, who died unmarried; seventh, Charlotte, married to the Rev. C. Langton, of Hartfield; eighth, Frances, who died unmarried; and, ninth, Emma, who married her cousin, Charles Darwin, F.R.S., author of the "Origin of Species," &c.

The next child of Josiah Wedgwood was Thomas, who died without issue, of whom I shall have more to say presently; and the remaining children were three daughters,

Catherine, Sarah, and Mary Anne, who all, I believe, died unmarried.

At the time of Josiah Wedgwood's death, the sole partners in the firm were himself, his son Josiah, and Thomas Byerley—Mr. John Wedgwood, the eldest son, having previously withdrawn from business, and become a banker in London. The active business management at this time devolved mainly on Mr. Byerley, whose experience and skill were of great value. In 1800 the partners were, however, the brothers Josiah and John Wedgwood, and Thomas Byerley, which arrangement continued, as I shall relate, until the death of the latter in 1810.

That Mr. John Wedgwood, familiarly called "Jackey" by his father, took at one time an active and confidential part in the manufacture at Etruria, is proved by the following fragment of a letter from his father, the Great Josiah, by which it will be seen that the mixing—the most "ticklish" part of the potter's art—was entrusted to him during his father's absence. The letter runs thus, and is extremely interesting as showing the care which Wedgwood bestowed on the details of the business, even when away from home:—

"Mr. Wood wrote to you last night to get some of the Cameos of fine white Clay made as soon as possible, of proper subjects, for inlaying from the size of the Statues to the small Gems; but if you have not a sufficient quantity of fine Clay, *proved to be good*, then to begin with the Bracelet sizes & less.

"I have now rec^d^ the tryals, 1332, which you apprehend to be over-fired. They are just the reverse, & only want *more fire* to make them excellent. The Gems made of this body sho^d^ be fired in the very topmost sagar of the Bisket oven, with only a thin Disk or Bat over them to prevent their being discolour'd by the flame. I suppose it works pretty well; & as I think it will agree pretty well with the common Bisket, you may wash a few Batts for the Medusa heads, Diomeds, &c., to try if it will answer, & by that means you may get up an assortment sooner than you can if you wait to have Clay enough all of the same kind. But this will not do for those Statues where Arms, &c., are to be added; for those it will be necessary to grind some 1332 in a Dish, and face this with some . . . . Joseph may set some more grinders to work . . . . a number of the Cameos, such as the Statues, Diomeds . . . . . The new Boys as soon as may be. Fine heads, not . . . . relief, and so down to the small Gems, as soon as they can be made. I have wrote to Jackey to weigh some more 1332 for Joseph; but you may use any of your Nos. up that you find good, and some that are not good in the Bisket will be better in the white oven, such as 1207, 1194, 1225; but 1194 will be good very high in the biskett oven 1308, 1309.

"Jackey will mix some 1194 & 1205, both of which will be very good at the top of the Bisket oven."

Mr. Thomas Wedgwood, who suffered from constant ill health, took no part in the management of the business. He was a man of refined tastes, devoted, so far as health permitted, to scientific pursuits, and was widely and deeply respected. To him and to his brother Josiah, conjointly, Samuel Taylor Coleridge was indebted for that substantial assistance which proved the turning-point of his life, and enabled him to devote his talents to literature. The aid thus liberally and disinterestedly given by the Wedgwoods is so nicely spoken of by Mr. Coleridge's biographer, Cottle, that I cannot forbear quoting the following passages from his interesting narrative. Mr. Cottle says:—

"Mr. Coleridge, up to this day, February 18th, 1798, held, though laxly, the doctrines of Socinus. On the Rev. Mr. Rowe, of Shrewsbury, the Socinian minister, coming to settle in Bristol, Mr. Coleridge was strongly recommended by his friends of that persuasion to offer himself as Mr. R's successor; and he accordingly went on probation to Shrewsbury.

"It is proper here to mention, in order that this subject may be the better understood, that Mr. Poole, a little before the above period, had introduced Mr. Coleridge to Mr. Thomas and Mr. Josiah Wedgwood. These gentlemen formed a high estimation of Mr. C's talents, and felt a deep interest in his welfare. At the time Mr. Coleridge was considering whether or not he should persist in offering himself to the Shrewsbury congregation, and so finally to settle down (provided his sentiments remained unaltered) into a Socinian minister, the Messrs. Wedgwoods, having heard of the circumstance, and fearing that a pastoral charge might operate unfavourably on his literary pursuits, interfered, as will appear by the following letter of Mr. Coleridge to Mr. Wade:—

"'Stowey.—My very dear friend,—This last fortnight has been eventful. I received one hundred pounds from Josiah Wedgwood, in order to prevent the *necessity* of my going into the ministry. I have received an invitation from Shrewsbury to be the minister there; and after fluctuations of mind, which have for nights together robbed me of sleep, and I am afraid of health, I have at length returned the order to Mr. Wedgwood, with a long letter, explanatory of my conduct, and accepted the Shrewsbury invitation.' . . .

"The two Messrs. Wedgwoods, still adhering to their first opinion, that Mr. Coleridge, by accepting the proposed engagement, would seriously obstruct his literary efforts, and having duly weighed the 'explanatory letter' sent them by Mr. C., addressed him a conjoint letter, announcing that it was their determination to allow him for his life one hundred and fifty pounds per year. This decided Mr. Coleridge to reject the Shrewsbury invitation. Mr. C. was oppressed with grateful emotions to these his liberal benefactors. He always spoke in particular of the late Mr. Thomas Wedgwood as being one of the best talkers, and possessing one of the acutest minds, of any man he had known. While the affair was in suspense, a report was current in Bristol that Mr. Coleridge had rejected the Messrs. Wedgwood's offer, which the Socinians in both towns ardently desired. Entertaining a contrary wish, I addressed a letter to Mr. Coleridge, stating the report, and expressing a hope that it had no foundation. The following satisfactory answer was immediately returned:—

"'My very dear Cottle,—The moment I received Mr. Wedgwood's letter I accepted his offer. How a contrary report could arise I cannot guess. . . . . I hope to see you at the close of next week. I have been respectfully and kindly treated at Shrewsbury. —I am well, and now and ever your grateful and affectionate friend, S. T. Coleridge.'"

Other allusions to this truly generous action on the part of the brothers Josiah and Thomas Wedgwood occur in the same work, and Coleridge himself, in his "Biographia Literaria," says:—"While my mind was thus perplexed, by a gracious Providence, for which I can never be sufficiently grateful, the generous and munificent patronage of

Mr. Josiah and Mr. Thomas Wedgwood enabled me to finish my education in Germany. Instead of troubling others with my own crude notions and juvenile compositions, I was thenceforward better employed in attempting to store my own head with the wisdom of others." *

De Quincey, speaking of the friendship which existed between Coleridge and the Wedgwoods, says :—"Coleridge attended Mr. Thomas Wedgwood, as a friend, throughout the anomalous and affecting illness that brought him to the grave. The external symptoms were torpor and morbid irritability, together with everlasting restlessness. By way of some relief, Mr. Wedgwood purchased a travelling carriage, and wandered up and down England, taking Coleridge with him as a friend. By the death of Mr. Wedgwood, Coleridge succeeded to a regular annuity of £75, which that gentleman had bequeathed to him. The other Mr. Wedgwood granted him an equal allowance."

Mr. Thomas Wedgwood, who was never married, died in the year 1805, at Gunville, Dorsetshire. He was a man of considerable scientific attainments. During his father's lifetime he prosecuted his studies with his aid and that of Alexander Chisholm, and made such progress in his researches into the properties of light, &c., that in 1792, three years before the death of Josiah, he communicated to the Royal Society an account of his "Experiments and Observations on the Production of Light from different bodies by Heat and by Attraction." His continued experiments and researches resulted in the discovery of the process of photography, and in 1802, in conjunction with Sir Humphrey Davy, who assisted him in his experiments, he made those discoveries known by a paper printed in the "Journal of the

* The most graceful, elegant, and truly *worthy* memoir of Samuel Taylor Coleridge which has ever been written—and, indeed, the only one which can be read with real pleasure—is the one recently given in the *Art-Journal* for February, 1865, from the pen of his friend and associate, Mr. S. C. Hall, F.S.A. To this memoir—a written portrait, word-painted by a most worthy and able artist—I cordially direct the attention of my readers.

Royal Institution of Great Britain," under the title of "An Account of a Method of Copying Paintings upon Glass, and of making Profiles by the Agency of Light upon Nitrate of Silver; with observations by H. Davy." This is the first recorded attempt at fixing the images of the camera-obscura (which Wedgwood appears to have used from a youth) by the chemical influence of light. But for the death of this deep-thinking and wonderful man (Thomas Wedgwood), which took place about two years after this time, doubtless the world would have largely benefited by his labours in this particular field. As it was, he died before he had succeeded in permanently fixing the pictures he had obtained, and it was left to later experimentalists to perfect that wonderful art which he had discovered, and of whose success he had laid the foundation.

Mr. Josiah Wedgwood, the elder brother of Mr. Thomas Wedgwood, just named, was also a man of considerable taste, and of high attainments. He was one of the founders of the Royal Horticultural Society, and took an active part in public affairs. In 1832, he was elected one of the members of parliament for the then newly-constituted borough of Stoke-upon-Trent, but retired from its representation in 1835. He died at Maer.

In 1810, Thomas Byerley, upon whom the bulk of the direct management of the concern had devolved from the time of the death of the Great Josiah, died, and was buried at St. Anne's, Westminster—the church where he was married, and where Mrs. Byerley's mother (Mrs. Bruckfield) and his infant son were previously buried.

During the period of the war then going on with France* —a weary and a troublous time for the commerce of this

* I have heard it related that during this war large orders were received from France by the Messrs. Wedgwood, and other potters of the district, for marbles. These were made in great quantities, shipped off to the Continent, and there used as bullets. During the same war, I believe, goods to the value of several thousand pounds, which were in their warehouse in France, were destroyed.

country—Mr. Byerley had worked incessantly and earnestly at the business, and had succeeded in maintaining for it its high position; but the exertions and anxieties overpowered him at length, and he sank. He "was a grave, reserved, but kind being, and those who knew him learnt to appreciate his goodness, and to love as well as reverence the dignified urbanity that characterised his deportment." He was devotedly attached to his uncle, the Great Josiah; and many circumstances which have come to my knowledge show that attachment to have been mutual.

On the death of Mr. Byerley, the business was carried on by Josiah Wedgwood alone, until Martinmas, 1823, when he took his eldest son Josiah (the third of that name) into partnership, the firm being carried on under the style of "Josiah Wedgwood and Son." Four years afterwards, at Martinmas, 1827, the other sons having been taken into partnership, the style was altered to that of "Josiah Wedgwood and Sons."

In November, 1841, Josiah Wedgwood, senior, of Maer Hall, retired from the business, and it was carried on by his sons until the following April, when Josiah Wedgwood, junior, also retired. The style of the firm, however, continued to be, as it is to the present day, "Josiah Wedgwood and Sons."

The manufacture of china, which had, for reasons already given, never been attempted by the Great Josiah, was commenced at Etruria about the year 1808 or 1809, in the time of Mr. Byerley, who considered that it would be an advantageous addition to the works; but was only carried on for a very few years, probably only nine or ten, and then finally discontinued. The china ware thus made was of extremely good quality, both in texture of body, in colour, in glaze, and in decoration. It was not made to any great extent, and is now very scarce. In Mr. Gladstone's possession is an excellent specimen—a coffee mug, the ground of a small pattern, in blue, with Chinese figures in tablets, in red and other colours. Examples also occur in other private collections, and collectors will find in the Jermyn Street Museum, London, and in Mr. Mayer's museum, Liverpool, excellent and characteristic specimens.

The mark on the china is the simple name

WEDGWOOD

in small capital letters, printed on the bottom in red or blue colour.

Some of the china is painted, and other examples which I have seen are printed in blue. The example in the Jermyn Street Museum is decorated with flowers and humming-birds in bright oriental colouring, and is well gilt.

"Stone china" was also at one time, to some little extent, made at Etruria, examples of which are now rare. It ceased to be made about the year 1825. It was remarkably fine in body, and its decoration exceedingly good.

In 1815, on the 15th of January, Mrs. Wedgwood, widow of the great Josiah, died at Parkfield, in the eighty-first year of her age, and was, a few days later, buried in the parish church of Stoke-upon-Trent, near her husband. On the north wall of the chancel of that church, close by the monument of her husband, engraved on page 359, is a Gothic memorial tablet of plain and very poor design, recording her death. It bears the following inscription :—

Sacred to the memory of
SARAH,
Widow of Josiah Wedgwood,
of Etruria,
Born August the 18th, 1734.
Died January the 15th, 1815.

The productions of the firm at this time—and, indeed, through each successive change in the proprietary down to the present time—were, as they had been in the time of the first Josiah, divided between the "useful" and the "ornamented." The "useful" consisting of services of every kind in fine earthenware, and in all the varieties of bodies hitherto introduced, to which additional patterns were constantly added; and the "ornamented" comprising all the immense variety of exquisite articles which had been made by the great founder of the works, with additional vases, medallions, and other pieces.

In 1843, on the 23rd of August, Mr. John Boyle became a partner in the firm; but his connection was only of short duration, and sixteen months afterwards, on the 4th of January, 1845, he died.

On the 2nd of March, 1846, Mr. Robert Brown,* of Cliff Ville, became a partner with the Messrs. Wedgwood; but, dying on the 26th of May, 1859, Mr. Francis Wedgwood was again left sole proprietor of the works. In November of the same year he was joined in partnership by his son, Mr. Godfrey Wedgwood, and in 1863 by his second son, Mr. Clement Wedgwood, and the works are still carried on by them—Messrs. Francis Wedgwood, Godfrey Wedgwood, and Clement Wedgwood—under the old style of "Josiah Wedgwood and Sons."

The Marks used by the Wedgwoods have been but few, and will therefore in a few words be disposed of in this memoir. The mark has in all cases, except during the partnership of Thomas Bentley, on that particular branch of the manufacture in which he had an interest, been the simple name of Wedgwood. In some instances the name is impressed in large capitals—

WEDGWOOD

in others, it appears in small capital letters—

WEDGWOOD

and in others, though not so commonly, in the ordinary type—

Wedgwood

* Mr. Brown was a man of enlarged understanding, of great experience, and of wonderful business talents. He realised a handsome fortune entirely by his own industry and exertions, and was possessed of a refined taste, which aided him materially in his progress.

On a few pieces the name occurs thus—

WEDGWOOD
ETRURIA

On those ornamental goods (vases, medallions, &c.), in the production of which Thomas Bentley had an interest—for it will be remembered I have already stated that the partnership between himself and Josiah Wedgwood extended to the "ornamented" branch only, and had nothing whatever to do with the "useful"—the general mark used was the circular one here shown. In this the letters are *raised*, not sunk, as in the other marks. Another used at this time was as follows—

WEDGWOOD
& BENTLEY

and another—

Wedgwood
& Bentley

both of which are, of course, impressed marks.

With regard to these marks of "Wedgwood and Bentley," it may be well to remind collectors that whatever pieces may come into their hands bearing these names must have been made in the twelve years between 1768 and 1780.

Besides these marks, a variety of smaller ones—letters, flowers, figures, and numbers, both impressed and in colours, are to be seen on the different varieties of wares. These, it will be easily understood, are simply workmen's marks, or marks denoting period, &c., and which, being private marks, concern only, and are of interest only, to the proprietors themselves.

And now, while speaking of *marks*, a few words may opportunely be introduced on a matter which is somewhat puzzling to collectors, and about which they will doubtless be glad to receive enlightenment. It is this: in many collections pieces of one kind or other will be found bearing the mark

WEDGWOOD & Co.,

and others with the mark of

WEDGEWOOD,

sometimes impressed, and sometimes in colour. The latter, it will be observed, has a central E, which the real name of Wedgwood does not possess. These I have heard variously appropriated by collectors to Wedgwood and Bentley, to Wedgwood and Byerley, and to a dozen other supposed periods and people. I am enabled to state that these pieces, many of them highly creditable and excellent productions, were not made by the Etruria Wedgwoods at all, but that the latter (the "Wedgewood," and sometimes the "Wedgwood") were the manufacture of Messrs. William Smith, and others, of Stockton, against whom Messrs. Wedgwood applied for and obtained an injunction restraining them from using the name of "Wedgwood, or "Wedgewood."

The following official notification will well explain this matter, and prove of considerable interest to collectors:—

"Vice-Chancellor of England's Court,
"Lincoln's Inn, 8th August, 1848.

"In Chancery.

"*Wedgwood and others* against *Smith and others.*

"Mr. Bethell on behalf of the Plaintiffs, Francis Wedgwood and Robert Brown (who carry on the business of Potters, at Etruria, in the Staffordshire Potteries, under the Firm of 'Josiah Wedgwood and Sons'), moved for an Injunction against the defendants, William Smith, John Walley, George Skinner, and Henry Cowap (who also carry on the business of Potters, at Stockton, in the County of Durham, under the Firm of 'William Smith and Company'), to restrain them and every of them, their Agents, Workmen, or Servants, from stamping, or engraving, or marking, or in any way putting or placing on the ware manufactured by them, the Defendants, the name 'Wedgwood' or 'Wedgewood,' and from in any manner imitating or counterfeiting such name on the Ware manufactured by the Defendants since the month of December, 1846, or hereafter to be manufactured by the Defendants, with the name 'Wedgwood' or 'Wedgewood' stamped, engraved, or otherwise marked or placed thereon.

"Mr. Bethell stated that the trade mark 'Wedgwood' had been used by the family of the Wedgwoods for centuries; he would not, however, go further into the matter at present, because Mr. Parker appeared for the Defendants; and it might become necessary—with whom, and himself, it had been arranged by consent on Mr. Parker's application on behalf of the Defendants, for time to answer the Plaintiffs' Affidavits—that the Motion should stand over until the Second Seal in Michaelmas Term next; and that in the meantime the Defendants should be restrained as above stated; except that for the words, 'since the month of December, 1846,' the words, 'since the month of July, 1847,' should be substituted.

"Mr. J. Parker said he appeared for the Defendants, and consented without prejudice; and on his application for time to answer the Plaintiffs' Affidavits, the Court made an order accordingly.

"On the 9th day of November, being the Second Seal in Michaelmas term, 1848, Mr. E. Younge, as counsel for the above-named Plaintiffs, moved for, and obtained, a perpetual Injunction against the Defendants in the terms of Mr. Bethell's Motion, substituting for the words, 'since the month of December, 1846,' the words, 'since the month of July, 1847;' the Defendants consenting to pay to the Plaintiffs their costs.

"Solicitor for the Plaintiffs,

"SAMUEL KING,

"Furnival's Inn, Middlesex."

CHAPTER XXII.

ETRURIA WORKS.—PRODUCTIONS OF THE PRESENT DAY.—SOLID JASPER AND JASPER DIP.—MAJOLICA.—MR. MINTON.—M. EMILE LESSORE.—PARIAN.—INLAID WARE.—QUEEN'S WARE.—PEARL BODY.—ROCKINGHAM WARE.—POROUS WARE.—RED WARE.—BLUE PRINTING.—VIEWS OF THE WORKS.—"SUN AND PLANET" MOTION STEAM ENGINE MADE BY WATT.—THE VILLAGE OF ETRURIA.—THE VILLAGE INN.—ETRURIA JUBILEE GROUP.

HAVING now spoken pretty fully of the productions of the Etruria Works, and of their great founder, and remarked upon their characteristics in the earlier periods of their career, as well as in those of a later date, it remains only to bring my narrative down to the present time, by saying a few words on the different classes of goods manufactured by the Messrs. Wedgwood at the time I write, and of some of the specialities of their various productions. As in the "olden times" of the great Josiah, so it is now at Etruria. The self-same moulds are used; the self-same principles are acted upon and carried out; the same mixture of bodies and glazes, with but (in some instances) trifling modifications, are in daily use; the same system is employed, and the same varieties of goods are manufactured, as was the case in his days; and, consequently, the vases, the medallions, the services, and all the other goods which he made, seventy, eighty, or ninety years ago, may be, and are, daily reproduced for customers of the present time. It is true that the ornamental goods of the present day have not quite that charm of super-excellence about them which those made in the days of the first Josiah possess; but it must be conceded by collectors that a great deal of that charm consists solely in the knowledge that they *are* the productions of his own time, and in the established fact that nothing produced since then can equal them in finish, or in softness and beauty of surface. Taken as productions of the present time alone, it is pleasant to feel that Messrs. Wedgwood's jasper and other ornamental goods stand as far in advance of their competitors as those of the great Josiah did in advance of those of his own time.

I have already stated that Messrs. Wedgwood still produce their "jasper," their "basaltes," their "red," their "cream-coloured," and, indeed, all the other wares for which the works in the olden times were so famous. The jasper goods are still—as they have ever been since the first production of that marvellous body—their principal feature—the great speciality of their works. In this, since the days of Turner, they have never even been approached, and their goods still maintain their old and high reputation. All the famous works of the olden time—from the Portland Vase down through all the chaste and beautiful varieties of vases, plaques, medallions, services, &c.—are still made in all their beauty, with the addition of many new and ever-varying designs and combinations.

The jasper is produced in dark and in light blue of various shades (with, of course, the raised figures and ornaments in white), in sage-green, in pink, and other tints. It is also produced both in "solid jasper"—that is, the solid coloured body throughout—and in "jasper dip," which is the white jasper body with the colour laid on the surface. The "solid jasper" was reintroduced in 1856.

Another speciality of the ornamental productions of the Etruria Works of the present day—for it is but of recent introduction—is that of "majolica," which is produced of extreme beauty and of high artistic excellence, as well in dessert and other services as in pieces of a more strictly and solely ornamental character. The manufacture of majolica was, it is of course well known, revived by Mr. Minton, whose firm in that, as in many other varieties of pottery, takes the lead in point of excellence of decoration. The manufacture of majolica was commenced at Etruria in 1860, and in this style, I believe, Messrs. Wedgwood now produce as much in quantity as is done in any other establishment, while their quality and style of decoration is of commensurate excellence. In the purely artistic portion of the majolica—the paintings on plates, dishes, slabs, and other pieces—those produced at Etruria are fully equal, both in force of drawing, in purity of style, and in depth as well as delicacy of colouring, to any produced at Sèvres; while in choice of subjects they are far superior to those of the Royal factory. In quantity, too, I believe that the productions in this particular and wonderfully artistic and beautiful style are multiplied by six at Etruria, while they are divided by ten in cost. The principal painter of these majolicas is M. Emile Lessore, an artist of considerable repute, whose works are much sought after.* His majolicas have the advantage of bearing his name, written on the painting itself, either in full, "Emile Lessore," or "E. Lessore." Whether in pastoral, emblematical or other groups, or in the nude figure, this artist's productions bear the stamp of originality, and are characterised by great freedom and power of touch, and by harmonious and rich colouring. The future collector will be pleased to know that the pieces bearing the name of M. Lessore, and the Wedgwood mark, have been produced since 1859.

* M. E. Lessore possesses first-rate abilites, and his works are far superior to those of any other artist in this striking and beautiful style. His name is well known as a painter in oil; but of late years, having turned his attention to producing paintings on pottery, M. Lessore has succeeded, by the liberal and enlightened aid of the Messrs. Wedgwood, in founding a school of decorative art on pottery which bids fair to be of lasting duration, and in which the works of Rubens, Raphael, Titian, and other great masters are interpreted in such a way as to render them applicable to fictile purposes. M. Lessore was, I believe, for a time, at the Royal Works of Sèvres.

In majolica a dinner service of unique pattern, with figures and foliage on the rim, recently designed, will no doubt prove very successful. In majolica, too, as in the "malachite," the "mottled," the "agate," and other wares, dessert and toilet services, and a variety of both useful and ornamental articles, are made—ranging from the large-sized garden seat (a fine one, formed of bamboos, is specially deserving notice), and the gigantic vase, down to the small and delicately-formed ladies' ring stand. In the "mottled" ware a marvellously rich and striking effect is produced by the combination of the most brilliant colours; while in the "malachite" the beautiful green and darker wavings of the stone are well imitated.

"Parian" was made by the Messrs. Wedgwood at Etruria about 1848 or 9, and was of good quality.

Another variety of ornamental work is the "inlaid" ware, in which a variety of articles, including services, are made. The effect of this style of ornamentation is much the same as the "Tunbridge ware," which, of course, is well known to my readers. It is striking from its novelty, and pleasing from its very simplicity.

Turning now to the "useful" and more strictly commercial part of the works, I must first of all note that the "cream-coloured" ware, the veritable "Queen's ware" of the olden time, is still made to an enormous extent, and is still sought for and purchased throughout the world. Of a delicate creamy whiteness in colour, light and pleasant to the touch, true and close-fitting in the "potting," and covered with one of the most faultless of glazes, this ware still "holds its own," and maintains its wonted supremacy. In it, services and every variety of useful articles are made; and it is pleasant to add, that the pieces are still made in the old moulds used in the great Josiah's time, with only such modifications as fit them for more modern notions. For instance, the "turin" modelled by Flaxman, and charged for in his bill, which I have printed, is still made, with only the addition of newly-designed handles; and hundreds of others of the "ancient forms" are still, in the same way, preserved and produced.

The next principal variety of useful ware is the "pearl" body—a body of great hardness and durability, of a pure pearly white, and glazed to the utmost perfection. In this, as in the cream-coloured, services and useful goods of every description are manufactured, both in plain white and printed. The same body is used also for many of the decorated varieties, and is highly glazed. The "pearl" ware is not a "pearl of great price," but one for ordinary use and of moderate cost.

"Rockingham ware," of a very superior quality and of a good colour, is made largely at Etruria in teapots, coffee-pots, services (the cups white inside), and other articles.

The "porous ware" used for water bottles, butter coolers, &c., is also made at the present time; and the "mortar ware" is still made, and keeps foremost rank in the market.

In the "red ware"—a rich colour and fine body—services and a large number of other articles are produced, and are frequently ornamented with raised figures, &c., in black, with good and striking effect.

Blue Printing was introduced at Etruria at an early date, and has, of course, with black, &c., been continued to the present day.

These are the principal varieties of wares in the "useful classes," and it will be sufficient, in closing, to make the one general remark, that the services now made at Etruria, whether dinner, tea, dessert, or toilet—whether of the more ordinary descriptions "for the million," or of the more elegant and costly "for the few"—are all thoroughly good, and all produced with that care and nicety which have ever characterised the place and its proprietors.

The markets to which the goods are sent are more widely spread than perhaps will be conceived by the uninitiated, and it is not too much to say, that, besides the home trade, which is very extensive, the "Wedgwood ware" of the present day is sent, as it used to be, to every quarter of the globe.

In a former chapter I have given a view of one portion of the Etruria works—the "Black Works," as that portion was called—and I here re-introduce it, and at the same time add two others, for the purpose of giving my readers some idea of their extent and their general character.

The first view which I give of these famed works shows

the front of the manufactory. In the foreground is the canal—the canal carried out by the enterprising spirit of Wedgwood, and formed by the indomitable skill of Brindley—which passes close to the works; where there is, as will be seen, excellent wharfage; it has branches opening directly into the manufactory itself, so that boats may be laden and discharged with the greatest ease. To the left of the view will be seen the "hovels" and kilns; and in the centre—the large pedimented building with the bell-turret—are the "show-rooms," the offices, the "museum," &c.; and at the extreme end of the view, to the right, will be seen the lodge, &c. These works, it may be remembered, were planned and built by the great Josiah, and possess, therefore, an unusual degree of interest.

The next illustration shows a part of the interior of one of

the yards, which I have selected as much from its historical interest as from its picturesque character. It is one of the "useful" works where so much of the "Queen's ware" and other of the staple manufactures of the place has been made;

but it is most especially "interesting" as showing the stone steps—those to the left hand—by which Josiah Wedgwood constantly ascended to his counting-house, and the bridge by which he crossed the yard from his office to the ware-rooms and works.

The whole of this part of the works has an air of venerable age about it, and the very atmosphere seems to breathe of the presence, as it were, of the master mind of its first and greatest owner. But not only in this part of the works. The same remark will apply to nearly every portion of the place, and perhaps more especially so to the engine and

THE "BLACK WORKS," ETRURIA.

engine-house, which have an appearance of antiquity about them possessed by no others in the kingdom. The steam-engine to which I refer was one of the first made by James Watt, and has worked uninterruptedly since his day to the present hour, and still does its work as well and "sweetly," as the engineers say, as ever. It is a condensing engine of forty-horse power, and its great curiosity consists in its being worked with the "sun and planet" motion, instead of the "crank." It is the only engine of this construction in existence, and therefore possesses an unusual amount of interest.

The third illustration is the "Black Works," the first portion of the manufactory which was erected. In this part it will be remembered that the Portland Vase was produced, in it Flaxman worked, and in it most of the exquisitely beautiful ornamental wares have been, from the first day of its erection down to the present, produced.

Of the village of Etruria I have before said a few words. It consists of one long straight street, running down from the canal bridge, at the works, to the railway station, with some shorter side streets, and contains, I believe, about two hundred houses, almost entirely inhabited by Messrs. Wedgwood's workpeople and their families. The houses are far better than is generally the case; and it is pleasant to add that the people, as a rule, have a more comfortable, happy, and "cared for" look than is usual in the Potteries. Etruria has its church, its dissenting places of worship, and its schools, which are principally supported by the Messrs. Wedgwood. It has also its wharf, its "Etruscan Bone Mills," its foundry, its immense iron-works, its newly-erected forge, and many other important features; and it has, too, its village inns, its post-office, and its hucksters' shops. I have said that there are village inns at Etruria: two of these, the "Bridge Inn" and "Etruria Inn," are close to the works. The first, the "Bridge Inn," kept by Mrs. Jones, a worthy matronly old lady, who all her life-time has been connected with the Wedgwoods, as nurse and otherwise, closely adjoins the works, to the left of the view of the front in the engraving just given, and here the visitor will find the old spirit of Wedgwood pervading the whole place. In one room Sir Joshua Reynolds' beautiful portrait of Josiah Wedgwood—the fine mezzotint by S. W. Reynolds—is faced by photographs of the present generations of the family; and in another, the same portrait of

Josiah Wedgwood has for its companion an interesting group of portraits of Mr. Francis Wedgwood and nine of his workmen, whose average term of servitude with the firm was at that time more than fifty-four years. This truly interesting group bears an inscription worthy of being preserved. Here it is :—

"Etruria Jubilee Group of Francis Wedgwood, Esq., and nine workmen, whose average time of servitude is 54½ years, November, 1859. From a photograph by John Emery. Front row, sitting, from left hand of group, Moses Brownsword, Enoch Keeling, Francis Wedgwood, Esq., William Stanway, Thomas Mason. Rear row, standing, from left hand of group, James Boulton, William Adams, John Adams, John Finny, Benjamin Lovatt."

Of these workmen all but Thomas Mason are still living, and still work in their old rooms, at their old, old occupation, where now they have been engaged for more than sixty years. Born in the village, commencing work when mere children, they have continued through the "seven ages" on the spot which gave them birth, and there, when their sands are run, they will rest—not where the "rude forefathers of the hamlet sleep," for the hamlet is, as I have shown, of comparatively modern formation, but with their fellow-labourers in Wedgwood's field of industry.

No stronger testimony, surely, could be given to the kindly excellence of the Wedgwoods as employers than that which this group affords—showing, as it does, the master surrounded by a number of his workmen who have been faithful servants for so many years. It is interesting to note that in the person of one of these men, William Stanway, an absolute link with the great Josiah is kept up. This man began to work at Etruria the very year of Josiah Wedgwood's death (1795), and has remained there ever since—a period of sixty-nine years.

CHAPTER XXIII.

WEDGWOOD MEMORIALS.—THE WEDGWOOD STATUE AT STOKE. —ADDRESS OF THE PROMOTERS.—WEDGWOOD MEMORIAL INSTITUTE AT BURSLEM.—MR. GLADSTONE LAYS THE FIRST STONE.—HIS VIEWS ON THE ADVANTAGES OF THE PROPOSED INSTITUTION.—CASKET MADE BY MESSRS. DAVENPORT.—TROWEL BY MR. MACINTYRE.—MR. W. WOODALL.—CAPTAIN FOWKES' ARRANGEMENT OF THE ROOMS.—MR. BERESFORD HOPE'S PROJECT FOR EXTERNAL FICTILE DECORATIONS.—DECORATIONS DESCRIBED.—WEDGWOOD MEMORIAL JUG.—MESSRS. C. MEIGH AND CO.'S EARTHENWARE WORKS.—HAPPY ARRANGEMENT BY WHICH EACH OF THE THREE TOWNS POSSESSES ITS MEMORIALS OF WEDGWOOD.

AND now a word or two on what has been done of late years, and what is now doing, to do honour to, and to perpetuate the memory of, the great and good Josiah Wedgwood, the founder of the Etruria Works, whose full biography I have the proud satisfaction of having been the first to write, and the history of which I have here, for the first time, prepared and given to the world.

It is true that the works of Josiah Wedgwood form, and will remain, his greatest, proudest, and most lasting monument, but it is equally true that to him, above most men, it was fit that not only a national and public monument should be erected, but that an institution, such as he would have gloried in supporting, should be founded in connection with his name, and in the district which he had so much benefited, and, indeed, raised to its high state of prosperity. It was fit that a public monument should be erected, and it was equally fit that an educational and art institution should be established to his memory; and these, happily, have been accomplished.

In 1859, the project of a public statue to Josiah Wedgwood was broached. This laudable project originated with Mr. Joseph Mayer, of Hanley, and was carried out to a successful issue by Mr. Edwin Allbut, the secretary. The circulars and papers issued by its promoters thus well expressed the feeling of the district:—

"It is a time-honoured custom that an intellectual and grateful people should seek to perpetuate the memory of its distinguished men by erecting STATUES to their honour. The bronze and the marble do not simply recognise the genius that once emanated from a single soul; they also declare that its scattered rays now light up many intellects, and are widely diffused among the race.

"From all England's worthies it would be difficult to select one to whom this remark would be more applicable than the late JOSIAH WEDGWOOD. Though dead, his memory still lives amongst us, in a thousand beautiful and classic forms which he introduced, and by the improvements and inventions by which he converted a rude manufacture into one of the highest developments of art. In him were blended classical taste, scientific skill, and practical ability; and this rare union of qualities, warmed and vivified by a temperament singularly poetic and artistic in its manifestations, was entirely devoted to one great practical object, involving the elevation and employment of his fellow-men.

"Throughout the length and breadth of England, the name of Josiah Wedgwood is a 'household word.' In this particular district, honoured by his birth and residence, and enriched by his genius, there is not an employer—hardly, indeed, an operative—who cannot more or less fully repeat the story of his active and useful life.

"It is perhaps owing to this remarkable familiarity with his name, that no monument has been hitherto erected to his memory. But nearly two-thirds of a century have now elapsed since his decease. Longer delay might be mistaken for ingratitude; and although time can never obliterate the benefits he has conferred, the few contemporaries who can still personally identify them as the direct result of his perseverance and genius are fast passing away, and with each succeeding generation tradition becomes fainter.

"Impressed with these views, a number of gentlemen assembled at Stoke-upon-Trent, on Monday, January 24th, 1859, John Ridgway, Esq.,* in the chair, when it was resolved—

"I.—That the lapse of more than sixty years since the death of Josiah Wedgwood, F.R.S., has applied the test of time to his works, and shown that they possess the lasting power of pleasing, not dependent on having been suited to the fashion of his day; which, combined with the permanent and general usefulness of his labours, seems to point him out as a fit subject for a public monument.

"II.—That a statue be erected to his honour by public subscription, the character and locality to be left to the decision of the subscribers.

"Among the distinguished men who have too long waited for a befitting recognition of their worth and services stands pre-eminently Josiah Wedgwood. France has long honoured her Palissy; Germany her Boettcher; Italy her Lucca del Robbia; and all those countries assign equal honour to our Wedgwood. Only his own country has, however, hitherto seemed reluctant to provide that memorial which his genius, his moral worth, his personal example, and his signal services to his countrymen justly deserve. Wedgwood, however, has never been forgotten; and recently a tide of reaction in favour of permanently honouring his memory by a national monument has steadily set in; and the lovers of genius, art, practical sagacity, and moral earnestness, will be inexcusably to blame if, before that tide ebbs, they have not secured a lasting public tribute to his memory. At first sight, it may seem that to put the monument into the shape of a handsome building devoted to some useful public purpose would answer the double end of honouring the dead, and furthering the welfare of the living; but, to do anything well, we must be content to kill one bird with one stone; and this scheme is no exception to the rule. The utility must be suited to the present time, and therefore liable to grow out of use. It must needs be connected with a considerable yearly outlay, which must be met either by annual or occasional subscription, or an endowment. If in the first way, perpetual trouble, anxiety, and failure are entailed on the trustees, and certain eventual ruin, or at best its separation from all monumental purposes. If in the second way, will the general public be willing to raise so large a sum as will be needed for purposes which, to be

* Mr. Ridgway was the first mayor of Hanley.

useful, must be local? Or suppose such a sum raised and vested in trustees, how many of the contributors, if they could awake two hundred years hence, would be satisfied with the then application of their bounty? A statue, on the other hand, is for all time, and is local only so far as it can only stand on one spot. It entails no expense after the first outlay, requires no trustees, and, with proper care, artistic merit may be ensured—in short, the universal consent of mankind has settled the matter long ago that a monument ought to be a statue; and we shall do well not to run counter to such an authority.

"The spread of knowledge, the increased intelligence among all ranks of the people; the immense progress of the physical sciences, and the enlarged interest in the fine arts, which have signalised the last twenty years, have unavoidably brought the exquisite art of the potter into fresh notice and interest, and as unavoidably brought Josiah Wedgwood into additional prominence as England's great and most famous potter. None more willingly accord this pre-eminence to him than those among his contemporaries and successors, whose achievements best entitle them to dispute it with him.

"All feel that he deserves this in virtue of the twofold genius which enabled him alike to satisfy the poorest and the least artistic of the land with a strong, cheap, cleanly household ware, and to delight the richest and the most fastidious in taste with vessels so pleasing in form and colour that it was an education to the senses to look at and handle them; and their surpassing excellence as pieces of useful pottery was forgotten in admiration of their beauty as works of Art. His name, moreover, has gone round the world; and Wedgwood ware is as famous as that of Sèvres and Dresden, and competes even with that of China and Japan. Nor was Josiah Wedgwood more estimable as a potter than as a man. Laden with poverty in his early years, he found only an impetus to labour in the load. Sorely tried with sickness, he spent the enforced leisure of one long illness in studying the chemical and other scientific principles, the foundation of the potter's art, and rose from his sick bed to apply them with unheard-of success to the improvement of it. The protracted convalescence from another malady, involving a severe surgical operation which maimed him for life, was beguiled by the study of those æsthetical laws the mastery of which soon made him, if possible, more famous as an artist than even as a manufacturer. When his genius, patience, and perseverance, aided by restored health, made him a successful and wealthy man, he showed himself a generous and considerate master to those in his employment, and was an object of love and honour to the wide circle who enjoyed his friendship. His liberal support of some of the most distinguished literary and scientific men of the country, and the important assistance which he rendered several of them in their memorable undertakings, are matters of history. His enlightened patriotism and public spirit are equally familiar to all students of his lifetime, and will doubtless, before long, receive justice at the hands of some competent biographer. Such men are exactly those who should be remembered alike as benefactors of their fellows, whom, though they ask it not, one of the noblest instincts of our nature commands us never to forget; and as examples of honest, noble workers in the Great Taskmaster's eye, whose lives are precious daily lessons to all the children of our common empire. Great Britain cannot afford any longer to want a monument to Josiah Wedgwood."

The idea of a statue was carried out to a successful issue by its promoters, who having collected a sufficient amount of subscriptions, commissioned Mr. E. Davis, of London, to prepare the figure. The bronze statue of Josiah Wedgwood now stands on a kind of neutral ground, on the confines of the towns of Stoke and Hanley, in the open square in front of the railway station at Stoke-upon-Trent, within a few minutes' walk of the church where he is buried. He is represented standing, bare headed, and holding in his left hand the Portland Vase, whose emblematic figures he appears to be in the act of descanting upon. The pedestal bears in front the words "JOSIAH WEDGWOOD;" on one of its sides, "Born 1730;" on the other, "Died 1795;" and at the back—facing the hotel—"Erected by Public Subscription. Inaugurated by the Earl of Harrowby, 24th February, 1863."

The other project—that of founding a Memorial Institute—has, happily, also been carried out. The proposal was first made in 1858, and inaugurated on the 27th of January, 1859, by the Right Hon. the Earl of Carlisle; and though for a time it waned, has never been lost sight of, and the institution is now, at the time I write, gradually rising from the ground—the almost hallowed ground—within little more than a stone's throw of the birthplace of the great potter. This proposition for the founding of an institution was the first movement which had been made to do him public honour, and it was shortly afterwards met by the counter proposition to erect a statue. Thanks to this opposition, both the statue and the institution are provided for the Potteries. The first stone of the "Wedgwood Institute" at Burslem was laid on the 26th of October, 1863, by the Right Hon. W. E. Gladstone, M.P., her Majesty's Chancellor of the Exchequer, who took occasion in the course of one of the ablest and most eloquent addresses which even he has ever delivered, to pay a just and warm tribute to the excellencies, the character, the ability, and the high attainments of Wedgwood.

From this address of Mr. Gladstone's, I have already made some quotations in former chapters. His idea of the establishment of the institution being national rather than local in its interest and purpose, remains to be given. "When," said Mr. Gladstone, "I received, through one of your respected representatives, an invitation to co-operate with you in the foundation of the Wedgwood Institute, at the place which gave him birth, and on the site of his first factory, I could not hesitate to admit that a design of this kind was, at least in my view, not a local, but, when properly regarded, rather a national design. Partly it may be called national, because the manufacture of earthenware, in its varied and innumerable branches, is fast becoming, or has indeed become, one of our great and distinguishing British manufactures. But it is for another and a broader reason that I decide to treat the purpose you have now in hand as a purpose of national rather than merely local or partial interest. It is because there are certain principles applicable to manufacture by the observance or neglect of which its products are rendered good or bad. These principles were applied by Wedgwood, with a consistency and tenacity that cannot be too closely observed through the whole of our industrial production. These principles being his, and being true, were also in no small degree peculiar to his practice. and deserve to be in the permanent annals of art especially associated with his name."

Later on in the day the Chancellor of the Exchequer said :—

"If this is a day dedicated and devoted to the commemoration of Wedgwood, let me observe that there is one mode of commemorating him beyond all others, and that is by following in his footsteps; and you have now undertaken—you have now given a pledge —by your energies, to erect a building which you mean to call the Wedgwood Institute. Let me presume to tell you that you have thereby entered upon no mean or trivial enterprise; you have thereby undertaken no slight responsibility. If under the name of Wedgwood—of the Wedgwood Institute—there should be erected in this town—which, I must say, appears to me to have shown singular public spirit in the nature of the buildings already raised for public purposes—if there should be raised under the name of the Wedgwood Institute anything mean, anything inadequate, anything at variance with the principles to which he was devoted, that institute, instead of being an honour, will be a discredit to the town of Burslem. I cannot help hoping that in that institute we shall set forth, and set forth in the fullest efficiency, the means for prosecuting Wedgwood's art—that you are determined that that institution shall be a powerful instrument of public improvement, a means of improving the taste of the community, and of raising the faculties and minds of the working classes to that level which they are capable of attaining. To do this two things will be necessary. One is to instruct them through the medium it may be of books or lectures, or both, and the other is to present the best models to their eye. And here I must confess it is a matter of deep regret that in this neighbourhood—this great, wealthy, and populous neighbourhood—there should at this moment, with the exception of certain limited private possessions of individual manufacturers, be no great collection available for public purposes, and showing forth the wonderful achievements of the art of the potter. That art is, perhaps, nearly the oldest in the world—the oldest, I believe, in which the aid of fire was called in as an auxiliary to the industry of man. But, old as it is, it is no less new than old; it is as full of vigour, it is as full of capability, it is as full of promise for the future, it is as full of forms of excellence, as yet undeveloped, as if it were an invention of yesterday. For one, I do not hesitate to say, that those who are connected with this manufacture ought never to rest contented with less than this—that they shall claim for it the honour of being one of the fine arts, as practically one of the fine arts as is the art of architecture, which, like the art of pottery, aims at once at the attainments of objects of practical usefulness and the exhibition of the beautiful. I was greatly grieved, in seeking enlightenment on your local affairs, to find there was a difficulty which interfered with the creation of a museum worthy of this district, in which collections of the specimens of the beautiful creations of Germany, of Italy, of France, of China, of Japan, and of almost every other civilised country in ceramic art, should be exhibited to your population. It appears, forsooth, that Burslem is one place, and Hanley another, and Stoke a third, and there may be some more, and that on that account there is no museum in existence. I must confess I cannot conceive a more unsatisfactory mode of explaining a fact in itself so much to be regretted. If it be true that there are these different places—if it be true that in each of these places there are men capable of leading the community—if it be true that there are so many intelligent assemblages of Englishmen qualified for and accustomed to self-government, and engaged in pursuits of the highest interest and utility, and greatly conducive to wealth—do you tell me, because there are four or five such places, therefore they cannot muster even one museum? This appears to me to be a solecism which verges on the ridiculous. But then it seems that if the manufacturers of Burslem propose a museum, they are met by the manufacturers of Stoke, who justly observe that the same article cannot be in two places at the same time. That is undeniable, and the employer of labour in Hanley and elsewhere may say the same thing; but then, the just conclusion is, not that there ought not to be *any* museum, but that there ought to be three, or four, or five. Now let me point out that the economical view of the case is, as it appears to me, entirely in favour of those who found the first museum. What I mean by founding a museum is, that you should do here what has been done elsewhere. . . . . . If you have a museum, it will teach the best methods of production, it will offer new inducements to the best class of masters and workmen to settle in Burslem, and your rates will become lighter than they are now. I most sincerely hope you are disposed to concur in the feeling that this undertaking, to which you have pledged yourselves, is an undertaking that concerns the character and honour of the town, as well as one that promises great things for its future prosperity. If only it can be brought home to the minds of

Englishmen, that the memory of Wedgwood is a precious deposit —that the pursuit of his methods and the application of his principles are a means of wealth—a means of social improvement—a guarantee for advancement in civilisation—if only these can be brought home to the minds and perceptions of Englishmen, so that they shall resolve upon a definite course—then there is nothing to fear. What an Englishman resolves upon is usually accomplished, and what an English community resolves upon still more rarely fails. If you resolve upon this pursuit with all your energies, it will redound to your honour, and not less will it redound to your profit. Great will be the credit that you will gain; but let no man suppose this is a light matter. Let no man think that we have to-day taken part in an idle ceremonial. Those who intend to be followers of Wedgwood, must address themselves to the task as one of a serious and responsible description."

It will be interesting, in connection with the Wedgwood Memorial Institute, to note that in the cavity in the foundation stone which was laid by Mr. Gladstone, was placed a chaste and beautiful china casket, the manufacture of Messrs. Davenport & Co., containing the following record:—

"Wedgwood Memorial Institute, Burslem.—The Foundation-stone of this building, erected by public subscription, and dedicated to the uses of a Free Library, a School of Art, and a Museum, in honour of the eminent potter, Josiah Wedgwood, F.R.S., F.S.A., who was born in Burslem on the 7th of July, 1730, was laid by the Right Honourable William Ewart Gladstone, M.P., D.C.L., Chancellor of the Exchequer, on the 26th of October, 1863, in the Twenty-seventh year of the reign of Her Most Gracious Majesty Queen Victoria. Chief Bailiff, William Edward Twigg. Trustees, Joseph Edge, William Ford, Isaac Hitchin, James Macintyre. Chairman, John Sheriff Hill. Honorary Secretary, William Woodall. Architect, George Benjamin Nichols. Builders, Thomas Blissett Harley, Alfred Dean."

This document was of vellum, the writing being executed by Mr. Nichols, the architect, in richly illuminated Old English characters. The aperture containing the casket was covered in with a china slab, bearing a similar inscription.

The trowel presented to Mr. Gladstone is an excellent

specimen of the potter's art. It was manufactured by its donor, Mr. James Macintyre, of Burslem, from designs furnished by Mr. W. Maddock. The body is of the finest china, but so splendidly decorated that the trowel has very much the appearance of being made of enamelled gold. The ground colour is delicate amethyst, over which is traced light green scroll work. Mr. Gladstone's arms, the arms of the Local Board of Health, and a suitable inscription, are enclosed in medallions upon the blade, and these medallions, together with the blade itself, are surrounded by a deep rich border of figured gold. The inscription is as follows:—"Presented to the Right Honourable William Ewart Gladstone, M.P., Chancellor of the Exchequer, on the occasion of his laying the foundation-stone of the Wedgwood Memorial Institute, Burslem, on the 26th day of October, 1863." The blade is connected with the handle by an elegant device in silver, by Mr. Mayer, of Liverpool. The back of the blade is ornamented in the same style as the face, and has in the centre a medallion enclosing the Portland Vase.

The institute is now, happily, a great fact, and ere long the town of Burslem will have in full operation one of the most valuable and important educational institutions which has yet been established in the provinces. The scheme has been energetically carried out so far by the committee and its hard-working and enlightened secretary, Mr. W. Woodall: subscriptions have flowed in; the "Public Libraries and Museums Act" has been taken advantage of; and everything done to render the scheme, what it promises to be, a great success.

The "Wedgwood Institute" is, almost primarily, intended to be a museum. Its principal room has been specially designed for the purpose by Captain Fowke, and for future requirements the whole of the upper floor can be thrown *en suite* into apartments, wholly top-lighted, for this use. It has been so designed through the conviction continually forced upon its promoters that the absence of such a museum is a reflection, not only on the public spirit of the district, but of the nation at large. It is much to be hoped that the new museum will be one which shall be a credit to the nation, an honour to the district whose manufactures and arts it is intended to illustrate, and worthy of the name of Wedgwood which it bears. The project of the museum is one which commends itself to people of every class, and it is to be hoped that donations of specimens of fictile art of every kind may so abundantly be received as to enable the executive to arrange the contents chronologically and educationally. The Institute is intended, it appears, not only to be a memorial to a potter, but a monument in pottery. The competition suggested by Mr. Beresford-Hope for external fictile decorations, resulted in the selection of Messrs. Robert Edgar and John Kipling as the best artists, and they have since elaborated an architectural composition of effective appearance, in which terra-cottas, majolicas, jaspers, and mosaics, are exquisitely introduced. Of this peculiar feature of the building, the following extract from the description by the artists themselves, gives a pleasing idea :—

"The designers propose to introduce into the blank space of the first-floor wall a series of terra-cotta panels, representing the twelve months of the year, by half-length female figures, all variously designed and modelled in relief. These will be contained in a moulded framework of architectural character, and surmounted by a triangular pediment, the space enclosed by which will contain the sign of the zodiac corresponding to each month, and will be surrounded by brilliant-coloured mosaic. The whole of this part of the design will be executed in red terra-cotta, of a colour and texture which will show out against the red-coloured brickwork with which the exterior of the building is to be faced.

"A cornice in buff-coloured terra-cotta will surmount the story in which these panels are placed, and will be crowned by a rich ornamental cresting in the same coloured material, the roof above being covered with a deep rusty green coloured tile, such as we have ascertained can be secured in the immediate neighbourhood of the building.

"Between the two stories a coloured frieze is to be introduced, two feet six inches in depth, divided into eight compartments, which will represent so many of the industrial processes of the modern manufacture of pottery. It was originally intended by us that those subjects should be modelled and coloured in the manner of Della Robbia. But as the expense of producing in this case would form a very serious item, and make a large inroad on the whole sum allotted to us for our design, we were very reluctantly compelled to abandon the idea of carrying out this feature in relief, and resort to painting the same subjects on the flat. It would be a matter of congratulation to us if we could hope that the introduction of the Della Robbia ware would ever be practicable at some subsequent time before the work is actually undertaken. When we consider, however, the secondary object for which the ceramic design is conceived, there is one argument which should probably reconcile us to these subjects being painted on the flat as compared with the modelled treatment. If the Wedgwood building is to serve as a pattern card, so to speak, of the uses to which modern pottery can be put in architecture, and of the market prices at which it can be produced, it is no doubt desirable that all the ceramic work should be of a kind and be introduced in such a manner as will best answer to the modern notions of economy in building. In regard to this particular feature of our design such a result will no doubt be best obtained by having this frieze of subjects manufactured in numbers of flat pieces, as tiles, rather than in large modelled and moulded slabs, which would necessarily be much more costly in the process of making and in the risk of firing.

"The windows of the ground floor are proposed to be decorated with buff coloured terra-cotta, in various modelled designs, somewhat after the type of the windows in the great court of the Hospital at Milan. The space contained within the arched window head will be filled with red Mansfield stone, to serve as a framework, or background, for richly coloured portraits of the most celebrated potters of ancient and modern times, and also on the side, elevations of Flaxman, Brindley, Bentley, and other distinguished contemporaries of Wedgwood. These portraits will be painted in majolica colours on large circular plaques, and the remainder of the space, or spandril, outside of them, will be in enamel mosaic.

"The porch, or front entrance to the building, is designed to form a central object on the ground floor. Varieties of ceramic material are employed in its principal parts. The shafts on each side of the door, which carry the archway over the entrance, will be fluted in buff terra-cotta, and the flutes filled in with rich mosaics. In the face of the porch, and over the archway, three small panels, in Wedgwood Jasper-ware, are introduced, and are surrounded by an enamel mosaic ground. The small panels will probably contain some heraldic subjects connected with the Wedgwood family and the town of Burslem.

"In the more architectural features moulded and ornamental brickwork will be used, and the entire façade of the building, both in its constructive and decorative parts, will thus be almost entirely composed of ceramic material."

Altogether there seems to be every probability that the memorial will be one of which not only the Potteries, but the nation, may well be proud.

Among the minor memorials to Wedgwood, which the love and veneration felt by the inhabitants of the pottery district he so much benefited, for the character and genius of that great and good man, have originated, one of the most pleasing, because one which can find its way into the homes of the workman, is "a memorial jug," which has been produced in parian by Mr. C. Meigh, of the Old Hall Earthenware Works, at Hanley. The jug is the design of Mr. Henry Baggalley, modeller, of Cobridge. It is ten and a half inches in height, and of good form. On one side is a medallion portrait of Josiah Wedgwood, six inches in height, in bold relief. This portrait is moulded from Sir Joshua Reynolds' portrait, and is very successful. On either side of the medallion are figures of Art and Commerce; the latter figure also supporting, with Science, a pedestal bearing the Portland Vase, which forms the lower part of the neck of the jug. On the other side, on a medallion of similar size, is the crest of the Wedgwood family; and the ribbon bears the dates of the birth and death of Wedgwood. The handle is appropriately formed of a figure of Fame, holding out a wreath of laurel over the head of the "Prince of Potters." The "Old Hall Works," at Hanley, at which this pleasing memorial has been produced, were established about a hundred years ago, by the grandfather of the present Mr. Charles Meigh, and have been worked without intermission by the family until the last four years. The works are now carried on by the "Old Hall Earthenware Company," the principal shareholders in which are Mr. Charles Meigh, jun., and other members of that family. All the usual varieties of earthenware are there produced, and of every quality, from the very plainest for common household use, to the most highly decorated for the mansions of the wealthy. Parian statuary is also produced of excellent quality, and stone ware is likewise made in a variety of ways. The Old Hall Works employ, I believe, on an average, no less than five hundred hands.

The three great pottery towns of Stoke, Burslem, and Hanley, have in many instances shown a jealousy or a rivalry of each other. There has frequently been a want of hand-in-hand feeling among them which has had to be deplored. In the case of the Wedgwood memorials that feeling has, I am happy to say, though unintentionally, resulted in good to all. Stoke and Hanley opposed Burslem in her scheme of a Wedgwood Institute and School of Art, and Burslem opposed them in their proposed Wedgwood statue. As it is, Stoke and Hanley have succeeded in erecting the statue; Burslem is building its institution; and Hanley of itself has reason to feel proud of its museum, which possesses the indentures of Wedgwood's apprenticeship, a good selection of his productions, and the cabinet containing the results of his researches.* Thus all three are

* In the museum at Hanley are many interesting specimens of the different varieties of "Wedgwood ware," which the collector will be interested in examining. Among these are remarkably good examples of flowered vases of Japanese style, and of large size, both with a light ground, with birds and flowers in bright colours, and with a black ground with similar decorations, and an open work basket of bamboo. In the same museum is preserved as truly interesting a relic of the latter days of the great Josiah as that of his early time—the indenture of his apprenticeship—to which I have before referred. I allude to the cabinet—a large one containing a multiplicity of drawers—in which he arranged his specimens of clays and other earthy substances, his fossils, and the results of his trials into their properties. In this cabinet all these objects, although, of course, many times disturbed, and in most cases injured, still

benefited; and it is pleasant to feel that these three towns have vied with each other in doing honour to the memory of the man to whom they were each and all so lastingly indebted.

remain as they were placed by him, and there they are now—thanks to that commendable spirit which induced the executive of the institution to secure them by purchase—likely to remain, as lasting mementoes of his skill and industry. The cabinet contains, among a mass of other matters, some hundreds of Wedgwood's and Chisholm's trials of glazes, &c., all carefully numbered; of trials of bodies, with, in some instances, the degrees of heat to which they have been subjected; of small earthenware vessels in which his samples of clays, &c., were kept, and of other things of equal interest. These small earthenware vessels (mostly of fine Queen's ware) are generally oblong square in form, of various sizes, from an inch to three or four inches in length, and they have each a small projection, inwardly, at the top, on which the number could be affixed. Nothing could show the care which Wedgwood bestowed on the details of his business better than these little vessels, which are almost all marked with his name, and are remarkably well formed; and it is truly pleasant, on withdrawing the bars and opening the drawers of this cabinet, to feel that one is as it were in the presence of the great man, surrounded by his secrets, and admitted into all the intricacies of his private laboratory. It is very much to the credit of the committee of the Hanley Mechanics' Institution that they have secured to the Potteries this memorial of the great head of its native art.

CHAPTER XXIV.

JOSIAH WEDGWOOD.—CHARACTERISTICS.—HIS GREAT SUCCESS AND WEALTH.—COPY OF HIS WILL.—ALEXANDER CHISHOLM.—WEDGWOOD'S ACQUAINTANCE WITH MEN OF INTELLECT AND SCIENCE.—DR. PRIESTLEY.—SUMMARY OF WEDGWOOD'S CHARACTER.—POEM ON A STAFFORDSHIRE TEAPOT.—WEDGWOOD'S LABOURS INCREASE THE COMMERCE OF THE KINGDOM.—STAFFORDSHIRE HAS REASON TO BE PROUD OF HER SON.

JOSIAH WEDGWOOD, whose life I have thus attempted to trace, was, without exception, one of the most wonderful of all the "self-made men" which our nation of great and noble geniuses has ever produced. Not only did he stand out as a clear statue from the men of his own time, but in high and bold relief from those of every time and every age. Original in thought, far-seeing and clear in his perceptions; with a mind capable of grasping the most difficult problems and working them out to a successful issue; with a firmness of purpose, and a determination which carried him safely through all his schemes; a power of wrestling with and overthrowing every obstacle which came in his way; a genius which soared high above his fellow-labourers in art, and led them on to success in paths unknown to them before; with an energy, a perseverance, and an industry which never flagged; an unswerving fixedness of purpose which yielded not to circumstances, however adverse they might seem; with a heart warmed by kindliness, goodness, and charity to all men, and a mind imbued with that true religion—a conscientious discharge of his duty to God and man; with a strict probity and a scrupulous adherence to all that was honourable and right, Josiah Wedgwood hewed out for himself a path through the world-jungle which surrounded him, that led him to the highest point of worldly prosperity, and earned for him a name which has been, and always will be, received with honour.

When he started life he had, as I have shown, the poor and miserably small sum of twenty pounds, left him by his father, to establish himself in business, and battle with the world upon. When he died he was able to leave very large landed estates, manufactories, and houses, to his widow and sons, and sums of £30,000 to each of his sons, and fortunes of £25,000 to each of his daughters, and all this, with the exception of the help which his wife's fortune gave him, the result of his own skill and his own industry.

In the early chapters of this memoir I gave the indenture of apprenticeship of Josiah Wedgwood, and a copy of the will of his father, in which the "score pounds" is left to him; and I cannot do better in this my concluding chapter than give my readers a copy of his own will, in which the extent of his property is shown, and the legacies to his children and others are defined. This will, which is preserved in Doctors' Commons, I now for the first time make public. It is as follows:—

"The last Will and Testament of me, Josiah Wedgwood, of Etruria, in the County of Stafford, made the second day of November, in the year of Our Lord One thousand seven hundred and ninety-three, in manner and form following (that is to say): I give and bequeath unto my dear and affectionate Wife, Sarah Wedgwood, all that messuage or dwelling-house situate at or near Etruria aforesaid, with the buildings, gardens, and appurtenances thereto belonging, late in the holding of Mr. Thomas Wedgwood; and also all that field or piece of land in which the same stands, containing eight acres or thereabouts; and also all that close, piece, or parcel of land lying contiguous to the said dwelling-house, called the Horse Pasture, containing by estimation twelve acres or thereabouts; and also all that piece or parcel of land situate at Etruria aforesaid, heretofore purchased by me from Mr. Hugh Booth; To have and to hold the said messuage or dwelling-house, pieces or parcels of land, hereditaments and premises, with their and every of their appurtenances, unto my said Wife, Sarah Wedgwood and her assigns, for and during the term of her natural life. And from and after her decease, I give and devise all and singular the said messuage or dwelling-house, pieces or parcels of land, hereditaments, and premises, with their and every of their appurtenances, unto my Son, Josiah Wedgwood, his heirs and assigns for ever. Also I give and bequeath the sum of Three thousand pounds unto my said Wife, to be paid to her within twelve months next after my decease. Also I give and bequeath unto my said Wife so much and such part of my household goods and furniture as is mentioned and specified in the Schedule or Paper Writing hereunto annexed, marked with the Letter A. Also I give and bequeath the sum of Ten thousand pounds unto my Executors hereinafter named, upon trust that they, my said Executors, do and shall place the said sum of Ten thousand pounds out upon some good and sufficient public or private security or securitys, at interest, to be approved of nevertheless by my said Wife, and do and shall pay to, or permit and suffer my said Wife to receive and take the interest, dividends, and produce of the said sum of Ten thousand pounds, as the same shall from time to time become due to and for her own use and benefit for and during the term of her natural life. And from and after the decease of my said Wife, I direct that the said sum of Ten thousand pounds shall be applied for and towards payment and satisfaction of the several legacys or sums of money hereinafter given by me. And I do hereby direct that the provision hereinbefore made or intended for my said Wife shall be in lieu, bar, and satisfaction of dower and thirds at Common Law. Also I give and devise unto my said Executors, for the use of my said son, Josiah Wedgwood, his heirs and assigns for ever, that part of Etruria Estate which I now occupy, upon the north side of the Turnpike Road leading from Newcastle to Leek, with the house I now live in, the outbuildings belonging to the same, with the pleasure grounds and all appurtenances thereto belonging, being about sixty-five acres; and also another part of the Etruria Estate, now in the occupation of Richard Hall, being about sixty-eight acres; And also another part of the Etruria Estate, now in the occupation of Thomas Ford, being about forty-five acres; and also the Estate late a part of the White House Estate, on the south side the Turnpike Road leading from Newcastle to Leek; and likewise the land purchased from Thomas Heath, with a small meadow on the north side the said Road, and lying in the Parish of Woolstanton; and likewise a meadow lately purchased from John Marc, of Handley,—all in the holding of Richard Billington, being altogether about Eighty-one acres; and also a piece of land on the south side of the same Road, now in the holding of Daniel Haywood, being about two acres; and also an Estate bought from George Taylor, and now in the holding of Jonathan Adams, being about nine acres; and also a small piece of land adjoining the land bought from Hugh Booth, together with a part of the Hough Meadow, and now in the holding of John Ryder, being about four acres; and also an estate called the Spittels, situate in Penkhull, in the Parish of Stoke upon Trent, and lately purchased from James Godwin, containing sixty-three acres or thereabouts; and also an Estate adjoining to the Spittels on one side, and to Stoke Lane on the other, situate in Penkhull aforesaid, in the Parish of Stoke upon Trent, late in the holding of Humphrey Ratcliff, containing fifteen acres or thereabouts; and also a piece of land called the Woodhills, situate in the Parish of Stoke upon Trent, lately purchased from Ralph Baddeley, and now in my own occupation, being about eleven acres; and also all buildings, tenements, houses, farm-houses, out-houses, pot works, warehouses, workshops, and other buildings, of what kind soever they may be, situate, standing, and being upon any of the land or premises above named, and not hereinbefore devised; and also all my share of the models and molds of the Manufactory in Etruria aforesaid. Also I give and bequeath the sum of Thirty thousand pounds unto my son John Wedgwood. Also I give and bequeath the sum of Twenty-nine thousand one hundred and ten pounds, and likewise twenty shares in the Monmouthshire Canal, unto my Son Thomas Wedgwood. Also I give and bequeath the sum of Twenty-five thousand pounds unto my daughter Susannah Wedgwood; and which said several legacys or sums of Thirty thousand pounds, and Twenty-nine thousand one hundred and ten pounds, and Twenty shares in the Monmouthshire Canal, and Twenty-five thousand pounds, so given to my said Son John Wedgwood, and to my said Son Thomas Wedgwood, and to my said Daughter Susannah Wedgwood, I do hereby direct shall be paid to them as soon as conveniently may be after my decease, together with interest for the same in the mean time, after the rate of four pounds and ten shillings per centum per annum. Also I give and bequeath the sum of Twenty-five thousand pounds unto my Daughter Catharine Wedgwood, to be paid to her as soon after her age of twenty-one years, or day of marriage, which shall first happen, as conveniently may be, with interest for the same in the mean time after the rate of four pounds and ten shillings per centum per annum. Also I give and bequeath the sum of Twenty-five thousand pounds unto my Daughter Sarah Wedgwood, to be paid to her as soon after her age of twenty-one years, or day of marriage, which shall first happen, as conveniently may be, with interest for the same in the mean time after the rate of four pounds and ten shillings per centum per annum. Provided always, and I do hereby direct, that in case my said Daughters Catherine Wedgwood and Sarah Wedgwood, or either of them, shall happen to die unmarried before the age of Twenty-one years, then that the legacy or legacys of her or them so dying shall sink into and become part of the residue of my personal Estate, and be applied and disposed of accordingly, as shall hereinafter be mentioned. Also I do hereby declare it to be my will that all the rest, residue, and remainder of my said stock in trade, goods, wares, implements, materials, and utensils of trade, and other matters and things used by me, in or belonging to my said Manufactory, except the models or molds therein used or kept, shall, at the time of my decease, sink into and become part of the residue of my personal estate, and be applied and disposed of accordingly. Also I give and bequeath all and singular my household goods and furniture not hereinbefore given to my said Wife, together with all my books, prints, books of prints, pictures, and cabinets of Experiments, of Fossils, and of Natural History, unto my said Son Josiah Wedgwood. And I do hereby commit the Guardianship and Tuition of such of my said children as shall not at the time of my decease have attained the age of twenty-one years unto my said Wife and my said Son John Wedgwood, until such children shall attain the said age. And I do direct that the fortunes or portions of such of my said children shall in the mean time be managed by my said Wife and my said Son John Wedgwood, and a competent part of the interest and produce thereof be applied for their maintenance and education, and the residue of such interest and produce be suffered to accumulate for their benefit and advantage in such manner as my said Wife and Son John Wedgwood shall in their discretion think most meet and proper. Also I give and bequeath one annuity or yearly sum of twenty pounds unto my Brother in Law, Philip Clark, for and during the term of his natural life. Also I give and bequeath one annuity or yearly sum of Twenty pounds unto my Niece, Sarah Taylor, for and during the term of her natural life. Also I give and bequeath one annuity or yearly sum of Twenty pounds unto Mr. Alexander Chisholm, for and during the term of his natural life; recommending it to my Son Josiah Wedgwood to give him any further assistance that he may stand in need of, to make the remainder of his life easy and comfortable. And I do hereby direct that the said several and respective annuitys of Twenty pounds, Twenty pounds, and Twenty pounds shall be paid and payable quarterly, at the four most usual feasts or days of payment in the year, (that is to say) on every twenty-fifth day of March, twenty-fourth day of June, twenty-ninth day of September, and twenty-fifth day of December, by even and equal portions, free and clear of and from all taxes, charges, and deductions whatsoever; the first payment thereof to begin and be made on such of the said days as shall first and next happen after my decease. Also I give and bequeath the sum of Ten Guineas unto the said Alexander Chisholm, as a testimony of my regard for him. Also I give and bequeath the sum of Two hundred pounds apiece unto all and every the children of my Nephew Thomas Byerley, who shall be living at the time of my decease, to be paid to them at their respective ages of twenty-one years: Provided always, and in case any one or more of the said children shall happen to die without issue before he, she, or they shall attain the said age, then I direct that the legacy or legacys to him, her, or them so dying shall go and be paid unto and amongst the survivors or survivor of them equally, share and share alike, in case there shall be more than one, at such time and in such manner as is hereinbefore directed and expressed of and concerning the said original legacys or sums of Two hundred pounds: Provided also, and in case all the said children shall happen to die without issue before they shall attain the said age, then I direct that all the said legacies or sums of Two hundred pounds so given to them as aforesaid shall sink into and become part of the residue of my personal estate, and be applied and disposed of accordingly. And I do hereby expressly direct and declare that no interest shall be allowed or paid upon the said respective legacys or sums of Two hundred pounds in the mean time from my decease to the time that the same shall become payable by virtue of this my Will; such legacys or sums of Two hundred pounds being given by me in lieu of legacys or sums of One hundred pounds, which it was originally my intention to have directed to be placed out at interest, and to have accumulated for such children of the said Thomas Byerley as aforesaid until they should attain the age of twenty-one years. Also I give and bequeath unto each of my Nephews Thomas and John Wedgwood, Sons of my late Nephew Thomas Wedgwood, of the Upper House in Burslem, the sum of Two hundred pounds each, to be paid to them at their respective ages of twenty-one years: Provided always, and in case they shall either or both of them die before they arrive at the age of twenty-one years, I direct that the legacy or legacys of the party or parties so dying, of Two hundred pounds so given to them as aforesaid, shall sink into and become part of the residue of my personal estate, and be applied and disposed of accordingly. Also I give to my Servant George Jones the sum of twenty guineas, as a token of my remembrance of his faithful services to me. Also I give and bequeath to the several persons whose names shall be mentioned and comprised in the Schedule or List hereto annexed, signed with my name, and marked with the letter "B," the mourning Rings or other small legacys or sums of money which shall be therein specified and expressed. Also I give and bequeath unto James Caldwell, Esq., of Newcastle under Lyme, in the County of Stafford, the sum of One hundred pounds, which I desire he will accept as a testimony of my friendship and esteem for him. And I do hereby direct and appoint that my said Nephew Thomas Byerley shall, under the direction of my Executors, settle my accounts and manage and conduct the collection of my debts and other matters relating to the settlement of my concerns in business; and that a Salary of One hundred pounds per annum be allowed and paid to him for such particular service, so long as he shall be employed therein, over and above all charges and expenses attending the same. And it is also my Will that an estate at Burslem, late in the occupation of Joseph Wedgwood, consisting of a newly erected dwelling house, a set of pot works, with other buildings, and a field called the Cross hill, containing altogether about two acres; and likewise an estate in the Parish of Astbury, in the County of Chester, called Spengreen, and now in the holding of Thomas Johnson, containing about seventy-five acres or thereabouts; and also a piece of land on the east side of the Bridge in Congleton, in the said County of Chester, being about two rods; and also all the rest, residue, and remainder, messuages, lands, tenements, hereditaments, and real estate, money, securities for money, debts due and owing, personal Estate and Effects of what nature or kind soever or wheresoever, not hereinbefore particularly devised or disposed of, together with such or so much of the several sums of money hereinbefore mentioned and bequeathed as shall, by means of the contingencies and directions hereinbefore expressed, shall all of them sink into and become parts of the said residue of my personal Estate. And I do hereby give, devise, and bequeath the same unto my said Executors, for the payment of the legacys and annuities hereinbefore mentioned; and provided there should be a residue after the above mentioned payments, then I direct that such residue shall go and be divided unto and amongst my said children, John Wedgwood,

Thomas Wedgwood, Susannah Wedgwood, Catherine Wedgwood, and Sarah Wedgwood, their heirs, executors, administrators, and assigns, equally, share and share alike, as tenants in common, and not as joint tenants; and if there should be any deficiency of real or personal estates for paying the said legacys and annuitys, such deficiency shall in that case be born equally amongst and made up by those my said children above named, (that is to say) John Wedgwood, Thomas Wedgwood, Susannah Wedgwood, Catherine Wedgwood, and Sarah Wedgwood, share and share alike, in proportion to the amount of the legacys to them herein left and bequeathed. And I do hereby nominate, constitute, and appoint my said Wife, my said Son John Wedgwood, and the said James Caldwell, Esq., Executrix and Executors of this my Will. And lastly, I do hereby revoke all former or other Will or Wills by me at any time heretofore made, and do declare this only to be my last Will and Testament. In witness whereof I have to this my last Will and Testament, contained in six sheets of paper, and have to each of the first five sheets thereof set my hand, and to the sixth and last sheet thereof my hand and seal the day and year first before written.

"Jos. Wedgwood. (L.S.)

"Signed, sealed, published, and declared by the said Josiah Wedgwood, as and for his last Will and Testament, in the presence of us, who in his presence, and in the presence of each other, have hereunto subscribed our names as witnesses thereto; the several following words being first interlined: money—my—happen—said.

"Alexr. Chisholm.
"Thomas Mitchell.
"Joseph Rutland.

"John Wedgwood, of Etruria, in the County of Stafford, Esquire, maketh oath, and saith that he has searched among the papers and writings of his late Father, Josiah Wedgwood, late of Etruria aforesaid, Esquire, deceased, in order to find certain Schedules or Paper Writings referred to in the last Will and Testament of the said Josiah Wedgwood, and therein mentioned to be annexed thereto, and respectively marked A and B. And this Deponent further saith that he has not been able to find such Schedules or Paper Writings, or either of them; and this Deponent further saith that he has never heard or been informed, nor does he believe that the said

Josiah Wedgwood ever wrote or made out, or caused to be written or made out, such Schedules or Paper Writings, or either of them.

"JOHN WEDGWOOD.

"Sworn at Newcastle under Lyme, in the County of Stafford, the 29th day of June, 1795, Before me, JOHN LLOYD, a Commissioner.

"Proved at London, 2nd July, 1795, before the Judge, by the Oath of John Wedgwood, the Son, one of the Executors, to whom Administration was granted, having been first sworn by Commission duly to administer. Power reserved of making the like grant to Sarah Wedgwood, Widow, the Relict, and James Caldwell, the other Executors, when they shall apply for the same."

It will be seen how, in this will, the kindliness of Wedgwood's disposition here and there cropped out. To his old servant and associate, Alexander Chisholm, he left a gift of ten guineas "as a testimony of my regard for him," and also an annuity of £20 a year for life, "recommending to my son, Josiah Wedgwood, to give him any further assistance that he may stand in need of to make the remainder of his life easy and comfortable." To others he left remembrances; but it is much to be regretted that his intention of leaving "to the several persons whose names shall be mentioned and comprised in the schedule or list hereunto annexed, signed with my name, and marked with the letter B, the mourning rings, or other small legacies, or sums of money, which shall be therein specified and expressed," was defeated by no such "list or schedule" having been found to exist. Memorial rings are, however, in existence, bearing the name of the illustrious potter and the date of his death, one of which is now in the hands of Mr. Hall.

Wedgwood, during his lifetime, drew around him men of talent and of learning, and they in return were only too glad to cultivate his friendship, for he was at least their equal in intellect and in philosophical and scientific acquirements.

Dr. Priestley, an old friend of Wedgwood's, in the midst of his troubles, after the disgraceful and savage riots at Birmingham, was invited to make a stay at Etruria, and his house was ever open to receive men of every rank and station who had the passwords of bright intellect and of scientific or art eminence to recommend them. He was a liberal contributor to the annuity to Dr. Priestley. In religion he was an Unitarian, and was on intimate terms of friendship with Mr. Willet, the minister of the old Presbyterian Chapel at Newcastle, whose ministry he attended. His religious views, however, were never allowed to influence his actions, whether of friendship or of business. He wisely felt that there was good in all, and that a man's religion was a question between his own conscience and his Maker, and not one on which commercial relationships or ties of friendship ought to hinge.

One who knew him well, wrote of him soon after his death, "He was most kind, and he did all he could to make us comfortable. He made a present of one hundred pounds to my little boy. He made me take him (my boy) out in his carriage every day, and being a most superior man, his conversation was very instructive and interesting. Many gentlemen visited him, particularly at breakfast, and I was very much amused and improved by the society of this good man's friends. Oh, money! what an enchantress art thou! thou canst raise fairy ground around us, and make men and everything else smile upon us. The frequent visits of this wonderful man, whose portrait is now before me, was in the end a misfortune—we lived when he was with us very luxuriously—which was not very easy to change when he left us; he was so kind to me and to his godson; who was called after him, that I loved him dearly, and felt most desolate when he left us, and we sank into our usual insignificance—my husband always having work neglected while our visitor was with us, and now must be done. This period of his visit was very consoling."

In the works of Sir Charles Hanbury Williams occurs a poem, called "Isabella," describing the morning occupation and visitors of Lady Isabella Montague (*circa* 1770). Of one of her admirers, a Mr. Bateman, it is said:—

"To please the noble dame the courtly squire
Produced a tea-pot made in Staffordshire!
So Venus looked, and with such longing eyes,
When Paris first produced the golden prize.
'Such works as this,' she cries, 'can England do?
It equals Dresden, and excels St. Cloud;
All modern China now shall hide its head,
And e'en Chantilly must give o'er her trade.
For lace let Flanders bear away the bell;
In finest linen let the Dutch excel;
For prettiest stuffs let Ireland first be named;
And for best-fancied silks let France be famed;
Do thou, thrice happy England, still prepare
Thy clay, and build thy fame on earthenware.'"

Little did the writer think that through the skill, the enterprise, the industry, and the perseverance of one man, Staffordshire would, indeed, soon equal Dresden and out-do St. Cloud in works both of utility and beauty. Little did he think that "thrice happy England" would, literally, still prepare its clay, and "build its fame on earthenware." Little did he think that within a dozen years from the time when he penned those lines, the great man whose industry had tended to bring about so wonderful a result, would stand in the House of Commons and give his evidence that at that time from fifteen to twenty thousand persons were employed in the potworks of Staffordshire alone, and double that number received employment in preparing the materials—the coal, the flint, and the clay—for their use. But so it was. And the district of the Potteries has gone on increasing in size and in importance from that day to this. It is indeed a great fact—a fact of which Staffordshire has reason to be proud—that the man who did most to bring about this happy state of things—who laid the foundation on which the nation

"Builds her fame on earthenware,"

was a son of her own native soil, who was raised up to do her honour, and to add to our national prosperity. The man who did all this was JOSIAH WEDGWOOD.

INDEX.

C.

D.

M.

N.

O.

P.

Q.

R.

S.

THE END.

CPSIA information can be obtained
at www.ICGtesting.com
Printed in the USA
LVHW101021190422
716440LV00024B/296

9 783752 590609